Penguin Books

THE QUEST OF BEN HUR

Born in March 1919, Karl Tunberg has written the scripts for more than forty major films, including *Ben Hur, Beau Brummell* and *Because You're Mine*, and has received two Academy Award nominations. He received his B.A. from the University of Southern California and has subsequently taught at university. As well as writing film scripts he has also produced many films, but now devotes all his time to writing. He has also been President of the Writers' Guild of America.

Owen Walford was born in August 1950 and received his M.A. from the University of Southern California, studying and subsequently teaching classical Greek and Roman history. He is now a full-time writer.

A bestseller from the outset, the original novel *Ben Hur* was written by Lew Wallace, an American Civil War General, diplomat and historical romancer, and first published in 1880. It was successfully adapted for the stage and was in demand for film adaptation as early as 1907. Sam Goldwyn bought the film rights in 1923 and after three years' work, dogged with mishaps and at a cost of four million dollars, the huge silent film was shown in 1925, being greeted with great acclaim, particularly for the brilliantly filmed chariot race, and set the pattern for future epic productions. The remake of *Ben Hur* by Metro-Goldwyn-Mayer is the one that most people now remember; it was completed in 1958 and starred Charlton Heston as Ben Hur. One of the most successful films of all time, it held box office records for several years, only latterly exceeded by films like *Star Wars* and *Close Encounters of the Third Kind*. This book continues the story of Ben Hur where the film ended.

KARL TUNBERG AND

OWEN WALFORD

THE QUEST OF
BEN HUR

PENGUIN BOOKS

Penguin Books Ltd, Harmondsworth, Middlesex, England
Penguin Books, 625 Madison Avenue, New York, New York 10022, U.S.A.
Penguin Books Australia Ltd, Ringwood, Victoria, Australia
Penguin Books Canada Ltd, 2801 John Street, Markham, Ontario, Canada L3R 1B4
Penguin Books (N.Z.) Ltd, 182-190 Wairau Road, Auckland 10, New Zealand

First published 1981

Made and printed in Great Britain by
Richard Clay (The Chaucer Press) Ltd, Bungay, Suffolk
Set in Linotype Granjon

AUTHORS' NOTE

Rome. Down through the ages the name has meant many things to many people. In the popular view, it has often conjured up the images of bloodshed, rampant sexuality, gladiators, orgies, luxury and slavery. And certainly these things did exist in ancient Rome. Yet the Roman historian Tacitus, writing of his own time, could describe 'tyranny, debauchery, rapine' as 'excesses that were quite un-Roman'.

He was right. The qualities which made Rome great were gravity, piety, dignity, courage, orderliness, and practicality – to name only a few. The Empire shaped our present culture with its laws, political institutions, literature, and, above all, the religion it bequeathed to us.

To later generations, Rome would become the centre of Christianity. It became the capital of the faith. The Christian religion would probably not have survived in the west without the protection and sponsorship of Rome.

Christianity itself assimilated much of what was great about pagan Rome, and went on to mould the world we live in today. Some of us are religious, others are not, but for all of us, Christian beliefs, ideas, and thought patterns continue to affect and colour every aspect of our existence. Without this great spiritual edifice, all our lives would be very different, and probably far less rich.

But in the first century, Christianity was not a great edifice – it was a despised and fugitive sect, considered subversive by the government and scorned by intellectuals. There were hundreds of rival religions, sects, and strange beliefs – all seeking to provide the individual with the emotional satisfaction and spiritual sustenance which the pagan state religion failed to give.

Yet the Christian religion, at first one of the smallest and most insignificant of these sects, was the only one to survive . . .

A mere hundred years before our own time, the classic novel *Ben Hur* dramatized the origins of Christianity and ended with the conversion of Judah Ben Hur, a young Jew, who lived in Jerusalem in the days of Christ.

But Judah Ben Hur lived on, suffering many misfortunes, experiencing strange adventures. He became part of a new movement struggling to establish itself in a hostile world. That tale must be told . . .

BOOK ONE

THE EMPEROR

CHAPTER ONE

They were late in bringing out the condemned man, but the people packed into the courtyard still waited silently.

The Centurion regarded them with disgust. He wiped away the trickle of sweat which ran from under his helmet. How he hated this pestilent land! Everywhere a man looked there was nothing but sand, goats and horse dung. A little after dawn now, it was already hotter than the vapours of Aetna. No wonder there was so much madness in the air, murder in men's eyes.

He gazed round sombrely. Would his score of men be enough, should the madness chance to flare up here and now among this unwholesome multitude? The segmented, metal chest-plates gleamed dully in the corners of the courtyard where he had positioned his soldiers, strategically but unobtrusively.

Another glance at the hushed, expectant crowd reassured him. There would be no disturbances today, unless, of course, the people were deprived of their spectacle.

A murmur ran through the onlookers, and all turned towards the great gates as they creaked open. Two lictors of the Jewish court dragged their prisoner into view. He was a small man, and his hands were bound behind him. His eyes were still blinking in the sunlight, after being snatched from the darkness of the prison.

There was a movement from the other end of the courtyard, and a tall man emerged, stately in his white beard and long robes, escorted by two more lictors. The Centurion knew him by sight. He was Ananias, the High Priest of these people.

The Centurion cursed softly as more sweat dripped from his helmet. He wished they would get on with it so he could return to the cool shade of his barrack room in the tower of Antonia, but he had to stand here in the brutal sun to make sure there was no trouble, while these people administered their queer justice. The Roman government had allowed the Jewish Sanhedrin autonomy, as long as it didn't interfere with the peace of the province. But the 'ins' and 'outs' of the local justice made no sense to the Centurion. It had been said that the condemned man was one of the Nazarenes, a sect persecuted by the Jews. But why this group should be so harshly treated the Centurion neither knew nor cared.

Ananias, eyes fixed on the Temple which towered over Jerusalem, concluded his prayer. Then the High Priest faced the ashen victim.

'Yeshua Ben Hannan,' Ananias intoned, 'the Sanhedrin has condemned you to die for your outrage against your God and your forefathers. Have you anything to say?'

Ben Hannan replied defiantly, in spite of his quavering voice. 'You can kill me. You can kill a thousand more like me. But you can't stop the truth. I spit on you and your Sanhedrin!'

Impassively Ananias made a sign to the lictors. Two of them grasped Ben Hannan's arms and forced him into a kneeling position. A third drew a heavy sword from beneath his cloak and raised it high. Grunting with effort, he brought the blade down. There was a strangely metallic thud as the victim's head was severed cleanly from his body.

Ananias leaped backwards with astounding agility for a man of his years, snatching his robes aside to avoid the splatter of blood.

Joseph stood in the blazing heat in front of the sprawling house on the outskirts of Arimathea. There was a bench in the cool shade of the archway which opened on to the spacious courtyard, but he did not feel like sitting down. Ignoring the merciless sun which scorched his white hair, Joseph continued to pace in front of the gate. Then, for the thousandth time, he stopped and stared anxiously down the long, dusty ribbon of the Jerusalem road. At last there seemed to be a horseman approaching, but the horizon was shimmering in the heat, and he wasn't sure whether or not it was a mirage.

Throwing aside his staff, Joseph set off at a trot down the road. 'Judah!' he shouted. 'Judah!'

In a moment Judah Ben Hur was riding up to Joseph, reining his horse to a halt. Ben Hur's leathery, seamed face broke into a warm smile at the sight of his friend. With the lightness of an athlete, he swung his supple frame from his beast and embraced Joseph.

'Blessed be the womb which bore you!' Joseph exclaimed. 'We've been expecting you all day! You were so long we feared for your safety!'

Ben Hur laughed. 'Oh, I'm safe enough. What the heat has left of me, that is.'

'We have some chilled wine in the house. Come.'

So saying, Joseph turned. Ben Hur, leading his horse by the bridle, walked beside him towards the gate. In the sweltering afternoon, the two men moved slowly.

'Whatever delayed you?' asked Joseph.

'Nothing. I left early this morning.'

'But my house is only a short ride from Jerusalem,' said Joseph.

'I stopped on the way.'

'Stopped? Where?'

'Nowhere in particular. I just wanted to be alone. To think.'

Joseph paused, appraising his friend. 'I thought you had put aside your doubts.'

'They have come back, Joseph. I loved Esther. To take another wife will be very difficult.'

'Esther has been dead two years. A man should have a woman.'

Joseph patted Ben Hur's arm. 'The moon was full last night. A good omen for arranging a marriage.'

Ben Hur gazed at Joseph soberly, then embraced him again. 'You are right. Let us go and seal the betrothal.' He slapped the saddlebags on his horse. 'Wait until Leah sees the gifts I have brought her!'

Slyly Joseph touched a finger to his right eyelid. 'Wait until you see Leah! How old was she when you saw her last? Eight, I think. Well, she's fifteen now. You'll think a year's betrothal much too long. You'll want to bed her tonight!'

In the cool shade of her chamber, Leah grew more and more impatient. She had been there all day, but she had no intention of venturing out into the burning sun. Whiter than most, her skin flushed easily in the heat. For the hundredth time she gazed into the polished bronze of her mirror. The amber reflection reminded her of one of those profane statues which men said that King Herod had imported from Greece back in the days when her father had been a little boy.

How creamy was her complexion, smoother than alabaster! It only made her dark eyes and full lips the bolder. She considered the grace of her shoulders and the roundness of her full breasts. Well she knew there would be no man who could resist such charms. Her father had warned her many times that vanity was a sin, but she saw no harm in admiring what God had given her.

She rose, running her hands along her sides and pressing her gown to her body. Had her mother been just as beautiful? It was hard to imagine a man like her father as a lover of a woman, yet he must have been. Leah wished her mother had not died in childbirth. There was no other female in the house. No one to talk to, no one to confide in.

But none of that mattered now. She was about to be betrothed to Judah Ben Hur. Since her childhood, that wonderful and compelling figure had occupied an exalted place in Leah's imagination. People constantly recounted his marvellous adventures, his great achievements in Rome, his travels all over the world. In the eyes of her father and his friends, Ben Hur could do no wrong. She would never forget the first day she had seen him. Ben Hur had just returned from a journey to Rome, and he had come to the house with her father. Leah had expected a striking-looking man, but he was even more handsome than she had imagined. She knew, of course, that he was of middle age. But the years had not dealt harshly with him. Indeed ... they only enhanced his comeliness. From that day forward, Leah had loved Judah Ben Hur with an adoration bordering on worship.

She caught her breath. There was the banging of the great gate outside. The babble of voices in the courtyard told Leah that her intended husband must have arrived.

Her mouth dry with excitement, she glanced into the mirror. She dipped her fingers into the bowl of sweet-smelling nard paste. It came all the way from India and it was very expensive, but she used it liberally, rubbing it into her smooth cheeks. Then she lifted her purple gown, and applied it to her belly and thighs as well.

Hastily Leah let her garment drop as a gentle rapping was heard at her door.

'Come in,' she called.

The door opened, and her father stood there.

'You are more beautiful than a bed of spring flowers!' he exclaimed. He sniffed the air and gave a little laugh. 'And you smell better too.'

'He's really here?' Leah asked with breathless excitement.

He nodded, and Leah started eagerly for the door. But Joseph detained her, holding up his white silk prayer shawl.

'Haven't you forgotten something?' he asked.

Impatiently she darted back to the table and picked up her own tallith. Father and daughter wrapped themselves in their shawls and faced Jerusalem. Holding his hands aloft, Joseph intoned the words, and Leah followed suit.

'Blessed be the glory of God! Not to me, Lord, but to you alone, the glory! But if it please you, O God, bless this day and the betrothal of our house to the house of Hur.'

When the prayer was concluded, he removed his shawl. Leah did likewise. The girl stepped to the small window and closed the wooden shutters, plunging the room into shadows.

Taking Leah by the arm, her father led her out into the hall. They moved slowly and with stately dignity.

Suddenly Leah stopped, clutching her father's arm.

He looked at her in surprise.

'Leah! What is it?'

'I'm afraid ...'

'Afraid?'

She shook her head. The words would not come. She could never put them in a way her father would understand. How could she tell him the nature of her dreams? How could she explain her fear they would no longer be dreams when she came face to face with the man in the next room?

Gently Joseph took hold of her. 'Come, child ... You must do as you are told ...'

Trembling, Leah allowed herself to be led down the passage. Then they turned towards the archway at the far end which opened into the atrium. Leah could see Ben Hur, the open ceiling bathing him clearly with light.

She drew in her breath sharply. His tunic-clad figure was trim and spare as ever. His hard limbs gleamed like ivory, and his hair was still thick and youthful.

Impulsively she threw off her father's hand and ran forward, through the arch, into the brightness of the far chamber. Kneeling before the startled Ben Hur, she took both of his hands.

'Judah Ben Hur,' she vowed, 'I will make you a good wife!'

Joseph hurried up behind her. 'Leah!' he exclaimed. 'Restrain yourself.'

Ben Hur smiled. 'I like her the way she is.'

Raising her up, he continued for a moment to look into her eyes. She could clearly see the seams in his weathered face and the slight wrinkles around his mouth. But to Leah, they only made him more romantic.

'She is even lovelier than you boasted,' Ben Hur was saying. 'The gifts I have brought her will seem plain in comparison.'

Joseph grinned. 'Knowing you, Judah, I doubt if anything you brought could be plain.'

From a table in the centre of the atrium, Ben Hur picked up a wide belt of gold mesh, studded with jewels.

'This girdle is a small size.' He glanced at her. 'But it will circle your waist easily. How I envy it!'

Leah took the belt and ran her hand over its bright surface.

Ben Hur pointed at a silver box, embossed with beautifully moulded figures of men and animals. 'For generations this marriage casket has been in the family of my adoptive father, Quintus Arrius.'

'Is it Roman?'

Again Ben Hur smiled his warm smile. 'In a manner of speaking. It was made by a Greek craftsman who lived in Rome.'

'How I would love to go to Rome!'

'You will,' Ben Hur promised. 'I have a house there. A villa just off the Flaminian Way.' He indicated the silver box. 'But open it.'

With trembling fingers, Leah obeyed. A moan of pleasure escaped from her lips at the sight of the rings, brooches, lockets and bracelets shining inside the casket.

A commotion in the courtyard made Ben Hur start. Leah, entranced by her newly acquired treasures, seemed oblivious to it, but Joseph had heard and looked worried. A door opened and banged shut. Heavy footsteps tramped down the hall. Then a huge figure appeared in the archway to the atrium.

A full head taller than Ben Hur, he was of middle age. He

was clean-shaven in the Roman fashion, with a florid complexion suggesting more than a passing acquaintance with wine. He wore a sweat-stained tunic, which was stretched tightly around his huge girth. Joseph's manservant hovered apologetically behind the giant.

'It's all right, Shem,' said Joseph, waving his hand at the servant, who disappeared promptly and with obvious relief.

The newcomer's glance swept the company. 'No doubt you're looking forward to a joyful future,' he observed caustically.

'Did you come all the way out here just to ask that, Peter?' Ben Hur inquired.

The big man turned his back on them, stalking over to a small stand where there was a pitcher of wine. Unceremoniously, he poured himself a drink and downed it.

'While you were out here, occupied with your mating dance, they killed Yeshua Ben Hannan!' said Peter.

There was a moment of shocked silence.

'Who is Yeshua Ben Hannan?' asked Leah timidly.

Her father rounded on her, his eyes blazing. 'Go to your room, and don't come out until I send for you!'

Leah flinched. She hesitated only a moment, then turned and fled.

'When was he arrested?' Ben Hur asked.

'Just yesterday. The generous and tolerant Sadducees accused him of bringing Gentiles into the Temple. They tried him immediately, and did not even wait the required time to kill him.'

'They're looking for any excuse to strike at us!' Joseph exclaimed bitterly.

'Do the others know?' Ben Hur asked.

'Only a few. I came to you first.'

'I think we should meet at the tannery tonight.'

'We've been there too often,' warned Peter.

'I know,' said Ben Hur. 'But this is vital. I've been considering a plan for some time. I have always thought it too daring – only to be attempted at the most propitious moment. But now – perhaps the time has come.'

'Then let us meet,' Joseph agreed.

Finally Peter nodded as well. 'I will get word to the others.'

'Hurry,' Ben Hur urged him.

Peter poured himself another cup of wine, downed it and left the room as abruptly as he had entered.

'I am sorry for Leah,' Ben Hur told Joseph. 'To have the celebration interrupted like this – it must be a terrible disappointment.'

'Don't concern yourself, Judah. I'll make her understand. Now you must be on your way.'

Ben Hur squeezed Joseph's arm. 'I'll see you tonight.'

The old man gazed after him as he went out. Then he turned wearily and moved back into the hall.

At Leah's door, he knocked softly. There was no answer. He waited another moment, then entered.

She was sitting on the couch, staring starkly at her reflection in the bronze mirror. She was no longer weeping, but her cheeks were stained with tears.

Joseph approached her. He stroked her head gently. 'Tears are for pleasures ended ... Yours are still before you.'

'He went?'

Joseph nodded. 'It was urgent.'

'I ought to be the most urgent thing for him.'

'You are. But he has other responsibilities.'

'What other responsibilities?'

'Nothing you should worry about. Just think of your life ahead. You have a golden future.'

She regarded him dubiously.

'Trust me, Leah,' he insisted.

Impulsively she put the mirror down, jumped to her feet and hugged her father.

Joseph chuckled. 'I take it you are no longer afraid ...'

'Afraid?'

'You said you were.'

'You shouldn't listen to me.'

'I always do.'

'Then go and rest. It has been a tiring day for you.'

He nodded and started for the door, but Leah caught his arm.

'Father – who was the man who was killed?'

He shook his head sadly. 'There is too much ugliness in the world. Must it touch you as well?'

'You treat me as if I were a – a vessel of glass. Something too delicate to hold the truth. But I'm *not* delicate, father.'

Joseph regarded her sombrely. For an instant he felt the urge to confide in her. But he suppressed it. She was indeed fortunate to be able to complain of being too sheltered! There were many times when he wished he could make the same complaint.

'Change your clothes,' he ordered. 'We're leaving for the Temple shortly.'

He closed Leah's door and moved into the corridor. Only a few steps took him to another entrance.

This room was dark. The shutters were barred, but Joseph did not open them. Closing the door softly, he crossed the spacious but simply furnished chamber to a chest which stood by itself against the wall next to his sleeping couch.

Taking up the key which hung on a chain around his neck, Joseph unlocked the great box and lifted the lid almost reverently. From under a cloth coverlet, he took out a silver chalice.

It was an ordinary drinking goblet, though perhaps somewhat larger than usual and devoid of any decoration or embellishment. But in the gloom of the room, its polished metal seemed to emit a peculiar luminescence.

Joseph closed the chest and set the chalice on the lid. Kneeling down on the floor, he grasped the cup in both hands, closing his eyes. A new strength emanated from the cup into his fingers, flowing up his arms and permeating his whole body . . .

The street was so narrow that two carts could not pass abreast, and it was cut into steps to mount the gradient of the steepest hill in Jerusalem.

Ben Hur did not like that full betrothal moon, for it drenched the city in a light almost as bright as day. At frequent intervals he stopped in shadows to make sure he was not being followed, chafing the whole while to be at his destination. Suddenly his foot slammed into a large stone which projected unseen from a wall. An excruciating pain shot up his shin, and he had to bite his lip to hold back a curse.

He waited a moment, then slipped the last few feet to a darkened recessed entrance and rapped twice. A small panel in the door opened, and two eyes peered out at him. Then the slit closed, and the door opened, revealing Peter.

'Took you long enough,' he hissed.

Without waiting for an answer, he turned his back on Ben Hur and led the way up a narrow, winding stairway to the large torch-lit loft of a disused tannery, which still smelled faintly of the animal urine used in the curing of hides.

Twenty or thirty people, mostly men, but with a sprinkling of women, were gathered in one corner of the room, talking softly.

Ben Hur knew them all. Some were dear friends. There was James, brother of Jesus, who had accompanied Ben Hur through some of the most difficult years of his life. There was Matthew, still apologetic for the wrongs he had once done as a tax collector. And there was John, scholar and writer, who could discuss philosophy with the best of the Greeks. And Peter, of course. Peter, that solid fisherman, boastful and strong, yet so humanly weak that, when faced by soldiers, he had denied being a follower of Christ. Not once, but three times. Long forgiven by Jesus, Peter had never forgiven himself and was blustering his way through life, trying to make up for that one lapse.

These were men Ben Hur would have liked to spend more time with. But it was not possible. He could only see them in hurried, furtive meetings.

The conversation ceased, as people became aware of Ben Hur's presence. A small man, who seemed familiar, but whom Ben Hur could not quite place, came forward, holding out both hands in greeting.

'Judah!' he exclaimed.

Finally Ben Hur realized who it was, and took him by the hand. 'Paul!' said Ben Hur warmly. 'You've grown a beard since I saw you last.'

'To disguise myself,' Paul admitted. 'I'm getting a bad reputation. It seems I talk too much.'

Ben Hur smiled. 'I hope you never stop.'

He started towards the others, but Paul held his arm. 'I've been preaching in many lands,' the little man continued. 'I stopped here in Jerusalem for the Pentecost on my way to Antioch.' Then his face sobered. 'When I heard the news, I was almost sorry that I had come. But I am eager to tell you everything. It has been so long and we have so much to share.'

'Later, Paul,' Ben Hur said gently. 'There's something I must discuss with everyone. And I'll particularly value your counsel.'

With Paul following, Ben Hur joined the company on the other side of the loft. They had resumed their conversation, but now turned expectantly at Ben Hur's approach.

'My friends,' Ben Hur said. 'I am most grateful for your being here tonight. I know well you take a risk every time we meet. I am sure you all feel the same way as I do about what has happened, but I have not come to grieve over Yeshua. His memory can best be served by what we do from now on. Our mistake has been trying to ride two horses at the same time.

'We accept Gentiles, but the Pharisees and the Sadducees will not. We believe that the Messiah has come, has spoken to men and has told them what they must do. To the Jews, this is sacrilege. Yet we still call ourselves Jews and worship in the Temple. But for God there is neither Jew nor Greek, master nor slave, man nor woman. Christ spoke to *all men*, and we must not be prevented from doing this as well. As the Jewish people have done, we must win recognition from the Romans and the protection of their laws. I am a Roman citizen, of equestrian rank. I shall go to Rome and appeal to Caesar myself.'

'But, Judah!' Paul exclaimed. 'A Roman emperor would be likely to favour the Sanhedrin over a small group like us. He –'

Ben Hur held up his hands. 'Please! Hear the rest of my plan. And then voice your objections, by all means. The man who now rules the Empire is different from those who have preceded him. I believe that Nero will listen to our case. If you doubt this, I say to you – look at what he has done in the four years he has been Emperor of the Romans. He has lowered taxes, spared his enemies, restored the judicial powers of the Roman Senate. He has guaranteed that the poor of Rome should eat. He has freely given forty million sesterces of his own money to the public treasury. Surely this man is no stranger to justice and virtue!'

There was no dissenting voice. So Ben Hur continued. 'You are all aware that I knew Jesus and heard him speak – as did many others among you here. But I believe I can bring our faith to a man who did not hear Christ, because of the strength of the doctrine itself. Have we no faith in the words of our Master? Surely any decent man will realize what hope these words will bring – especially to the downtrodden. I propose to convert the Emperor to the faith of Christ! If the Emperor of Rome becomes Christian, the rest of the world will most certainly follow.'

There was silence in the room. Finally a murmur ran through the listeners.

'It's a startling idea!' breathed Matthew. 'You really think you could do it?'

'Yes,' said Ben Hur.

'Judah ...' Joseph said slowly. 'I too think it is a daring and inspired proposal ... But one thing I fear greatly. You have put your fortune at our disposal. Your funds support us. You are vital to us. For that reason you have always kept your true faith a secret. If you reveal yourself now, you will become a marked man.'

'Not if Caesar is on my side.'

Joseph regarded him doubtfully. 'And if he is not? What if he is not so receptive as you think?'

'It must be worth the risk,' Ben Hur insisted. 'Anything would be better than the way things are now. Is any one of us really safe? Even you, Joseph. It's a long time since you buried Christ, but don't think that your fellow rabbis have forgotten that sign of your true sympathies. Believe me, if they found the right pretext, they'd have you in front of their council before you could say a prayer.'

There was a chorus of agreement.

'I can see that everyone else is with you, Judah,' said the old man. 'I only hope that God is with you ...'

The warm night wind tousled Ben Hur's hair, as he placed the last of the blankets into his saddlebag. He wondered. Had he done everything? He had ensured that his steward would have access to money, so that the great house could function and the servants be paid, even if his absence were prolonged. And he had gone to the men's courtyard of the Temple and prayed for the success of his journey.

Impatiently he glanced at the sky. It was beginning to get light. Why was Peter taking so long with the extra horse? Ben Hur was impatient to be on his way before daybreak.

His eyes wandered over the familiar outlines of the house. He thought of Esther again. Hardly anything had changed since she had lived here. That lovely and warm woman had given him so much of her brief life. He could still hear the shouts of his children echoing from the walls.

But then the plague had come and taken his family with it, swept away the very foundations of his happiness. He had tottered, but he had not fallen. The one thing which had eased the pain of their deaths was his faith that he would see them again, perhaps in the not too distant future.

The clatter of hooves on cobblestones interrupted his reverie.

Ben Hur hurried to the gate, and pulled back the heavy wooden latch. But when he had swung the gate open, he gazed in astonishment at the rider. It was not Peter. It was Leah.

She dismounted and walked her horse into the courtyard. Ben Hur shut the gate and strode over to her.

'Leah! There is no one with you? You have come here –'

'I know what you are going to tell me,' she said. 'There are brigands on the roads. It is dangerous.'

'That does not alter the fact that you should not be travelling alone at this time of night.'

She stared at him coldly. 'My father tells me we are no longer betrothed.'

'Did he tell you why?'

'Yes. You are going on a long journey. You may never come back.'

'It is the truth. To ask you to wait for me would not be fair.'

Her expression did not change. 'Could you not have come yourself to tell me this?'

'I had no time to come to you.'

'What is this mission?' Leah demanded. 'No one will tell me a thing about it.'

'Believe me, it is safer for you not to be involved.'

Leah gazed at him steadily. 'Very well. I will say no more about that. I will ask you something else. Why do you lie to me?'

'In what way have I lied?'

'You say you had no time to tell me you were leaving. That is not true. You were afraid to face me – that is the real reason. I despise cowards.'

Ben Hur took her by the shoulders. 'Please believe me. I *am* in a hurry. It is against the law to travel on the Sabbath. I must reach Caesarea before then.'

She shook her head. 'You are not being honest, Judah. There is more to this than your hurry to be off.'

He hesitated. 'Perhaps I have not been fair to you. You know what happened to my wife and children?'

She nodded. 'My father told me.'

'I – I cannot take leave of them, Leah ... To contemplate another life – I would feel disloyal ...'

'I am glad we are no longer betrothed!' she burst out, wrenching free of him. 'You are no good to any living woman – you are in love with a dead woman! Perhaps you should crawl in the tomb with her – your life is over!'

In a sudden flash of anger, he slapped her.

She buried her face in her hands and burst into tears. Instantly Ben Hur was sorry. He put his arms around her and stroked her long, glistening hair.

'Forgive me, Leah. You did not deserve that. I *have* lived too long with the dead.'

Her tears ceased, but she drew away. Ben Hur took her by both arms and pulled her back to him. He held her until the tenseness went out of her body. She felt soft and small – yet Leah was the only one who had dared to speak to him like this. Her words had jolted him.

'You have made me look at myself again,' he said finally.

'A man like you should not stop living,' she murmured.

'I have no intention of that,' he said with sudden determination. 'If I have a future, I want you to share it. Let us resume the betrothal.'

'You say that now. Perhaps tomorrow you will change your mind again.'

'No,' Ben Hur insisted. 'I mean it, Leah.'

'You have said your journey will be hazardous. What if you never come back?'

'That is a risk we must take.'

'Perhaps if you know what awaits you,' she said softly, 'you will hasten your return ...'

Before Ben Hur's astonished eyes, she removed her cloak and slid out of her stola. There was nothing underneath. She stood there in front of him, naked, her glorious young body silvered by the moon of Nisan.

On the high stern deck of the great ship, Ben Hur breathed the sea air deep into his lungs. Next to him was the rounded canopy, where the ship's master was sitting, protected from the sun. The gilded swan's head which decorated the vessel's stern gazed out sightlessly at the open, whitecapped sea.

Ben Hur smiled wryly. He had been just as blind as that wooden bird. Until the other night, he had always thought of Leah as an ingenuous, pliable child. But now it was clear to him that she was driven by a formidable determination to get exactly what she wanted. She had left him speechless when she had calmly removed her clothes. Apparently the standards of behaviour expected from a girl of her breeding meant nothing to her.

Ben Hur had been sorely tempted in that moonlit courtyard. But he had forced her to put her clothes back on, then escorted her to her father's house.

Roused from his bed, Joseph had been surprised but delighted to learn that the betrothal had been resumed. He had made a few chiding noises to show his disapproval of his daughter's unorthodox visit, but he obviously had not the slightest idea just how far she had been prepared to go.

Ben Hur was glad Leah had been so aggressive. If he was to beget another family, he could think of no better line than the house of Joseph to unite with his own.

The shrill cries of the Egyptian seamen distracted him. He watched as the naked brown-skinned men laboured in the warm sun, heaving on the braces which controlled the great yardarm. The wind must have shifted slightly while he had been occupied with his thoughts. His eyes travelled up the huge, swelling square sail to the small triangular topsails set above it. He had been lucky to obtain passage on an Alexandrian mail ship which had stopped at Caesarea. In such a craft he would have a better chance of a fast voyage. Only mail ships were allowed to carry their topsails at all times, even in harbours and restricted areas where other craft were prohibited from doing so.

A yell from the master sheltered under his canopy told the sailors they had swung the yard far enough. Ben Hur noted how swiftly the seamen leaped to obey. He well knew that the province of Egypt was largely populated by the poorest peasants in the Empire. For one of them the life of a seaman on a merchant ship was an escape indeed.

Behind him Ben Hur heard a desperate groan. The huge figure of Peter sagged against the rail like a limp sack of grain. After a moment, the sack straightened up.

'Seasick, Peter? I thought you spent so many years as a fisherman.'

Peter groaned again. 'The Sea of Galilee is a very different kettle of fish from a great ocean.'

'But there is not a wave anywhere,' said Ben Hur. 'The Sea of Galilee can be much rougher than this.'

'It's not so much the waves I hate. It's that I can't see land. Anywhere. But – if you really want to know the truth – I was sick all the time on the Sea of Galilee.' He sighed. 'That's why I gave up being a fisherman, and became a teacher.'

Ben Hur chuckled and patted Peter's shoulder reassuringly. 'Have patience. We're one day from Brundisium at the most. The rest of the journey is by land.'

'I'd feel better if I didn't have such doubts,' Peter muttered.

'What doubts?'

'About this mad scheme of yours. You talk about this man Seneca. How well do you know him?'

'I've met him a few times. He was a friend of my adoptive father.'

Peter's scowl deepened. 'Why should this Roman help a band of renegade Jews? Maybe he hates Jews.'

Ben Hur smiled. 'In that case we must retrieve our foreskins.'

Peter laughed weakly.

'In all seriousness,' said Ben Hur, 'if Seneca will not introduce me to Nero, there are others. I am not without connections in Rome.'

Peter's face went white. He clutched his stomach, then leaned over the rail and retched. Finally, with a moan, he stood erect. 'What if the wind dies? Your "one day from Brundisium at the most" could turn into weeks!'

'Perhaps you might worry less, Peter, if you felt better. I should lie down, if I were you.'

Peter clutched the rail unsteadily. 'If we ever go back to Jerusalem,' he vowed, 'I'll walk!'

He staggered over to a coil of disused rope and sank down on it miserably.

Ben Hur watched with a smile. Then his face sobered. He had made light of Peter's doubts, but that did not mean he had none of his own.

CHAPTER TWO

Why was Seneca avoiding him? Troubled, Ben Hur stared through the open shutters of the window at the portico which bordered the peaceful garden of his villa. Impatiently he brushed aside a fly. Twice now he had paid a visit in person to Seneca's house in Rome, and on neither occasion was Seneca there – or at least so Ben Hur had been told. Today he had sent Phaon, who had no better success.

He turned back to the kindly-faced, white-haired man who stood waiting patiently by the table.

'Who was it you spoke to?' Ben Hur wondered.

'The freedman,' Phaon replied.

'What were his exact words?'

'He merely told me that the Renowned Seneca was not in residence. But he assured me that he would inform the senator that you wish to see him.'

Ben Hur moved over to the table and sat down with a sigh. Phaon held up a bundle of papyri.

'The accounts, young Arrius.'

Ben Hur smiled inwardly. He would always be *young* Arrius to these people, even though he was middle-aged now, and the elder Arrius was long dead.

Phaon continued to wave the papyri at him. 'You've been putting off looking at them too long. Tomorrow is rent day.'

'I'm sure they're in order.'

'Of course they are! But I've told you before – you should still look at them. If I may say so, you are more highly regarded by your tenants than other great landlords. That's because I have always insisted that you take the trouble to be familiar with their affairs when you are here. You cannot fool a farmer, young Arrius. Either you know what his land yielded, or you don't. It is your personal interest in such things which makes them realize they are in your heart, even when you're over the sea. That way –'

'All right, Phaon. All right. You have made your point. I give you my word that by tomorrow morning, I'll look at your excellent accounts.'

'Thank you, young Arrius,' he said, placing the pile of papyri on the table in front of Ben Hur.

The elderly man scrutinized Ben Hur's face knowingly. 'You're worried. You're not getting enough sleep.'

'I'll try to rectify that.'

Phaon nodded, and left the room.

The documents on the table in front of him were the furthest thing from Ben Hur's mind. He stared at them with unseeing eyes. Was there any significance to Seneca's mysterious unavailability? Perhaps he should pay yet another visit to Seneca's house. Or would that be too demeaning?

His thoughts were interrupted when the door of the tablinium opened, and the tall figure of Electra stood there, clad in her usual long grey tunic. She held a tray laden with platters.

'My husband said you were in here,' she announced. 'It's time for your meal. Sea urchins, cooked in spices, honey and oil. Some egg sauce is on the side. I made it yesterday, but it's always better the second day.'

Electra sailed into the room, unceremoniously swept Phaon's accounts from the table and plonked the tray in front of Ben Hur. The scent of the highly seasoned dish titillated his nostrils. He found himself devouring the food.

As usual, Electra's presence began to grate. She stood over him doggedly, arms folded, watching him eat. Ben Hur had given up all hope of changing this annoying habit of hers. On several occasions in the past, he had suggested that she go away and return for the tray later, but she never did, always hovering round, engaging him in unwanted conversation or, worse, criticizing him for his habitual speed in eating.

Today she was silent, which was a bad sign. It usually signified that she was gathering her energy for a particularly explosive outburst.

Ben Hur could remember when he had first met Electra and Phaon, her husband. They had been the slaves of the elder Quintus Arrius when Ben Hur, a lonely stranger, had been brought into this home. Twenty odd years had gone by since then, but neither husband nor wife seemed to have changed at all. Phaon was Greek, while Electra was Latin, but it had pleased Arrius to give her a Greek name to match her husband's. In a jesting spirit, he had dubbed her Electra, for she had always been fierce, dominant, and even vengeful on occasion.

In his will, Arrius had manumitted them both, but neither would accept freedom. Both chose to stay on here, for it was their home. And Ben Hur was glad of this, because they cared for the villa, and ran the business of the estate in his absence.

'Must you eat your sauce so fast!' Electra barked suddenly. 'I've long since ceased to worry about your digestion. But you might at least pause to consider that what you gulp down in one second I take half a day to create.'

'I've tasted every bite,' Ben Hur protested. 'It's delicious.'

'You like it!' she exclaimed, somewhat mollified.

'I do indeed.'

Once again Electra scowled. 'You would've had more to eat,' she muttered. 'I had three roast parrots, cooked in figs, bay leaves and rubbed with honey. But when I went to get them, they were gone. And there he was – sitting there picking teeth. He'd eaten the lot – that slave of yours!'

'Peter is no slave,' Ben Hur corrected her.

'Then what is he? He *does* nothing ...'

'He's a teacher.'

'Hah!' Electra snorted derisively. 'What does he teach? Gluttony?'

'I'll speak to him about those parrots,' said Ben Hur, rising and preparing to escape.

'And while you're at it, mention that haunch of venison which disappeared yesterday.'

'I'll mention the haunch and the parrots.'

'On second thoughts,' Electra whispered, 'don't. Not a word. I'll cook a parrot especially for him. With a thistle in it!'

Outside, he breathed in the morning air with a sigh of relief, and strolled along the handsome portico which led to the other wing of the house. He paused abruptly at the sound of a tremendous splash, followed by a chilling animal wail. It came from the bath-house further along the walkway. Ben Hur strode forward, turned right under a small archway and opened a door.

In a spacious, circular room, well lit by two open windows and a round aperture at the apex of its dome, Peter reclined like a great white whale in the tepid pool. He waved happily when he saw Ben Hur.

'The cry I heard!' Ben Hur exclaimed. 'Was it you?'

'Of course!' Peter boomed.

'But it sounded like a hyena.'

'That's right. They used to come down to the shores of Galilee at night to drink. I often talked to them. There was no one else to talk to.'

Peter dived under and came up, blowing out a stream of water. 'The hyenas were better company than some men I've met,' he said. 'I'm referring to certain respected rabbis in the Sanhedrin.'

Ben Hur smiled and began to shed his tunic.

'What a wonderful bath this is!' Peter exclaimed rapturously. 'Nothing like being clean to make a man feel virtuous.'

'Our Master said that the cleanliness *inside* a man is what matters,' Ben Hur pointed out, removing his shoes.

'He was right, of course,' Peter burbled, half-submerged. 'But I see no harm in keeping a man's outer parts as virtuous as his innards.'

At that moment the door of the bath-house was flung open, and Electra stood there. She looked at the two naked men with no change of expression.

'Arrius, put your tunic on. There is a noble gentleman here to see you. The Most Renowned Seneca.'

With that, the door banged again, and Electra was gone.

Finally Peter broke the silence. 'Well – what are you waiting for? I'll save the water for you.'

Ben Hur nodded, slipped back into his tunic, tied on his shoes, and left the bath-house.

Hurrying along the portico, Ben Hur entered the triclinium, then passed through another doorway into the bright, spacious atrium.

There stood Seneca. He was a portly, balding man, dignified in his toga with its wide purple stripe proclaiming him a senator. At the moment Seneca's heavy-lidded eyes were glued to the multi-coloured fish which darted here and there round the atrium pool. He seemed oblivious to Ben Hur, who waited in the doorway.

'Welcome, Most Renowned Sir,' Ben Hur said finally.

Seneca did not move, continuing to stare at the water. 'A moment,' he murmured. 'A fish in this pool. The fellow with the black blotch on his fin ... I'd swear he was here in your father's day!'

Now Seneca turned to Ben Hur with a puzzled frown. 'But that can't be, can it? Fish don't live that long. Or do they?'

'Accounts of their life-spans vary.'

'Perhaps I'll write a treatise on fish,' Seneca mused. 'They must be happy there. Swimming round, unaware they are mortal. They are more fortunate than men.'

Then Seneca's frown deepened, and he shook his head. That can't be true. If men did not know they were mortal, they would not have philosophy, and then they would be unfortunate indeed! The more one ponders on nature, the more one realizes that everything has its price. You've been looking for me, young Arrius.'

So rapid was Seneca's shift of thought that it was a moment before Ben Hur answered. 'Why ... yes! That's right! I have been! You've been very inaccessible.'

'Apologies are a waste of time, explanations are not. You should see my house at Nomentum! It's rather like this – but much larger. That's where I've been. I always go there when I get tired of Rome, and that's why you couldn't find me.'

Ben Hur bowed slightly. 'I am only glad you finally got word I was looking for you.'

'Word usually seeps through to me. It's good to see you again, young Arrius.'

'And it is good to see you too, Most Renowned Sir.' He moved to a small table by the pool and picked up a Samian-ware jug. 'Your house may be bigger, but I'm sure your Falernian is no finer. May I offer you a cup?'

Seneca's heavy-lidded eyes twitched slightly. 'You know, of course, that I am a follower of Zeno. And Zeno said that a good man does not drink. His actual words were "No person who drinks is entrusted with a secret. The good man is entrusted with a secret. Therefore, the good man will not drink."'

Ben Hur shrugged and started to put the jug back.

'One moment,' Seneca continued quickly. 'Zeno was not always right. In fact his argument on this matter was quite fallacious. One could easily reply to Zeno "No person who sleeps is entrusted with a secret. The good man is entrusted with a secret. Therefore, the good man will not go to sleep."' Seneca cleared his throat. 'And, therefore, young Arrius, I will have that drink.'

With a laugh, Ben Hur poured two cups full of wine and handed one to Seneca. The senator passed it under his nose two or three times first, then sipped it gratefully.

'Arrius the elder was one of my closest friends ... And you know what Aristotle said about friendship. It is "a single soul dwelling in two bodies", though, unfortunately, only one of us is left. Therefore, young Arrius, perhaps I'll see about arranging an audience with the Emperor for you ...'

Ben Hur was astonished. 'How did you know what I wanted?'

'Why else would you seek my company? A sententious, garrulous old bore like me? Everyone wants me to introduce him to the Emperor.' Seneca gave an evil little chuckle. 'Naturally I turn a deaf ear to most.' His heavy-lidded eyes regarded Ben Hur penetratingly. 'Might I ask *why* you want to see the Emperor?'

Putting his cup back on the table, Ben Hur spoke crisply and with assurance. 'The Sanhedrin in Jerusalem is abusing the privilege which the Roman Government has allowed it. They are persecuting any group they don't approve of. And with no outside hindrance.'

Seneca sipped his wine. 'And which of these persecuted groups do you represent?'

Ben Hur hesitated. Should Seneca learn what Ben Hur had in mind, there was no way of predicting how he would respond. Many were violent in their disapproval of the Christians.

'I think,' said Ben Hur cautiously, 'that all groups and beliefs should have equal protection from Rome. As long as their activities are lawful, of course.'

'And you came all the way from Jerusalem to bring this to the attention of the Emperor?'

'That's right.'

'Yet you were in Rome less than a year ago. You didn't pursue the matter then?'

Ben Hur felt a little coldness inside. He had not known that Seneca was aware of his last visit to Rome. Ben Hur shrugged casually. 'Affairs in Judaea have grown much worse since then.'

'Has this situation injured you in any way?'

'No.'

'Then you are here on behalf of others?'

'Is that so surprising?'

'Altruism is always surprising.'

Seneca put his cup down on the table. 'I still think that fish was here in your father's day. It must be the oldest living fish.'

Abruptly he moved round the pool and strode to the hall entrance. Just under the arch, he paused and swung round with a little smile. 'You'll be hearing from me, young Arrius, if I am favoured by the Gods, or God – or whatever you might worship.'

Then the senator turned and made his stately way down the short, mosaic-floored passage to the entrance.

Ben Hur followed him. Standing in the hallway, he could see Seneca as he joined his small retinue of attendants waiting outside, including a musician, who immediately began to play his lyre. Seneca climbed into a sedan chair, first carefully picking up his toga to make sure it did not get dusty. Then four powerfully muscular slaves hoisted the poles of the litter on to their shoulders, and the great man was borne away, his retinue tagging along on either side.

The lyre player began to sing, as he strolled close to the litter. His voice was high and clear. His words floated back to Ben Hur in the fragrant summer air.

> Alas and alack! What a nothing is man!
> We all shall be bones at the end of life's span:
> So let us be jolly as long as we can . . .

The song, echoing over the fields, could still be heard after the procession had rounded a bend in the road and was out of sight.

With a frown, Ben Hur turned back towards the atrium. There had been an undercurrent in Seneca's manner which Ben Hur did not like. He had not expected Seneca to be so suspicious. It could well be that if the senator learned of a clandestine sect of Christians in the capital, he might decide he had more to gain by denouncing them as subversives than by helping them.

Ben Hur came to a decision. Abruptly he turned back and strode out of the house. Crossing the small but well kept garden, he came to a gate. Lifting the latch he passed through the fence into a wild uncultivated stretch of woodland which separated the villa itself from the fields of the nearest tenant farmer. Here the grass grew as high as a man's waist, and heavy undergrowth impeded progress every few feet. Ben Hur could not see very far in front of him, because of the denseness of the foliage, but he knew exactly where he was going. A few more feet of trudging brought him to a little hollow, where the branches hung thickly. Parting the leaves, he suddenly found himself in the presence of a temple. It was made of Parian marble, and set on a miniature podium. Its beautifully carved Corinthian columns were exactly like those found on much larger buildings all over Rome. The elegant little monument was overgrown with weeds, and birds had nested on its roof.

It was the tomb of Quintus Arrius.

A wave of emotion swept over Ben Hur. Long-forgotten memories thrust painfully back into his consciousness. He had never known his natural father, who had died when he was an infant, but Arrius had more than made up for that lack. Arrius had taken him into his home and given him a new life.

Ben Hur recalled the care with which Arrius had supervised the construction of this temple. The design was cunning and well suited to Ben Hur's present purpose.

Moving round the building, he approached the rear. Coming up to the base of the structure, he ran his hands along the smooth, precisely cut stones, until he found one which was slightly recessed. He pushed. As it had twenty years ago, it swung aside easily, revealing an entrance to a secret chamber below. Ben Hur lowered himself through the opening and descended a short flight of steps.

The shaft of light coming through the open entrance dimly illuminated the underground crypt. About sixty feet in length, it was in the shape of a small basilica. Its ceiling was an oblong barrel vault, and the far end rounded into an apse. A row of arches travelling down its length opened into small side chambers. Bare and devoid of furniture, this had once been a place where Arrius had practised certain secret rites of his own, shared only by intimate friends. Other than these few people, not even his household staff knew that a room existed under the mausoleum. Slaves had surreptitiously built the secret chamber while they were constructing the temple above, and once their task was finished, they had been sent to Arrius' other estate in distant Cilicia.

Arrius had been a devotee of Mithras and had initiated Ben Hur into that religion. Its God was a God of light and truth. Mithras was an intermediary between man and God, and his adherents practised baptism, a rite somewhat different from the bizarre and orgiastic rituals of many other cults.

Ben Hur reflected that there were many strong similarities between the worship of Mithras and the doctrines of Christ. Was it possible that Mithras and Christ were leading men to the same God? Of course, there were differences. Mithras was a man's religion, even prohibiting female initiates. And though Mithras preached honour and virtue, it was the virtue of men rather than women.

But Ben Hur was convinced that Christ's message combined many inspired elements of other cults, and therefore came closest to revealing the true nature of God.

Now Ben Hur ascended the short flight of steps, groped for a handle and found it. He pulled, and the stone which concealed the entrance slid shut again. The underground hall was plunged into darkness, but descending back down the steps, Ben Hur unerringly made his way along the nave until he came to the far end. Reaching the apse where the altar had once stood, he felt carefully along the curved surface of the wall. He found what he was looking for – another handle – and he opened a small door. Ducking his head, Ben Hur crouched low and entered a narrow subterranean passage, being careful to close the door behind him.

Crouched thus, creeping gingerly along, Ben Hur made his way for perhaps five or six hundred feet, until the ground began to rise. If nothing had fallen into disrepair, more steps should lie ahead. Sure enough, Ben Hur came to them. There were only four, and when Ben Hur climbed them, the top of his head brushed a trapdoor. Lifting his hands he felt along its edges until he touched yet another lever. He pushed, but the door was stuck. Grasping the handle in both hands, he pushed again with all his might. Finally the heavy stone yielded. Ben Hur shoved it to one side, then climbed laboriously through the opening. Again he was in a chamber, and the stone which he had just pushed aside was one of the flagstones of its floor. A huge marble sarcophagus rested in the middle of the room. Ben Hur knew it contained the remains of Arrius' wife.

Now he replaced the stone and moved the few feet to the entrance. Twisting the handle, he opened the great double door and emerged on to the portico of another small temple similar to the one which he had entered.

He blinked in the bright sunlight, his eyes having become accustomed to the dark. Stretching before the tomb was the Flaminian Way, its paved length pleasantly shaded by plane trees. Other tombs in different architectural styles could be seen bordering the road at varying intervals. Now Ben Hur turned, closed the double doors behind him, then descended the three steps of the podium to the roadside.

Arrius had gone to such lengths to create secrecy for himself and his closest friends because the worship of Mithras was not considered respectable for a Roman of his class. But for Ben Hur and the Christians secrecy might be a matter of life and death.

Phaon wearily bent over and picked up the heavy bridle. As he did so, the mule aimed a vicious kick at him which barely missed. Phaon shook his head sadly.

'I never did like mules,' he murmured, leading the beast out of the stable into the hot afternoon sun.

'Phaon!' shrieked Electra's voice.

He stiffened and squinted into the sun towards the villa. A moment later his wife's form came hurtling down the path towards him at full gallop. She brandished something.

'You have no more brains than an owl!' she stated emphatically. 'You forgot your hat.'

'But I don't need a hat,' Phaon protested.

'If you don't take your hat, you're not going!'

'But I have to. Tomorrow's rent day. I've got to be sure the tenants will appear ...'

'You'll be three hours in the sun,' Electra pointed out. 'Your brains are too addled as it is.'

'Very well, then,' Phaon sighed with resignation.

Electra clapped the hat on his head and strode back up the path towards the villa.

Phaon mounted the mule and dug his heels into the animal's side. It ambled slowly off.

Leisurely the beast picked its way through the olive grove near Ben Hur's villa. When it reached the edge of the trees, and descended a small slope to the bank of a stream, Phaon was starting to doze. There was only one path in the vicinity, and the animal knew it well. He could relax.

Suddenly he sat erect. Two men stood waiting in the path ahead of him, one bearing a wicked-looking knotted cudgel. Phaon recognized them almost immediately as two of Seneca's freedmen. The shorter man was the very fellow he had spoken to this morning at Seneca's house in Rome. Phaon was perplexed. What were they doing out here?

As Phaon drew abreast of them, the men stepped forward, one on each side of the mule. Taking the animal by the bridle, they brought it to a halt.

'Greetings,' said the one with the cudgel.

'Your honour's good health,' Phaon replied courteously.

'We want you to come with us,' explained the other – explaining nothing.

'I have duties to attend to. I must be on my way.'

'After we're finished with you,' said the one with the cudgel.

Phaon gulped. He wondered what was in store for him.

Abruptly the two men led him off the path into some brush. The going was tortuous and rocky. Soon the terrain began to slope upwards. The mule, clearly resentful at being led off his beaten track, stood stock still, refusing to go further. Savagely the man with the cudgel lifted his weapon and brought it down hard under the animal's tail. The mule brayed and scrambled forward again. Phaon began to perspire. Irrationally, he was grateful that his wife had forced him to wear the hat.

Finally the ground levelled out. They were in a grassy meadow. A clump of trees lay ahead. Coming from it, growing gradually louder as they drew closer, was the clear sound of a man singing, accompanied by the notes of a lyre.

They came to a clearing. And there a strange sight met Phaon's eyes.

Taking his ease on the grass, surrounded by his retinue, was Seneca. All were enjoying a meal of cheese and fruit. At the sight of Phaon, Seneca waved to his companions, who rose and made their way off among the trees to one side.

The two freedmen led the mule up to the great man, then retired discreetly into the trees with the others.

'Parmenides says this universe is no more than a semblance of reality,' Seneca murmured finally. 'Perhaps a deceptive semblance. But that mule is very real. Would you remove it?'

Obediently, Phaon dismounted and slapped the mule. But the beast would not move. Now Phaon began to beat it in earnest. The animal, however, doggedly remained where it was.

'Never mind,' said Seneca. 'Never mind. Perhaps it is a reality without any substance at all. Zeno says that nothing exists. And this conversation won't take long anyway.'

Phaon bowed humbly. 'Anything which pleases you, Most Renowned Sir.'

'Men have good report of you, Phaon,' Seneca stated.

Phaon was surprised and pleased. 'Do they?'

'Indeed they do. You must serve young Arrius very well.'

'Your words are most kind, Renowned Sir.'

'Euclid says "The shortest distance between two points is a straight line." Therefore I will get straight to the point. I confess your devotion to Arrius has made me envious. I would like you to work for me.'

'Oh no! I could never leave young Arrius.'

'I would never ask you to. Indeed not! In fact, the task I have in mind for you is contingent on your remaining in his employ.'

Phaon said nothing.

'I have an insatiable need for knowledge,' Seneca continued. 'It pervades my whole life. As Zeno said, "It is better to be wise than to be king." No ... On second thoughts, he didn't say that. *I* said it. The introduction to my treatise "On Knowledge", I believe ... At any rate, I find I am woefully ignorant about young Arrius. And ignorance is a state of affairs I cannot tolerate.'

Phaon licked his lips. 'With all due respect, Renowned Sir, I could never be an informer, if that is what you are suggesting. I could not be so disloyal.'

Seneca regarded him thoughtfully, then reached behind him and picked up a bag. He weighed it experimentally in his hand and then placed it in his lap.

'Thinkers have never agreed about the nature of loyalty,' he murmured. 'The Cynics hold that loyalty is the greatest single obstruction to the development of mankind. I don't agree. I think loyalty has a definite value. At today's prices, about three denarii.'

He reached into the bag and took out three coins, which he placed suggestively on the ground nearby.

Phaon shook his head resolutely. 'Please don't ask this of me. Young Arrius has done so much for me. I owe him everything.'

'Ah. Now you are talking about a different quality. Gratitude. Perhaps that is worth a little more. Maybe four denarii.' Seneca extracted four more coins and placed them beside the others.

Phaon gulped. 'Renowned Sir – don't ask me to do anything against young Arrius. I love him like a son.'

Seneca raised an eyebrow. 'Love? Now of all the virtues, that is perhaps worth the least, if indeed it is a virtue. Many *give* it away. But let us say it is worth a denarius.'

The Senator took out a single coin, putting it with the others.

'I am sorry, sir,' Phaon insisted. 'I cannot.'

Seneca took up the money and returned it to the bag. 'Admirable!'

Phaon blinked with surprise. 'You are not displeased with me?'

'Not a bit! You have only proved what men have said about you. You are an honourable man, Phaon. A mountain of virtue.'

The freedman blushed.

'The true test of man's integrity,' Seneca went on, 'is his imperviousness to bribery. The great Cicero himself said, "I prefer a man without money to money without a man."' Seneca shook his head sadly. 'Few men shared Cicero's principles. They killed him, you know ...'

Phaon glanced at Seneca sharply. For an instant their eyes held, then Phaon hastily looked away.

'That is an interesting hat you are wearing,' Seneca observed.

The freedman touched it self-consciously. 'My wife says it protects me from the sun. She gets very upset if I don't wear it.'

'Oh dear! I am so glad you told me. When we send your head to her, we'll be certain it is in the hat.'

Two figures, wrapped in cloaks against the chill of the night, hurried along close to the buildings on one side of the street. A wagon, almost as wide as the road itself, laden with amphorae, trundled past, forcing the pedestrians to flatten themselves against the wall to avoid being run down, the larger of the two dropping the torch he was carrying. It fell in a pool of water and went out with a hiss. Peter ground his teeth in frustration, lunged forward to retrieve it, but leaped back as another vehicle sloshed past.

Angrily he wiped the mud from his sleeve.

'The middle of the night!' Peter exclaimed. 'Where do all these wagons come from?'

'It's illegal for wheeled traffic to use the streets of Rome during the day – they must be left clear for the pedestrians,' Ben Hur told him.

Two more wagons rumbled by.

A moment later Ben Hur and Peter arrived at a fork where the street branched in four directions, each one twisting a snaky path into a mysterious black mass of buildings.

'Why don't you face it?' Peter growled. 'We're lost!'

Several other carts passed, forcing them to take refuge against a stone latrine by the road.

'I suppose you're right,' murmured Ben Hur. 'Lost isn't a bad description for where we are ...'

'How could *you* be lost? You've been to the Vicus before, haven't you?'

'Yes. The first day we arrived.'

'Then why can't you find it now?' Peter demanded.

'Because it looks entirely different at night. Rome is an extremely confusing city.'

'Why did we have to come at night?' Peter persisted. 'All this secrecy seems pointless.'

'It's not pointless. Better that our journeys down here are not generally known ...'

Ben Hur stepped into the path of an approaching horseman and hailed him. But the stranger only kicked his mount to a gallop, raising his whip threateningly. Ben Hur leaped back to avoid being trampled to death and returned to Peter with a scowl. 'Try to stop someone for directions – they think you're a footpad!'

'I'm ravenous!' Peter moaned. 'I wish I'd eaten before we left. I don't relish starving to death out here.'

Ben Hur said nothing.

'I would've eaten,' Peter grumbled, 'but my mouth was too sore. You'll never believe what happened. Last night I woke up and felt like a morsel of something. I found a lovely roast parrot all dressed and prepared in your scullery. But when I bit into it – Jehovah's mercy! It had a *thistle* in it! How it got there, I can't imagine.'

Paying no attention to Peter's muttering, Ben Hur gazed round in bewilderment, searching vainly for some familiar landmark. A hunched figure in a chariot raced by. Once again mud splattered both men.

Peter shook the grime from his cloak. 'This Vicus of the Wheelwrights ... is it a big place?'

Ben Hur nodded.

'Then why can't we find it?'

'The city is divided into about three hundred of such districts.'

'I've got a suggestion,' Peter said hopefully. 'Let's go back to the villa.'

'I wish we could,' said Ben Hur, 'but I don't think I could find the way back either.'

Peter glared at him malevolently.

Ben Hur cleared his throat. 'I suggest we just keep going. I can't believe we're going that far away.'

'I'll tell you what I'm going to do. I'm going to stop one of these drivers, even if I have to pull him out of his cart!'

Peter turned grimly towards the road, but then paused, sniffing the air like a gun dog.

'What is it?' asked Ben Hur.

'Can't you smell it?'

'Smell what?'

'Roast mutton.' Peter sniffed again. 'I'm never wrong about such things.' Peter pointed towards one of the mysterious alleys which branched off into the darkness. 'It's that way. Let's go!'

'No! First we've got to find the Vicus.'

'Forget the Vicus,' said Peter, starting forward. 'I'm hungry!'

Ben Hur fell into step beside him. Both men lurched back to avoid another wagon, but then continued onwards.

'Besides,' said Peter, still sniffing, 'the gentlefolk who are dining on that juicy, succulent mutton will doubtless be able to tell us where the Vicus is.'

Faster and faster Peter walked, until Ben Hur could also smell the overpowering odour of cooking meat. Then from a narrow passage which meandered off to their right through an archway, the sound of loud voices and singing could be clearly heard.

When they turned into the alley, an astonishing spectacle of gaiety and light leaped at them out of the darkness. A wooden pole set across the entrance barred the place to wheeled traffic, and the whole area was brightly lit by scores of torches, flaring from the closed shop fronts. Big trestle tables piled high with food were set out on the street. People were crowding round them, chattering, singing and drinking, obviously having a good time. The mutton in question was being cooked on spits over fires which blazed between the tables.

Peter licked his lips. 'Wonder who is giving the celebration ...'

Ben Hur pointed to a little niche set into a street corner wall. There were inscriptions all round the shrine.

'This must be a festival of the street corner gods,' said Ben Hur. 'Every street corner has its Lares. Their festivals are celebrated frequently.'

'It's a nice custom,' Peter stated. 'And it certainly doesn't violate any of my beliefs. Let's get some of that mutton.'

Ben Hur took him by the arm, and again indicated the shrine. 'Look just above the niche.'

Peter did so. Carved on the keystone of the little arch was a wheel.

'Thank God for you and your nose!' Ben Hur exclaimed. 'This

is the Vicus of the Wheelwrights. With all the shops closed, the lights and festivities, I didn't recognize it. Let's find Barnabas.'

'Barnabas will have to wait until I eat,' Peter stated emphatically. He headed for the nearest of the great cooking fires, where a plump young woman was slicing off great pieces of meat and piling them on wooden platters, which she handed to all who approached. Without even looking at the two newcomers she put plates in their outstretched hands.

Immediately Peter began to wolf the food. 'I love you!' he boomed with a mouth full of meat.

The woman looked up, and when she saw Peter, she smiled invitingly. With a suggestive swish of her large hips, she turned to an earthenware jar, pouring a cup of wine, which she handed to Peter.

'Are you married?' Peter asked.

'No.' She smiled again and added coyly, 'Not yet.'

Peter gulped down the wine. 'What a pity!'

Ben Hur pulled him by the arm. 'Come ... we must find Barnabas.'

'Can't *you* find Barnabas?' Peter grumbled. 'Would you have me rudely turn my back on this nice lady?'

'You are looking for Barnabas the rim-maker?' the woman asked. 'The one who is married to Phoebe?'

'That's right,' said Ben Hur.

She glanced round at the roistering celebrants. 'I don't see them. But they must be here somewhere. If you can't find them, ask my father. He's the magistrate.'

'Where is he?'

'At the big table. His name is Nigrinus.'

'Thank you,' said Ben Hur, taking the reluctant Peter by the arm.

'I'll be back,' Peter promised the woman.

'I'll be here all evening.' She winked. 'And I'll save you some meat.'

The two wormed their way through drunken, shouting people.

'Do you think we should?' Peter whispered.

'Should what?'

'Well ... if her father's a magistrate ... He might be suspicious.

We're strangers in the area. You said you didn't want to call attention to your visits down here.'

'Don't worry,' Ben Hur reassured him. 'He's not that sort of magistrate ... He's just the leading citizen of the Vicus for the year ...'

By now they had reached the big table. Cups of wine were pushed in their direction.

'Which is Nigrinus?' Ben Hur asked the man next to him.

The man pointed to a small, swarthy fellow sitting at the head of the table. Ben Hur made his way over to the magistrate, followed by Peter.

'We're looking for Barnabas,' Ben Hur explained.

Nigrinus surveyed them curiously, and spoke in a voice unexpectedly deep for a man so small. 'You're new here, are you not?'

'We're old friends of Barnabas,' said Ben Hur.

'Sit down and have some wine,' Nigrinus rumbled.

'Later,' said Ben Hur. 'It's very important we find Barnabas.'

'I'm sorry about Barnabas,' Nigrinus said.

Ben Hur and Peter exchanged a look of alarm.

'What's happened?' Peter asked apprehensively.

'I just hope it isn't the fever,' Nigrinus mumbled. 'He was taken ill. He and his wife are shut up in their shop.' Nigrinus pointed to a row of shops fronting on the street. A light glimmered in one of them.

'I wouldn't go there if I were you,' said Nigrinus. 'If it's the fever ...' He shook his head ominously.

But they ignored the warning and made their way to the shop. Ben Hur rapped twice.

A door opened, and a woman stood in the oblong shaft of light which glowed within. She was demure, plain and young, her face devoid of artifice or make-up. She peered into the darkness, then smiled when she recognized Ben Hur.

'Judah! Come in.'

He did so, and Peter followed. Phoebe closed the door behind them. Piles of wheels and rims in various stages of construction littered the room.

'What brings you here at this time of night?' she wondered, glancing at Peter questioningly.

'I've brought someone for you both to meet,' Ben Hur replied.

She nodded, and, with another curious look at Peter, went into the back room. A moment later, she returned with a tall man.

'Welcome, Judah,' said Barnabas.

Ben Hur indicated Peter. 'This is Peter from Galilee.'

Barnabas appraised Peter with interest.

'So you're Peter!' Phoebe exclaimed. 'We've heard about your work for the church in Jerusalem.'

'Truly,' said Peter, with feeling, 'I hope I can do far more for the church in Rome.'

'They told me you were ill,' said Ben Hur to Barnabas. 'You don't look very ill.'

'I'm not,' muttered Barnabas with disgust. 'I just wasn't in the mood to drink, celebrate, and pretend to do homage to their inane gods. There are more gods in this city than there are men! But what news have you?'

'I've met with Seneca,' Ben Hur said.

A flicker of interest crossed Barnabas' taciturn face. 'And?'

'He'll try to arrange an audience.'

'What does that mean?'

'It means – it will take time. Therefore we must be patient. However long it takes, the result will be worth it.'

'But we can't wait!' Phoebe exclaimed. 'They've arrested Paul in Jerusalem. The Sanhedrin!'

There was a moment of silence, as Peter and Ben Hur glanced at each other in shock.

'When did you hear this?' Ben Hur asked finally.

'Silas arrived this morning and brought word.'

'Paul appealed to the Roman Governor,' Barnabas said. 'If the Governor sends him back to the Sanhedrin, we can say farewell to Paul.'

'Judah,' Phoebe broke in. 'Your mission is more important than ever. Silas says you are the greatest hope for all of them in Jerusalem.'

'You must get to the Emperor,' Barnabas insisted.

Ben Hur held up a placating hand. 'I dare not hurry this. And even when I've seen the Emperor – it will take time for me to win his confidence. We must be cautious. Many lives may depend on it. Not only Paul's.'

'I followed them to the Vicus of the Wheelwrights,' Phaon said.

'But I could go no further. The place was blazing with lights. I would have been seen.'

He eyed Seneca and his grim companion apprehensively. Phaon knew the other man's face. He was Burrus, commander of the Praetorian Guard, an official all men feared.

Burrus moved closer to Phaon menacingly. 'Then you didn't see whom he met?'

Phaon gulped. 'Well . . . he spoke to several people. I didn't recognize any of them. It seemed as though he was . . . looking for somebody.'

'The fact is – you don't know whom he met,' Burrus stated flatly.

The freedman glanced around the grove of trees as if searching for an escape. Finally his pleading eyes went to Seneca. 'As I told you, it was too light. Had I approached closer, I would surely have been recognized. And my usefulness to your worships would be gone.'

'It may be gone now . . .' Burrus growled at Phaon, who retreated hastily.

The commander of the Praetorians threw back his toga, revealing a stump of a right arm. 'How would you like yours chopped off at the same spot?'

Phaon said nothing.

Seneca sighed. 'That's enough, Burrus. You'll seize any excuse to remind us of your heroic past, won't you? Doubtless you're going to tell us the same old story about how you lost that arm leading your men against Herman the German.' Seneca turned to Phaon with a conspiratorial smile. 'Between you and me,' he confided, 'I suspect our Praetorian friend's arm dropped off because of an advanced case of pox!'

He took a pouch of coins from his toga, shook it suggestively, and handed it to Phaon. 'It takes a good servant to please two masters.'

Phaon looked at the ground.

'I trust we'll hear from you again soon,' Seneca suggested.

'Oh, you will. You will indeed,' Phaon croaked.

'Naturally you'll send word when you have something to report.' He indicated the grove of trees. 'Let us call this our usual meeting spot.'

Bowing deeply, Phaon retreated backwards through the trees, not daring to face away from two men so exalted. When he reached the clearing, he turned and ran to his mule, mounted and rode off.

The Praetorian commander grinned at Seneca. 'Was I threatening enough?'

'Just right,' said Seneca. 'His teeth were chattering, yet he didn't fall dead.'

Now Seneca frowned. The afternoon sun deepened the creases in his brow. 'Arrius is an equestrian. Son of an ex-consul. Yet in the middle of the night, when any respectable man is at his dining couch or with his mistress or with the boy he loves, this Arrius is prowling around the slums of Rome. What would he want in the Vicus of the Wheelwrights? And even if he did want something, he'd send someone else for it! In the daytime.'

Burrus shrugged. 'Maybe he visits a low-born woman who cannot come to him.'

'I would've thought so. But in this case, I suspect not. Too many things about the man do not make sense. He's been to Rome many times. I've met him before. He always kept to himself ... minded his own business. Now suddenly he wants to see the Emperor. And his reason is far too noble. When I tried to make him more specific, he merely became more evasive.'

'When you put it together like that,' Burrus admitted, 'it does indeed make him sound suspicious. Of course, you were always a master with words.'

'There's more,' Seneca pointed out. 'His companion Petros or Peter. He's not a slave. He's not a gentleman. He does no work. He's said to be a teacher. I have never seen him before. Yet suddenly here he is with young Arrius. Night and day. They are inseparable. Who is *he*?'

Burrus sighed wearily. 'Are you asking me or the trees? If you're asking me, I'll have Arrius and the fat one tortured separately. And then I'll tell you.'

Seneca shook his head. 'That's merely a last resort. Torture has too many disadvantages. In the first place, a man will say anything to escape more pain. The truth is still difficult to find ... But a much more important reason – should young Arrius suddenly disappear, it might alarm whoever his associates are. And then we'd *never* know the truth.'

'You philosophers waste so much time vaporizing that everything goes up in smoke. Tell me, then, do you have a better way?'

'A much better way,' Seneca replied. 'I'll make a friend of him. Cultivate him. Entertain him. And I know he will welcome the friendship for the advantage he thinks it will bring. Zeno, of course, has something to say about such friendships. "Those who begin a friendship because it pays them will similarly cease the friendship because it pays them." In this case, that suits my purpose perfectly.'

CHAPTER THREE

The mid-day sun was directly overhead. It was very warm, and the litter bearers were perspiring heavily as they placed the two sedan chairs on the pink gravel in front of the main entrance. One of the chairs shook slightly as the bulky form of Peter extracted itself and the big man stood up. He appraised the huge sprawling house which lay before him, while Ben Hur paid the carriers.

Both men were transfixed at the sight of Seneca's villa. The entrance was a portico a quarter of a mile long. At the far end of it were several enormous domed structures, and, beyond these, the palatial house itself. The capitals of the seemingly infinite columns were all gilded, the gold leaf shining brightly in the sun. Attendants clad in neat scarlet tunics waited at the entrance to receive the guests, who were filing in, the women elaborately coiffured, their hair flashing jewels, the men in togas nearly all sporting the purple stripe.

Just to the left of the imposing entrance stood a smaller circular outbuilding, its roof also supported by gilded Corinthian pillars. Round this structure the numerous horses of the guests were tethered. There were also sedan chairs set on the gravel, their bearers lounging by them, eating, sleeping or talking in small groups.

Peter blew his upper lip in wonder. 'He doesn't exactly live like a shepherd, does he?'

'Money is not one of his problems,' Ben Hur observed. 'He has written, however, that "One should cultivate a relationship with poverty", the idea being, I suppose, that even in prosperity, one must prepare for adversity – just in case it should strike!'

Peter thought this over, then nodded sagely. 'That makes a great deal of sense. I suppose he must have other, meaner places to live, when he feels in the mood for a little hardship.'

Ben Hur grinned. 'He has other places all right, not including his house in Rome, but *this* is the meanest.'

The big man shook his head in disbelief. Ben Hur beckoned, and both started for the entrance. They walked for a few steps, then Ben Hur stopped and faced Peter warningly. 'I'm going to tell you again, Peter . . . no wine today.'

Peter regarded him indignantly. 'I am invited to an occasion like this – and you expect me not to drink wine!'

'That's right. Why do you think we were invited? For the joy of our company?'

'Some have considered my companionship pleasant,' Peter replied haughtily.

'Seneca is suspicious – he plans to pump us for information, and I know you are a prime target unless you're sober – *and* prepared.'

'I think *you're* the suspicious one!' Peter answered hotly. 'Did it ever occur to you that he might be acting from motives which are perfectly straightforward – kindness and hospitality? Surely one should be prepared to look on the good side of people first. If you show a little love to other men, you might just get some in return!'

Ben Hur laughed. 'Matthew once told me that Jesus took you aside and laid on your shoulders the task of guiding his people when he would no longer be here. Or in Matthew's words – he gave you the keys to his kingdom.'

Peter looked embarrassed. 'He always did have a higher opinion of me than I deserve.'

Ben Hur shook his head. 'I think he knew better than you . . .' He turned and led the way to the huge doorway.

A red-clad servant bowed deeply to Ben Hur. 'Most Eminent Sir, you are everlastingly welcome.' Appraising Peter's unmarked toga, the servant gave him a supercilious nod, but said nothing. With sweeping gesture, he indicated the way.

Ben Hur and Peter crossed the threshold and entered the portico. As they went, they could hear the servant uttering the same welcome to the next group of guests, but with different forms of direct address.

'Tell me, Judah,' Peter whispered. 'He called you "Eminent". Those men behind us are "Grand", "Splendid", and "Illustrious". I'm nothing. What is the meaning of all this?'

'It is a very elaborate form of etiquette,' Ben Hur told him. 'And it is rigidly observed. The Emperor is "Exalted". All other senators are "Renowned". In special cases – "Grand". But among Equestrians, there are many gradations. At the top is "Most Illustrious", meaning you are worth three hundred thousand sesterces or more. Next is "Most Outstanding" – anywhere from one hundred thousand to two hundred and ninety-nine thousand sesterces. Below him – "Most Perfect". He's worth about a hundred thousand. The lowest is "Most Eminent". A mere sixty to one hundred thousand is all he's got.

'What comes below that?' Peter wondered.

'People like you with no stripes on their togas. They are sometimes invited, but never noticed. That's the safest place to be ...'

They arrived at the end of the walkway, only to find themselves in a circular ante-chamber, branching off into three more corridors. However, another red-clad servant was stationed there, indicating they should take the middle entrance. They did so, and, after another interval of walking, found themselves in a huge domed room filled with shouting people. The walls and ceilings were ablaze with large and costly circular mirrors. The floor was a gleaming expanse of marble. Columns stretched upwards, not for any structural purpose, but merely to display the copies of Greek statues which surmounted them. There were eight or nine different pools of varying temperatures. Into the largest one, water cascaded down from three different levels. Naked people of both sexes were everywhere, frolicking and laughing as if cares and worries belonged to another world.

Immediately, red-liveried servants came up and led the two guests to marble stalls in one corner of the room. This was the disrobing area.

Peter extricated himself with some difficulty from the cumbersome folds of his toga. 'It just occurred to me,' he commented, 'if you're so suspicious of Seneca, why did you come here at all?'

'There's no reason to antagonize him. And I have hopes still that he will help – if I can convince him I'm not a person to be feared. And I may meet others here ... One never knows.'

Peter fell silent, gazing at a formidable one-armed man, with a craggy, jutting jaw, tossing a ball back and forth with a group of several young men. When anyone of the group dropped a ball, he did not bother to pick it up, but merely took another from a slave who stood nearby with a basket of inflated skins.

'That's Burrus,' Ben Hur whispered to Peter. 'A man *not* to antagonize.'

'You know him?' Peter whispered back.

'No. But he has been pointed out to me on numerous occasions.'

Burrus snapped his fingers. Immediately two slave boys came running up, bearing between them an enormous gold pot suspended from a pole, which they had been carrying round to various guests. When they had positioned the receptacle in front of Burrus he proceeded to urinate without stopping his ball game.

Just then a newcomer hurried up to Ben Hur. His face was artfully made up to give the pale, cadaverous complexion favoured by Roman dandies, and his elaborately curled hair was held in place by a net.

'Arrius, my nomadic friend!' the effete stranger cried. 'How wonderful to see you again!'

'Petronius!' Ben Hur exclaimed. 'When did you get back from Bithynia?'

'Scarcely more than a month ago. And I'm still thanking the Gods that I'm in Rome again. Being a Provincial Governor is no life for a man of sensibility.'

'I was surprised when I heard you'd accepted the appointment.'

'Believe me,' Petronius asserted, 'it was only from dire need. My finances were so low a provincial post was about the only way to recoup them.'

Ben Hur eyed him sardonically. 'I assume, then, that you came back with your pockets lined.'

'It took three years of my life. My first year of office was devoted to extracting money to bribe the senators who appointed me. My second year was occupied with squeezing out more funds to pay the lawyers.'

Ben Hur frowned. 'Lawyers?'

Petronius nodded sadly. 'For defence against extortion charges which the Bithynians are bound to bring against me.' He smiled. 'But the loot from my third year in office I'll keep for myself!'

Ben Hur could not restrain a laugh.

Petronius gave him a conspiratorial nudge. 'Enough small talk. I've got something much more interesting to reveal to you. I want you to meet the most lovely woman who ever set foot in Rome.'

'First,' Ben Hur insisted, 'I want *you* to meet someone.'

Petronius adjusted his hair-net. 'Someone lovely, I hope.'

'Not exactly,' said Ben Hur, indicating Peter, who came forward.

'Peter is a dear friend of mine from Judaea,' Ben Hur announced. He indicated Petronius. 'This is Gaius Petronius – the most brilliant writer and the most unprincipled man in Rome.'

'I don't believe that,' Peter declared. 'Everyone has principles.'

Petronius scrutinized Peter's bulk from head to toe. 'What arena did Arrius dig you from?'

'The arena of life,' Peter asserted. 'I kill people with love.'

Petronius laughed. 'I like that! No wonder Arrius esteems you. And, I assure you, your friend Arrius is a worthy fellow. He saved my life, you know.'

'He did?' Peter threw a look at Ben Hur. 'He never mentioned it to me!'

'Arrius is far too modest for that. But the good deed deserves to be told. You see – I made the mistake of ridiculing the Emperor Caligula in a poem. Unfortunately, Caligula lacked a sense of humour. However, Arrius here was generous enough to shelter me, until there was thankfully a change of rulers.'

Patronizingly, Petronius took their arms. 'And now, it is time to come along and feast your eyes on this female.'

Petronius propelled them towards another pool. They passed cubicles faced with Numidian marble from which the slapping sounds of massaging could be heard. In the front of one of these recesses the curtains were not fully drawn, and Ben Hur could make out the recumbent form of Seneca, his heavy-lidded eyes shut with ecstasy as he enjoyed his massage. But apparently he could see through closed eyes, for he raised a plump arm when Ben Hur went by.

'Young Arrius,' he murmured, just loud enough to be heard. 'I'm looking forward to conversing with you later ...'

There was no time for reply because Petronius pushed them towards the steaming, perfumed water of a hot bath. Ben Hur and Peter gazed around expectantly for the beautiful woman promised them, but the only occupant of the pool was a startlingly handsome man. He was perhaps in his early thirties, muscular, and with the profile of an Apollo by Polyclitus.

'What have you done with your wife?' Petronius demanded of the Apollo.

He shrugged. 'You know what she's like. When you said you were going to introduce her to someone, she fled like a startled fawn.' The Apollo turned to Ben Hur with a smile. 'I'm Marcus Otho,' he said.

He reached up and clasped Ben Hur's hand in the Roman fashion, then emerged from the bath.

'I'll go and get her,' Otho decided. He made his way off among the people.

Peter frowned. 'Why should she be afraid to meet us?'

'She's amazingly shy and modest,' Petronius told them, 'and yet she has nothing to be shy or modest about. Not only is she the greatest beauty in Rome – she's intelligent, learned, wealthy. But she hates to go out in public, because people make such a fuss of her.'

At that moment, Otho returned, leading a woman, who, in contrast to the other females present, was wrapped from head to foot in a large towel. What was visible of her, however, surpassed even Petronius' description. Her skin was unbelievably creamy and smooth in texture, and her chestnut-coloured hair was piled high in an elegant coiffure, exposing her delectable neck. Her large, expressive eyes had the questing quality of one who is constantly being surprised by life.

'Come on, you silly creature,' Petronius cried, 'will you take that ridiculous rag off! How can you bathe wearing that!'

With a sudden motion, Petronius reached out and jerked the towel away. Otho laughed. His wife hastily slid into the pool – but not before the men caught a glimpse of her exquisite body. Her gently rounded contours were thrillingly provocative. Her hips and breasts, though not large, were all the more exciting for their subtle charm.

'Poppaea, my nymph,' said Otho. 'You are lovely.'

'My husband is a wonderful man,' Poppaea said in a soft voice, 'but I wish he'd treat me like a human being for a change, instead of some goddess.' She sighed. 'I can't wait to grow old and ugly!'

'You'll never be ugly,' Otho insisted.

'And even if she were,' Peter broke in suddenly, 'you wouldn't see it. That's because you love her. And love makes everything beautiful.'

Otho, Petronius and Poppaea stared in astonishment at Peter, who flushed with embarrassment, then dived into the water.

At that moment there was a loud clashing of cymbals. The bathing-house fell silent. A red-clad servant stood in the doorway, flanked by two others holding bronze cymbals.

'The first course is now being served in the triclinium,' he announced, 'and all are invited to enter.'

Immediately a score of scarlet-uniformed servants appeared, and moved among the baths, distributing rolls of heated linen to the guests.

'It's time for me to say farewell,' announced Petronius.

'You've only just arrived,' Otho protested. 'You can't be leaving already!'

'Escaping is the word,' Petronius stated. 'Seneca is bound to read his latest literary production. It will spoil my meal, I'm afraid.'

'Professional jealousy?' Ben Hur wondered.

'Not a bit!' Petronius asserted. 'We are not in the same profession at all. Seneca writes about Philosophy. Such things put me to sleep. I cannot stand abstractions. I write about people the way they are – perverted, dishonest, contemptible. In short, human beings.'

Snatching a towel, Petronius patted Poppaea on the posterior and hurried away.

As soon as Ben Hur and Peter were dry and had donned their clothes again, they followed those who were already filing out through an open door.

They found themselves passing through a hall with walls decorated by an elaborate mosaic frieze.

'Must be a story of some sort,' Peter observed.

'It is Seneca's life,' said Ben Hur.

Ben Hur pointed out the remarkable scenes composed in patterns of polished stones, glass and wood. They showed Seneca as an eager young man, coming to Rome from his native Spain to study grammar, rhetoric and philosophy under the white-bearded teacher Attalus. The pictures catalogued Seneca's early career in public service, a story of rising success, followed by sudden reversal, when Seneca was banished by Claudius. Next, Seneca's return to favour under the same Emperor was portrayed, along with his appointment as official tutor for the young Nero. The pictures continued the story, including the signal honour of Seneca's consulship, up to quite recent times.

The mosaic ended suddenly in a blank wall.

'I suppose the panels are filled in every time there's a momentous event in his life,' Peter speculated, 'and this space is intended for the great events yet to come.'

Ben Hur nodded and pointed to the final section of wall, enclosed within a black frame. 'That part is reserved for his death scene, to be filled in after it happens.'

At the end of the hall was a huge wardrobe, with a built-in shrine, containing images of the household gods, framed scrolls of Seneca's philosophical treatises, and a mysterious gold casket.

'No doubt the box contains the clippings of his first beard,' Ben Hur whispered. 'The coming of age custom ... like our Bar Mitzvah.'

At last they followed the other guests into a subdued but elegant red-panelled triclinium, and sought out couches surrounding a long, low table. Peter chose a place immediately beside Poppaea. Ben Hur was about to recline next to Otho, when a servant tapped him on the shoulder.

'You are the Most Eminent Quintus Arrius?'

Ben Hur nodded.

The servant gestured towards two couches which lay empty at the head of the table.

'The Most Renowned Seneca has requested that you be at his side for the feast.'

Ben Hur followed the red-coated attendant and reclined on the couch next to the one reserved for the host. He was aware of the curious glances from many of the other guests.

An odd-shaped vial, made of lapis lazulae and gold, was set in front of Seneca's place at the table. It was the only such vessel to be seen and obviously intended for the exclusive use of the host. Ben Hur was speculating what it contained when he noticed something which alarmed him. Peter, freed from the restraint of Ben Hur's presence, was already pouring two cups of wine. Ben Hur watched with dismay as the big man handed one to Poppaea, drained his own and promptly refilled it.

At that moment, a singing chorus of slaves entered, some bearing bowls, others holding odd-looking instruments. Not ceasing their shrill song, the slaves spread out, and moved among the guests. Ben Hur found his hands being immersed in a bowl of iced water. Another slave removed Ben Hur's shoes and began to pedicure his toenails. Each guest received the same attentions. Not once during their ministrations did any of the slaves cease singing.

A creaking noise was heard beyond the door. The next instant a huge wooden horse was trundled into the room. On a platform attached to the front of this strange apparition were hundreds of toy soldiers, representing the unsuspecting Trojans drawing the beast into the walls of their city. Each little warrior was made of dried fruits, pastry, nuts and other delicacies.

The horse stopped just before the table. A trap-door opened in its belly, and Seneca climbed out, holding a scroll. The delighted guests shouted with laughter.

Seneca held up his hands for silence. 'Welcome, welcome,' he said. 'Today we dilute neither the wine nor the pleasure. But to whet your appetite, before we enjoy this banquet, I should like you to savour some words of undying wisdom from my latest essay.'

Untying the scroll, Seneca began to read. 'To reduce oneself to a frugal diet is truly to forestall the blows of fortune. I am not a follower of that hedonist Epicurus, but occasionally he *did* have a point. He used to observe certain periods in which he would be niggardly about satisfying his hunger, just to see how much he would really miss the elegant cuisine which was his custom. It is said that during these periods of abstinence, he fed himself on a half-drachma a day.'

Seneca cleared his throat and continued. 'Barley porridge or a crust of bread and water do not make a very cheerful diet – but nothing gives greater pleasure than to derive satisfaction from even *such* fare.'

Seneca looked up solemnly. 'However, I have often observed that one is best able to appreciate a virtue from its complete opposite. Therefore, let the feast begin.'

Tossing the scroll aside, Seneca clapped his hands. The guests shouted their approval and laughed.

At that moment a half-dozen servants entered, and a seventh trundled in a water organ. Almost immediately, he crouched over the keys and began to play, while the others broke into song.

> Nothing but bones, that's what we are.
> Death hustles us humans away.
> Today we're here and tomorrow we're not,
> So live and drink while you may!

As the refrain was repeated, more slaves marched in, bearing trays and huge platters. Two of them bore a dish as long as a man, offering it to Ben Hur. It was divided into the twelve signs of the zodiac – chickpeas over Aries, a slice of beef over Taurus, boar's testicles and kidneys in honey over Gemini, sugared flower petals over Cancer, African figs over Leo, and other delicacies so numerous Ben Hur could not decipher their astrological significance.

Hungrily he was helping himself to everything when he felt the creeping sensation of someone staring at him. He turned. There, close by, was the one-armed Burrus, who had taken his place on the couch just to the right, without Ben Hur being aware of him. Their eyes met. Burrus nodded and smiled as pleasantly as his fearsome face would permit, then turned his attention to the astrological tray, which was now being presented to him.

'I see you two are getting acquainted,' murmured Seneca's voice on Ben Hur's left. Ben Hur looked round, just as Seneca sank languidly on to his couch.

Another dish was held in front of Ben Hur. On a silver tray lay fat capons garnished with myriad vegetables, cooked fruits and honeycombs. At the four corners of the tray stood little gravy boats all shaped like the satyr Marsyas, with phalluses for spouts. Ben Hur pointed to a particularly succulent-looking bird, and a servant carved him several large pieces of meat, helping him liberally to gravy and sweet garnishings as well. Immediately another servant was by Ben Hur's side, filling his goblet with wine.

'The Falernian is not as good as yours,' Seneca said graciously, 'but I'm sure you'll find it quite fine.' He picked up the lapis lazulae vial and offered it. 'I recommend you try some of this in your wine.'

Ben Hur regarded the mysterious container warily. 'What is it?' he wondered.

'An aphrodisiac. The recipe was written down by none other than Hippocrates himself. And Hippocrates was still fathering children in his nineties. It is made from the marrow of a stag's horn. The beast is driven until it can run no longer, and its antlers cut off immediately. The marrow, saturated with the blood of the animal, is full of its vital energies, which are in turn transmitted to you when you ingest it.'

'Thank you,' said Ben Hur, 'but I don't need it.'

He hesitated, once again aware of another's eyes upon him. Turning, he found Burrus still watching him.

Just then a terrified servant scurried up to Seneca's couch. 'Most Renowned Sir,' he gasped. 'I beg your pardon for this intrusion, but the Emperor is approaching! At this moment he is in the portico!'

The dismayed look which passed between Seneca and Burrus was not lost on Ben Hur, and all his suspicions hardened into certainty. Seneca and Burrus *were* his enemies. Whatever their reasons might be, they were determined to keep him away from the Emperor.

As the great doors of the triclinium were thrown open, four servants scuttled in and feverishly began preparing a couch at one corner of the table for a new occupant. Next, an impressive-looking man strode into the room and approached the table. Ben Hur recognized him instantly. He was Epaphroditus, imperial freedman, head of the civil service and secretariat. He was always at Nero's side during official occasions and state ceremonies. It was a face known to nearly everyone in Rome.

The room was buzzing with speculation by now, and Epaphroditus gestured for silence, looking round the assembly with a smile.

'You have an uninvited guest,' Epaphroditus announced. 'But it is his urgent wish – and I'm sure you'll treat it as a command – that you continue to enjoy your festivities as usual and treat him merely as one of the company.'

Epaphroditus bowed and strode from the room. The diners fell silent, glancing at each other expectantly. Now about a score of men filed into the room. They were clad in togas bordered with the narrow purple stripe of the Equestrian Order. The newcomers took up positions behind the couch which had been so hastily prepared.

Finally a figure appeared in the doorway. He was a young man, wearing a toga. Of medium height, with a slight tendency to corpulence, he sported a gold circlet around his bronze-coloured hair, which was somewhat longer than the fashion.

Lucius Domitius Ahenobarbus Nero Caesar beamed at everyone in the room and held up a large sack in his right hand.

'Hello,' he said.

Immediately the Equestrians stationed behind his couch clapped as loudly and furiously as if Nero had uttered some marvellous witticism.

'I hope you're all having a splendid time,' said Nero.

Again the Equestrians applauded.

'I beg you to regard me as just another gentleman on this occasion.'

The Equestrians acclaimed this for a full minute.

'And you can always tell a gentleman,' said Nero, 'by the way he throws his money about.'

He delved into his sack and began throwing handfuls of gold denarii to the guests. Laughing, entering into the spirit of the occasion, many of the men made a game of it, competing among themselves to gather up the coins and pile them in front of their most favoured ladies.

For a time Nero continued to throw money. Then he stopped, and strode purposefully across the room to where Poppaea reclined. With a flourish, he upended the sack, and the remaining coins cascaded into a golden pile in front of her. She beamed delightedly, and for an instant his perfervid eyes held hers. Then he turned away, and snapped his fingers. Immediately a servant came running with the Emperor's lyre and handed it to him. The Emperor regarded the assembly with a conspiratorial grin.

'Now,' he announced, 'I will confess my real purpose in being here.'

The Equestrian claque beat their palms furiously.

'I've composed another song. But an unheard melody is never sweet,' Nero commented, raising the instrument, 'so here I am to present my humble effort to you.'

More applause came from the Equestrians.

Nero held up his hands for silence, then struck a chord, and began to sing, staring fixedly at Poppaea the whole while.

Ben Hur listened with some wonder. The Emperor's voice was clear and truly lovely, and the young man sang with real feeling.

> Loveless hearts shall love tomorrow, hearts that
> have loved shall love anew.
> Spring is young now, spring is singing, in the
> springtime the world first grew;
> In the spring the birds are wedded, in the
> springtime true hearts pair,
> Under the rain of her lover's kisses loose
> the forest flings her hair.
> Now in the shadow of the woodland She that binds
> all true loves' vows,
> She shall build them bowers tomorrow of Her own
> green myrtle bows.
> There Dione high enthroned on Her lovers lays
> Her law.
> Loveless hearts shall love tomorrow, hearts that
> have loved shall love once more.

Finally the song was over, and now not only the claque applauded, but the whole room as well. Nero looked around with pleasure and what seemed to be a genuine surprise.

'You liked it!' he exclaimed. 'You really did!'

The cheering mounted and Ben Hur clapped enthusiastically along with the others, for he had truly enjoyed the performance. He noticed that Peter was on his feet, applauding and stamping as well. Finally the noise died away.

'No artist could ask for a better audience,' said Nero, 'and now I beg you to return to your dining. Enjoy yourselves.'

As usual, the claque pounded their hands. At a gesture of dismissal from Nero, however, they ceased their applause, began to mingle with the guests and help themselves to food.

Nero returned the lyre to his servant, who had materialized at his side. Then, politely acknowledging the congratulations of others around him, the young Emperor made his way to the group near Poppaea.

He addressed himself to Otho. 'How nice to see you, Marcus. And the pleasure is doubly increased by finding you here with your delectable wife.'

He beamed at Poppaea, and continued. 'You were at the Festival of Ceres, but you have not graced us with your presence since. Where do you keep yourself?'

Poppaea blushed. 'Mostly in my garden,' she murmured demurely.

Nero laughed loudly. 'How delightful!' Then he waved a minatory finger at Otho. 'But do you think it fair, Marcus, to introduce me to this flower and then hide her away?'

Otho shrugged. 'One cannot fault her if she likes to keep to herself.'

Nero regarded him knowingly. 'Oh, come now ... You can't deceive an old partner in crime. I know you very well, Marcus. You want to keep this little bloom all to yourself. If you took her about with you, your jealous nature would allow you no rest, with all the admiration she would draw. But you're certainly going to bring her to the Circus for the games tomorrow, aren't you?'

Otho and Poppaea glanced at each other. 'I hadn't planned on it ...' Otho began.

'No excuses!' Nero exclaimed. 'You must both join me there – that's a command. Fortunatus is racing, and he's the greatest driver in the world!'

'Not so!' a voice exclaimed.

All three swung round in amazement. It was Peter who had spoken. His face red with wine, he stumbled to his feet.

'Who are you?' Nero wondered.

'My name is Peter,' Peter answered thickly.

'Indeed. In Greek, Petros means "rock". I must say, you certainly look like a rock. So you don't think Fortunatus is the best charioteer in the world?'

'No, I don't!'

Otho jumped up and took Peter by the arm. 'Don't you know better than to contradict the Emperor!' he hissed.

Peter glanced round the suddenly quiet room. The realization that he had committed an indiscretion hit the big man like a shot from a catapult. He gulped with embarrassment. 'B–but,' he stammered. 'H–he said to treat him just like one of the company.'

'Come along!' Otho muttered, trying to draw Peter away.

'Let him alone!' Nero said sharply. 'I want to hear what he had to say.'

Obediently Otho withdrew, and Nero faced Peter again. 'Now, Petros, if Fortunatus is not the best, who is?'

'He's right here in this room.' Peter pointed to Ben Hur. 'Over there. Quintus Arrius.'

Ben Hur was stunned. A moment ago his hopes had soared to the very heavens. Fate had brought him into the same room with the Emperor. It was an opportunity he had never dared to expect. But now Peter had trampled over everything.

Finally Nero shook his head and spoke. 'Arrius . . . Arrius . . . No, I've never heard of any charioteer by that name.'

'When he raced in the Circus,' Peter blurted out, 'he was known as Judah Ben Hur.'

Abruptly Nero turned his back on Peter and strode to Ben Hur. For a moment the Emperor stood there, his face working emotionally. Then he dropped to one knee, doing homage to Ben Hur. A gasp swept the room.

'Judah Ben Hur!' Nero exclaimed, rising again. 'The famed Judah Ben Hur! As a boy, I was told of your fabulous races!'

'Most Exalted Sir,' said Ben Hur, 'I am deeply flattered and touched that you do not hold my past in the Circus against me.'

'Against you!' Nero exclaimed. 'Three hundred and two victories in five years! That's the most astounding record in history! My father, who had a stable of his own, could never stop talking about you.'

'I was under the impression that men of such noble birth despise charioteers.'

'Those are not true nobles. True nobles look up, never down. But tell me, Ben Hur – how did you come to be called Quintus Arrius?'

Ben Hur hesitated. It was a question he was not eager to answer – certainly not with this sea of curious faces staring at him. He was just about to attempt an evasive reply when the Emperor held up his hand for silence.

'Tell me another time!' Nero said airily. 'I've got a wonderful idea. I can't wait to see Fortunatus' face when he finds out.' He laughed uproariously, slapping his thigh.

'Finds out what?' Ben Hur wondered.

'That he's racing against *you* in the Circus tomorrow!'

'Me?' Ben Hur gasped.

'That's right. I'll cancel the team race, and pit just you against Fortunatus. Can you imagine anything more magnificent?'

'But, Most Exalted Sir,' Ben Hur protested, 'I haven't raced in years!'

'I'm sure you've lost none of your skill. One doesn't forget a thing like that.'

Immediately a chorus of shouts went up from the guests, urging Ben Hur to compete. Apparently whatever the Emperor favoured, they favoured too – no matter how outrageous.

'I'm pleading with you,' Nero was saying. 'If you race, I will actually be able to say that I have seen Ben Hur in the Circus!'

Ben Hur knew that Nero was wrong about the skill of a charioteer. It was a thing easily lost, and which was maintained only by constant practice. But in spite of this risk, it was a chance worth taking. Should he win, he might rise high in the Emperor's favour.

Ben Hur bowed. 'Of course, whatever you desire I will be happy to do ...'

Nero beamed his approval. Putting his arm around Ben Hur's shoulder, he led him towards the couch reserved for the Emperor.

'I want you to sit next to me,' Nero urged. 'Have some wine, and tell me about that time you drove a seven-in-hand unyoked and defeated four teams ...'

As he took his place next to the Emperor, Ben Hur glanced across the room. Seneca and Burrus were still watching him.

CHAPTER FOUR

As the early morning sun lifted over the eastern seats, the huge, empty Circus, nestling between the Aventine and Palatine Hills, was suddenly filled with pinkish light. The enormous obelisk, which rose from the spina in the infield, cast a long, dark shadow across one side of the track. Near where the shadow pointed to the lowest tier of seats like a giant's finger, two men were waiting anxiously.

At the distant thunder of horses' hooves, Peter involuntarily gripped Barnabas' arm. The tiny form of a lone chariot appeared round the curve at the far end of the Circus, nearly half a mile away.

The vehicle grew rapidly in size as it stormed closer. Ben Hur could be recognized as the driver. In another moment the chariot sped up to Peter and Barnabas, sliding to a halt as Ben Hur reined in the horses with a powerful, heaving motion of his shoulders. The greenish copper dust of the track was still drifting in the morning air as he climbed down. Removing his gauntlets, he regarded the men with a grim smile.

Barnabas spoke first. 'As a wheelwright, I've seen them come and go. But never a lap like that one!'

'That was just a practice run,' Ben Hur replied quietly, 'but in a real race – I will have little chance. I'm an old man.'

'You're as fast as you ever were,' Peter insisted stoutly. 'And those horses the Emperor has given you are magnificent.'

'I'll never be able to hold them. Perhaps for a lap or two – but never seven!' Ben Hur flexed his fingers. 'My hands won't last.' He moved to the front of the chariot where the seven yoked horses waited patiently. He patted one of them. 'The Sicilian horses are the strongest in the world. Keeping their heads in on the curves – they'd pull my hands right out of my wrists!'

'Perhaps you should get a team slightly less strong,' Peter suggested.

'Then I'd have no chance. With this team, there's still a small chance. Most charioteers will save their horses for the finish. But it might be worthwhile to give these beauties their heads right at the start. Since Fortunatus is my only opponent, if I can just get in front of him, I can block him every time he tries to pass.'

'Block Fortunatus!' Barnabas exclaimed bleakly. 'That's something very few drivers have been able to do! And it's less likely today than ever.'

'Why do you say that?' demanded Peter.

'Fortunatus *has* to win. He needs money desperately.'

'You know him?' Ben Hur asked.

Barnabas nodded. 'Of course. He frequents the Vicus of the

Wheelwrights. Most charioteers do. He hasn't paid Scorpus for his rim-work for the past two months or more. It is well known that Fortunatus spends all his money on wine, dice and his three mistresses. A little circus of his own.' Barnabas grinned. 'What do you expect from a Syrian!'

Before Ben Hur could answer, a slender young man in a tunic came up.

'Which of you is Quintus Arrius?' the stranger inquired.

'I sometimes answer to that name,' said Ben Hur.

'Eminent Sir, I am Agerinus, freedman to the Lady Agrippina. She wishes to have a word with you.'

'Who is Agrippina?' Peter wondered.

Agerinus glanced sharply at Peter, obviously surprised at his display of ignorance.

'Agrippina is Nero's mother,' Ben Hur informed Peter. He indicated the horses. 'If you will unyoke them, I'll be back shortly.'

Ben Hur followed the young freedman down the track, under the entry arches into the paddock. There, waiting on the green dust, was a sedan chair, with the four bearers standing nearby. Ben Hur noticed that each man wore, sheathed at his belt, a short, broad-bladed gladius, the deadly sword of the Roman soldier.

Agerinus strode up to the sedan chair, rapped twice on the door, then opened it.

Ben Hur had never met Agrippina, and he did not expect her to be a woman of such great beauty. She was mature, but one of those females who bloom fully in middle years. Though tall, she was perfectly formed. Her body was clearly distinguishable, for she was wearing the short tunic of a man.

Her full, sensuous mouth parted in a smile, and she held out both hands in greeting to Ben Hur. 'So you are Quintus Arrius! Please forgive this unheralded visit, but I had to speak to you before the Circus.'

Ben Hur bowed. 'Unheralded, but not unwelcome.'

She glanced at Agerinus, who withdrew to where the swordsmen were standing.

'I've heard quite a bit about you, Quintus Arrius,' said Agrippina. She gestured towards the Circus. 'This was your world once – a cesspit! Charioteers, gladiators, ex-criminals – the dregs of humanity.

Yet you rose above that. Very few have ever done so. You are unique.' She paused for a moment. 'My son admires you, but for the wrong reasons. He admires your career in the Circus, not the way you escaped it.'

Ben Hur offered no reply.

'You haven't raced for many, many years,' she continued. 'You're out of practice. You could very well get yourself killed this afternoon.'

'I am touched by your concern,' said Ben Hur coolly.

Agrippina shrugged. 'I don't want to see anyone suffer. I'll admit, however, my worry is chiefly for my son. Being Emperor is a very precarious profession – far more dangerous than being a charioteer. The Emperor is only secure as long as he has the support of people in high places. Many of these people will resent the spectacle of an Equestrian being forced to compete in the Circus. By implication, it is an infringement of their prerogatives. Who knows when one of them may be next? But quite aside from the friends he may lose, I worry about my son's preoccupations. His mind ought not to be on trivial and savage entertainment – it ought to be on affairs of state.'

'You are a very attentive and concerned mother,' Ben Hur observed.

Agrippina smiled again. 'My son has called me the best of mothers. I beg you not to race today.'

'But your son has commanded me to race. You're suggesting I disobey him?'

'You need not fear his anger. I am not without some influence over him. Trust yourself to me. I will be your protectress ...'

Ben Hur hesitated. It occurred to him that Nero was possibly still susceptible to his mother. Agrippina was a formidable name, and it was well known that her will carried great weight. But would she be here pleading, if she truly controlled Nero?

'I am sorry,' he said coldly. 'I gave my word I would race today. I will race.'

For an instant her eyes narrowed in fury, but it vanished immediately. When she spoke, her voice was as clear and collected as ever. 'Is that your final word?'

He nodded.

'You are making a mistake,' Agrippina warned. 'I could have been a useful friend for you to have ...'

The savage howl of derision which poured from a hundred thousand throats was the most sickening sound in the world, Ben Hur thought. He was no stranger to it, and he knew what it meant. The mob sounded like that only when there had been an accident.

His eyes moved around the bare stone room. None of the other charioteers paid the slightest attention – any more than he had twenty years ago when he had been one of them. He smiled bitterly. He had thought those days were over, but here he was in the chamber next to the paddock.

Ben Hur shifted his weight slightly on the bench, immersing his hands once again in the bowl of brine in front of him.

Now he could hear the stamping feet of the spectators, demanding the next contest. There had been fifteen races already, eight-in-hands, seven-in-hands, even a ten-in-hand, and a team race; but the crowd was thirsting for more. The stamping and shouting increased. There was still one more event to go before he would meet Fortunatus in the great match race, which was to be the feature of the day.

He clenched his teeth as the brine bit into his hands. Even after this morning's meagre practice they were already cracked and sore.

Just then the curtain which hung over the doorway was swept aside, and two attendants bore in the proof that Ben Hur had guessed rightly about the cause of the mob's savage roar. On a stretcher lay the hideously mangled body of a charioteer. The gashes inflicted by the wheels which had run over him were streaming with blood, and his flesh hung in ribbons.

'He was thrown on the first turn. Couldn't get his dagger out in time to cut the reins,' an attendant explained to everyone in general. 'That five-in-hand must've dragged him for half a lap.'

Eyes flickered in the direction of the dead man, but no one seemed particularly affected.

Ben Hur had seen the sight many times, yet he could never get used to it. Abruptly he rose, picked up the bowl of brine, and went outside.

The paddock was humming with activity. Horses were being yoked and unyoked. Grooms were running to and fro. Chariots were on wooden blocks, their axles being removed and greased. Wheelwrights and smiths were busy everywhere.

In a corner of the paddock covered by an awning, shouting stable-boys were smearing the contestants for the next race with a protective coating of boar's grease. Now the men climbed into their chariots. Tying the reins to their belts, they flicked their whips and moved out from the canvas-covered enclosure towards the starting gates.

Ben Hur made his way through the noisy, odoriferous throng towards his chariot. One of its wheels was off, and the axle was propped up on blocks. Barnabas sat beside it, filing away industriously on the metal wheel rim.

A tall, cadaverous-looking man, who leaned on a staff, was watching him. Both turned as Ben Hur walked up. Barnabas indicated his companion.

'Judah, I want you to meet Silas, a brother of ours from Asia.'

Ben Hur nodded. 'I've heard good things of you, Silas. You worked with Paul in Antioch. I'm glad to have you with us in Rome.'

'It's a privilege to be here,' Silas croaked in a strange whistling voice. 'They have told me of your mission, Ben Hur. Truly, you are an inspired man!'

'I hope that inspiration will sustain me today,' Ben Hur said grimly.

He sat down on a stool and reimmersed his hands in the bowl.

'I will go and look for a seat,' Silas wheezed. 'I hate the circus, but this race I would not miss for anything.'

He hobbled away, leaning on his staff for support as he went. Ben Hur glanced after the bent figure. The story of how Silas had been crippled was well known among the Christians, but it was something that no one talked about. Ben Hur felt a sudden depression. Resolutely he put the thought from his mind.

Barnabas looked at Ben Hur's hands as they soaked in the salt water. 'Is that helping at all?' he wondered.

'I hope so. It hurts enough.' Ben Hur peered round the teeming paddock. 'Where's Peter?'

'He ought to be here soon. I sent him to the Vicus for a spare wheel.' Barnabas squinted along the rim. 'Just in case I don't get this one as true as I'd like ...'

He put the wheel down and rolled it up to the chariot. Pausing at a sudden commotion in the enclosure, he looked off across the paddock, then tapped Ben Hur on the shoulder.

'Look,' Barnabas whispered, 'Fortunatus ...'

Ben Hur glanced in the direction Barnabas had indicated. Everyone made way for a small retinue which was approaching. Fortunatus strutted in front of his retainers. Though lithe and tigerish, he was an extremely short man, and wore enormous lifts under his leather shoes. Heading the group of sycophants which followed him were three gaudily bedecked females, who were not in the prime of youth. The others were hangers-on of various sorts, including a notarius, who was clutching a tablet and stylus. Ben Hur realized that Fortunatus must be illiterate, and employed this man to record things of importance and to transact business.

There was something regal about the famous charioteer's progress towards his vehicle. Most greetings he ignored, deigning to nod to only a few. Ben Hur smiled wryly. It was common knowledge that not five years ago Fortunatus had been a wretched slave, condemned to a life of servitude for forgery and theft. Then one day his master had commanded him to stand in for an ill charioteer ... And Fortunatus was launched on his meteoric career.

Ben Hur knew from personal experience how the hand of fate could change a man's life.

Now Fortunatus arrived at his chariot, and inspected the vehicle very carefully. He was just turning his attention to the horses when his groom whispered to him, indicating Ben Hur. For an instant the Syrian appraised his opponent; then his swarthy, pock-marked face broke into a crooked little grin. Snapping his fingers and pointing to one of his horses, he muttered a brief command to the groom, then came swaggering towards Ben Hur, his jewel-encrusted dagger flashing in the sun as he walked. The women and the notarius followed. There was sudden silence and cessation of activity in the enclosure. All eyes were on the coming confrontation.

As Fortunatus drew closer, Ben Hur noticed the trappings of the Syrian's inflated self-esteem. His tight black curls were pomaded carefully into position. He wore his tunic open almost to his navel, exposing his hairy chest. Hung around his neck on a gold chain was a large round amulet. Ben Hur could see from its engraving that it was full of magic and endowed with great power. The heavy sweetness of Fortunatus' perfume contrasted startlingly with the stench of dung and boar's grease which pervaded the whole paddock.

Barnabas got warily to his feet as Fortunatus came up. Ben Hur remained seated. The little charioteer stood there a moment, hands on hips, feet apart, and contemptuously surveyed his rival.

'So!' the little man shouted for all to hear. 'You will race Fortunatus! Ha! Do you think it is wise, old man? You will make widows of your grandchildren! Ha!'

He laughed uproariously. The three women cackled along with him. A titter ran through the enclosure as well. Ben Hur said nothing, merely continuing to soak his hands in the brine and staring at Fortunatus steadily.

'Why don't you save your breath for the race, Fortunatus?' Barnabas demanded indignantly. 'You may need it!'

This sent Fortunatus into a paroxysm of shrieking laughter. Tears streamed down his cheeks. Finally he wiped them away and turned to his mistresses. 'He thinks I need breath!' He howled with laughter again, pointing to Ben Hur. 'For an old man like that! I need breath!'

The three females laughed as well, competing with each other to be the loudest. Suddenly Fortunatus' mirth was gone. 'Shut up!' he shouted.

The three women fell silent immediately. 'You sound like hens laying eggs!' he spat. 'This is an old man here. You show no respect for his years! Now go away!'

The mistresses retreated fearfully. Then Fortunatus turned back to Ben Hur. His glance fell on the bowl of brine. 'What is this? Your hands hurt?'

Still Ben Hur said nothing, but his eyes didn't move away from Fortunatus for an instant.

Fortunatus stepped closer and peered into the bowl with exaggerated solicitude. 'Brine for the bad hands? This is no good! Piss is much better. Here! I will piss in it for you!'

With that, he reached under his tunic, and pulled out his penis, holding it for all to see.

Ben Hur took one hand out of the brine and drew his dagger. 'One drop,' he said quietly, 'and I'll cut it off.'

For an instant Fortunatus was taken aback. Then he laughed uproariously again. Covering his penis, he strutted back towards his chariot.

'I wish he *had* pissed,' Barnabas muttered, turning back to the wheel.

The activity in the enclosure resumed, and Ben Hur rose with a sigh, shaking the brine from his fingers. Soaking the hands any longer would be pointless. Now for the painful task of putting on the driving gauntlets . . .

Suddenly a pair of enormous arms clasped him in a bear hug. He turned to find himself staring at Peter. Ben Hur noticed the big man's face was red again. Standing next to Peter was a stout young woman who seemed vaguely familiar.

Barnabas regarded Peter with a scowl. 'Where's the wheel?' he demanded.

Peter gasped. His cherry-coloured face turned a slightly deeper shade of red. 'Judah,' he whispered, 'I'm so sorry . . . How can you forgive me? I'm a useless lump of blubber. I'll go back to the Vicus immediately and get it now. I'll run all the way!'

Barnabas gave Peter a withering look. 'It's too late. We'll just have to trust to the wheel we've got. How could you possibly forget *why* you went to the Vicus?'

Emotionally Peter took Ben Hur by the arm. 'Judah . . . please say you forgive me.'

'Of course I forgive you. An extra wheel isn't going to help me anyway . . .'

Peter beamed, his good nature restored completely. 'I love you, Judah! And I did bring something for you. Or rather *she* did.' He indicated the woman. 'You remember Urgulania.'

It all came back in a flash. 'Indeed I do,' he said. 'She fed you so well with mutton that night at the Vicus.'

'That she did. And she has brought you broth made from that same mutton today. It will give you strength.'

Encouraged, the plump woman edged forward. She held out a small flask.

'Most Eminent Sir,' she said, 'the brains and guts and bones have been simmering for a whole week. Everything has boiled away except for the vital humours. You must drink it now.'

Ben Hur removed the stopper. A powerfully pungent odour assailed his nostrils. In four gulps, he drained the thick, clotty liquid. Immediately he felt a warmth in his midriff, which soon spread into his limbs. 'My deepest thanks and gratitude to you,' he said. 'Already I feel as though I could run *three* races.'

A trumpet fanfare stopped his heart. It was time.

His chariot was off the block, wheels attached. The team of black Sicilian horses was hitched, and the grooms stood by, waiting for him. Barnabas held out the heavy driving gauntlets. Conscious that Fortunatus was watching, Ben Hur pulled the gloves on to his throbbing hands, forcing himself not to show the pain.

He sprang on to the platform of the vehicle, allowing Barnabas to tie the reins to his belt.

'May God go with you!' Barnabas cried.

'Remember, Judah,' called Peter, 'this race is just the beginning for us.'

Ben Hur was about to flick the reins when something caught his attention in the corner of the paddock. He turned. It was a man standing unobtrusively behind a group of wheelwrights at work. He made a movement as if to retreat, but then apparently changed his mind. Hesitantly he moved forward, and, as he stepped from under the awning into the sunlight, Ben Hur recognized Phaon.

He approached Ben Hur's chariot uncertainly, stopping right next to the wheel. 'Young Arrius,' he said, 'I was concerned about you. At first I couldn't bear the thought of watching the race. But there was no help for it. I had to come.'

Ben Hur was deeply touched. 'You're a loyal friend, Phaon.'

Impulsively, Phaon reached round his neck and took off his amulet which he offered to Ben Hur. 'Wear this, young Arrius. It has a spell in it.'

Apologetically, Ben Hur held up his gauntlet-encased hands. 'I doubt if I could hold it.'

'If you will permit me,' said Phaon.

Ben Hur obliged, bending over, allowing Phaon to hang the medallion around his neck. Momentarily Ben Hur detected an odour which seemed familiar. Then he realized what it was. It was the same perfume which Seneca wore.

There was a second blast of trumpets. The attendants moved away from the two gates allotted for the start. With a slap of the reins,

Ben Hur urged his horses forward. He heard the crunching of Fortunatus' chariot wheels just to his right, but he kept his eyes fixed straight ahead. As his chariot arrived before the rope barrier of the gate, he tugged gently on the reins. The wonderfully trained beasts stopped instantly. Their powerful necks gleamed in the sunlight as they tossed their heads. An eerie silence descended over the huge circus. The stands were filled with an immense sea of faces, all staring expectantly towards the starting gate.

Framed by the archway, the green-dusted track stretched before him. Bisecting it was the centre island of the spina sporting its obelisks, monuments and statues. At one end was a revolving pole on which were mounted seven gilded dolphins, and, at the other, seven gilded eggs.

Halfway down to his left, the imperial box could clearly be seen, draped with purple. Ben Hur knew that Nero was sitting there, waiting expectantly to see him perform. He smiled wryly. The opportunity to win the Emperor's favour seemed heaven-sent, yet it also seemed tantalizingly beyond his grasp.

Ben Hur stole a glance to his right. He expected to find Fortunatus' jeering eyes on him, ready to taunt him further. But no – the Syrian was staring soberly ahead. Both of his hands clutched the amulet round his neck. He kneaded and rubbed the talisman reverently. Obviously when it came down to the event itself, Fortunatus was deadly serious.

Turning his attention back to the track, Ben Hur gauged the distance to the first turn. He must be in front the moment they burst from the gates. And he must stay there.

A third trumpet blast caused every eye to turn to the starter's box, where stood the imposing figure of Calpurnius Piso, the consul, holding up the starter's cloth. For a moment, the official stood motionless, savouring the suspense.

Ben Hur shifted his stance, planting his feet well apart, assuming a slight crouch. He held his reins high.

Abruptly, Piso let his arm fall.

With every ounce of his strength, Ben Hur lashed his horses. The team leaped forward, and the green dust rushed up to meet him as hooves bit into the sand. Shouting encouragement, stinging the animals with his whip, he headed straight for the stone wall of the spina.

But something flashed across Ben Hur's vision. It was Fortunatus! Beating his horses savagely, the Syrian was also going flat out. And he was ahead! Poised on the balls of his feet, crouched over, reins held high, he passed Ben Hur on the outside and cut in front to take the wall.

Clearly Fortunatus had guessed what Ben Hur's tactics would be. No doubt it was the bowl of brine which had given Fortunatus the vital clue. Fortunatus' horses would be exhausted before the first lap was over. But what would that matter if the Syrian were in front and could keep Ben Hur from passing?

The crowd, obviously expecting the usual slower start, exploded into bedlam at this display of driving.

Split seconds later, the chariots were rounding the first curve. Ben Hur held in as tightly as he could, not daring to give ground. The pressure of the powerful horses on the reins tore into his hands, sending shock waves of pain up both arms. His body shuddered with protest, but he hung on grimly. In a moment the curve was behind, and they were thundering down the straight again. His hands told him, however, that he could never make another curve that tight again.

But his team was still fresh and strong. He just might be able to pass now ... With a convulsive wrench to his right, he swung the beasts outside Fortunatus. More pain flowed up his arms. Slowly Ben Hur began to draw abreast, but the Syrian was ready. He swerved his thundering team away from the spina, blocking Ben Hur, driving him towards the opposite wall.

At the last moment, he was forced to apply a slight pressure on the reins to avoid collision with the wall. Fortunatus drew ahead. Working his way behind the Syrian, Ben Hur tried to inch his horses to the other side. But Fortunatus was there first, blocking him yet again.

Ben Hur ground his teeth with frustration. He had no choice but to follow Fortunatus, hoping for a chance to break through.

He hung on grimly for what seemed an eternity. They swept round the track again. The green dust kicked up by the spinning wheels and pounding hooves covered his face and burned his eyes. Ben Hur's stomach knotted as he realized the Syrian was gradually but inexorably drawing ahead. And the reason was apparent. Staying close to Fortunatus meant tight turns, and Ben Hur simply could not make them. Once more they made the circuit of the track, holding the same positions.

A swift glance at the spina told him that three of the dolphins and eggs had turned over. That meant four laps to go ... He hurtled into another turn, holding the beasts in as hard as he could. It was such agony on his hands that sweat poured from under his headpiece, trickling down his chest and back. His gauntlets were wet too.

This time, when the chariots pounded out of the curve into the straight, Fortunatus had increased his lead. Ben Hur had used every vestige of his will to overcome the pain and hug close to the wall, but his strength was just not enough. Obviously Fortunatus knew it as well, judging by the mocking looks he threw back from time to time.

Bitterly Ben Hur glanced at his gloved hands. Red rivulets were running down his wrists. It was not sweat which had dampened his gloves!

He choked with rage. He could not – *would* not – just keep following Fortunatus – eating his dust! Savagely he pulled his team towards the outer wall, but again Fortunatus was there ahead of him, blocking any possible attempt to pass. Ben Hur tried the inside – but with the same result.

Twice more the racers hurtled round the course. Thunderous applause crashed from the audience as Fortunatus streaked back and forth across the track, dexterously blocking his opponent. His ability to keep Ben Hur from passing was uncanny. Was he anticipating Ben Hur's moves?

Ben Hur lifted his reins, as if he were going to swing to the outside again. Sure enough Fortunatus veered outwards, but swerved back immediately when Ben Hur didn't change direction.

Once again Ben Hur feinted to the right. Fortunatus anticipated as expected. But instead of swinging to the right, Ben Hur yanked his horses to the left as hard as he could. The light chariot nearly overturned, tilting dangerously up on one wheel, only righting itself when Ben Hur hurled his weight to one side. Fishtailing wildly, Ben Hur's chariot shot abreast of Fortunatus, while the Syrian was still fighting to bring his team back again.

The crowd were on their feet, throwing things on to the track. The applause was so deafening Ben Hur couldn't hear his horses' hooves.

He was even with Fortunatus! They ricocheted along, hub to hub. Ben Hur's right horse was literally touching Fortunatus' left horse, and foam from the panting beasts was flying back at him. But Ben Hur knew he couldn't keep the advantage. His hands were throbbing with agony, and he could see the next turn looming up ahead. He could never make it tight enough.

A wild thought shot into his brain. An acrobat had once told him that the muscles in a man's jaw were as strong as any others in the body. Stuffing the reins into his mouth, he clamped his jaws shut, biting into the leather like a frenzied animal. Now with his free left arm, he guided the horse into the turn so tight against the spina that his hub grazed the stone, sending up a shower of sparks. With his right, he wielded the whip, stinging the outside horse on the flank.

The axle whined in protest, but the chariot sped into the straight. The last dolphin turned, indicating the final lap. Gripping the reins in his hands again, Ben Hur risked a quick glance back. He had gained! He was now a few precious feet ahead of Fortunatus!

The chariots flew into the straight. The younger man gradually drew abreast of Ben Hur on the outside. Ben Hur threw a look at his opponent. Fortunatus was livid. The mockery had gone from his face. His eyes were slits of hatred.

Ben Hur shouted to his team, whipped them again. For a moment, the chariots careened along, neck and neck. Fortunatus, screaming curses, tore off his helmet and threw it at Ben Hur's lead horse. But the magnificent Sicilians held fast, their hooves biting steadily into the dust. The speeding vehicles still held even.

Suddenly the tip of Fortunatus' whip tore into Ben Hur's face. He flinched with pain. Now came a shower of blows as the enraged Syrian lashed furiously at him.

For an instant, Ben Hur tried to avoid the attack, but there was no escape. In desperation, he lashed out with his own whip. The tip wrapped around Fortunatus' neck. Ben Hur jerked savagely. As the whip came free, Fortunatus' amulet went flying into the air. The younger charioteer lunged desperately for this talisman, grabbing out wildly, but it had long gone. The Syrian's horses reared up as he fought for control of his team, but Ben Hur was ahead.

As the racers stormed down the final stretch, Fortunatus succeeded in bringing his horses under control. Furiously he attempted to pass, but it was too late.

The stunning ovation which erupted from the audience echoed and re-echoed between the Aventine and Palatine Hills. Ben Hur slowed his team to a walk and turned them gently about, aiming them for the imperial box. He felt a twinge of sympathy for Fortunatus, whose face was grim with shame and despair. Then, his vehicle still moving, the Syrian leaped to the ground, throwing the reins to a groom who trotted alongside. As the audience hissed their derision, Fortunatus made his way to the paddock.

When Ben Hur reached the imperial box, he brought his weary animals to a halt. He glanced upwards. Nero was on his feet, waiting to receive the victor. Behind him stood his claque of Equestrians. Ben Hur dismounted, but instead of going immediately to the Emperor, he strode to his horses, which were tossing their heads nervously, their sides heaving with exhaustion. Ben Hur went to each animal, caressing and patting it. Only when he had calmed them did he turn back to the Emperor.

Slowly he mounted the steps to the box, for he too was tired.

Beaming, Nero waited impatiently, holding a laurel wreath in his hands. Finally Ben Hur reached the box.

'Ben Hur!' shouted Nero. 'Or I should call you Quintus Arrius! Today history has lived again.'

The claque applauded furiously. Nero waved them to silence; then, with an impatient gesture, he dismissed them. Immediately the claque resumed their seats at the rear of the imperial box. Now the Emperor turned back to Ben Hur. 'Truly,' he cried, 'you are the best!'

'I thank your Exalted Person for the compliment, and I only hope the race was not too dull,' Ben Hur said wryly.

Nero shouted with laughter and held up the wreath. But then he paused, and drew it back. 'No . . . you should not be crowned by me today. Let it be done by the most beautiful woman in Rome!'

Nero turned away, and Ben Hur noticed that Poppaea was sitting next to the imperial chair. The other occupants of the box were

Otho and Agrippina. Poppaea rose, and Nero handed her the crown; then he turned grandly back to Ben Hur.

'Now go ahead and crown him,' he urged.

Demurely Poppaea stepped forward and placed the wreath on Ben Hur's head.

More deafening applause filled the Circus.

Nero laughed again. 'To the victor, the spoils!' He patted Poppaea patronizingly. 'But not all of them. Not this time!'

Ben Hur glanced towards Otho. Surprisingly, the handsome Equestrian was paying no attention, gazing absently off into the distance. Ben Hur's eyes travelled to Agrippina. She was staring straight at him, but her face revealed not the slightest hint of her thoughts.

CHAPTER FIVE

The door closed, and Ben Hur was left alone in the bright little anteroom. He glanced round. The walls were adorned with painted arches which framed gay pastoral landscapes of birds and budding flowers. He crossed to the window. It looked out on an intimate sunken garden, with an open roof somewhat like an atrium. The secluded spot was verdant with sculptured bushes and plants, but no one was there.

Frowning, he turned back into the room and sat on one of the benches which lined the walls. This was certainly not what he had expected.

After his triumph in the Circus Maximus, he had been treated like a visiting king, commanded to sit next to the Emperor for the rest of the games, and presented with a miniature golden chariot as a token of the imperial esteem.

And that had been the last he had seen of Nero. Ben Hur had stayed at his villa for more than a week, but had received no further sign of favour. Peter had grown restive, urging him to take advantage of his new-found fame to precipitate a meeting with the Emperor. Moreover, Peter had been visiting the Vicus regularly and reported that the other Christians were similarly impatient. Ben Hur, however, had insisted he could not make the first move. That was up to the Emperor.

Finally, today, the summons had come. But it had been delivered in a surprising and alarming fashion. An abrupt centurion of the Praetorian Guard had ordered Ben Hur to present himself at the imperial residence on the Palatine Hill. And to make matters worse, two other Praetorians had escorted him on the journey. Like their superior, they had not been friendly.

Ben Hur looked up as the door opened and a sombre, toga-clad man beckoned to him. Epaphroditus was normally the one who escorted those in the imperial favour, but Ben Hur did not recognize *this* man. In the corridor, Ben Hur found his Praetorian escort waiting. They fell into step beside him, as Ben Hur followed the toga-clad personage down the hall. His apprehension mounted as they reached the door at the far end. The man in the toga opened it and stood aside. When Ben Hur entered, the door closed behind him.

He found himself in an austere, sparsely furnished hall. The only concession to ornamentation was a plain row of Doric columns which flanked each wall. The sun's rays which filtered through the skylight fell directly on three men. Nero was sitting on a curule chair, and next to him stood Burrus and Seneca.

Ben Hur waited for one of the three to speak.

Finally Nero broke the silence. 'Greetings, Arrius.'

'Most Exalted Sir ...'

'A rather disturbing matter has come to my attention,' Nero whispered, in such a low voice that Ben Hur could hardly hear him. 'I understand that before we met, you were seeking an audience with me. These gentlemen suspect your motives. But I don't want to strain my voice any further. I'm giving a recital tonight.' He waved at Burrus. 'He'll do the talking.'

'And I'll tell you why we suspect you,' Burrus snarled. His voice echoed in the bare chamber. Tapping the piece of papyrus he was holding, he continued. 'You're a convicted assassin!'

Burrus let the impact of his words sink in before he went on. 'Doubtless you assumed the truth about your past would go undetected, but our Governors keep careful records. The crime occurred in the reign of Tiberius. You were then the Prince of Hur, one of the noblest families in Jerusalem. When our new Governor,

Valerius Gratus, entered the city, he was nearly killed by a stone hurled from a roof. Everyone was astonished when you, the scion of such an exalted and pro-Roman family, confessed to this deed.'

Another silence engulfed the room.

'Well? Is this the truth – or not?' Burrus demanded.

'It is the truth,' Ben Hur admitted quietly.

Nero's eyes were hurt and reproachful. 'You *did* do it?' he gasped in his normal tones, abandoning his whisper.

'I *did* confess, but I did *not* throw the stone.'

'The tongue has no bones,' Seneca murmured. 'It will wriggle any way a person wills it.'

'The falling of the stone was an accident,' stated Ben Hur. 'My sister dislodged it. She was on the roof of the house, leaning over the parapet to get a better view of Gratus' entry procession into the city. The feeling against the Romans was so bitter at the time that no one would believe it wasn't deliberate. So I took responsibility for the mistake.'

Burrus slapped the piece of papyrus again. 'It says here that you claimed it was an accident at the time – but no one believed you.'

'Epicurus said that frequent confession is good for a man's soul,' Seneca observed. 'However, Zeno disputed this. As far as I'm aware, no philosopher has ever raised the issue of whether confession ought to be the truth. Now –'

'Jupiter's eyeballs!' Nero yelled. 'Will you shut up! I had to listen to this dung all day when I was in school, but I don't know! That's the only good thing about being Emperor!' He turned to Ben Hur. 'Now ... tell us what happened once you had taken the responsibility.'

'I was condemned to slavery. That's how I became a charioteer. Arrius adopted me.'

'Did Arrius know your story?' Nero wondered.

'Yes, he did.'

'What did he think of it?'

'He believed it.'

'Why?'

'He knew that I had too much to lose by making such an attempt, and too much to gain by not making it. And had I been fool enough to do it, I would have chosen a more certain method.'

'Arrius was said to be a virtuous and upright man. If he accepted you, that's good enough for me.'

'Exalted Sir ...' Burrus began.

'Shut up!' Nero shouted again. He rounded on both Burrus and Seneca, his voice high with exasperation. 'You two pederasts get out of here! And take your fatuous charges with you!'

Seneca and Burrus bowed respectfully and managed a graceful retreat from the room.

When the door had closed behind them, Nero slumped into his chair, his face flushed. 'My poor voice ...' he murmured. 'I suppose I'll have to cancel the recital ... Fancy letting those two sycophants get me all upset!' Ruefully he massaged his throat, appraising Ben Hur. 'You've had a rough life, haven't you, Arrius? I know what it is like. I've had a rough life too! Everyone thinks that because I'm Emperor, I've spent my entire existence on cushions draped with gold. Don't you believe it!' He rose again, warming to his theme. 'My father once put out a man's eye deliberately. He was the most evil man I've ever known. He died in prison, you know ... My mother was exiled when I was little. She left me with my aunt, who lived in squalor and poverty. I was abominably mistreated – even poisoned once. After all, I was a possible heir to the purple.' He sighed. 'And now that I *am* the ruler, life is even more difficult. People strive after power as though it were desirable. If only they knew the truth! Responsibilities allow you no sleep at night. Everyone is after you for a thousand reasons. All wanting something!' Nero sank back into his chair, shaking his head.

'One should look on the other side,' Ben Hur pointed out. 'It goes without saying that a ruler is in a unique position to do good for the world. And you have.'

'I have? You think so?'

'Wherever I travel, men speak well of you.'

'Really!' Nero exclaimed. 'I'm very pleased to hear that. I certainly try my best.'

Ben Hur decided to risk everything. 'You've shown such enlightenment, in fact, that I think you might be interested in a unique and wonderful teaching. Very few men know of it yet.'

Nero frowned. 'Is it philosophy?'

'One could call it that. But –'

Nero held up a hand. 'I don't want to talk about philosophy. Anything which smacks of philosophy I get sick of in no time – thanks to Seneca. Now chariot racing – that's a different matter. That reminds me – how are your hands?'

'Mending extremely well, thank you.'

'Let me see them,' the Emperor demanded.

Ben Hur held out his hands. The wounds had left bluish scars, but were nearly all healed.

'What a magnificent feat!' Nero exclaimed. 'With your hands in that condition – defeating Fortunatus! It was a race Rome will talk about for a long time. I'm glad your hands have healed, Arrius.'

He rose again, and began to pace thoughtfully. 'It's the most wonderful sight there is! A man controlling all that strength in those animals! Now *that* is real power! The power that an emperor has is nothing in comparison. It exists only in men's minds. It –'

Nero turned at a knocking on the door.

'Yes, yes!' he called impatiently.

The door opened, and the toga-clad man stood there. 'The Armenian ambassador ...'

Nero groaned. 'Another pederast! You see why I have no peace. We'll talk again soon, Arrius. I like your company.'

The young Emperor strode to the door and followed the other man out. Ben Hur was left alone in the audience room. He savoured a quiet jubilation. At least he need no longer worry about his past. In a way he was grateful to Burrus for accusing him.

Gripping the folds of his toga, he crossed the room and went out into the hall. As he strode along, his mind was seething with plans. His great design was beginning to fall into place. The only problem which remained was how best to inspire the Emperor.

It was too dark and much too cold to get out of bed. Ben Hur resisted with all his power the hand which was shaking his shoulder. He pulled aside, rolled over and tried to go back to sleep. But there was no escape. The shaking continued, forcing him into wakefulness.

'Young Arrius, you must get up!' Phaon was saying.

Finally Ben Hur struggled to a sitting position.

'It's the middle of the night! What is it?'

'The Emperor wants you. Now!'

'Now?'

'That's right. Epaphroditus is outside, waiting for you.'

Ben Hur rolled off the couch as Electra staggered into the room grumbling to herself, carrying an oil lamp. 'What a night! First that slave of yours, Peter, wakes me up breaking into the kitchen and stealing more food . . .'

'I've told you a thousand times,' Ben Hur growled, 'Peter is *not* a slave.'

'He's drunk!' stated Electra, as if that proved her point. 'You can hear him snoring all over the house.'

Phaon held out Ben Hur's tunic. 'Put it on, young Arrius.'

'I might as well start making the bread now,' Electra snarled. 'I'll never sleep this night!'

Leaving the oil lamp on the table, she left the room.

Ben Hur laced up his tunic, then bent over and pulled on his heavy Gallic leggings. Phaon held out a cloak. 'You should take this too, Arrius. It is not warm out.'

Throwing the garment over his shoulder, Ben Hur fastened the bronze chain around his neck, and ventured out into the freezing portico. His mind was too numb even to speculate on what might lie behind this bizarre intrusion.

Soon he passed through the atrium and made his way down the short entrance hall to the front door, where Epaphroditus was standing.

'If you will please hurry,' Epaphroditus said, 'he is waiting.'

The freedman turned, wrapped himself tightly into his cloak, and started down the gravel walkway. Ben Hur followed. The night was fairly clear, and Ben Hur's eyes adjusted to it quickly. He could make out the black shapes of bushes and trees. By the main road, grooms waited with two horses.

Ben Hur and Epaphroditus mounted and rode in silence to the Flaminian Way, past the tombs bordering the road, which were silhouetted against the night sky.

Suddenly Epaphroditus wheeled to the right, on to a cart track which led off into the fields. It wasn't long before the freedman turned off the wagon track as well. Slowing their horses, the two men picked their way down into a hollow, then climbed a ridge.

There, in front of Ben Hur, was an eerie spectacle. Blazing torches were set out in a long narrow oval which stretched over the entire meadow. Another line of torches formed a smaller oval in the centre. The whole meadow was illuminated by a dancing red glow, which lent the shadows a life of their own.

Epaphroditus beckoned, and Ben Hur followed him down the slope into the lighted area. As they drew closer, Ben Hur could make out the distinctive belts on the attendants which identified them as imperial slaves. Epaphroditus led the way past the flickering, hissing torches, until they reached a darkened grove of carob trees at one end of the meadow.

Under the overhanging branches waited two yoked seven-in-hand chariots. In one of them stood Nero, dressed as a charioteer, complete with dagger, gauntlets and leather helmet.

'Arrius!' Nero exclaimed. 'At last you're here. Put on your gauntlets and let's go.'

Ben Hur was astonished. 'Go where?'

'Racing, of course.' He indicated the other chariot. 'That's the same chariot you drove to victory over Fortunatus. And the same team.'

Ben Hur moved over to the Sicilian horses. He patted them, and they seemed to recognize him, whinnying and tossing their heads at his touch.

'Inside the chariot,' Nero continued, 'you'll find your harness.'

Ben Hur moved back to the Emperor. 'Are you serious?' he demanded.

'Of course I am,' said Nero, making a sweeping gesture towards the torches on the meadow. 'We have our own circus. Not quite as big as the Circus Maximus, but the turns are sharper – and no mobs to distract us.'

Ben Hur still couldn't believe what was happening. 'But why?' he wondered.

'That pederast Fortunatus was supposed to be the best in the world,' Nero replied. 'Yet you defeated him. Therefore, you're the best. And if I defeat you, I'm the best.'

'Have you ever raced?'

Nero laughed. 'Have I ever raced! My spare time is consumed by three things – practising my lyre, practising my poetry, and practising with my chariot. Of course, I can't appear in the Circus – all that rubbish about the proper decorum and other such rot. Anyway, this is a golden opportunity to test myself, and I don't mean to miss it, Arrius. I know it sounds immodest, but I've watched thousands of races, and to be perfectly honest – I've never seen one driver I didn't think I could beat.'

'But out here on this meadow!' Ben Hur protested. 'It's madness. Potholes, stones ... the chances are you'll be thrown and dragged to death.'

'My men have cleaned the track.'

'All it would take would be one stone.'

'If I'm tossed, I'll cut myself free.' Nero pulled out his dagger and waved it. 'It could happen just as easily to you. And your dagger's waiting – along with the other gear in your chariot. Get it on, Arrius.'

Ben Hur was suddenly suffused with anger at the sight of Nero's petulant face. 'Very well ... I'll race. But don't hold me responsible for what happens.'

Abruptly he turned his back on Nero and stalked over to the other chariot. He mounted it, and found the equipment. First he put on the helmet, then the harness and the dagger. He tied the reins to his belt, and pulled on the gauntlets.

He glanced towards Nero, who nodded back to him and flicked the horses with his whip. Ben Hur did likewise, and the two teams made their way out to a line of attendants with torches who marked the starting position of the improvised course.

Epaphroditus was ready with a white cloth.

'He'll give us the start,' said the Emperor. 'What do you say to seven laps, Arrius?'

'Whatever you want. After the first lap, you'll be so far behind you won't see me anyway.'

Epaphroditus' eyes narrowed at Ben Hur's insolent tone, but Nero merely smiled. 'We'll see ...' He turned to Epaphroditus. 'Don't keep two gentlemen waiting.'

Epaphroditus raised the cloth.

Ben Hur's eyes measured the twin lines of torches which stretched off into the meadow in front of him. Assuming his usual stance, he waited.

The freedman brought the cloth down.

Ben Hur lashed his team. The powerful beasts bounded forward. A glance to his left told him that Nero had made a creditable start and was abreast of him. Ben Hur waited a moment or two, allowing his horses to settle into their pace. Then, stinging them with his whip, he pulled a little ahead of his opponent. Without warning, he veered over at Nero, driving him into the row of torches which marked the boundary of the course. Nero's horses reared wildly.

'Jupiter's eyeballs!' Nero screamed in panic.

Manoeuvring his chariot in front of Nero, Ben Hur deliberately slowed. Nero wrenched his reins to the right and tried to pass. Ben Hur let him go for a moment, then easily overtook him, forcing the Emperor into the right-hand line of torches, knocking them spluttering out in the grass.

'A dog use your mother!' Nero shouted, fighting to control his team.

Ben Hur lashed his horses, the crack of the whip echoing into the night, and they sped off down the track.

The horses thundered into the turn and straightened out on the backstretch. Nero had been right. The course was well laid out, and so far Ben Hur had encountered no obstructions. As he approached the second turn, he took a quick look backwards and saw Nero well behind him.

They circled the track twice, with Ben Hur's lead steadily lengthening. As he rounded into the third lap, Ben Hur saw Nero in front of him, not behind him. Ben Hur was one full lap ahead.

Coming up rapidly behind the Emperor, Ben Hur started to pass. Surprisingly, Nero reined in. 'Stop, Arrius!' he shouted.

Ben Hur tugged on the reins, and both chariots drew to a halt.

He waited, watching Nero, who stood motionlessly in his chariot. For a moment nothing happened, then Nero spoke.

'Come over here.'

Ben Hur climbed down grimly. He cursed Nero inwardly for putting him through this, but he rebuked himself more. Why couldn't he control himself? He had humiliated the pride-inflated Emperor, and no doubt everything was ruined now.

He stopped in front of Nero's chariot and looked up at him. Nero glanced round surreptitiously. 'Do you seriously think I hoped to outrace you?' he whispered. 'Only a self-made eunuch would be that stupid!'

'Then why did you challenge me?'

'Because I wanted to find out what kind of a man you *really* are. If you were like the rest, you would have let me win. But you didn't. You've proved you're no sycophant. Perhaps at last I've found an honest man!'

Abruptly, he flicked his horses with his whip and galloped away into the blackness.

Slaves were pulling out the stakes and extinguishing the torches. Grooms had led Ben Hur's chariot away. Epaphroditus had vanished, and so had all the horses.

In a very short time everyone had gone, and Ben Hur was left alone in the middle of the meadow.

Only when he began the long, weary walk home was he absolutely certain the whole thing had not been a dream.

The morning sun had already lifted well into the sky, and the Forum was jammed with people as Rome went about its business. There were hawkers selling their wares, merchants negotiating vociferously, and others who were merely socializing, oblivious to the tumult around them.

Pushing his way haughtily through the crowd, Agerinus cleared a path for his mistress's sedan chair. The chair itself, borne by four stalwart slaves, was flanked as usual by Agrippina's armed guards.

Suddenly the banging of tambourines and jangling of bells was heard. A solemn procession of the eunuch priests of Cybele, resplendent in their yellow robes, was making its dignified way through the Forum. Everyone paused respectfully in their business as the eunuchs waddled by. Even Agerinus halted, signalling imperiously for the sedan chair to do likewise.

Agrippina stuck her head out of the window, then, seeing the cause of the delay, she withdrew into the compartment.

She settled again on the cushions and closed her eyes patiently. It was inconvenient having to traverse the city and fight the Roman traffic every time she wanted to visit her son.

Nero had insisted that she move to a house on the Pincian Hill. It was high, and he had told her repeatedly the air would be good for her health. Indeed it was a lovely house, but Agrippina was not taken in by her son's solicitude. His real motive was to get her out of the palace, so that she would have less control over him.

There was no doubt that her influence over her son had been growing less these days. Others who were formerly intimate with the Emperor were having the same experience, but Agrippina had always prided herself on occupying a special place in Nero's life.

After all, she had been extraordinarily close to him, looking after his interests, grooming him for his career. On his own, Nero would never have become Emperor. But Agrippina had married Claudius, and had arranged Nero's marriage with Claudius' daughter Octavia. She had also browbeaten the old Emperor into adopting Nero, thus cementing his claim.

Soon Nero had cast off poor Octavia, virtually ignoring her. He had started an affair with a slave girl, Acte. Both Agrippina and Seneca had opposed this, but Nero had refused to listen. For a time Agrippina had feared she was becoming estranged from her son, and it was only with the greatest difficulty that she had won his confidence again. Finally, however, she succeeded where Seneca failed. Nero had abandoned Acte.

But now an even worse possibility loomed. Poppaea. This was no slave girl. Not only was Poppaea married to another man, which could provoke a troublesome scandal in itself, but she was a woman of wealth, influence and position. She would be a definite threat to Agrippina. And Agrippina did not like the way her son had been following Poppaea round like a lost puppy. She had noticed his smouldering looks, the surreptitious touches and all the other symptoms of infatuation.

This had been going on for some weeks now, but Agrippina had hesitated to take any action. This morning, however, was different. The omens had been bad, extremely bad. On a farm behind the Pincian Hill, a pig had been born with hawk's claws. A swarm of bees had settled on the pediment of the Capitoline Temple only a few hours ago. Such portents could not be ignored.

She felt her ample hips being thrown back in the swaying sedan chair as the bearers began the laborious ascent of the Palatine Hill. The bedlam of the Forum was growing somewhat fainter.

Agrippina could not endure uncertainty. She had a great need to know how things stood. It gave her security. During the crises of her life, she had always known what course to take towards her goal. Perhaps that was the reason why she had always won. Until now.

She checked herself. She must not become alarmed! She had always employed a certain method of controlling her son. She had used it sparingly and judiciously, but it had always proved infallible. It would be again. Agrippina's career was a living proof of its efficacy.

Finally the sedan chair was placed on the ground. Agerinus held open the door and Agrippina climbed out. She glanced at the sweating bearers, then turned to her freedman. 'See they get wine,' she said. 'And I'll be some time inside, so give them a meal as well.'

'They will be grateful,' said Agerinus.

Just then Epaphroditus appeared from the great portico which fronted the palace. He strode up to Agrippina with outstretched arms. 'The Lady Agrippina! Welcome!'

'Is my son in the palace?'

'He is. But he is conferring with the Armenians at the moment.'

'Again?'

Epaphroditus nodded. 'I'm sure you remember how loquacious they are.'

'Indeed I do. And it's time the conference was cut short. It is important that I speak with my son. I'll be in the baths.'

Epaphroditus bowed. 'I'll attend to it.' He turned to go.

'Epaphroditus!'

He faced Agrippina again. 'Yes, Revered Lady?'

'Don't keep me waiting ...'

Epaphroditus bowed deeply and moved off.

Mounting the steps, she entered the great portico, striding past the sunken garden, avoiding the entrance to the audience hall where she knew the ambassadors would be, not stopping until she reached the doorway to the small basilica behind the palace. In the peristyle, Agrippina passed three servants, whose faces lit up with genuine pleasure when they saw her. They bowed respectfully.

'Nestor, how good to see you!' said Agrippina. 'And you, Laetitia. How well you look. And Gaius. You are thinner than ever.'

She patted his huge stomach and all the servants laughed delightedly. She knew these people were her friends.

With a wave, she took her leave, making her way onwards and turning into the bath-house.

It was empty. The pools steamed invitingly, but Agrippina was not ready to bathe yet. She moved over to a couch and took off her cloak, revealing a short tunic underneath. Now she reclined and settled to wait, aware that she made a very attractive figure.

Soon the door was thrown open, and Nero entered, his face full of irritation. 'What do you mean by interrupting my conference? Perhaps you want to take over the negotiations yourself. Doubtless these Armenian pederasts wouldn't know the difference between a Queen and an Emperor anyway.'

'Is that any way to talk to your mother?'

'Not to an ordinary mother. But you don't qualify.'

'An ordinary mother would never have poisoned her own husband, and her husband's son – so her spoiled son could sit himself in the seat of power.'

He looked at her malevolently. 'What are you going to do about it? Undo it?'

'I may remind you I'm not totally without influence,' Agrippina warned.

'I think about that all the time ...'

There was an interval with no words. Abruptly Agrippina got to her feet. 'My son,' she said soothingly. 'Why is there need to quarrel?'

'Because you refuse to realize I've grown up.'

'I'm only here to help you.'

'I've heard that before. What are you working up to this time?'

'A whore named Poppaea.'

'Don't you think Otho might object to that description of his wife?'

She laughed. 'I know what you're going to say. She's charming, talented, lovely. I'll admit she has every asset – except goodness.'

'You don't know her.'

'Do you?'

There was a moment of silence. Nero moved over to one of the pools and stared into it. Now Agrippina reclined again on the couch and watched him.

'It would be foolish to start something with Poppaea,' she said finally. 'You are supposedly married and so is she. If you use your imperial prerogative to transgress such barriers, you will not only be setting a bad precedent, you will alienate many people. And you need all the support you can get. You need good will. After all, your claims to the principate are not what they might be.'

Suddenly Nero rounded on her. 'You think I care about that! I don't! I wish I weren't Emperor. I hate this life!'

Agrippina rose and took him by both arms. 'Lucius, we've had such wonderful dreams, and so far we've made them all happen. If we remember our bonds of affection, nothing need ever change.'

Suddenly tears came to his eyes. 'You're right ...' he muttered. 'I should listen to you.'

Undoing the belt which bound her tunic, she let it drop to the floor. He stared at her. Moistening his lips, he moved slowly forward. She took his hand and pressed it against her.

'You came from here,' she whispered. 'You have been back many times. How could any two human beings be closer?'

His whole body shivered with desire, and Agrippina felt a flash of triumph. Her power was not dead. She would enslave him again as she had so many times before.

Ever since he was a child, she had recognized the unusual ferocity of his passions. Noting the frequency of his pubescent erections, she had cunningly capitalized on this.

She had always managed to be present while he bathed. She would pat him and massage him, while she talked inconsequentially about other things. And one day, quite casually, she had masturbated him. This grew to an expected part of an afternoon's bathing. It had only been a small step from this to more exquisite joys. Agrippina prided herself on being an experienced courtesan. And she had used all her arts to give him the maximum pleasure possible. This had reached the point when the mere threat of withholding an afternoon's delights was enough to bend his will to hers completely.

Agrippina suppressed a sudden scream when she felt his teeth.

The shadows of the Forum were long, and the afternoon sun was low in the sky. The bustling pace of the morning had slowed, and only a few groups of people moved here and there.

From her sedan chair, Agrippina stared at this marble-studded heart of the city, and reflected on how its mood could change from the beginning to the end of a single day. She was being borne back to her lovely but sterile house on the Pincian Hill. And what then?

Suddenly she stiffened at a familiar sound. It was that same strident clamour of tambourines and bells which she had heard this morning. She leaned out of the window of the sedan chair as the bearers halted to make way for the yellow-robed priests of Cybele. They too had ended their day of devotion and were returning from their temple. Their prayers, sacrifices, and voluntary emasculation were all as futile as her own pursuit of power. It was a warm afternoon, but Agrippina suddenly felt cold. It was a bad omen.

She had succeeded for today, but it could not last – any more than the prayers of those priests would last. Agrippina's time was growing short. Inevitably her female charms would wane. Poppaea's were just reaching their peak. There could only be one result to such an unequal contest ...

With melancholy eyes Agrippina watched idly as another sedan chair was placed on the ground near a statue which flanked the entrance to the Forum of Julius Caesar. But she sat up with new interest as the occupant of the chair got out. It was Seneca.

Alert now, Agrippina watched as the senator glanced around, as if to see who was present. Then he moved with ponderous dignity to join an elderly man clad in a tunic, who had been waiting obsequiously by the statue.

At that moment Agrippina's sedan chair lurched forward again, and soon she could no longer see Seneca or his companion. But there had been something familiar about the person Seneca had met. Agrippina frowned thoughtfully. She couldn't quite place him, and her neat mind rebelled at not being able to fit everything in its proper place.

Then it came to her. It was that freedman Phaon, manservant of Quintus Arrius. Of course, it was not unusual that Seneca would stop to speak to Phaon. After all, Seneca was acquainted with Arrius. Should the senator run into Arrius' freedman, it would be natural enough for them to greet each other.

But was this not a good omen? The sight of Arrius' man had brought to her mind an avenue she had never considered. Even if her hold over her son should weaken, perhaps there was another way to forestall Poppaea and maintain control ...

She had learned from various sources that Arrius lived a secluded and strangely solitary life. Apparently he consorted with no women, nor did he have a predilection for boys. Yet this man was rising high in the esteem of her son. Such a man was not to be dismissed lightly. Agrippina decided that she would get to know him better.

CHAPTER SIX

Tossing his whip to a groom, Nero tore off his gauntlets and leather headpiece. He glanced anxiously at Ben Hur. 'Well?' he asked.

Ben Hur climbed down from his chariot. 'You have a good pair of hands. If you'd been born a slave, you might well have become a champion driver.'

Nero flushed with pleasure. 'Coming from you that is high praise indeed!'

'Exalted Sir, it is only the truth. You have improved amazingly.'

'Never mind the "Exalted Sir". Call me Lucius.'

'Very well, Lucius.'

The young Emperor waved to his groom, who led Nero's light racer into the trees which bordered the flat meadow. There the groom was joined by others, who unhitched the horses and began to rub them down.

Nero turned to Ben Hur, who was divesting himself of his harness as his vehicle was also led away.

'Sometimes I wish I *had* been born a slave ...' Nero murmured thoughtfully.

'I've *been* a slave,' Ben Hur reminded him. 'And I don't recommend it!' He grinned. 'You are better off where you are.'

Nero laughed. 'Since I value your advice, I will give up the thought of abdicating.'

'Believe me,' said Ben Hur, 'if you were to abdicate, it would grieve me terribly.'

The young man regarded Ben Hur curiously. 'You really mean that, don't you?'

'With all my heart.'

'It does me good to talk to you!' Nero exclaimed. 'You give me faith in myself.' Impulsively, the Emperor put an arm round Ben Hur's shoulders. Then, hastily, he withdrew, flushing with embarrassment.

In spite of Nero's ingrained cynicism, he seemed to be groping for sincerity.

'I always expect the worst from people, not the best,' said Nero. 'I am surrounded by sycophants – like Seneca and Burrus – who care for nothing but their own advancement. But you, Arrius ... I truly believe you are not interested in using me for your own ends.'

Ben Hur felt a twinge of guilt. In a sense, he was indeed planning to use Nero.

Suddenly Nero snapped his fingers and squinted off towards the sun which was beginning to dip behind the western hills. 'Pederasts!' he exclaimed. 'Pederasts! These cursed Armenians! I have to meet them tonight. More jabbering about nothing. Who gives a toss about their stinking little country!'

He clapped his hands. Immediately four bearers shouldered a sedan chair, and emerged from the nearby grove of trees.

'I'm sorry you must leave,' said Ben Hur. 'I was hoping you could come to my house this evening and have some wine.'

'Another time, Arrius,' said Nero, starting for his chair. Then he stopped, and faced Ben Hur again with a strange smile. 'Yes! Another time ... In fact, Arrius, let us make it very soon.'

He gestured for the bearers to wait, then moved back to Ben Hur, taking him confidentially by the arm. 'I want you to arrange a little dinner for me ...'

'It will be my pleasure.'

'I knew I could count on you ...' Nero's voice lowered. 'Would it surprise you to know that I have more than a passing interest in Otho's wife?'

'Not really,' said Ben Hur drily.

Nero chuckled. 'Invite them to your villa – wife *and* husband too. The first evening they have free. I'll drop in unexpectedly.' He slapped Ben Hur in the stomach. 'And mind you – look surprised to see me.'

'Why do you need me for this?'

'I'm watched like a fish in a bowl. If I break wind, the Senate knows about it the same day. And my mother is the worst of my guardians. I go to all the trouble of providing her with a gorgeous house on the Pincian Hill ... does she stay in it? No! She still comes to the palace every day – and night. Never stops telling me what to do! You think people have any confidence in a head of state who must go to his mother for every decision? And she presumes to rule my personal life! She hates Poppaea. Insults her. I don't dare have her at the palace.' He paused. 'Now, Arrius, do you understand why I need you?'

'I suppose I do,' Ben Hur said cautiously.

'Good! Here is what I want you to do. Once this merry gathering is well under way, distract Otho. See if you can't take him away, even if only for a short time. I just need a chance to collect some honey from that little flower.'

'But the lady in question is married,' Ben Hur pointed out. 'Apparently happily.'

'I'm married too. What has that got to do with it?'

'You should consider Otho. He seems devoted to his wife, and she to him. Surely almost any other woman would jump at the chance of a night with you.'

Nero eyed Ben Hur resentfully. 'I don't want any other woman. I want Poppaea!'

Ben Hur shrugged. 'You can do what you please, of course. I can only advise you. The Emperor must be a man above reproach. More so than other men. He must set an example.'

'Jupiter's eyeballs! Are you my censor too? I thought you were my friend!'

'That's precisely why I'm telling you. What kind of friend would I be if I didn't?'

'You're taking advantage!' Nero shouted. 'You're presuming on my good will!'

Ben Hur met his eyes steadily. 'In future, then, I will keep my true feelings to myself.'

Instantly Nero's anger disappeared. 'I–I'm sorry ... Of course you must speak your mind. The fact that you have done so is very important to me.' He paused. 'Now that I think of it, you're right.' He sighed and looked at Ben Hur beseechingly. 'But please . . . invite them. At least I'll be able to enjoy her company, without my mother dripping venom in the background. If I do adore the flower – it will only be with my eyes. I promise.'

Electra cleared away the last of the platters. She had served a fricassee of roses for a final sweet, topping off a truly perfect banquet. Poppaea had commented favourably on the dish, and the Emperor had asked for a second helping. As a result, Electra had been dumbstruck, much to Ben Hur's relief.

'Don't forget,' Poppaea said demurely, as Electra started out, 'I want your recipe.'

Flushing with pleasure, Electra ducked her head and fled from the room.

Ben Hur glanced wearily at Nero, who had indulged rather heavily in wine. Surprisingly, the Emperor had been in a taciturn mood, and now seemed somewhat sleepy, paying little attention to Otho, who, quite the contrary, had kept up an animated conversation the entire evening.

'The Emperor Claudius wrote a history of the Etruscans,' Otho was saying. 'He was fascinated by them. He researched their language, which few people today still understand – even historians. He found their alphabet to be superior to ours in many ways. He even went so far as to have the Senate officially adopt some of their letters into the Latin alphabet.'

'I've seen inscriptions with strange undecipherable characters mixed with Latin letters,' said Ben Hur. 'Are they Claudius' additions?'

Otho nodded.

'But the style never caught on,' Ben Hur persisted. 'What happened?'

'The attempt died with Claudius,' said Otho, with a sidelong glance at Nero, who sprawled on a couch near Ben Hur, sipping a cup of Falernian.

'You sound more and more like Seneca,' Nero belched.

'I don't take that as a compliment, Exalted Sir,' Otho murmured.

'It isn't,' said Nero with a yawn.

Casually, he picked up Poppaea's cup and his own, holding out both to his host. Ben Hur got to his feet. Taking the cups, he moved to a jug on a table in the corner of the room and refilled them.

His sense of relief was growing steadily. Apart from the surprise and consternation occasioned by the Emperor's 'unexpected' arrival, the evening had been uneventful. True, Nero had made a sarcastic gibe or two. But, on the whole, the young Emperor's behaviour had been above reproach. He had made no advances whatsoever towards Poppaea. Ben Hur actually found himself enjoying the evening, for Otho had revealed himself to be an unexpectedly interesting man. It turned out that he had an inquiring mind, and was a serious scholar, deeply immersed in Etruscan history. Other unusual pursuits occupied him as well, the most notable being his collection of rare scents and perfumes from the far corners of the world.

Ben Hur carried the replenished cups back to the table, and gave one to Nero and the other to Poppaea. Then he turned questioningly to Otho. 'Some more for you?'

'Why not?' said Otho.

Nero groaned as Ben Hur replenished Otho's cup. 'That means he's going to talk all night! But I won't be here to listen.' He rose, finishing off his wine. 'I need my strength for tomorrow, so I think I'll be heading homeward.'

Otho and Poppaea got to their feet also. A trifle unsteadily, Nero turned to Ben Hur. 'I am very grateful for such an enjoyable evening,' he said.

Ben Hur bowed. 'And I too,' he said with feeling.

He was jubilant. Nero was leaving! There had been no embarrassment.

'I do hope my going won't put a stop to your conversation,' Nero went on, smiling at Otho. 'I wasn't contributing very much to it anyway.'

Abruptly he turned to Poppaea as if a thought had just occurred to him. 'As a matter of fact, you were not contributing much either.'

'No,' Poppaea agreed, 'I wasn't.'

'You weren't bored, were you?' Nero wondered.

'Beyond belief,' she said flatly.

Confused, Ben Hur glanced at Otho, who continued to sip his wine, apparently totally unconcerned.

'No gentleman permits a beautiful woman to be bored,' Nero announced. He took her by the arm. 'But never fear. Rescue is at hand. I'll take you home while these two continue their discussion. Would you like that?'

'I'd love it,' said Poppaea in velvety tones. Again she looked steadily at the Emperor. Their eyes held for a long moment.

Ben Hur appraised Poppaea with new eyes. All along she, not Nero, had been the aggressor.

The Emperor waved to Ben Hur. 'Do not bother to escort us out. We can find the way.'

They left.

Glancing at Otho, Ben Hur waited for some protest, but there was none. After an awkward silence, Otho spoke.

'You're embarrassed.'

Ben Hur nodded.

'Don't be,' said Otho. 'This was inevitable.'

'Nevertheless, I don't enjoy being party to it.'

Otho made a deprecating gesture. 'Don't feel responsible.'

Ben Hur said nothing. He refilled his cup with wine, then sank back on to his couch, his mind consumed with troubling thoughts. He was not disturbed about Nero's seduction of Poppaea. She had shown herself only too willing to be seduced.

But he had misjudged Nero. His ability to estimate a man's character had always stood him in good stead in the past. Yet now, when the stakes were the highest, it had failed him. Nero had felt completely free to violate his promise. Doubtless he would feel equally free to violate other promises.

'I insist that you do not take this to heart, Arrius,' Otho was saying. 'If it had not been you, it would have been someone else. Your house happened to be the most convenient place for him to meet her without attracting too much attention.'

Ben Hur regarded Otho curiously. 'You amaze me.'

'Why?'

'Because you act as though nothing had happened. Another man has just walked out of here with your wife.'

'That "other man" is the Emperor.' Otho rose, helped himself to some wine, then returned to his couch.

'I'll admit my feelings are somewhat bruised,' said Otho. 'But that is better than a more fatal sort of injury – which might result if I offered Nero too many obstacles.'

'Come now! Nero is no tyrant. He does not go beyond the law.'

'You've been away from Rome too long.'

Ben Hur studied him. 'Surely you misrepresent the case. Perhaps he's irresponsible. But, publicly at least, he has always shown the highest respect for justice.'

Otho laughed. 'You refer to the so-called "great age of Enlightenment"? The young God-like Emperor, who descended in a fiery chariot from heaven to bestow divine benefits on mankind? It's a lie, Arrius! This "Enlightenment" was the work of others – Seneca for one. He may be a hypocrite, but he's not without some principles. And Agrippina – she is dedicated to the good of the Roman state. Those two were able to put their ideas into practice while Nero was still young. But now he wants to be his own man – and that is *not* a very admirable man. Seneca is losing control. It is even worse for Agrippina. She has already been excluded. Her life is miserable. Every day she takes an antidote for fear of being poisoned.'

Ben Hur was silent. He told himself Otho's words were merely the bitter outpourings of an offended husband ... But the accusations could not be dismissed quite so lightly. Ben Hur could not forget Nero standing in the meadow, excoriating his mother as the worst of all guardians.

'Then let us look on the bright side,' Otho was saying with heavy sarcasm. 'If my wife is so determined to make herself an Empress, at least the legal headaches of a divorce will be made easy. Of course, I might suffer a sudden accident, but I doubt it. I haven't obstructed them. No ...' he mused, 'it is much more likely my services will be demanded in some distant corner of the empire ... a *long* way from Rome.'

He downed the wine in one gulp and got to his feet. Ben Hur did likewise.

'I have enjoyed your company, Arrius,' said Otho. 'I'm only sorry my wife's ambitions have embarrassed you. May I have your hand?'

He held out his arm, and Ben Hur clasped it in the Roman fashion.

*

It was late in the afternoon when Ben Hur returned to the villa. Even an entire day's tramp in the country had not succeeded in bringing peace to his troubled mind. The question was still there – had he been dazzled by his vision of the future? Was he attempting an impossible task?

The sound of a baritone voice floated from the bath-house. It was Peter, who had apparently returned to the villa during Ben Hur's absence. Peter, with his insistence on the all-conquering power of love, was the one person Ben Hur could not tolerate this evening.

Ben Hur turned and left the garden, plunging into the tall grass of the meadow. Soon he was in the grove of trees bordering his land, and thankfully out of sight of the villa. He wandered on, straying almost without purpose, until his steps brought him into the clearing where stood the tomb of Arrius the Elder.

Ben Hur breathed a silent prayer for guidance and strength. Suddenly he realized he was praying to the spirit of his departed father. It was said that a man in extremity would invoke whatever power he believed in most strongly. Did this mean he was losing faith in God? Irritated, he dismissed the thought as a mere philosophical quibble.

But just as he did so, the answer came to him. A warm glow of light seemed to flood his heart and bring reassurance at last.

What a fool he had been to doubt his purpose! Nero might be irresponsible and whimsical, but were not all men? And Christ had said that no man was beyond hope.

Certainly Nero's intentions were good. Not once, but many times, he had confided to Ben Hur his desire to be an exemplary ruler. If the desire was there, could it not be realized? Ben Hur told himself he must dismiss Otho's insinuations. If anyone had a reason to be prejudiced – surely it was Otho!

Ben Hur had been guilty of giving up too easily. His task was to shore up his *own* faith.

Serene at last, he made his way out of the woods. He crossed the grassy expanse of meadow and was just about to re-enter the garden when he came face to face with Peter.

'I've been looking for you all day!' the big man boomed accusingly. 'Where have you been – roaming off by yourself in the fields?'

'Enjoying my own company,' said Ben Hur. He regarded Peter curiously. 'You look happy ...'

'I am indeed!' Peter grinned. 'I'm betrothed to Urgulania!'

Ben Hur embraced him warmly.

'It reaffirms my faith in Christ!' Peter asserted.

'In what way?'

'If I hadn't left the life of a fisherman, I never would've followed Christ. And if I hadn't followed Christ I never would've come to Rome with you. And if I hadn't come to Rome with you, I never would have met Urgulania.'

'Your logic is worthy of Seneca himself,' Ben Hur observed.

'I have only one regret. I won't be living in your house any more, Judah. I have packed all my belongings – not that they were very many.'

'You are getting married so soon?'

Peter shook his head. 'You don't understand. The sooner I move into the Vicus, the sooner I'll have her father's approval.'

Ben Hur frowned. 'He doesn't approve of you?'

'When I asked him for her hand, do you know what he said? He told me to learn a trade and *earn* his consent! Can you imagine the insolence of the fellow! Oh, well ... I shall learn a trade.'

'Didn't you tell him you are a teacher?'

'No!' Peter exclaimed. 'He would have asked me what I teach. And he's not ready for that yet. He's still sacrificing cats to Anubis – that two-headed dog from Egypt!'

Ben Hur smiled. 'What trade are you learning then?'

'Barnabas has promised to teach me the wheelwright's art. I'll have to move into his shop, like any other apprentice.'

Without waiting for a reply, Peter slapped Ben Hur on the shoulder and went bounding away in the direction of the road. Ben Hur watched him with amusement. He remembered an old Jewish saying, 'He best thrives who best wives.' Ben Hur hoped it would be true of Peter.

He hoped it would be true of himself too. But Leah was a long way off, and it would be a long time before he would ever see her again.

The sleep left him. Like an animal sensing danger, Ben Hur was instantly wide awake. There was someone else in the room with him! Afraid to make a noise, he lay still in his bed, every nerve tingling in anticipation of an attack, his ears straining into the darkness.

Even though he could hear nothing, he could feel the other presence. Ben Hur hardly dared to breathe, but his hand crept towards the table where his dagger lay.

Then the sound came. Barely audible, but distinct ... a slight scraping of a leather shoe sole on the mosaic floor, over by the shuttered window.

Ben Hur froze. The sound was not repeated ... Once again his right hand began its stealthy journey. His fingers reached for the dagger, but the sheath was empty!

'I have the dagger,' whispered a voice in the darkness.

It was Nero!

Ben Hur recalled hearing that the Emperor's father was insane. Had this streak of madness been passed to his son?

'Why did you take my dagger?'

'You might have thought me an assassin,' muttered Nero's disembodied voice. 'Killed me before you knew who it was.'

'I'll get a light,' Ben Hur suggested.

'No!' Nero exclaimed sharply. 'No light ... I don't want to be looked at ... not now ...'

Something solid thumped on to the bed.

'There's your dagger ... I don't want it any more. I'm afraid of it ... I might kill myself!'

'Why?'

'Arrius – I am the most miserable of men. I wish I'd never been born!' His words came faster. 'I had to talk to someone! I couldn't be alone! You're the only one, Arrius. The only one!'

'How did you get in here?' Ben Hur wondered.

Nero said nothing.

Ben Hur's nerves tingled again. Obviously neither Phaon nor Electra had heard Nero's entry. He had slipped into Ben Hur's bedroom without waking anyone. It made Ben Hur realize how insecure he really was ...

'Are you still angry with me?' Nero asked suddenly.

'Have I been angry with you?'

'I broke my promise to you. I took Poppaea away. I know a

promise is a sacred thing between two gentlemen. But, Arrius – in her presence, I can think of only one thing. I can't resist her! Even if I can't marry her, she's the only woman I will ever care about.' He sighed. 'I'll admit I was wrong to break my word. I *want* to be an honourable man. I want to do good! But sometimes there is another part of me which does wrong – even though I don't want to.'

'We're all like that.'

'Are you like that, Arrius?'

'Of course I am. But I don't despair of life – I know the part of me which urges me towards good is God.'

'God? What God?'

'The same God who lives in all men. We should heed Him.'

'I feel no God in me. I'm Emperor, but I'm nothing. My life is nothing!'

'It need not be. There is much to do – another great Empire to conquer.'

'Nonsense! Rome rules almost the whole world. It would be foolish to acquire any more lands. There's too much to manage as it is. Julius Caesar and Augustus conquered most of it. Claudius added Britain. All that's left for me is to make sure the whole monstrous establishment runs smoothly.'

'I'm not talking about that Empire. I'm talking about man's spirit. His soul. The Empire of God.'

'How do you know about such things, Arrius? How does anyone?'

'I learned from a great teacher in Judaea. He showed me that a man can achieve a knowledge of God – that a man's soul may live for ever. Not in suffering, as in this life, but peace and joy.'

'Nothing lives for ever,' Nero said sadly.

'Every year the trees, flowers and grass die, yet in spring they come to life again,' Ben Hur pointed out.

'A tree is not a man,' Nero replied. 'And neither is a blade of grass.'

'The man who taught me these things died,' Ben Hur said softly. 'But he rose from his tomb and lived again.'

'Jupiter's eyeballs!' Nero whispered incredulously. 'Are you sure of this? Did you see it?'

'I did not see it. But I know men who did.'

'What a wondrous thing! Is it true, Arrius? I want to hear the whole story.'

'Very well,' Ben Hur said.

'But now I want light. I want to see your eyes when you tell it. Sometimes the eye tells more than the tongue.'

'I'll get a lamp then. I'll only be a moment ...'

Rolling from his sleeping-couch, Ben Hur took up his cloak, which lay on the nearby stool. Wrapping himself in the garment, he groped towards the door. Opening it, he stumbled a few feet along the portico, then entered the triclinium, where a scented taper was burning, safely mounted on its metal stand over a bowl of water. Ben Hur took one of the oil lamps stored in a niche cut into the opposite wall. Now, moving to the table on which the taper glowed, he held out the lamp to the flame. The wick ignited.

Ben Hur left the triclinium, carefully shielding the flame from the vagrant breezes of the portico, and re-entered his bedroom.

But Nero was nowhere to be seen! Holding the light high, Ben Hur looked round to be sure the flickering shadows had not deceived him. But there was no trace of his nocturnal visitor. Then he noticed the shutters had been slid open.

Ben Hur placed the lamp on the table and strode to the open window.

The darkened trees and shrubbery of the garden, which seemed so neat and well-ordered by day, were by night a chorus of grotesque creatures from the nether world, swaying before an invisible power. A shadowy form ghosted across his vision and perched on a branch adjacent to the house. It was a great horned owl.

Hastily Ben Hur closed the shutters. He sat on the bed, but any thought of sleep was gone. The owl was a sinister omen ...

CHAPTER SEVEN

The steady measured beat of eight oars drove the barge up the Tiber. Looming ahead in the murky darkness of the night was the mausoleum of Augustus, its marble columns and gilded capitals barely visible on the right-hand bank. Lights flickered uncertainly here and there along both shores.

Epaphroditus sat in the stern of the vessel, which curved up behind him like a high-backed chair. His glance travelled to the passenger sitting in the similar curve of the prow, his features clear in the light of a torch held by a slave seated in front of the rowers.

Quintus Arrius was the new favourite, but he did not look happy. Epaphroditus could see the tense, thin lines of worry stretched between the other man's eyebrows. He noted the slightly vacant way Arrius was watching the naked backs of the oarsmen – without really seeing them. The freedman smiled inwardly with contempt. He had known many imperial favourites, and they all had that worried look. Arrius was perhaps different from the others, for he had once been a slave. At least, so men said. But Epaphroditus did not consider the difference significant. After all, Arrius had been born an aristocrat and had grown up as one. A short interval of servitude would hardly change a man's basic way of thinking.

Epaphroditus was grateful he had been *born* a slave. He wasn't hampered by the standards and the inhibitions of the upper class. If Epaphroditus wanted something, he had to contend with only one limitation. Could he get away with it?

He knew he was well liked. It was because he always smiled, no matter what he was thinking. A slave had to smile, and the habit had stayed with Epaphroditus after he was manumitted. So affable was he that even when he struck – as he occasionally had to – his victim was never prepared.

Epaphroditus was not deceived by his own good fortune. Even though he had been freed long ago and was now among the greatest of gentlemen himself, his old ways of thinking, moulded by the demands of survival, had stayed with him and would never change. There were many others like him rising to positions of prominence all over the Empire. Those who lived by the old aristocratic ethics could not compete against such ruthless opposition. The freedman class was the wave of the future!

The bend in the river was drawing closer. Epaphroditus clapped his hands and indicated a dilapidated wooden jetty, looming blackly ahead. Obediently the helmsman moved the steering oar, and the prow of the barge swung towards the bank. A moment later the craft glided up to the dock. The rowers hauled in their oars, and two of them leaped out, holding the boat fast by its gilded stem.

Epaphroditus picked his way over the thwarts towards Arrius, who stood up, dusting off his tunic.

Ben Hur turned as Epaphroditus stepped respectfully in front of him. The freedman bowed deeply and gave him a warm smile. 'Most Eminent Sir, I hope you have enjoyed the journey.'

Epaphroditus pointed to a dark hole of an alley behind the shadowy warehouses. 'That will take you to your destination. The Milvian Bridge is just round the bend. I wish I could accompany you further, but the Emperor did not want the imperial barge seen in the area.'

'My thanks,' said Ben Hur, stepping on to the dock.

'One other thing,' Epaphroditus called after him. 'The tavern is on this bank, just at the foot of the bridge.'

Ben Hur set off down the dock, mounted some steps and turned into the alley. The place was filled with refuse, and he had to pick his way. Soon, however, he reached a wider road. He strode along until he could see lights reflected in the river again. And there was the Milvian Bridge, its six graceful arches of tufa and travertine spanning the Tiber.

Ben Hur glanced at the road leading to the bridge. He could see the tavern right next to it, a soft light glowing behind its shuttered windows. The wine shop was a low, ramshackle structure, in contrast to the shabby six-storey tenements which towered all round. A strange place for the Emperor of Rome to spend an evening. And yet the message had been clear. Nero would be waiting in the tavern for him. Ben Hur hoped the Emperor would have an explanation for his mysterious disappearance the night before. He also prayed that Nero would be alone, so they could continue the conversation which had started so promisingly.

He quickened his pace, but he was tired. It had been a day of anxiety. Worry and doubts about Nero's sanity, hours of introspective debate, had sapped his strength.

Early in the afternoon Epaphroditus had arrived with the summons from Nero. Ben Hur had hesitated, for he had not forgotten the omen of the great horned owl. A sensible man would have stayed inside his house until a more propitious sign came his way.

Or he might have sent for a sorcerer to give him a safeguarding charm. But this would have taken too long. Crossing the forces of evil had made Ben Hur uneasy, but he'd done it. For seeing Nero immediately was all-important.

Now Ben Hur reached the door of the wine shop. He stopped, overpowered by the stench of the threshold, where the drunken customers habitually came to puke. Steeling himself, he held his breath and entered.

The room was long and low, illuminated by smoky tapers held in metal stands. With windows closed, the air was stifling. Ben Hur glanced round. Several men wearing leather aprons sat at one of the trestle tables. They looked like smiths or artisans. Two others lounged at the opposite corner of the room. Judging by their scars and powerful muscles, Ben Hur had a feeling they were not strangers to the arena. Not far away a stout prostitute, who had apparently abandoned all hope of being gainfully employed, was addressing herself to a pot of wine.

Seeing no sign of Nero, Ben Hur made his way distastefully to the most remote table he could find and sat down. The proprietor started towards him, bringing wine, but Ben Hur waved him away, wondering how long he would have to wait for the Emperor.

He noticed another occupant in the room, a villainous-looking tough with long hair and a shaggy black beard sitting on a stool in the corner. His rough, homespun habit and cloak of goat's hair were in obvious contrast to the urban garb of the others present.

Ben Hur did not like the way this scavenger was staring sullenly at him. Growing increasingly uncomfortable, he thought about going outside and waiting. A plague on Nero! Why should he choose a place like this to meet?

The bearded man crossed the room and stood right next to him. He seemed to cringe as he spoke.

'Illustrious sir,' he whined, unctuously, 'might I share this table with you . . .'

Without waiting for an answer, he sat down.

'You can have it all to yourself,' said Ben Hur, getting to his feet.

The other caught him by the tunic. 'You wouldn't be so cruel as to walk away from one of life's unfortunates, would you? A poor, derelict shepherd from Calabria who has lost his sheep ...' He chuckled gruffly. 'You'll never miss a denarius or two, and it'll warm me with a pot of wine ...' Suddenly the voice changed. 'You don't know me, do you?'

Stunned, Ben Hur sat down again, staring at the ragged fellow. The eyes behind the made-up folds of flesh were suddenly familiar.

'I'm a wonderful actor,' Nero said. 'If I ever abdicated, I could make my living on the stage ... A simple craft will keep a man from want.'

Ben Hur remained silent, contemplating this fresh eccentricity.

'I'm sorry about last night, Arrius. When you went to get that lamp, I suddenly realized how late it was. Poppaea was waiting for me at the Temple of Vesta. I had to be on my way before it got light.'

'But what are you doing down here, dressed like a Calabrian bandit?'

'Affairs of state,' Nero whispered solemnly. He grinned through the black beard. 'You think I'm mad, but I'm not. How else can I get to know my people? What they really think? Do you imagine they'd tell the truth if they knew the Emperor was listening?'

Ben Hur appraised him warily. This was either the act of an imaginative statesman or a madman.

'Surely you could find a less hazardous way to keep yourself informed.'

Nero laughed, indicating the two big men sitting at the opposite end of the room. 'They look like gladiators, don't they?'

Ben Hur glanced at the bulky fellows, who continued to drink their wine placidly.

'Well, they *are* gladiators,' Nero giggled. 'Diomedes and Juba. The best. If anybody gives me trouble, I just do that ...' He snapped his fingers silently.

Nero sighed. 'This place is dead tonight. Let's go somewhere else ... I know! Calpurnia's!' He leaned closer to Ben Hur with a conspiratorial leer. 'It's a cat house! You'll never believe it, Arrius – when you pay Calpurnia, the freedwoman counts the change with her thing! I'm not joking – she picks up coins with her thing!

That's what I call education.' He sighed with ecstasy. 'You can find anything there. They've got two Syrian girls who do it with each other – while you watch. Boys too. There's a dwarf. And a big lady who was in the arena. Men who can't get it up at home even take their wives to Calpurnia's!' Nero rose. 'I don't go there much any more because I always run into Seneca – but we'll chance it tonight.'

'I thought the purpose of these nocturnal excursions was to inform yourself about your people,' Ben Hur observed wryly.

'There's no better place than a whorehouse to feel the pulse of the public,' Nero stated. 'People from all walks of life go there. Whores are the first to know what's going on.'

He rose and snapped his fingers, audibly this time. On the other side of the room, Diomedes and Juba put down their cups and got to their feet. Ben Hur did likewise and followed his bearded guide out into the dark street, the gargantuan shadows of the bodyguards keeping pace not far behind.

'I'll promise you one thing,' Nero declared. 'When I get rid of all the sycophants and self-seekers – my mother, Seneca, Burrus, the whole poxy lot – I'm going to have nothing but whores as my advisers. Then I'll really be in touch with the people!' He bellowed with mirth.

Soon they had left the clammy air near the Milvian Bridge, and were plunging into the murky blackness of a maze of alleys. When they came to a stop at a crossroads, one of the gladiators sidled up to Nero.

'Exalted Sir,' he whispered, 'shall we get torches?'

'You talk like a eunuch, Diomedes,' Nero sneered. 'Are you afraid of the dark?'

'No, Exalted One, but I like to know where I'm going.'

'I know where I'm going. Just follow me.'

They rounded a corner. Nero hurried ahead as if he could not wait to reach the delights of Calpurnia's. Ben Hur was sure of one thing. There would be no discussion of religion or philosophy tonight!

Ahead, the shrill wail of gemshorns, chanters and shawms spilled out of a tavern, followed by a fat man who staggered down the steps, sweat drenching his three chins. He collapsed into the miry road with a groan, and broke wind with an incredibly loud noise.

Nero sauntered over to the recumbent figure and prodded him with his foot.

'Your legs have given out?' Nero inquired.

The drunk farted again. Nero kicked him harder.

'You're polluting the air.'

The fat man blinked up at his tormentor. 'Go and bugger a dog,' he muttered.

Affecting mock concern, Nero turned to his companions. 'Would you say this poor fellow has had too much to drink?'

The gladiators grunted their assent.

Nero again addressed himself to the drunk. 'What about your family? No doubt you have children. No doubt it is the money for their food you are spending on drink ...'

'Bugger a dog,' the drunk repeated.

'I think you need a lesson,' said Nero. 'When we've finished with you, there won't be a spot on your body which doesn't ache. You won't be in any condition to raise your arm, let alone take a drink!' He turned to his companions. 'Let's toss him!'

With alacrity Diomedes and Juba leaped on the fat man, pinning him down, despite his vociferous protests. He fought back wildly and struggled to draw a dagger from his belt, but shrieked when Nero's foot came down on his wrist. Nero grabbed the dagger and threw it away into the darkness.

'You can't be too careful,' the Emperor commented to Ben Hur. 'Even when they're drunk ...'

'Did you ever think about letting him alone? Ben Hur suggested.

'I don't like to see Romans drunk,' Nero replied virtuously.

He returned to his sport. Diomedes had taken off his cloak and spread it on the ground, while Juba was rolling the struggling victim on to it.

When Nero had joined them, all three seized the edges of the garment, and, with a great simultaneous heave, tossed the flabby man into the air. The victim fell back into the cloak with such force that he knocked it to the ground. His howl of pain was cut short as the breath was knocked from his body.

'Careful!' yelled Nero. 'You'll break his back. Hold it higher.'

Ben Hur watched with distaste as they tossed the drunk again and again. Nero was shrieking with delight, the tears streaming down his face into the beard.

'Enough!' he shouted finally.

Roughly the three men turned the cloak over, dumping its contents on to the road. The fat man lay there inert.

Ben Hur moved towards the victim with concern, but Nero stopped him. 'Don't worry, Arrius ... He's not dead.' He chuckled. 'It's very hard to kill a drunk.'

Ignoring the Emperor, Ben Hur leaned over the motionless figure. Rasping snores attested that the fat man was very much alive.

Nero plucked Ben Hur's arm. 'Come on!' he said impatiently. 'We're wasting valuable time!'

For a time, they threaded through the twisting, winding alleys. Nero led on unhesitatingly. Suddenly there was more music coming from an archway ahead, this time accompanied by the shouts of many people.

'The Vatican bear pit,' Nero whispered. 'Perhaps we should stop there ... But no! It's Calpurnia for us tonight.'

He hurried off, and Ben Hur moved with him.

'I was at the bear pit the other night,' the Emperor confided. 'They were so intent on watching those beasts gouge each other to pieces that I lifted four money pouches, and no one was the wiser. I am an expert pickpocket. If I ever abdicated, I could make my living that way –'

Abruptly, Nero seized Ben Hur by the arm and pulled him into the shadow of a doorway. The bodyguards likewise flattened themselves against a wall.

Coming towards them were two youths carrying flaming torches ahead of a sedan chair. The litter was a handsome one, leather, with ornate ivory window frames.

'Jupiter's eyeballs!' Nero whispered. 'This is too good to be happening!'

'Now what?' Ben Hur asked apprehensively.

'It's Montanus. The most pompous ass in the Senate. Of course, in public I have to treat him with respect, but tonight ... tonight we have a little sport!'

'Don't you think we've had enough sport for one night?'

Nero looked aggrieved. 'I may never get another chance like this. I don't intend to pass it up.'

Snapping his fingers, Nero ran from his place of concealment. Diomedes did likewise and beckoned for Juba to follow. With blood-curdling shrieks they charged down on the advancing torch-bearers, who hurled their flaming batons into the mud and fled in panic. Reaching the chair the gladiators began pummelling the pole-bearers, who dropped their burden and retreated fearfully against the wall. Immediately the gladiators seized the poles and began to shake the chair violently. Cries of rage and pain came from within.

Ben Hur had seen enough. He moved from the doorway and strode forward, but before he could intervene, Nero and his comrades turned the chair on its side. The door flew open, and Montanus tumbled out, sprawling into the mud.

The senator extricated himself from the tangles of his cloak and struggled to his feet. The sweat of terror dampened his brow as he faced his bearded assailant.

'You blackguard!' Montanus blustered. 'Make way, or I'll call the watch.'

'Go ahead!' Nero mocked. 'Call them! They won't hear you!' He picked up the hem of Montanus' toga, displaying its broad purple stripe to his henchmen. 'Well, well ... we've bagged a senator, it seems.'

'That's right,' Montanus gasped. 'I *am* a senator, and, in the name of the Senate, I demand that you let me pass.'

Nero laughed. 'And what are you going to do if I don't?'

Montanus could barely restrain his trembling.

'L–let me pass, I beg you!'

Nero grinned conspiratorily at his gladiators, who chuckled throatily. 'He wants to pass!' Nero jeered. Suddenly he turned on the senator, thrusting his face close to Montanus. 'I'll let you pass. But first I'm going to take your money! Then I'm going to take that beautiful chair you parade yourself in. Next I'm going to strip off that toga, every stitch of clothes you've got on, all your jewels, your rings – everything. And I'm going to leave you sitting in the mud of this street as naked as the day you were born!'

Montanus moaned. 'Don't do this to me! Please!' He fumbled

in his toga and extracted a bag, offering it to Nero. 'Here! Take my money! It's all I've got. But let me have my chair and go my way.'

Nero snatched the bag, tossed it thoughtfully, surveying Montanus intently the whole while. Then, without warning, Nero's hand shot out, groped under the folds of Montanus' toga and reappeared with an even larger bag of coins. Nero brandished it in Montanus' face. 'All you've got, was it? You lie like a Parthian!'

He nodded to his cronies. Diomedes and Juba launched themselves on Montanus' sedan chair and savagely began to pry off the ivory inlay with their daggers.

'My chair!' Montanus howled. 'Not my chair! Please!'

Ben Hur took an involuntary step forward, but stopped. What could he do? Remonstrating with Nero would be useless.

When the gladiators had stripped the last of the ivory from the litter, Nero confronted Montanus again. Fearfully the senator backed away from his tormentor.

'You filthy scum,' Montanus cried. 'From this day hence, I swear I won't rest until you're caught. I have influence. I'm not just any senator. I'm *Montanus*, ex-praetor and ex-quaestor! My name carries weight!'

Nero stopped abruptly.

'Montanus!' he exclaimed. 'Not *the* Montanus!'

The senator drew himself up, a trifle pridefully. 'The same.' He held out his thumb. Nero pretended to peer in astonishment at Montanus' seal ring.

'A thousand pardons, Renowned Sir!' Nero spun round and faced his gladiators. 'We've made a terrible mistake. It's Montanus! Put the ivory back! Fix the chair! Immediately!'

The bodyguards leaped to obey.

Ben Hur watched incredulously. Nero had boasted of his acting ability, and he had not been exaggerating. It seemed to Ben Hur as if everyone in Roman high society was perpetually on stage. Apparently they all had numerous personalities and could choose at will the one best suited to the situation at hand. But the performance Ben Hur was witnessing now was by far the most skilled he had ever seen.

Nero hovered apologetically over the shaken senator. 'I never would have troubled you had I known it was Montanus. The man who wants to restore the Republic – to return to the Romans the freedom which they once had.'

Montanus eyed him cautiously. 'Where did you hear such things about me?'

Nero winked slyly. 'In the streets we learn many things – sometimes things which people in higher circles of society dare not say. Senator Montanus is against the government – and so am I. Senator Montanus hates the Emperor – and so do I. Is it not so?'

Montanus made no reply.

Nero held up the money bags. 'Any enemy of Nero's is a friend of mine. And I do not rob my friends ...'

'I am glad we are friends,' Montanus said warily, 'but I do not believe I've ever said anything against the Emperor.'

Nero withdrew the money bags immediately, regarding Montanus with pained eyes. 'Then you're *not* a Republican ... You *don't* oppose the Emperor ...'

The senator's eyes flickered furtively round the darkened alleys, where his bearers and torch boys were still cowering against the walls. When he spoke, his voice was a whisper. 'Well ... actually there is some truth in it. But you understand – we don't talk about such things.'

Nero patted Montanus on the shoulder. 'I understand. But fear not – you are among friends here in the street. You and I are allies. We both know that Nero is an ill-starred misfit. They say he was born feet first, you know ...'

'Indeed!' Montanus exclaimed, eyeing the money pouches greedily. 'That explains a great deal. By the Lares of my family, in the days of the Republic he would not have lasted long.'

Nero handed the money to Montanus, then turned back to the gladiators. 'Set his chair up properly! And shake the mud out of it!'

Grumbling, the gladiators moved to obey.

Now, solicitously, Nero began to wipe off Montanus' cloak. 'Once again, I beg your pardon, Most Renowned Sir. I would not be reduced to molesting people in the streets, had not Nero ruined my life. I was Chief Notarius to the Prefect of the Grain Supply. I had a respectable career ahead of me. Then I was thrown out of my post. All because that pederast Nero wanted to give it to one of his favourite freedmen.' Nero allowed his voice to drop to a whisper. 'The stories about the Emperor's depravity are unbelievable. But you are a senator, so you must know. Tell me, is it really true that the Emperor is unfaithful to his wife, and spends all his time playing the lyre?'

Montanus laughed. 'That's nothing. Child's play. Do you have any idea what else he's done? He poisoned the old Emperor – and his own brother.'

Nero took a deep breath. 'Appalling! It is hard to believe – even of Nero! Are you certain this is true?'

'It's true, all right,' said Montanus. 'And I could tell you more – but such things are better left unsaid.' Montanus glanced round. 'Sometimes the very walls have ears ...'

'Sometimes the ears are much closer than the walls,' Nero said silkily.

With a flourish, he pulled off his wig and beard.

Montanus looked as though he had been hit in the stomach. His mouth opened and closed, but no sound came out.

Ben Hur was repelled and disgusted. Yet a part of him was fascinated. The whole display was so unreal that he would not have believed it, had he not been a witness.

Nero seized Montanus by the toga and shook him violently, like a dog worrying a bone, then flung him aside. But Diomedes and Juba hauled Montanus up again and dragged him before the Emperor.

Nero slapped the senator violently. 'When I've finished with you – you won't be able to tell any more tales about me!'

Seeing Nero double up his fist to aim another blow, Ben Hur hesitated no longer. Leaping from the shadows, he grabbed Nero's arm and jerked him backwards. Indignantly Nero tried to twist free, but Ben Hur held him fast.

Diomedes and Juba seized Ben Hur, and pulled him away from Nero, who was sobbing with impotent fury. Ben Hur dropped to his knees, then rose sharply, bringing both clenched fists into Diomedes' groin. The powerful man gasped with agony.

Ben Hur spun, slashing with the back of his hand at Juba's throat. But the gladiator was even faster. He easily evaded the blow and grabbed Ben Hur's wrist, twisting his arm up sharply behind his back.

Diomedes drew his dagger. His eyes glittering menacingly, he advanced on Ben Hur.

'Stop!' cried Nero suddenly.

He plunged forward, pushing Diomedes back.

'Release him!' Nero commanded.

With a reluctant grunt, Juba slackened his hold.

With tears in his eyes, Nero faced Ben Hur.

'You were right, Arrius ...' Nero said. 'I am utterly mad,' Thank you for recalling me to my senses.'

'You can thank me by letting Montanus go his way.'

Nero made a gesture to Diomedes and Juba. 'Call back the senator's attendants.'

The gladiators trotted into the shadows, rounding up the cringing bearers and torch boys.

'From now on,' Nero said to Montanus, 'if you have criticism, come to me, and tell me to my face. You need not fear retaliation. It is only when such things are breathed behind my back that I resent them. You may go now.'

Montanus hastily picked up his money bags, which he had dropped in the scuffle. He climbed into his chair. The bearers lifted it, and carried him off at a run.

Nero faced Ben Hur apologetically. 'Tell me we're still comrades.'

With an effort Ben Hur forced himself to quell his uneasiness. He took the hand which Nero offered.

'We're still comrades,' Ben Hur said quietly.

'Good!' Nero exclaimed. 'Now let's go to Calpurnia's! By the wand of Mercury, I've never watched you humping a woman yet!'

Ben Hur smiled weakly. 'I'm no longer in the Circus. And I don't plan on starting tonight.'

'You're not still angry with me, are you?' Nero asked anxiously.

Ben Hur shook his head.

Again they clasped hands.

'I still see doubt in your eyes, Arrius. I beg you not to think ill of me. This will not happen again.'

'We will say no more about it.'

'Only on one condition. You come with me to Baiae in four days' time. For the festival, you know. It will be an intimate gathering. And best of all – my mother will not be there. I made a point of not inviting her.'

'Of course,' Ben Hur assented quickly, eager only to make his escape. He would have agreed to accompany Odysseus to the Isle of Cyclopes – if only to be away and alone to think.

'Splendid!' Nero cried. 'Baiae is lovely this time of year. And sea bathing is the best thing for the skin.'

Finally Ben Hur was able to extricate himself and take his leave. He strode off until he could smell the river at the end of the alley. He quickened his pace, feeling like leaving Rome and never returning.

Had Montanus been right? Had Nero poisoned the old Emperor and his own brother? These accusations were alarmingly similar to the ones made by Otho not long ago.

Even if these rumours were not true, it was becoming obvious that Ben Hur's mission could never succeed. A man like Nero could never be the instrument of the Christians' aspirations. And would those aspirations ever be possible in this cynical and selfish world?

At the end of the alley Ben Hur paused, gazing sombrely at the Tiber. Its turgid surface reflected a grey light, and he suddenly realized that it was dawn. Soon all Rome would be going about its business. He came to a decision. What must be done he would do now, while he was still here in the city, and then be quit of it for ever.

CHAPTER EIGHT

'There is no point in fighting for a hopeless cause.' Ben Hur surveyed the reproachful faces of his comrades. There was total silence in the little shop.

He went on. 'I take full responsibility. It was my plan, but Nero will never be won over.'

'You are wrong, Judah,' Silas rasped. 'Your design was the inspiration of God! You must not turn from it. Imagine – the Emperor of Rome himself, embracing our faith!'

'It could only happen with an enlightened emperor,' Ben Hur answered. 'Perhaps one day it will . . . But not now, not with Nero.'

'You can enlighten him,' Silas persisted. 'God will put the words in your mouth!'

Ben Hur made an impatient gesture. 'You expect too much! Nero is a jaded, dissolute young man. He's not interested in ideas or things of the spirit. Nothing will ever make him so.'

'Perhaps you should try to understand him,' Barnabas suggested. 'All his life he has been surrounded by bad influence. Bring out the good in him, Judah – the same good that exists in *all* men.'

Ben Hur hesitated. 'I can no longer make myself believe there is good in all men . . .'

Peter could not hide his dismay. 'In the past your faith was always so strong.'

'The more I see of people,' Ben Hur admitted, 'especially those surrounding the Emperor – the less faith I have.'

'Remember our Master,' Silas said firmly. 'He found something to love in all men.'

Impatiently Ben Hur rose. 'Silas – that strange sound you make when you speak – men say you were tortured on the rack for being a Christian. It tore something inside you. Is that true?'

Silas nodded mutely.

'Do you love the man who did that to you?'

'Yes.'

'You are the worst kind of liar! You lie to yourself!'

'Judah, please!' Peter protested. 'Let us not quarrel among ourselves. Even if you will have nothing more to do with Nero, let us remain united in Christ.'

'If we want to remain united,' said Ben Hur, 'we must leave Rome.'

'Why?' Peter demanded.

'Because Rome is not a city of God – it is not ready for the teachings of Christ. And if I stay here, I will have to continue my relationship with Nero.'

'Rome is the centre of the world!' Peter cried. 'Here, above all, we must build the church.'

'I cannot remain,' Ben Hur insisted, 'pretending to be a part of the Emperor's court. Already my life is becoming a lie. It is destroying me!'

'What do you propose, then?' Peter ventured. 'Will you go back to Jerusalem?'

'I think not. The Emperor would surely trace me there. I must find a place where no one knows me.'

Peter gazed at him sombrely. His words came with an effort. 'It will be very difficult for me to leave Rome. How can I? Not only am I betrothed to Urgulania, but I am betrothed to the Roman Church too. This I have vowed, Judah.'

'I understand. I know you are founding a home here. I would never think of taking you away from it.'

Peter's eyes did not leave Ben Hur's face. 'You are saying goodbye, then ...'

'Perhaps only for a time. When I know where I will be, I will find some way to communicate with you.'

Ben Hur held out his hand. Peter clasped it. The tears came to the big man's eyes.

'May God guide your steps ...'

'One day, Peter,' Ben Hur promised, 'we will be together again.'

The moment was painful. Ben Hur turned to the others, taking their hands in turn.

'Barnabas ... be sure to say goodbye to Phoebe for me.' He glanced at Peter. 'Urgulania too ...'

Ben Hur wanted to say more, but the words would not come. Blindly he turned and left the shop.

Only when he reached the archway at the end of the crowded Vicus did he pause to look back.

Peter was standing in the doorway of the shop. He raised his arm once, then disappeared inside.

The villa was unexpectedly quiet. At this hour the place was usually echoing with the sounds of the scullery and Electra's strident screeches at her husband.

'Phaon!' Ben Hur shouted.

There was no answer.

Then he remembered. This was their market day. Electra, shepherding her husband in his wide sun hat, would have left long ago to visit the produce sellers of the city. The day would be half gone before they had loaded the baskets on their mule and started their homeward journey.

Ben Hur felt a flash of irritation. After his sleepless, exhausting night, he would have welcomed a meal. But first he wanted a hot bath to draw the stiffness from his limbs. Then he would eat and plan his departure from Rome.

He made his way down the portico and turned into the bath-house. He hoped that Phaon had heated the water before leaving this morning.

Kneeling on the slate floor by the edge of the bath, Ben Hur tested its temperature. It was invitingly warm. Phaon was indeed the perfect servant! Such small evidences of consideration made life bearable – even at times like this.

He removed his shoes and tunic, then slipped into the pool. Sinking back on to the stone seat which circled the bath, he allowed his tension to dissolve into the water. Some time passed. He forced all disturbing thoughts from his mind, determined to find repose.

A door banged somewhere in the direction of the atrium. Someone was in the house. He wondered if it could be Phaon returning from the market. But these were not Phaon's footsteps ...

Ben Hur had no intention of allowing any intruder to catch him in the bath. He scrambled out, searching for something which might serve as a weapon.

Just then the door opened, and Otho stood there. He smiled apologetically.

'I am sorry to disturb your bath, Arrius. I knocked on your front door. No one answered. The matter was urgent, so we came in ...'

'We?'

'I've brought some friends with me.' Otho moved back to the door and called to someone outside. 'He's in here!'

Petronius entered, his hair perfectly curled above his chalk-white face, and his toga impeccably folded as usual. 'Arrius!' he cried. 'Forgive this invasion of your privacy.'

Another man entered behind Petronius. It was Montanus, his lips still swollen from Nero's blows.

'Again we meet, Arrius!' Montanus exclaimed. 'But under better circumstances this time; I am grateful to have the opportunity to thank you in person for your noble intervention last night.'

'I am glad I was able to help you,' Ben Hur replied. He glanced curiously at the others. 'Surely *all* of you haven't come here to thank me?'

'Indeed we have,' Petronius asserted. 'Montanus is one of our dearest friends. Any injury to him is an injury to us ...' Picking up a towel, he draped it over Ben Hur's neck. 'Do dry yourself, Arrius. We don't want you to catch cold.'

'Thank you,' Ben Hur grunted, as he began rubbing his limbs. 'If you'll just bear with me until I get my clothes on, perhaps I can offer you some wine.'

'That's the first sensible suggestion I've heard this morning,' Petronius said.

'Once again I must apologize for our unorthodox entry,' Otho insisted. 'But it really *was* important that we have a meeting before I depart.'

Ben Hur slipped into his tunic. 'You are going away?'

'As I predicted,' Otho said drily, 'I have been honoured with an important post – in a distant part of the Empire. To be exact, Governor of Lusitania. Both the Emperor and my wife are eager to see me on my way.'

Ben Hur put on his shoes and escorted them to the door.

On the sunlit portico, Otho took Ben Hur's arm confidentially. 'In point of fact, thanking you on behalf of Montanus was not our only reason for coming ... We've been wanting to have this talk for some time. We hesitated because we thought it might not be prudent. But what you did for Montanus last night changed our minds.'

They reached the tablinium and entered. Otho sprawled on the couch while Ben Hur moved to the cupboard, took out goblets and filled them with Falernian. Montanus carefully closed the door.

'I gather,' said Ben Hur sardonically, as he handed Otho a cup, 'that you have not come here to discuss Etruscan history.'

Otho laughed. 'No, Arrius. Roman history. Circumstances have changed since that evening when the Emperor appropriated my wife. At the time I received the distinct impression that you were not entirely happy with Nero, but I was not certain how deep it went. Now perhaps I have a clearer idea.'

Ben Hur gave the others their wine, then faced Otho again. 'You are saying that you would like to see a change of Emperors?'

'I would indeed. Nero's insanity will only get worse. Something must be done quickly. Some friends of mine – including those of us here – have formed a group aimed at a change of political power. You would be an invaluable asset to us. Nero trusts you. He will not be afraid to go anywhere alone with you. Not one of us enjoys so favoured a status. So you see, Arrius, you would be truly indispensable for us.'

Ben Hur shook his head. 'I want no part of conspiracies.'

Otho got to his feet. He placed an arm on Ben Hur's shoulder. 'I know you're a moral man, Arrius.'

'Indeed?'

'If you were not, you would never have dared to help Montanus.'

'You saved my life from a madman,' Montanus said fervently.

'The Roman Empire is at the mercy of this madman's whims and desires,' Otho persisted. 'Is that a moral thing?'

'No,' Ben Hur agreed. 'But, on the other hand, I don't propose to set myself up as a judge or executioner.'

'No one is asking you to set yourself up as anything,' said Petronius blandly. 'If you need any inner justifications, you can always tell yourself that circumstances forced you into it.'

Ben Hur put down his cup angrily. 'I just gave you my answer! If you can't think of anything else to discuss, finish your wine and take yourselves off!'

He strode to the door and opened it, then turned to face them. But none of them moved.

'Surely you have not given us a fair hearing,' Otho insisted.

'I have heard enough,' Ben Hur replied firmly.

'Perhaps he will listen to me,' said a voice from the door.

There stood the commanding figure of Agrippina, clad in her customary man's tunic. She stepped into the tablinium.

Otho cleared his throat discreetly. 'I was about to tell you, Arrius, that we had brought the leader of our group with us.'

Ben Hur appraised Agrippina cynically. 'The best of mothers ... Isn't that the way Nero once described you?'

'That was a long time ago,' she replied.

'I never knew maternal feelings were capable of being so easily suspended ... But I suppose anything is possible in Rome.'

Montanus and Otho exchanged an uneasy look, but Petronius seemed to be enjoying some private joke.

'Nero's father was a monster,' Agrippina said coolly. 'And the offspring is just like his sire. My son should not be ruling. He must be removed. I will not deny that I'm acting in my own interest. But my interest happens to coincide with the good of the state.'

'I may point out,' Petronius added, 'that joining us is actually the best thing you could do, Arrius. The life-span of imperial favourites is notoriously short.'

Agrippina nodded. 'No one is safe while Nero holds power. I can tell you who the next victim will be. His wife. Octavia is an obstacle to his plans for Poppaea. Our esteemed Marcus Otho will probably share the same fate for the same reasons. And you, Petronius, have committed the unforgivable sin of being a better poet than my son. He fears your biting tongue. As for me ... well, I can only say I am surprised every morning I wake up to find myself still alive.'

When no one spoke, Agrippina continued. 'My son has more enemies than friends. We have supporters even in the Praetorian Guards. After all, my father, Germanicus, once commanded them. When we have achieved our purpose, we will go to the Praetorian camp. They will proclaim me Empress!'

Ben Hur shook his head grimly. 'You are an ambitious woman.'

'And why not?' she demanded. 'No one is better qualified. I have been sister to an Emperor, wife to another Emperor, and now mother to still another Emperor. None of them was capable. In each case it has been *I* who did the actual ruling. I have more knowledge of governing than anyone alive. I should be the head of state.' She paused. 'Do you disagree?'

'I don't dispute your qualification,' said Ben Hur, 'only your methods.'

She dismissed the others with an imperious gesture. 'Leave us.'

The three men bowed to Ben Hur, and strode out of the room.

Agrippina studied Ben Hur with an odd little smile. She poured herself wine. Sipping it, she moved over to the window and stared out.

Beyond her, through the window, Ben Hur could see Otho, Montanus and Petronius as they mounted their horses and cantered away towards the road. Only Agrippina's sedan chair remained, the bearers lounging idly in the shade.

At last Agrippina left the window and faced Ben Hur.

'In many ways,' she said, 'a conspiracy resembles a marriage. The more you know of your prospective partner, the better your chances of success. Therefore, I've taken the trouble to learn a bit about you ...'

Ben Hur's senses tingled, but he forced himself to speak calmly. 'Too much knowledge can be a bad thing.'

Agrippina laughed. 'In this case it will do no harm at all. That girl you are betrothed to. In Judaea. My people tell me she is lovely indeed. Her name is Leah, is it not?'

He took a deep breath. 'Yes,' he said quietly. 'That is her name ...'

'But they say her father has been associated with some strange sects. My informers tell me he was caught up in the movement of that rabble-rouser Christ. They say Joseph of Arimathea even buried Christ after the execution. Now that took considerable courage – he defied the Jewish law.'

'Why do you concern yourself with Joseph?' Ben Hur demanded.

'I'm getting to that. He is willing to accept *you* as his son-in-law ... And your own way of life. One might almost suspect you were a Christian too ...'

'Can you prove that?'

'I have no wish to. I only want to be your friend, Arrius – to make your interests my own. I have no intention of denouncing you – just the opposite. Christians are not popular. In many cases they suffer persecution. But, when I obtain supreme power, I will pass laws to protect the Christians.'

Their eyes met. She smiled, but the warning was clearly there.

'These suspicions you have about my personal religion,' Ben Hur wondered. 'Do your comrades share them?'

'Of course not! I make it a rule never to tell anyone more than he needs to know. Any secrets you may have are safe with me.'

'Even if I don't co-operate with you?'

'I think you will ... once you've thought things over.'

'No! You –'

She put a finger against his lips. 'Don't say any more, Arrius. You need a few days to consider it. Weigh all the possibilities. We'll speak again ...'

She left the room. Ben Hur followed, escorting her through the house. They reached the front door and emerged. Ben Hur noticed her freedman Agerinus waiting with the bearers by her sedan chair.

'A word, please ...' he said, stopping her, 'while your freedman is still out of earshot ...'

'Agerinus is one of us,' she insisted. 'You can speak freely.'

The freedman joined them, bowing respectfully. Ben Hur did not take his eyes from Agrippina. 'I urge you not to go through with your scheme ...'

She did not answer, but that maddening smile stayed on her lips. She clapped her hands. The bearers lifted the chair and brought it over. Agerinus opened the door for her.

'Brutus wanted no part in the killing of Julius Caesar,' Agrippina said to Ben Hur. 'They were friends. But in the end Brutus chose duty over friendship.'

'Believe me, I know where my duty lies.'

She climbed into the chair. The bearers lifted it and trotted off.

Ben Hur watched them go. He wished with all his heart that he *did* know where his duty lay. But only one thing was certain – he would not be party to the killing of a helpless, unarmed man. Especially one who regarded him as a friend. It was equally obvious what action the conspirators might take if he persisted in his refusal to co-operate with them.

He turned back towards the house. Phaon was standing by the shrubs near the door, twisting his broad-brimmed hat nervously.

'You're back early,' Ben Hur observed.

Phaon nodded. 'I felt weary. I left Electra to finish the marketing.' He regarded Ben Hur curiously. 'I did not know you were expecting the Emperor's mother.'

'It was an unexpected visit,' Ben Hur replied.

The sun was high in the sky, and the daisy-flecked meadows basked in the heat. The only evidence of human existence was the stone-paved road which cut through the fields, stretching into the distance and up over the far range of hills like a giant ribbon. A flock of magpies pecked at the grass near the roadside, and crying gulls wheeled overhead.

Now an alien sound violated the pastoral quiet. It was the steady beat of drums, the wail of flutes and chanters, the clarion call of trumpets, distant at first, but growing steadily closer. Accompanying the music was the resonant rumble of many horses.

In panic the birds took flight. Then, over the range of hills, the cavalcade appeared. In the lead a hundred cavalrymen carried the imperial standards. Their armour was gilded, and they wore parade helmets with masks moulded into a variety of iron expresssions, some fierce, some benign. Following the soldiers were mounted musicians, and behind these came the imperial carriage itself, its embossed silver flashing brightly. Taking up the rear were yet more soldiers. These men wore parade helmets with masks facing backwards.

A solitary horseman flanked the imperial carriage. It was the proud figure of Epaphroditus, resplendent in his purple cloak.

Epaphroditus sniffed the air with delight. He could smell the sea. Baiae was not far ahead. Today was one of those rare days when everything was just right. The music stirred his blood. Ever since he had been a small boy, he had loved a military parade.

And his thoughts matched the music. Taking a holday from the capital was always pleasant. Rome was thronging with people, all seeking to circumvent Epaphroditus and get at the Emperor. At Baiae there were fewer petitioners, and Epaphroditus had little need to worry about potential rivals.

He had another reason to feel well disposed to the world. He had just won a victory. A small triumph, perhaps, but significant nevertheless. He had convinced Nero not to include Agrippina in the guest list. Though endlessly irked and hampered by his mother, Nero had nevertheless always adhered to the outward forms of filial duty and etiquette. But Agrippina was one of Epaphroditus' greatest rivals, and the freedman never lost an opportunity to strike at her. His smile of pleasure had been quite genuine when he had explained to that ambitious amazon that an invitation was unfortunately impossible because Poppaea would be in attendance. To some people, perhaps, Agrippina's absence at the festivities would be a mere oversight. But those cognizant of the ways of the court would know better.

A new noise distracted the freedman's thoughts. He looked behind him. Thundering down the road at a gallop and overtaking Nero's procession was a turma of cavalry.

Unlike those in the imperial cavalcade, these men wore no ritualistic embellishments such as gilded armour or parade helmets. They were equipped for combat, not ceremony, clad in mailed coats, carrying swords, lances and shields. Leading them was Burrus, accompanied by two civilians who wore plain tunics.

Epaphroditus lifted a hunting horn which hung on a chain round his neck and blasted it once. He held up his arm for the company to halt, then wheeled his horse and waited for the approaching soldiers. In a moment he could recognize the tunic-clad civilians at their head. One was Seneca, his flesh jiggling uncomfortably in the saddle, and next to him was a man Epaphroditus recognized as Quintus Arrius' freedman, Phaon.

The soldiers reined to a halt when they drew abreast of the imperial party. Throwing himself from his horse and ignoring Epaphroditus completely, Burrus strode to the door of Nero's carriage and rapped. Epaphroditus was furious. No one should approach the Emperor without paying due respect to the imperial freedman first. Epaphroditus made a mental note to remember Burrus' rude conduct, and mark the Commander for future retaliation.

The carriage door did not open. Impatiently Burrus rapped again. Finally the shutter above the door was raised, and Nero stuck his head out. 'Jupiter's eyeballs!' he bellowed. 'What is the meaning of this?'

Burrus bowed. 'My apologies for the intrusion, Exalted Sir, but I must speak with you immediately. I'm afraid it cannot wait.'

Nero cursed and banged the shutter closed again. After a moment, he emerged, lacing his tunic. The reason for the delay had become apparent as he turned to help Poppaea alight.

'Exalted Sir,' said Burrus with a glance at Poppaea, 'what I have to say is confidential ...'

'Very well.' Nero smiled at Poppaea. 'I'll be back in a moment.' He allowed himself to be led across the road to a clump of trees, where Phaon and Seneca waited. Phaon dismounted and bowed deeply to the imperial presence.

Seneca was helped from his horse by the two cavalrymen. There was an interval of animated conversation which Epaphroditus could not hear, but he could see that Nero was growing more and more disturbed. Suddenly the Emperor seized Arrius' freedman by the tunic and shook him violently. Immediately Burrus and Seneca pried them apart. Nero was obviously furious.

Burrus beckoned to Epaphroditus. Wonderingly the freedman dismounted, crossed the road and joined the others.

'There's a plot against the Emperor's life,' Seneca muttered. 'But he chooses not to believe it.'

'Make him listen to us,' Burrus pleaded.

A glance at the Emperor's choleric face told Epaphroditus that he must be careful, and he spoke diplomatically. 'If these men have some warning of danger, should you not heed them?'

'Pederasts!' Nero shouted. He made a contemptuous gesture at Phaon, who was quavering behind Burrus. 'This lying, favour-currying little sycophant! I'm surrounded by informers. I –'

'He's not lying!' Seneca cut in. 'Phaon is a truthful man. He has brought me reliable information many times in the past.'

'It can't be true!' Nero cried. 'Not Arrius!'

'Arrius!' Epaphroditus repeated with astonishment.

'He's been implicated in the conspiracy, along with the Emperor's mother,' explained Burrus.

Epaphroditus kept his face expressionless. But this was too good to be true. Arrius was another potential rival . . . until now.

'We have this man's testimony,' Seneca was saying to Nero, as he indicated Phaon. 'The conversation occurred outside Arrius' house.'

'It does not make sense,' Nero insisted. 'My mother has been up to no good for a long time – long before Arrius appeared on the scene. You're all jealous of him!'

'Epicurus said "It is impossible to be jealous of a fallen man." Now on most issues, of course, I do not agree with Epicurus, but on this –'

'You pompous old windbag!' Nero roared. 'By the sacred womb of Cybele – I'll have you made into a eunuch – if you're not one already!'

'Exalted Sir,' Burrus pleaded. 'Listen to reason. Why should Phaon implicate Arrius if it were not true? Surely it would have been enough for him to have merely told us what he knew of Agrippina?'

'There is no plausible reason why Arrius should be involved,' Nero insisted.

'If I may intrude, Exalted Sir,' Epaphroditus said, 'the reason should be quite obvious. Who has more access to your person than Arrius? Who is more trusted?'

Seneca focused his heavy-lidded eyes on Phaon.

'Repeat to us what you heard them say,' Seneca insisted.

'That B–Brutus did not want to kill his friend Caesar,' Phaon stammered, 'but he acted out of duty, and – and ...'

'Well?' demanded Burrus impatiently.

Phaon swallowed. 'Well ... Arrius said he knew what his duty was ...'

Seneca turned back to Nero. 'What more do you want?'

Nero gazed at him steadily. Suddenly he rounded on Epaphroditus. 'I invited Arrius to the festival. Is he coming?'

'I don't know, Exalted Sir,' the freedman replied. 'He is not with our company.'

'Send an escort for him immediately,' Nero said slowly. 'I would not want him to miss the festival. Not this one ...'

CHAPTER NINE

Nero had been in an exceptionally good mood all evening. It had been an intimate dinner in Nero's charming villa on the bay, with only those in the closest circle of the Emperor invited. Ben Hur was on Nero's left, and, but for Poppaea, the most favoured guest present. Surprisingly, in the midst of the festivities, Nero had sprung exuberantly to his feet, called for silence, and presented Ben Hur with a gold amulet.

'A token of my esteem, Arrius,' Nero had said, 'to express my appreciation of what a good and loyal comrade you have been. Even if fate should separate us, it can never rob us of what we've already had.'

Ben Hur was mystified by all this attention. It had begun when he was finishing his preparations for slipping away from his house and leaving Italy. He had just hidden the money he could not take with him under the floor of the bath-house when he had been surprised by the arrival of an imperial escort, sent as a mark of signal honour to conduct him to the celebrations at Baiae. There had been no choice but to mask his anger and frustration and go along with them.

And now that he was here, there was something even more puzzling – the presence of Agrippina. Looking radiant and more beautiful than ever, she had sauntered in very late. She had been greeted warmly by everyone, including her son. Yet on that unpleasant night at the Milvian Bridge, Nero had confided to Ben Hur his decision not to invite her. Had she brazened her way in, or had Nero changed his mind?

'Has your best friend just died?' a voice intruded suddenly.

Ben Hur looked up to meet Nero's jesting eyes.

'On the contrary,' he said with a gaiety he did not feel. 'Your excellent wine has gone to my head ...'

'The only cure for that is more wine,' said Nero, filling Ben Hur's cup.

Ben Hur had to drink it, and sit out yet another course of the interminable meal. When the banquet was finally complete, the guests filed into the bath-house for an immersion in the warm pool, which did not help Ben Hur's digestion at all. He noticed that tonight Poppaea displayed no maidenly reserve about disrobing and displaying her charms. Petronius, who had been a quiet guest all evening, was utterly indifferent to Poppaea's alluring form. It was a notable contrast to his avid admiration of her on the night of Seneca's banquet. After the bath, as slaves with strigils scraped the oil from their bodies, Petronius had made his position quite clear.

'Elementary rule for survival,' he had muttered. 'Keep your eyes – let alone your hands – away from the imperial upstart's female!'

Finally, when everyone was dried and had donned their clothes again, the entire company assembled to express in turn farewells and thanks to the host.

When Ben Hur paid his respects, Nero drew him aside. 'Perhaps you are wondering about my mother ... her being here, I mean. I had no intention of inviting her, but I discovered that she was staying just across the bay. I decided there was no reason to exacerbate our estrangement. After all, she *is* my mother. And sooner or later, she'll have to get used to things the way they are, myself and Poppaea, in other words.'

'You are right, of course,' Ben Hur agreed.

'And she's never cared much for you. That will have to change too ... So I want you to escort her home tonight. Make a friend of her ...' He lowered his voice confidentially. 'And while you are at it – see if you can find out how she reacted to Poppaea tonight.'

'But of course,' said Ben Hur with a bow.

He strode into the hall, eager to be away.

Once outside, in the crisp night air, he breathed deeply. The skies were clear and spiked with stars, and the path which sloped from the villa to the beach could be seen plainly. The guests made their way down in single file towards a group of attendants, who waited by sedan chairs.

Ben Hur caught sight of Agrippina and followed her across the short stretch of beach on to the quay. He reflected on Nero's request. Its deviousness was just the sort of thing Ben Hur had learned to expect from the Emperor. There seemed nothing out of the ordinary about it. Yet, as he strode down the dock, he could not shake off an increasing uneasiness. Nero's concern for his mother's good opinion did not quite ring true.

Hearing his footsteps on the wooden jetty, Agrippina turned.

'May I escort you across the bay?' he said, taking her by the arm.

The strange smile flitted across her face. 'That would be charming ...'

Lightly she stepped into the boat and took her place under the canopy at the stern. She indicated the cushions next to her and Ben Hur took his place.

Not far in front of them, the helmsman grasped the steering oar. Three other boatmen untied the lines and pushed off. Soon, under the powerful strokes of eight oarsmen, the light craft was gliding out over the black water.

Ben Hur watched the boatmen in silence. Agrippina laid a hand on his knee.

'What did you have in mind for tonight – business or pleasure?'

Ben Hur paid no attention to the question. 'Doesn't it strike you as odd?' he murmured. 'At first you were ignored. Then, at the last moment, invited. And with Poppaea there.'

Agrippina shrugged. 'The Emperor has to keep up appearances. I am his mother.'

Ben Hur lowered his voice even more, anxious to be sure that none of the crew could hear them.

'I have an ugly suspicion that there may be another reason.'

'What?' she wondered.

'I think Nero knows everything.'

Agrippina stared at him. Even in the dark, Ben Hur could see the astonishment on her face. 'Whatever makes you say that?' she whispered.

'I think he wants to get us alone – together. He has discovered what you and Otho are up to. He thinks I'm involved. Why else would he ask me to accompany you?'

'It wasn't *your* idea to escort me home?'

'No.'

For a second neither spoke.

'I wonder,' Ben Hur asked softly, 'what is in store for us when we reach your house . . .'

'I don't propose to find out,' she stated grimly.

Agrippina got to her feet and made her way to the steersman. 'Change course for Misenum,' she commanded.

The helmsman did not respond.

'Did you hear me?' Agrippina shouted. 'Change course!'

Still the man did not move. It was as if Agrippina had not spoken. Furiously she seized him by the tunic and shoved him aside, taking the handle of the steering oar herself. The boatman staggered, but quickly regained his balance – and grasped hold of Agrippina.

She swung round to Ben Hur. 'This is not my helmsman!'

Ben Hur leapt to his feet and attacked the helmsman, hurling him back against the stern post.

Then he saw something which made his flesh crawl. The rowers had silently shipped their oars. Two of them moved forward and took up station by the prow. The others advanced towards Ben Hur and Agrippina.

'They are not my crew!' Agrippina gasped. 'I do not know these men.'

The years fell away from Ben Hur ... Once again he was a desperate slave thrown into the arena, facing a row of implacable enemies. But they had worn armour and carried tridents and swords. They had stabbed him repeatedly, dealt him wounds which by all rights should have stretched him on the sand, but he had killed every one of them ...

Now the past lived again as he rushed madly at the sailors. The boat rocked wildly. Gripping the front man, he whipped him round and twisted the fellow's arm up behind his back. The man grunted with pain and with his other hand groped for his dagger. But Ben Hur caught his wrist, knocking the knife to the deck. Then, with all his power, Ben Hur forced the oarsman's arm upward until his shoulder snapped like a piece of rotten wood.

A strength which he had long forgotten surged once again through his limbs. He swung round, smashing his fist into the face of the next man, who stumbled and fell into the water with a splash.

But two more of the attackers were on him, overwhelming him, forcing him to his knees in the bottom of the boat. As he struggled, he caught a glimpe of Agrippina. Pursued by two other rowers and the steersman, she evaded them with astonishing agility. Like a cat, she darted to the knife on the deck and snatched it up, then confronted her enemies. Immediately, however, they picked up oars and struck her brutally with them, knocking her into the sea. Rushing to the side, they continued to club savagely at the water.

The men stationed in the prow were pulling at the planks of the hull. To Ben Hur's astonishment, they came away easily. Obviously they had been loosened in advance. The water gushed into the barge, which began to sink rapidly. Ben Hur's captors held him fast, forcing him into a kneeling position. Soon the water had risen to his waist, then to his chest. A pair of hands seized his hair and forced his head down under the water, holding it there.

He felt as though his lungs would split. Desperately, he fought the lassitude which was beginning to creep over him. The leg of the man holding his hair was close to him. With a sudden wrench, he twisted his head and bit into the leg with every vestige of strength he could muster, sinking his teeth deep into the flesh. The man's shriek of agony sounded strangely distant, but the grip on Ben Hur's hair slackened, then finally ceased. Ben Hur tore his head above the water, and gulped in the air, choking and spluttering. Blurred through his streaming eyes, he could see the boat was nearly submerged. But the hands were still holding him, trying to force him back under the water. Ben Hur struggled desperately. He knew that blows were landing round his head, but he hardly felt them. Gradually, inexorably, the strength of the two assailants overcame him, and his head was pushed back under. Then, amazingly, he was free, lifting his head above the water and breathing desperately.

The man who had been holding Ben Hur by the hair had released him and now stood up, staring down with disbelief at the bloody point of the dagger which had struck him from behind and was protruding from his belly. Abruptly the blade was withdrawn and the man pitched forward with a splash. But there was no sign of his assailant. His companion stared round wildly, forgetting all about Ben Hur. An instant later, like an avenging sea monster, Agrippina rose from the water behind the oarsman and plunged the dagger into his neck, leaving it there. His eyes staring hideously, the dying man groped for the gunwale of the boat. At that very moment, the barge sank beneath the waves.

With the boat gone from under him, Ben Hur floundered in the water. Agrippina's hand was under his arm, supporting him. 'Swim!' she hissed.

Summoning the dregs of his strength, Ben Hur obeyed. He swam for his life. With easy, powerful strokes, Agrippina kept pace beside him, glancing now and then to be sure he was still afloat.

Finally, his feet scraped the pebbles of the beach. Soon they emerged from the water, sinking to their knees, gulping the night air into their lungs.

At last Ben Hur found his voice. 'I am in your debt ...'

'Never mind,' she panted. 'I'll cancel all debts – if I survive this night.'

'From what I've seen, your instincts for survival are unsurpassed. When they knocked you into the sea, I thought it was the end of you. But it seems you can breathe in the water like a fish.'

She laughed wryly. 'I can thank my brother Caligula for that.

When he was Emperor, he suspected me of plotting. And I'll admit – there was some truth to it. After all, he was as demented as a three-headed eagle. Someone had to do something. Anyway – he exiled me to Capri, and I spent my time learning to dive for pearls.' She grinned. 'Tonight – for the first time in my life – I am grateful to Caligula.'

She sobered and got to her feet. 'But enough. The house where I am staying is not far. We must go there now.'

'That's the first place they'll look for us.'

'Nevertheless we'll have to chance it. I know my servants are loyal – no matter what. And they will be better than no protection.'

Ben Hur nodded. He could think of no alternative plan which offered any hope.

They trudged over the pebbles in silence. Soon they made their way into the shrubs which bordered the beach, where a small house nestled in the trees. They approached it, and Agrippina knocked at the door. After a moment, it was opened by Agerinus, holding an oil lamp. At the sight of them, his usual urbanity vanished.

'Gods –'

Agrippina entered, gesturing for silence. 'There is no time for explanations, Agerinus.'

'I understand,' said the freedma grimly. 'We are discovered. Is it not so?'

She nodded, then faced Ben Hur.

'We must go to Rome immediately. To the Praetorian barracks. I will have them declare me Empress tonight. It will be risky with Nero still alive, but I think they'll back me. Whatever the case, it is our best chance.'

'We'll never get to Rome,' Ben Hur pointed out. 'Nero must know by now that the accident was not fatal.'

'Perhaps we can gain some time,' said Agrippina. She turned to her freedman. 'You could do it for us, Agerinus . . .'

He nodded. 'Anything.'

'Go to the Emperor. Tell him we were assaulted by brigands on the bay, but that we managed to escape. He is not to worry about me. I am well and will visit him tomorrow.' She turned back to Ben Hur. 'If Nero thinks we do not connect him with the attack, there is a slight possibility he will feel less need for haste in planning his next attempt.'

Agerinus bowed. 'I will go immediately.'

He gave Agrippina the lamp he was holding and turned.

'Wait!' Agrippina called.

Agerinus paused questioningly. She stepped forward, taking his hand, squeezing it warmly.

'Thank you,' she said.

The freedman grinned. 'Thank me when you rule the Empire.'

Then he was gone.

Agrippina indicated a doorway on the right-hand side of the narrow, painted hall. Ben Hur stepped to it, pushed aside the curtain hanging across it and entered. He found himself in a storage room full of casks and amphorae. Agrippina entered also and beckoned for Ben Hur to follow. He did so, and she led the way into an adjoining scullery. Crossing to a wooden sideboard, she put down the oil lamp. Then picking up an earthenware jug, she filled two cups and offered one to Ben Hur.

'Goat's milk. We'll need strength.'

Eagerly Ben Hur took it, gulping down the cool liquid. Agrippina did likewise. Reaching for the jug, Ben Hur poured himself some more.

When he had finished, Agrippina spoke. 'I suggest we get mounted and on our way. The horses are fresh . . . even if we are not.'

Ben Hur followed her through the storage room, back into the main hall, then through the front door.

Immediately outside, both of them stopped short. Armed men were ringing the house. A group of them were approaching the entrance, but they paused at the sight of Agrippina and Ben Hur. One of them, clutching a bloody sword, held something aloft with his other hand. He shook it at them. It was Agerinus' head.

Agrippina gasped. Her strong fingers gripped Ben Hur's arm. 'Get back to the door,' she hissed, 'and open it slowly.'

Ben Hur inched backwards, until he could feel the frames of the door behind him. His fingers groped for the handle.

Agrippina boldly took a step forward.

'How dare you come here like this!' she exclaimed in a loud

voice of outrage. 'I am the Emperor's mother! Leave immediately!'

Ben Hur was amazed at her composure. She faced her enemies without a hint of fear.

'I order you to go!' she repeated.

The leader of the armed men only laughed. With a gesture which made his intent only too clear, he tossed Agerinus' head aside and started for her. His companions drew their swords and advanced also.

Ben Hur sprang forward to protect her. But at that moment, something heavy whistled through the air, slamming him backwards. Ben Hur stared down with disbelief. A javelin had gone right through his shoulder and pinned him to the wooden door! Only then did the terrible, searing pain stab through him.

Ben Hur struggled desperately to free himself, but the soft iron shank of the javelin had bent and the point was lodged firmly in the door.

Agrippina had seen Ben Hur's plight, but she did not run. For an instant their eyes met. Then, with supreme disdain, she faced her enemies proudly and grimly ... Immediately they were upon her, plunging their swords into her brutally. Impossibly, she remained standing, as if refusing to die, than at last she sank to the ground. One of the attackers took her by the hair, and severed her head with a single, swinging blow.

With a convulsive jerk, Ben Hur tore the spear point from his shoulder. He almost lost consciousness at the wave of fresh pain which engulfed him, but he managed to stay on his feet. Staggering through the door, he slammed it and rammed the bolt home.

He plunged down the hall, across the tiny atrium. Nearly falling through a curtained entrance, he stumbled down another hall. A side door opened, and two serving women peered out. At the sight of Ben Hur they shrieked, but he lurched past them, not stopping until he found the rear entrance. Pulling this door open, he flung himself into the trees. He wanted to find a lonely spot, where he could hide himself, and then die unmolested.

Suddenly there were horsemen advancing through the trees. He paused, tried to retreat, but they approached too rapidly.

'Stop!' cried a familiar voice.

Ben Hur hesitated, staring at the man. It was Petronius, flanked by two of his slaves. Petronius leaped from his horse and ran forward as Ben Hur's knees began to buckle.

'Be strong, Arrius,' Petronius begged. 'You *must* ride!'

The slaves had dismounted and came running up to aid Ben Hur. Helping him to Petronius' horse, the three lifted him bodily into the saddle. Ben Hur swayed. He was growing dizzy, and desperately he tried to hold on. But then Petronius mounted behind him, supporting him with both arms, kicking the horse to a run.

He struggled to open his eyes, but the lids were too heavy. Ben Hur did not know how long he had been unconscious. All he knew was the blazing fever in his head. His mouth was dry, and his tongue swollen. And his left side had no feeling at all.

Once again he tried to raise his eyelids. But the murky gloom was almost impenetrable. The only thing visible was a thin rectangle of light silhouetting the closed shutter. There was a faint humming in his ears.

He cried out, but no sound came. His throat was too dry, and his leaden tongue would not move.

His thoughts began to wander ... Where he was no longer seemed important. His soul drifted away from his body ...

There was a distant shape. It grew clearer, outlined in the hard light of a bright sunny day. It was that hill of Golgotha. Three limp figures hung from the crosses to which they were nailed. The swarms of circling birds told him they were already dead ...

Better dead than some of the living ... Two leprous faces looked up beseechingly. Could these be his own mother and sister! What had been Tirzah's beautiful mouth was a running sore. And his mother's nose had fallen away, leaving a blank between the squinting eyes.

The clean, work-hardened hands of the Carpenter's Son reached out and touched them – dared to caress those diseased faces. And then they were whole ... 'Whoever believes in me,' said the voice, 'shall never die ...'

But the man who had uttered those words was dead. Ben Hur could see him now, slumped to one side, drawn and sagging with pain ...

Judah Ben Hur gazed helplessly at the three crosses. It was not

Jesus in the centre – it was Peter. And flanking him were Barnabas and Paul.

'Cling to your faith!' Peter cried. 'Only love can save the world.'

But Ben Hur was shaking his head, denying him. 'Love brought you to do this, Peter ... Don't ask me to follow you.'

Then he awoke.

A voice spoke from a great distance. 'There is no hope ... I'm sorry. He's going to die ...'

An inexorable force was pushing him downwards. In a moment he knew the earth would close over him. But he would not die! He fought back desperately, struggling against pressure. His eyes opened. He was on a table in an elegant triclinium. The shutters were closed, but many oil lamps illuminated the room with their soft glow. A tall, bearded man whom Ben Hur did not recognize waited by a brazier full of glowing embers, stirring them with an iron, which he held carefully in gloved hands.

'Where are we?' Ben Hur croaked. He was amazed at the feebleness of his own voice.

'In my house,' said Petronius, appearing by his side. 'But do not worry. You are safe.'

'What about you?'

Petronius smiled. 'We are among friends. So far my role in this sad business remains undetected. I intend to keep it that way. As an added precaution, we've been moving you from place to place, but I don't think anyone has followed us.'

He held a silver cup to Ben Hur's lips. The water was soothing and life-giving. Eagerly he gulped it, slopping half of it onto his chest.

'You will die,' said Petronius, 'unless we cauterize your wound. The spear passed right through you.' He indicated the stranger by the fire. 'Diocles, my surgeon, has done his best, but the wound has not healed. In fact, it has grown more inflamed. This will be extremely painful.'

Diocles took the iron from the brazier. Its end was glowing red with heat.

'Doubtless you will scream,' said Petronius. 'But that might give us all away. So I'm afraid we must silence you.' He beckoned to one of the two slaves who stood by the door.

The slave produced a wad of cloth and inserted it in Ben Hur's mouth.

Diocles approached with the hot iron. 'Bite down,' he ordered, 'as hard as you like. Concentrate on not making a sound. Think about that *only*! It will help to distract you.'

The slaves eased him back on the table and held him in a vice-like grip.

Deftly Diocles removed the dressing to reveal the bluish, festering wound. Before Ben Hur realized it, the hot iron was pressed to the torn and swollen skin. An unbelievable pain flooded through him. He clamped his teeth into the cloth, struggling to hold back the shriek of agony which built up inside. But Diocles grimly forced the iron deeper and deeper into the wound. The burning flesh sizzled, and its smell filled Ben Hur's nostrils. The torture mounted to a terrible crescendo, tearing at his nerves. His head became a ball of fire, growing hotter and hotter until it seemed to burst. Then, mercifully, he faded into blackness . . .

Angrily Ben Hur peered through the half-open shutter. For what seemed a lifetime, this restricted view of Petronius' garden had been his only sight of the outside world.

He had become a stranger to himself. Ever since his arrival in Rome, the spiritual message of Christ had offered him less and less comfort. Now it seemed more hollow and futile than ever. It was like the garden visible through this window, a garden without sin, perfect, ordered and harmonious. But the world would never be like that. The Christians believed the soul was perfectible, but that no longer seemed possible. The code of the arena was closer to the truth. Survival was the only object of life, and staying alive needed no justification.

Impatiently he turned away from the window and picked up a small lead weight which lay on the floor near his sleeping-couch. With a sigh he sat down and began to push it over his head rhythmically. They had told him the exercise would strengthen his shoulder. But after performing it regularly three times every day for more than a month, it was becoming unutterably irksome.

Physically his recovery was complete, but his mind had grown feverish with inactivity.

There was a rap on the door.

'Come in,' Ben Hur called.

Petronius entered. 'Good morning,' he said pleasantly. He glanced at the weight in Ben Hur's hand. 'You have moved to a heavier one, I see.'

'The wounded shoulder is now stronger than the other one.' Ben Hur growled.

Petronius laughed. 'You are ready for action, aren't you?'

'I certainly am! I feel like a caged animal in here.'

'It is time you were out of your cage. So far your presence in my house has been a well-kept secret. But that cannot continue indefinitely. Much as I like you, Arrius, I must confess that your being here makes me nervous.'

'I gather they're still looking for me.'

'You can be certain of that. Of course, they've hushed the whole thing up. It was announced that Agrippina committed suicide. But, I assure you, it is just a ruse to smoke out the others who are involved.'

Ben Hur put the weight on the floor. 'Then I must endanger you no more. Do you think you could get me to my villa?'

'Don't be ridiculous! They'd soon find you there.'

Ben Hur rose. 'I will not go to the house itself. There is a place nearby where I shall be safe.'

'If you have to spend your life hidden here in Rome, you will be no use to anybody – least of all yourself.'

'Then you have something in mind ...'

Petronius pulled up a curule chair and sat down. 'The Praetorian Guard is an elite force. Not only do they protect the Emperor's person, they have all sorts of special privileges. For example, a Praetorian soldier who has served sixteen years can automatically join any provincial legion as an officer.' He surveyed Ben Hur. 'You would be about the right age.'

'But I haven't had sixteen years of military experience.'

'Have you had any at all?'

'Before I became a charioteer, I spent two years in the arena.'

'Ah ... Now that is almost as good as having been in the army.'

'You seriously expect me to enlist as a soldier?'

Petronius nodded. 'It will get you to Spain. While you were recovering, our friend Otho was sent there to take up his new post. He's quite safe and still apparently untouched by suspicion. Does Spain appeal to you, Arrius?'

'Indeed it does!'

'I will procure you a letter of introduction from Burrus himself to the commander of the Fourth Legion Macedonica, stationed in Spain. The letter will state that you wish to enlist with the rank to which you are entitled by your long service in the Praetorians. They've been recruiting on the Field of Mars for a week. They set out for Spain tomorrow.'

'But the letter – you'll forge it?'

'Not personally. For such things we need a professional. But you need not worry. The army will not look at it too carefully. Men aren't joining the legions like they used to any more ... The army is hungry for soldiers.'

Petronius got to his feet. 'We *still* intend to remove Nero. It is only a question of time. One day, when Otho has built up enough strength, he will return. And he will need capable officers to support him ... men like you.'

The Tribune, a lean man of middle age, barely looked at the letter Ben Hur showed him. But he did take a hard look at Ben Hur, as he returned the document to him. 'Gaius Severus ... sixteen years in the Praetorians ... you look thin for a Praetorian. After sixteen years, most of them get thick in the middle, with all that soft living in Rome.'

'Yes, Tribune,' said Ben Hur.

The Tribune regarded him with surprise. 'A polite Praetorian! Now I've seen everything!'

'Yes, Tribune.'

'I like that! "Yes, Tribune." You just keep saying that and you might survive.'

The officer pointed to a tent where a group of men waited with their packs and belongings beside them. They were dressed in plain tunics or other civilian garb.

'Sit down over there with the rest of them,' the Tribune commanded.

Obediently Ben Hur shouldered his bag, walked over to the tent and sat with the others on the grass. The group was guarded by about a dozen regular legionaries, all in full armour and bristling with weapons. He knew that such heavy escorts were provided for companies of recruits to discourage desertions. It was said that this precaution had not been necessary in former times. Many pointed to this as one more indication of social degeneration. Romans of today, they argued with considerable logic, were not what they used to be.

Two more recruits joined those in front of the tent. Then the Tribune himself strode over and surveyed the assembled group with contempt.

'On your feet!' he bellowed.

Shamblingly the men rose.

'We'll be on our way shortly,' the Tribune announced. 'But first there is a small formality.' He pointed to Ben Hur. 'You, Praetorian, tell those ignorant sons-of-bitches what it is.'

Ben Hur hesitated. It was an unpleasant moment. Feverishly, he ransacked his memory. Then, vaguely, he recalled a ritual he had witnessed in a field outside Jerusalem. 'The oath ...' he said tentatively.

'That is correct,' said the Tribune, 'and you bastards had better take it to heart, because you'll be repeating it every year. Now – say it after me.'

In unison, Ben Hur and the others intoned the words as the Tribune uttered them. 'I swear by the Gods, and especially by Jupiter and the Genius of the Roman State and by the Power of the Emperor, who, next to the Gods, should be loved and worshipped by the human race, to perform with enthusiasm whatever the Emperor commands, never to desert, nor to shrink from death on behalf of the Roman State. I also swear to follow my commander wherever he leads me, and never to leave the standard, nor do anything else contrary to the law.'

The Tribune beckoned to one of the armed legionaries. 'Publius,' he called.

A stocky Centurion strode forward, swinging his vine staff ostentatiously. The Tribune faced the recruits again.

'You will follow the Centurion. He will lead you at the military pace.' The Tribune grinned. 'That means fast. And you won't have many stops on the way. I promise you – your feet will hurt. But have no fear. When that happens you can walk on your knees. By the time you reach Gessioracum, you'll be ready to march anywhere!'

Ben Hur was alarmed. He was not sure he had heard the word correctly. He took a step forward. 'If the Tribune pleases, did you say ... Gessioracum?'

'I did,' the Tribune replied.

'But that's on the north coast of Gaul!'

With sarcasm, the Tribune turned to the group at large. 'This man is a geographer! It seems they teach geography in the Praetorians. I suppose they must do *something* to pass the time ...'

Ben Hur persisted. 'But, Tribune, I was given to understand that we were bound for Lusitania.'

'That was this morning,' said the Tribune harshly. 'It would've been nice, wouldn't it? Warm climate ... warm women ... peaceful province.' He scowled suddenly. 'But orders *do* change. You'd better get used to that. Seems they need recruits in Britain. New Governor up there – a real fire-eater. He's planning to conquer the whole island – even Caledonia.' He grinned again, surveying all the recruits. 'So it's going to be one long, cold march for all of you. And *lots* of fighting.' He glanced at Ben Hur. 'You ought to like that, Severus. It will be a big change from the Praetorians ...'

Sick at heart, Ben Hur moved back to the tent, shouldered his bag of belongings, and fell into line behind the others. The armed escort moved forward, flanking the recruits on both sides.

BOOK TWO

JOSEPH'S DAUGHTER

CHAPTER TEN

Joseph was bewildered. The house was clearly unoccupied and had been for some time. The windows were boarded up and the garden overgrown.

He glanced uneasily at his daughter. She stood there without words. It tore his heart to see the unspeakable disappointment in her eyes.

He turned to the bearers, who were waiting stolidly by the large sedan chair.

'This cannot be the right place,' Joseph insisted.

'You asked for the house of Arrius,' one of them replied. 'This is it. Many times I've delivered wine here.'

'Have a look,' Joseph ordered. 'See if anyone is on the premises.'

The man ducked his head and trotted off, followed by his two companions.

Joseph approached the gate. It was unlocked and swung open at his push. He walked slowly up the path, the flesh on the back of his neck tightening as it always did when he felt foreboding.

Heavy timbers had been nailed across the front door. Clearly it would be impossible to force an entry without tools.

'Something awful has happened to Judah,' said Leah, coming up beside him.

'Not necessarily,' he replied. 'There could be many explanations . . .'

'What?' Leah demanded. 'He had servants, didn't he? He would never leave his home like this.'

'Perhaps he was called away unexpectedly.'

'If we had come earlier, when I wanted to, perhaps this would never have happened.'

'Leah . . . we had no choice but to wait. His letters urged us to be patient.'

'The letters stopped! It was probably too late even then!'

'There is no reason to get upset.'

'Wasn't he on some dangerous mission?'

'You would not understand, Leah.'

'You've always kept secrets from me!' she flamed. 'You've always made my decisions for me! And all I ever had to do was obey! You'd think I had no mind of my own. You think I don't notice your secret meetings! Those people coming and going ... The way the conversation stops the moment they catch a glimpse of me –'

'Hush!' Joseph commanded.

At that moment the porters hurried up.

'We've checked the stables,' one of them told Joseph, 'but they haven't been used for some time. And all the entrances are shut tight.'

Joseph nodded grimly. 'Very well. Take us back to Rome. The Forum.'

He took Leah by the arm, but she pulled away. He eyed her anxiously as she stalked down the path ahead of him. She had come on this journey with such high hopes. And her excitement had mounted every day as they had drawn nearer their destination. She had created such fantasies about the life she would live here in the capital of the world. And Joseph had seen no need to temper her enthusiasm. But now – Judah's mysterious disappearance filled Joseph with a nameless dread. How much worse it must be for Leah.

Peter seemed to be trying to conceal his agitation.

'Yes,' he said. 'I was aware Judah intended to leave. But I had no idea the house was closed. You say the windows are boarded up?'

'Yes,' Joseph replied, 'and the garden has not been tended for weeks.'

Leah studied Peter. She remembered him from Arimathea. She had been impressed by his size then, but somehow, here in Rome, he looked smaller.

Her father frowned. 'But why would Judah leave like this? No word ... No letters ... Almost as if he were in trouble ...'

'He has been having difficulties ... He has changed.' Peter's eyes flickered uneasily towards Leah. 'But I think, Joseph, perhaps we should discuss it another time.'

Leah felt a flash of resentment. As usual, something was passing between her father and his friend which was not meant for her ears.

'You have no idea where he could have gone?' Joseph persisted.

Peter shrugged. 'He did not know himself when I last spoke to him. But he promised to communicate with me. He will, Joseph.'

'Did he say anything about me?' Leah asked eagerly.

'No,' Peter admitted, then added quickly, 'but you must understand that he was burdened with worries at the time. And there were many other occasions when he *did* speak of you – most fondly.'

Leah felt a surge of hope. She touched her father's arm. 'Come, we must find lodgings ...'

Peter laughed. 'My dear child. You have found them.' He put an arm round Joseph's shoulders. 'You will stay here with us.'

Leah glanced distastefully at the seedy shop. The open stall meandered into the street, where rough-looking men laboured in their dirty tunics for all to see. Added to the animal and human refuse in the road just outside were unsightly mounds of discarded rims, broken tools, or other unidentifiable pieces of rusty metal. The din was ceaseless, shouted conversations from every shop, the banging of hammers and the clanging of metal, the whoosh of bellows in the furnaces of smithies intensifying the hellish summer heat.

'I would be mortally offended if you would even think of staying anywhere else!' Peter was insisting.

'Very well, then ...' Joseph patted Peter's shoulder with affection. 'You are a good fellow ...'

Peter motioned to the porters. 'Bring the luggage inside!'

'Surely we're not going to sleep here!' Leah whispered to her father.

'Of course we are.'

'But there must be a better place,' Leah protested.

Her father was about to reply, but Peter interrupted. 'Come in and meet the others.'

Joseph paused only to pay the porters, then he and Leah followed Peter through the shop into the back room.

It was a dank, airless chamber. A group of people were seated on either side of a trestle table, eating doggedly, wasting no time in conversation. The room was oppressively hot, and the eaters were stripped to the minimum clothing, their skin glistening with perspiration while they masticated their food.

Leah's eyes swept the room. It was apparently a catch-all for everything. Piles of cordage, unfinished lumber and wheels were stacked in full view on the floor. Near the far wall, a pallet of straw and a few slop bowls revealed that someone slept here as well.

A bent, misshapen figure rose from the table and limped over to them. He embraced both Peter and Joseph, speaking in a peculiar rasping voice which was like no sound Leah had ever heard from a human throat.

'This is Silas,' Joseph told Leah. 'One of our greatest teachers from Asia.'

'Joseph's daughter!' Silas wheezed with great reverence. Then he bent and kissed her hand. His touch nearly made her cry out with revulsion.

The others had joined them. A couple was introduced to her as Barnabas, the shop owner, and his wife, Phoebe. Leah noticed that they treated her father with a respect verging on worship. She surmised that all these people were part of the same religious group. Leah was aware that her father had actually known the great teacher Christ, who was said to be founder of the sect. Perhaps this was the reason for the deference which was shown to Joseph.

Peter took Leah by the arm and pushed her towards a stout woman in the last stages of pregnancy.

'This is Urgulania,' he announced proudly. 'My wife.' He patted her stomach. 'She is bearing what I hope will be my messenger to the future – perhaps the first of many.'

'What glad tidings!' Joseph exclaimed. 'If ever a man should be a father – it is you, Peter.'

'You are so right!' Urgulania said. 'Look!' She held up a wooden doll. 'Already Peter has carved this for the little one.'

'For my son,' Peter added, with a grin.

'He insists it will be a boy,' Urgulania told them. 'I say it will be a girl.'

Peter made a deprecating gesture. 'Women know nothing about these matters. It will be a boy.'

'Let's not stand here arguing,' Barnabas interrupted. 'They must be hungry.' He smiled at Joseph and Leah. 'Come and eat. There's plenty of it.'

'But, father,' Leah blurted out, 'surely we cannot stay here!'

'You are not imposing,' Peter assured her. 'There is plenty of room for all of us.' He indicated the pallet of straw. 'Joseph and I will sleep there. We have a lot to talk about.' He pointed to a low door. 'And, Leah – you'll sleep in the back with Urgulania.' Peter pointed at his wife. 'She's so near her time she's no use to me anyway ...'

'Come, my child,' said Urgulania with a smile. 'I'll show you the room.'

'No, no,' Phoebe interjected. 'She can sleep with us in the loft. It is cooler.'

Leah moved to Joseph. 'Father – there is no need for us to live here,' she pleaded.

'We must,' Joseph replied.

'Why must we? We're not poor.'

'No, we're not poor. We have the greatest wealth people can have. Friends who love us, who want us to live with them, and who want to share with us everything they have.'

'Why must they share with us?' Leah demanded. 'They need what they have. And we have money of our own.'

Joseph hesitated. 'No longer ... Before we left, I gave everything to the church.'

Leah gazed dumbly at her father. It was a moment before she could trust herself to speak.

'Why?'

'It is something I have always wanted to do. I have never desired wealth. It has been weighing down my spirit all these years. I have always dreamed of seeing it benefit others. Christ said "A camel will sooner go through the eye of a needle, than a rich man enter the kingdom of heaven."'

'I don't care what your wonderful rabbi said!' Leah choked. 'What about me?'

'You really think I had no thought of you? If it had not been for you, I would have done it sooner. Don't you see? I waited until you were provided for. We came to Rome so that you could marry Judah Ben Hur. I knew he would care for you. Then I could devote my life to God ...'

Leah's voice trembled with indignation. 'But Judah is not here!'

'Yet God has not abandoned us. Peter has offered us a home. We can stay with him until we find Judah. You will be all right here, Leah.'

Leah burst into tears. 'I won't stay here! I hate this place. How could you be so cruel!'

With a cry of anger, she ran into the outer shop, banging the door.

'I'll go to her,' Phoebe offered. 'I think she will listen to me ...'

Phoebe went into the adjoining room.

Embarrassed, Joseph eyed the others. 'She meant no disrespect to Christ,' he explained. 'It is just that she knows very little of his teachings.'

The others were astonished.

'How can that be, Joseph?' Peter wondered. 'You – of all people – have not taught your daughter our beliefs?'

'I raised her as a Jewish girl. I have said little about our Master. You know how children are. If I imbued her with his life and teachings, she might talk. And in Judaea such beliefs must be kept secret.'

'That was a mistake. You should have been open about your beliefs – filled her with them, and taught her discretion.'

'Perhaps if she were a boy, I might have said more. But she's only a vulnerable girl. Would you expose your daughter to danger?'

Peter nodded. 'There is a limit to how much we can shield our young – boy or girl. I want my child to grow up believing what I believe – continuing what I have begun. We are all individuals, that is true, but we are also more than that. We are God's people. When the unity of the generations is broken, a people disintegrates into a collection of little ants – each pursuing his own thing, careless of who came before or who will come after.' He placed his hand on Urgulania's belly. 'On the day he – or she – is born, I will tell him – or her – of Christ's love.'

Joseph appraised Peter wonderingly. 'I see I have not only misjudged my daughter ... I have misjudged you as well. Jesus was right when he said that you are the rock on which we would build our church.'

'I am afraid we have not been building too well,' Peter said wryly. 'Followers have not been flocking to us. Our Master's teachings are strange. After all, few people in Rome like to hear that the things they value most, wealth and power, are the least important. These are shocking thoughts indeed. And the more we repeat them the greater our danger.'

Nearly a month had passed, and there was still no word from Ben Hur. Joseph could no longer ignore his inner disquiet. Judah was a man who kept his promises. Had he been able to communicate with Peter, surely he would have done so by now.

Joseph's eyes travelled to his daughter. As usual she was showing little interest in her food. These days she had grown more and more withdrawn, and the barrier which had always existed between them had become insurmountable.

The heat of the Roman summer had not helped her temper at all. They had been taking their meals in the shop, because the back room was unendurably stifling. But there was little relief anywhere.

A gurgling sound made Joseph look towards the other end of the table. Silas was having his usual difficulty in eating. His torture-damaged throat could only accommodate a tiny amount of food at once, and a large proportion of every mouthful found its way back on the plate.

Joseph sensed Leah's revulsion. She was gripping the table until her knuckles were white.

'Will you have some more wine, Leah?' Phoebe said, attempting to distract her. Leah shook her head mutely.

Phoebe served the others, but when she came to Peter, he covered his cup with his hand.

Barnabas stared at him. 'You, Peter – refusing wine! I don't believe it!'

'I must keep myself sober,' Peter explained. He grinned at Urgulania. 'She's as big as the Circus Maximus. The spectacle could begin at any time, and I must be ready.'

Urgulania looked at Peter lovingly. 'You will probably faint dead away when it happens. Besides, there is no need for you to worry. One of these good women will always be here – either Leah or Phoebe.' She glanced at Leah. 'My child, have you ever helped a midwife?'

Leah shook her head.

'No matter,' said Urgulania good-naturedly. 'I have attended many births, and I can tell you exactly what to do. The only difficult part is cutting the cord.'

'There will be nothing difficult about it,' Phoebe interjected hastily. 'The delivery will be a mere trifle. And since it is certain to happen very soon, I shall avoid leaving the shop if I can.'

Barnabas glanced at Leah, who was still staring at her unfinished platter of eel stew. 'You're not eating,' he observed.

'It is too hot,' replied Leah.

'Girls of your age must eat,' said Barnabas.

'What do you know about girls her age?' Silas wheezed. 'You never had any. Why don't you tell the child what is really on your mind? I can see what you are thinking by the way your eyes are devouring her plate. You would like her food.'

Barnabas looked a trifle sheepish. 'I do confess – I don't like to see such nourishing fare wasted. After all, God placed fowls in the air and beasts on the earth for man to eat. And naturally that includes eels – even though they are not specifically mentioned in the scriptures ...'

'You are welcome to it,' said Leah, passing him her plate.

'Thank you,' said Barnabas, breaking off a piece of bread and dipping it into the stew.

'Strictly speaking,' Silas wheezed, 'we shouldn't eat this at all. Eels are unclean.'

'How can they be unclean?' Barnabas demanded. They spend their life in the water.'

'The law *says* they're unclean,' Silas insisted.

'Someone once made that observation to Judah,' Peter recalled. 'D'you know what he said?'

Barnabas stirred his stew. 'What?'

'A man cannot be defiled by eating the wrong food. A man is defiled by having the wrong thoughts and doing the wrong deeds.' He sighed. 'How I miss Judah!'

Barnabas eyed him. 'You speak as though Judah were dead.'

Peter's face grew morose. 'It has been so long. What else can I think?'

'We must have faith,' Joseph insisted. 'His work in this world is not finished yet. Judah Ben Hur lives. Somewhere ...'

Abruptly Leah got to her feet. 'I have a headache,' she announced. 'I am going to lie down.'

Without waiting for an answer, she strode through the door into the back room.

'That was tactless of me,' Peter admitted. 'I should never have mentioned Judah.'

'You did no harm,' Urgulania said stoutly. 'If the child is never going to see Judah again – better she face the fact.'

Peter turned to Joseph. 'You said Judah still lives ... How could you know that?'

'Sometimes I have knowledge of things. I cannot explain it. It is a gift God has given me.'

'Why have you not used this gift to guide your daughter?' Barnabas asked acidly.

Joseph shrugged. 'Of course I have tried ... but the power often fails me. I have thought my gift is imperfect because I am imperfect.'

'We are all imperfect,' Peter asserted. 'But I need no gift to know what troubles Leah. She wants to live in a fine house, with many servants – not a hovel like this.'

'Hovel!' Barnabas exclaimed. 'This is the biggest shop in the Vicus!'

Peter made a deprecating gesture. 'The biggest pigsty on a farm is still a pigsty. And Leah finds the life of a pig uncongenial.' He glanced at Joseph. 'She has always had everything she wanted. All the things you could give her when you were still a rabbi. But that is finished now.'

Joseph nodded. 'It is finished indeed!'

Barnabas swallowed the last mouthful of his food and pushed his plate away and rose.

Those at the table fell silent and waited solemnly as Barnabas crossed to the door and disappeared into the back.

A moment later, he returned, bearing a tray. On it was a loaf of bread and an earthenware bowl filled with wine. He placed his burden on the table. All rose, the women covering their heads with their kerchiefs. After a moment of silent prayer, they resumed their places. Reverently, Barnabas broke the bread, giving each a piece.

'In the words of Christ,' he intoned, 'take, eat: this is my body. Do this in remembrance of me.'

All followed Barnabas' example and ate the bread. When they had finished, he picked up the bowl of wine.

'In the words of Christ, this cup is the new covenant in my blood. Do this, as often as you drink it, in remembrance of me.' Barnabas sipped the wine, and continued. 'For as often as you eat this bread and drink the cup, you proclaim the Lord's death until he returns.'

He handed the bowl to Peter, who sipped and passed it round the table.

When the ritual was over, Joseph got to his feet.

'If you'll excuse me, I'll go and see if my daughter's headache has improved.'

He strode into the shuttered back room of the shop. Leah was nowhere to be seen. Joseph stepped to the ladder which led to the loft and looked up. 'Leah!' he called.

There was no reply.

He raised his voice. 'Leah! Are you up there?'

Still there was no reply. Worried, he mounted the ladder.

The loft also was empty. Leah's bag lay on the floor by the side of the cot. He opened it and began to sift through its contents.

Peter's head appeared through the trap-door.

Joseph turned bleakly. 'She's gone ...'

'Perhaps she went down by the river where it is cooler,' Peter suggested.

The old man shook his head. 'She took all her betrothal gifts – all of her jewellery. She does not mean to return.'

'I'll call Barnabas,' said Peter. 'It's getting dark, and he knows the district better than I do.'

Hurriedly the big man disappeared down the ladder.

Leah slipped through the shadows cast by the dark tenements. Ahead the road forked into two narrow alleys. With only the slightest hesitation, she entered one of them.

She probed her way along, her heart pounding with fear. She knew what she was doing was hazardous. She considered turning back, but immediately rejected the thought. She had finally been able to muster the courage to make the move she had contemplated ever since her father had settled in that benighted Vicus. She had made her decision, and she was going to stick by it. It was time to face the fact that Ben Hur was probably dead.

She would follow the same advice she had given him on that moonlit night back in Jerusalem. She would *not* live with the dead. She would always cherish her dreams of him. But she had mourned her lost hopes, and there must be an end to mourning.

And no longer would she waste her life in that wretched Vicus with those sanctimonious people, who could think of nothing but their meaningless religion, while they ignored the poverty about them. The worst of the lot was her own father! Although she had never understood him, she had respected him at any rate. But even respect had gone now. In giving away his wealth, he had left her exposed to the cruelty of the world. She felt betrayed and suffused with a deep resentment.

Leah stopped again, peering into the darkness. The dim, irregular buildings rose up on either side, mysterious, like creatures in a mythical land.

Suddenly bizarre, glowing eyes appeared just ahead. The creature was taller than she – and it was coming towards her! Leah stopped in panic. It was too late to run. She did not know where to go. And then the eyes were close to her face. It was a cat, walking on a wall. She breathed a deep sigh of relief as the animal passed, looking at her curiously.

Now she could hear the steady, measured boom of a large drum. Then it was joined by the nasal wail of a shawm and the chant of many voices.

Leah moved towards the sound warily. Mingled with the song was the babble of conversation and laughter.

She increased her pace eagerly until she came to a courtyard filled with people. For a moment, Leah remained in the shadows and watched. There were forty or fifty of them, not including the musicians. All of them were gathered in small groups round smouldering fires. From time to time bundles of leaves were thrown on the flames, causing billows of even thicker smoke, which everyone in the vicinity would sniff eagerly until it dissipated. All the while they continued their song. Others, moving among the celebrants, distributed garlands of flowers. Leah was entranced but puzzled.

The people seemed supremely happy, yet there was something odd about them. Perhaps it was the way they moved, with an easy, languorous grace, touching occasionally, yet detached from each other.

No one paid the slightest attention to her. Resentfully she glanced round. Surely *someone* would notice her.

Her glance caught a man, reclining indolently with a group by a fire. His appearance was so strange that she could not avoid staring at him. He was not old, but he had no hair at all, not even eyebrows. Sitting with his back propped against a wall, he lounged negligently, his thin legs spread well apart. He had rolled up his tunic and removed his loincloth, exposing his genitals to the warmth of the fire.

He looked directly at her. His body made no movement at all, but his eyes flickered in a way which beckoned. In spite of a certain distaste at the sight of him, Leah found herself obeying him.

As she came up to the hairless man, he lifted his arm and crooked his little finger downwards at the flagstones next to him. Leah realized he was inviting her to sit, and she did so.

'My name is Leah,' she ventured.

His eyeballs spun with approval, but he still remained silent.

'What are you called?' Leah wondered.

Astonishingly the stranger bounded to his feet, and, with movement so fluid that it seemed he had no bones, he began to pantomime a story. Leah had no difficulty in recognizing the well-known tale of Paris and Achilles. She was enchanted as he acted out the legend, with the assassin stealthily drawing his bow and taking aim – then quickly shifting to the role of the victim being hit in the heel and dying tragically.

'I know,' Leah cried, 'your name is Achilles!'

He shook his head and once again drew his imaginary bow.

'Paris!' said Leah.

He nodded happily, and before Leah could catch her breath, he had turned three somersaults and was standing on his head.

The man must be mute! Leah was intrigued by his unique method of conveying his meaning. It was just as expressive as words – and much more fun.

With a backward flip he was on his feet again. Two leaps took him to a table, where he gathered some freshly cut flowers, then, like a bald Pan, danced back to her and twined them in her hair. He skipped off again, and returned with a goblet of wine. Leah sipped it, as Paris resumed his dance, scattering more green leaves on to the fire. The smoke billowed up thickly, and a pungent odour like burning grass assailed Leah's nostrils. Paris leaned over and inhaled the smoke deeply. He gestured for Leah to do likewise.

Almost immediately her head felt light, and she understood the lethargy of the others. She was exhilarated and lyrically happy, yet deliciously lazy at the same time.

Paris pulled her to her feet, as the musicians struck up an air. He began to lead her in an ecstatic dance, and she followed. It seemed to Leah as though the steps were extremely complicated. Yet, with Paris as her guide, she was performing them with ease.

A tremendous crash of cymbals was heard. Instantly Paris ceased his dance. Wonderingly Leah looked round. All present had stopped whatever they were doing and were getting to their feet. Another clash of the cymbals pulled Leah's attention to a doorway in the building at the rear of the courtyard. There stood an enormously fat man, clad in a voluminous yellow robe. He stood aside, and the entire company began to file towards the entrance.

She had no idea what was happening but curiosity soon got the better of her, and she joined the procession entering a small antechamber. She followed them to a stairway which led downwards.

She was in a long hall. Torches flickered from metal stands set in every column. At the far end was a raised dais, surmounted by what looked like an altar, where the bemused worshippers were gathering. More yellow-robed men stood there. Their uniform garment was most distinctive, and Leah guessed they must be priests of some sort. She wondered why they were all so fat. Did they spend their entire time eating?

Leah sat on the floor with the other celebrants. Two of the priests lit censers and began to swing them. Soon the air was filled with pungent incense. The yellow-robed men lined up in front of the altar and faced their audience, who devoutly bowed to the floor, kissing the stones. Not wanting to look strange, Leah did the same. Now one of the priests stood apart from his fellows, and, beating the rhythm with a tambourine, he began to lead the colleagues in a sonorous chant.

The sing-song lyric was easy to understand, and as the story unfolded, Leah's every sense tingled with horror. They sang of a hermaphroditic monster Adgistus, who roamed the earth long, long ago, ravaging the fields and crops. Dionysus, the ingenious God, undertook to defeat the monster by turning a mountain stream into wine. When Adgistus drank it, he went into a frenzy and castrated himself. A tree grew from the torn testicles planted in the ground.

The congregation joined in, singing ecstatically with the priests. The song told how an earthly woman, Nana, plucked the fruit of the genital tree and ate it. Nana became pregnant by the fruit and gave birth to Atthis, who grew to be a handsome youth. So beautiful was Atthis that the great mother Goddess, Cybele, seduced him. Atthis fell in love with her, and when the Goddess's fancy turned to another lover, Atthis was driven mad with grief, and, like his monster-father, castrated himself.

Their voices rising, the singers extolled Atthis, now a God, freed from mortal state and mundane desires. As the paean went on, Leah became aware that the room was growing darker. She glanced round. Approaching on either side of the hall from the far end were two more priests. Each held a metal snuffer; they were extinguishing the torches one by one.

Leah was suffocated by a feeling of panic. She sensed that the ritual was drawing to some sort of climax, and she did *not* want to be here to witness it. But her limbs were so frozen with fear that she could not move. Then the last of the torches was put out. The chamber was in total blackness.

Shuffling sounds told Leah of a mass movement all round her. There were other sounds too, gasps, groans, but, before Leah could make any sense of them, a pair of hands had seized her. She pushed her assailant away, grabbing him by the beard, but inexorably he pressed her down. She considered gouging his eyes, but she was afraid of what might happen to her if she offered too much resistance. So she submitted, while he pulled her tunic, ripped away her loincloth and forced her legs apart. She felt a sharp pain as he thrust his member into her. But immediately the pain began to lessen, and was replaced by a growing pleasure, which became breathless in intensity. She rose to a shuddering climax and he was not stopping. Now frenziedly Leah co-operated, eagerly meeting his thrusts with her own. She felt the hot rush inside her as he filled her with his lust. Then, suddenly, he was gone. But Leah lay there, quivering, overwhelmed, hoping to find him and draw him back to her, but she could find no one.

A light flared. Leah froze. A moment later, a torch blazed up, followed by another. Gradually the temple was relighted.

Leah glanced round, wondering which of the men had lain with her. All she knew of him was that he had a beard; but most of the men present did.

There was a movement on the altar. Two of the priests led out a naked man. Another priest approached from the opposite side of the dais with a knife. Leah gasped with horror. Did they actually mean to bring to life that terrible tale related in the chant? Were they going to cut off this man's genitals?

A door opened at the far end of the temple. A white bull was brought on to the dais. The naked initiate stepped down into a recess sunk into the floor just in front of the altar. The priests urged the bull forward, placing the beast so that its throat was directly over the man's head. Deftly, one of the priests slashed the bull's throat. The animal gave a strangled snort and swayed as its blood gushed all over the initiate, who frantically began to rub himself with it, catching some in his cupped hands and drinking it. Immediately everyone in the temple began to chant. Slowly the bull sank to its knees, then finally, with a shuddering, wheezing sound, it died.

Shaken, Leah got to her feet unsteadily. She had to get out. Furtively she began to slip away near the row of pillars on one side. But suddenly the chanting stopped. Everyone in the temple was staring fixedly at her. Two priests advanced.

The ugly fat men came very near and stopped.

'You do not belong here,' said one accusingly. 'The worship of Cybele is forbidden to all but initiates.'

'You must pay the penalty of a trespasser,' said the other priest, taking Leah's arms.

She struggled to free herself, but the man's grip was too powerful.

'Stop!' called a voice. 'She is my woman! I brought her here!'

Immediately the priests released Leah. A man came forward. It was Paris. And he had spoken. He was not a mute.

'I will take her,' said Paris.

Leah had not seen Paris anywhere during the ceremony. And it was certainly not Paris who had assaulted her in the dark. But apparently he had been present the whole time.

CHAPTER ELEVEN

The night air was cold and refreshing. Leah breathed it with relief.

She glanced at Paris. He smiled and offered his arm. Leah took it. She did not care where they went.

They walked in silence. Paris did not seem to desire conversation, and Leah was grateful for the opportunity to collect her thoughts. There had been frightening moments this evening, but the experience had been thrilling. Leah wondered how many more strange things the great city concealed. She had plunged into a vast sea of new sensations, and she did not want them to stop.

'The priests of Cybele,' she blurted out suddenly, 'what would they have done to me if you had not been there?'

'They couldn't do what most men would like to do to you. They are eunuchs.'

'How horrible!'

'They are holy men. They have made the supreme sacrifice for their love of Cybele. Just like Atthis did. That is why they are priests. Most worshippers of Cybele are not expected to castrate themselves. In fact, they are urged to celebrate their physical nature and thus revere all the more those who have chosen to go without it.'

Leah said nothing. She was mystified by the whole idea.

'In passing,' wondered Paris, 'since you are not a follower of Cybele, what were you doing there?'

'I was running away.'

'Running away? From whom? Husband? Lover? Keeper?'

'From my father.'

'He ill-treats you?'

'Oh no!' Leah exclaimed. 'He would never do that!'

'Then why did you run away?'

'I hate the way he lives. He *and* his friends. And he wants me to live like he does.'

'How does he live?'

'He is a Christian.'

'A Christian!' Paris exclaimed. 'No wonder you made an escape! Men say the Christians are the worst of all people – that they are hostile to mankind – that they practise unspeakable rites.'

'I have no love for them,' Leah agreed. 'But they cannot be worse than the followers of Cybele.'

'What a thing to say!' Paris exclaimed. 'The worship of Cybele is held in great esteem by all men – and with good reason. The Christians insist that everyone should believe as they do, but the worshippers of Cybele never try to win converts to their religion. They respect all other Gods and only ask that they be allowed to worship theirs.'

'My father says that there is only one God.'

'How ridiculous!' Paris exclaimed. 'The world is too big and too complicated for one God. Anybody can see that. There is not just "one" of anything. So why should there be one God? And what a wonderful thing it is that there *are* many Gods! A man can choose which one he likes best.'

'Why did you choose Cybele?'

'Because worshipping Cybele involves sex. Anything to do with sex I like. I have had sex in every way possible,' said Paris earnestly. 'With women and girls. With men and boys. And with many kinds of animals. But, in spite of that, I am always searching for more.'

'You are a strange man,' she observed. 'When I first met you, I thought you were a mute.'

'I *am* a mute. For long periods of time. It is my profession.'

'In what way.'

'I am a pantomimist. The greatest in the world. I can tell any story imaginable without speaking a word. I have performed before the Emperor himself.'

'The Emperor! What was he like?'

'A marvellous and intelligent man. He *adored* my performance.

He has had me back to play for him time and time again.'

'I have never seen a pantomime. Except what you did tonight ...'

'Just a frippery. A mere improvisation. When I perform, I do long, elaborate stories in full costume, with orchestras and choruses. Pantomime is the highest form of all acting. The greatest nobles in the land – senators and equestrians – come to my theatre to see me.'

'*Your* theatre?'

'You have not been in Rome long, have you?'

She shook her head.

'If you'd been in this city for any time at all, you would have heard of the Theatre of Cybele. It is one of the most famous. And I own it.'

'I'd love to see it. I wish I could be in the theatre!'

He looked her up and down. 'You never know ... There might be a something for you ...'

'Please!' Leah begged. 'It would be so exciting. And a blessing. After all – I must find some way to earn my bread.'

Once more his gaze flickered over her body. Experimentally, he reached under her tunic and fondled her breasts. His hand discovered the pouch hanging round her neck.

'What have we here?'

'Don't!' Leah cried. 'Those are mine!'

He gave her a playful little slap on the cheek. 'I wouldn't take anything from you. I'm only curious ...' He lifted the pouch from her neck and opened it, pouring some of the jewels into his hand. 'You stole them?'

'No! They were gifts. Now give them back.'

'You said you wanted to work for me ...'

'I do!'

'Then I must keep them – as a pledge for your good conduct.' He placed the jewellery into his own pouch, again patting her cheek. Then, suddenly, he gripped the flesh, pinching it very hard. She shrieked with pain. But he held her cheek tight, squeezing it viciously. 'Remember only one thing,' he said softly. 'Never disobey me. Never.'

Paris, resplendent in a flame-coloured cloak, wearing the mask of the jealous blacksmith God Vulcan, stood in the middle of the sun-drenched stage. He stretched his arms heavenward. The cymbals clashed, and the musicians split the air with their flutes.

Slowly Paris brought his arms down, and then, with fluttering fingers and sinuous swaying of his body, he began to weave his invisible net.

The smallest finger of Paris' left hand made a quivering motion. Leah knew this was not part of Paris' performance. It was the signal that he was ready for his next mask.

She was standing to one side of the stage to allow the Master plenty of room for his performance. Clad in only a tiny loincloth, her nipples gilded, she was meant to look as ornamental as a statue. Now she took a few graceful steps forward and offered Paris his new mask. Deftly, with an almost imperceptible motion, he took it, donned it, handing the old mask to Leah. As Paris assumed his new role, Leah retreated to her former position at the side of the orchestra.

Now she watched Paris, marvelling as always at the way he slipped into the part of the stealthy lover creeping to his assignation. The wail of the flutes sank to a sibilant, seductive throb.

Her eyes moved to the spellbound audience. The tiers of stone seats which rose in a semi-circle around them were filled to capacity, as they had been for every performance. As one, the audience leaned forward in their seats, watching Paris' gyrations intently. Save for the musicians, there was not a sound in the whole place.

With unerring skill, never uttering a sound, Paris brought to life the tale of Mars and Venus and their illicit affair. Paris always led off his performance by portraying a secret tryst between the lovers. As Mars, he was virile and attractive. As the yielding Venus, he was invitingly seductive. And as Vulcan, Venus' husband, Paris was ferocious, jealous and vengeful. With his artful motions, the pantomimist delineated the cunning trap Vulcan had set for the guilty pair, placing the magic net he had woven to snare the lovers in the midst of their embraces.

When the trap was sprung, Paris somehow managed to become the net itself, implacably holding the lovers. Shifting from one part to another, Paris depicted in turn Vulcan going to summon the other Gods to show them his catch, then each of the Gods, expressing their various reactions, all of which made a laughing stock of the cuckolded blacksmith, who beat his anvil in fury and dismay.

Finally the flawless performance came to an end. Paris bowed to howls of laughter and thunderous applause.

The artist turned as if to leave the stage, touching off a roar of protest. Once again he bowed. There was more applause. When he attempted a second exit, there were angry shouts for another performance.

Leah knew he would have to heed them. Paris was their idol, but he paid a price for their adulation. On one occasion he had been too tired for an encore, causing a riot in the upper tiers of seats, where the rougher sort usually sat. They had descended, putting to flight the aristocrats in the choicer seats below. Then they had stormed the stage and literally dragged Paris from his dressing room.

This afternoon Paris was taking no chances. He took up his cloak, put on his first mask, and prepared to launch into yet another rendition of the ribald tale. Leah knew that the theatre-goers were well acquainted with the story itself. It was Paris and his interpretation of legend that they came to see. And Leah herself never tired of it. As many times as she had witnessed his art, she was thrilled on each occasion by the extraordinary fluency of his physical language.

Once again Paris was alternately Mars and Venus, with the flutes whispering their licentious suggestions and Leah coming mutely forward to supply masks.

As she watched Paris act out the mock intercourse, her mind went back to their first night together. He had proved to be the most accomplished of lovers, spending the entire night in a bewildering variety of copulations.

She had become his mistress. In the weeks which had followed he had made love to her every night. Leah matched his vitality with her own and participated eagerly in these bouts. Yet the pleasure she felt was not the same overwhelming sensation she had experienced on that first night, when she had been ravished on the floor of the Temple of Cybele. Even now, at the mere recollection of the incident, she found herself becoming aroused.

Many times she had thought of wandering back to the Temple in the hopes of having the same experience. She had not, however, dared to try it. She was afraid of Paris, and had discovered that he could be very cruel. Once, while still learning her job as his stage assistant, she had made a mistake during the performance. Paris had bound her hands and feet and left her in the same position for a whole day and night. She had suffered excruciating tortures from hunger and lack of circulation. Never again would she do anything to displease him.

Speculatively Leah glanced at the nearer seats, surveying the first fourteen rows, reserved for senators and equestrians. Careful to remain absolutely motionless until Paris made the sign for his mask, she allowed her eyes to scan the faces.

Then she felt a slight surge of triumph. Her admirer was here again! Hardly a performance had passed without the presence of the tall Equestrian. He paid scant attention to the elegant gymnastics of Paris; always his eyes were fixed on Leah. His attraction to her had been dramatically confirmed when the Equestrian, introducing himself as Ostorius Minucius, had appeared one night at Paris' lodgings and offered to buy her. Angrily Paris had refused, pointing out that Leah was no slave.

'Then what is she?' Minucius had inquired.

'She's my woman!'

Leah remembered the contemptuous way the nobleman had surveyed Paris. 'You're an actor, aren't you? Surely there is nothing you would not sell – if the price was right?'

'Get out of here!' Paris had screamed, flinging the door open.

The moment Minucius was gone, Paris had rounded on Leah. 'You little slut! So you've been flaunting yourself. Enticing another man behind my back.'

'No!' Leah had cried defensively. 'I have done nothing.'

'Then why was he here?'

'You make me go naked before all those people. What do you expect?'

'I'll tell *you* what to expect. If it happens again, I'll kill you.'

Paris had cuffed her again and again to emphasize his point.

But Minucius had not given up. A few days later he had returned and repeated his offer. Even the Equestrian's rank, however, was no deterrent to Paris when enraged. In a towering fury he had vowed he would call the watch if Minucius showed his face again. Laughing at the actor's anger, Minucius had shrugged and sauntered away.

Paris had blustered, but he did not strike Leah this time. From then on, his treatment of her had improved noticeably, and he seemed more tolerant when she made mistakes.

She had even considered telling him that she was pregnant. But she had held back. In the first place, she was not certain yet. Her late menstruation might stem from other causes. And if she was with child, it could just as easily be the offspring of the ruffian who had despoiled her in the Temple.

Leah's eyes flickered to the front row, where Minucius was sitting. Her gaze met his. The Equestrian's brown eyes twinkled back invitingly. Leah was glad he had come. Paris must have noticed him too. Obviously Minucius was not deterred one bit by Paris' threats. She wondered if Minucius would make another offer for her – or perhaps he would try something else. Whatever the case, as long as Minucius persisted in showing interest, Leah was certain that Paris would continue to treat her more carefully. Now, perhaps, she could ask for a few things, possibly even the return of her jewellery.

Slowly Leah became aware that something was amiss in the theatre. There was movement and muttering among the spectators. They were not watching Paris.

Two men had entered through one of the corner archways. Leah could not see them very clearly, but they seemed to be searching for something as they moved along the passage leading into the orchestra. The newcomers paused, glancing towards the stage, blocking the view of people in the front row, who protested loudly.

Leah's heart stopped. It was all she could do to restrain her impulse to flee to the pit behind the orchestra. The newcomers were her father and Peter! And they had seen her. In panic, she glanced towards Paris, who continued his performance as impeccably as ever. But the crowd was restive.

Joseph and Peter came to the very edge of the stage, right in front of Leah. Her father's grief-stricken eyes gazed up at her. His face streaming with tears, Joseph's lips worked emotionally.

'Leah ... Leah ...' he said brokenly. 'I could not believe it, when

I heard you were here in this place of sin, flaunting the beauty which God gave you!'

With a supreme effort of self-control, Leah forced herself to concentrate on the top tier of seats, holding her body still. She would pretend that her father was not here ...

'Please come down!' her father begged. 'Clothe yourself and come back home with me. You will be forgiven. Everything will be just as it was before.'

Now Paris ceased his performance. Tearing off his mask, he hurled it to the floor, and strode furiously to the edge of the stage.

'Out!' bellowed the actor. 'How *dare* you break in here! How dare you! This is a performance!' His voice rose to a scream. 'Out! Out! Out!'

'We will not leave,' Peter stated defiantly. He pointed to Leah. 'Not until she comes with us!'

Leah could stand it no longer. Consumed with embarrassment and indignation, she stepped forward. 'Go away!' she cried. 'How can you do this! *You* are the one with no shame! Making a spectacle! In front of everybody!'

A dry sob burst from Joseph's throat. The old man tried pathetically to mount the stage, but the effort was too great for him.

Hisses and catcalls came from the audience.

Once again, Joseph tried to climb up. This time Peter helped him.

Glancing round desperately for a weapon, Paris finally picked up the angry mask of Vulcan, which he had just discarded. Peter clambered on to the stage and advanced towards Paris threateningly.

The actor backed away.

'You despicable despoiler of children!' Peter roared, knocking the mask to the ground.

Paris hesitated only an instant longer, then, abruptly, turned and fled.

Leah found herself facing her father and Peter alone. For a moment she was too mortified for words, while the anger of the theatre became more and more audible.

Joseph reached out a trembling hand, his agony showing plainly in his face. 'My child, Leah,' he sobbed. 'Please come back to me.'

Leah flung him back. 'Get away! Get away!' she gasped.

'Others have led you astray!' Joseph cried. 'But I will not let you destroy yourself!'

'Let me alone! I hate you! I never want to see you again!'

Joseph staggered backwards, as though he had been hit.

Just then, however, something sailed through the air and landed on the stage with a thump. It was a shoe. Immediately it was followed by a shower of other objects, everything from pieces of fruit to pottery.

The muttering of the audience was now a deafening roar. The gentry in the first fourteen rows were on their feet, trying in vain to hold back the human wave which was pouring over them from behind. Leah realized that the patience of the rabble had been tried to the breaking point. It was too late to stop them now. Before she could think about flight, they were swarming over the stage.

Several converged on her father, knocking him down. Peter lunged to his aid, tearing away some of the assailants, but he was overwhelmed by force of numbers. Soon the stage in front of her became a mass of shouting unkempt people.

Leah watched in terror. Then hands were on her. She whirled round. Two men were clutching at her. One was an obese, bearded fellow, and his companion was not much different, except for the disfigurement of a scar which nearly obliterated one of his eyes. The scarred one squeezed her breasts and rubbed his hand roughly over her belly. A third man joined them, his eyes glowing with excitement.

'Let's take her behind the theatre . . .' the newcomer breathed. 'Have her all to ourselves there . . .'

Leah kicked and twisted, but to no avail. They lifted her off her feet, and bore their squirming burden down the steps behind the pit. An arch led out behind the theatre. They carried her through it and pinioned her on the grass at the rear of the building.

The scarred one pressed his hot face close to hers. In terror and revulsion, she scratched wildly. He dealt her two stunning slaps, but before he could do more, he was jerked away by the obese man.

'I saw her first!' the fat one growled. 'Now hold her!'

While the others held her arms, he tore away her loincloth. Leah gazed up at his grotesque form as he prepared to mount her. Then something else came into view, behind her assailant. It was Minucius. He had thrown off his toga and gripped a heavy cudgel. With a resonant crack, he brought the weapon down across the fat man's head. Senseless, the would-be rapist pitched to the ground beside her.

The other molesters rose, turning to face the threat. Minucius charged, sending them spinning with dexterous swings of the club. In a moment, they too were helpless on the ground. But Minucius did not stop. He continued to pound them mercilessly, distributing his blows evenly between the three, until Leah was certain they must be dead.

Finally he stopped, standing still for a moment to regain his breath. Tossing the cudgel aside, he picked up his toga, which lay in a heap on the ground. Then he helped Leah to her feet, and draped the garment over her shoulders.

'Come,' he said.

He led her round to the façade of the theatre, which fronted imposingly on the squalid little street.

But Minucius did not stop here. He conducted her across the street, down a narrow alley. A short distance ahead, a large sedan chair lay on its side on the ground, directly in front of a wine shop. The bearers, who had obviously been in the tavern, were standing in the open stall, cups in their hands, staring curiously at the theatre, from which the sounds of the angry rioters still echoed.

At the sight of Minucius, they straightened up respectfully, placing their cups on the table.

'I'm sorry to spoil your afternoon,' said Minucius blandly, 'but it seems the show has ended early.'

Immediately the bearers placed the leather pads on their shoulders, hurried into the street and hauled the litter upright.

As Minucius waited for them, Leah appraised him covertly. He was of middle age, perhaps fifty, and not as paunchy from self-indulgence as most Romans that age. He was neither handsome nor ugly, but his gaze was firm and steady, and his features were pleasing enough. It was obvious from the way he conducted himself that he was a man of consequence, accustomed to giving orders and having them obeyed.

When the bearers had the chair ready, Minucius stepped forward and opened the door for Leah. 'You will do me the honour ...'

She climbed into the chair, squeezing herself into the cramped seat. Minucius got in with her and closed the door.

'I wonder if they killed Paris,' said Leah as the litter lurched forward.

'We can always hope,' replied Minucius, cynically. 'But I doubt it. Actors are indestructible.'

Leah had no answer. They sat for a moment in silence.

She stole another look at his profile. There was no doubt about his purpose. He wanted to savour her body – as all men did. But Leah vowed that this time she would not make the same mistake as she had with Paris. She had given herself too easily to Paris and he had treated her brutally. This time she would be more difficult to possess.

Lifting the shutter, Leah peered out of the litter, then turned to Minucius. 'Sir, you have been very kind. And I thank you with all my heart. We are well away from the theatre, and I will be quite safe here – if you'll let me out.'

'You're coming home with me,' he said flatly.

'Please,' Leah begged. 'Let me go.'

She half opened the door, but Minucius banged it shut again.

'You think I am a whore,' Leah protested. 'To be used just as you please.'

'I do not know what you are. But I intend to find out.'

She lunged again for the door, but Minucius was on her, pulling her back. They wrestled for a moment. However, the Equestrian was strong, and soon he had pinioned Leah's arms behind her back. The sedan chair swayed perilously, and the coarse laughter of the bearers could be heard outside.

'Find yourself another woman!' she flamed.

'You have no idea how much I desire you. I have since the first time I saw you in that silly statue pose with your breasts painted gold.' He twisted her wrist. 'But no words can explain it. You will only understand when you see for yourself.'

Leah was puzzled. 'See for myself? What do you mean by that?'

'When we get to my house, I will show you.'

CHAPTER TWELVE

Leah sank back into her seat silently. She was irked by the suggestion that it might be anything but her charms which would draw this man to her. She was not accustomed to men being niggardly in their praises of her beauty.

But she was intrigued. What might there be at this man's house which could possibly be connected with his attraction to her? She glanced at him. He seemed to be preoccupied with his own thoughts. It was almost as if he had forgotten Leah's presence.

Leah was jolted slightly when the chair was placed on the ground. The door was opened. She climbed out, looking round expectantly.

At first the house was not visible. All she could see was a gravel path leading into a thick grove of pines.

Minucius appeared beside her, taking her by the arm.

'The house is just behind the trees.' He smiled. 'I like seclusion.'

Soon they were among the pines, and Leah could make out the villa. It was a low, sprawling, whitewashed building with a tiled roof. Outwardly, it was neither impressive nor mean, but Leah had the feeling that it was spacious inside.

When they were almost at the door, it was opened by a female servant clad in a long stola. Obviously the woman had been waiting close by so that Minucius would not have to knock.

'I will call you when we are ready for supper,' said Minucius. 'Until then, Teuta, I do not want to be disturbed.'

The woman's eyes flickered curiously at Leah, then she bowed and disappeared.

Leah furtively appraised their surroundings. The darkened hall seemed quite bare.

'Come,' said Minucius.

She followed him towards the light spilling through an open doorway at the far end of the hall.

The room which lay before her was spacious, flooded with the golden glow of the setting sun, which poured in through the large open windows. The walls were covered with paintings, and the floors were inlaid with the most exquisite mosaics that Leah had ever seen. The whole chamber seemed to shimmer with many colours.

He smiled. 'You like it?'

'It's . . . it's overwhelming.'

'I only use it when I want to impress people. Actually I come to this part of the house very rarely. My quarters are very simple.'

He led her across the mosaic floor. Leah stared down at the colourfully depicted scenes as they went. They told the story of the planting of grain, through its harvest, and loading into large ships, which set out onto the sea with billowing sails.

'My family fortune came from the grain trade,' Minucius commented. 'I installed this floor as a tribute to my father. Fortunately I never had to soil my hands with earning money . . . thanks to him.'

Now they made their way down another corridor, until they came to a screened doorway on their right. Here he stopped, watching her intently. Leah had a feeling she was about to discover the secret of the house.

With a sweeping motion of his arm, Minucius pulled the curtain aside and invited Leah to enter.

She found herself in a diminutive vaulted chamber. There were no windows, the dim light being provided by scented tapers. The room contained only one object, a nude statue of a female figure, wrought from a marble whose texture was as smooth as human flesh. The figure was of surpassing beauty and symmetry, but it was the face which made Leah catch her breath in astonishment.

'It's me!' she whispered.

'It is certainly an uncanny likeness,' Minucius agreed. 'But it is hardly likely that the sculptor knew you. Praxiteles, who created it, died more than three hundred years ago.'

'Who is she?'

'She is Aphrodite, the Goddess of Love, portrayed as she was the day she rose from the waves.'

Leah gazed at the serene features of the Goddess. And, in truth, Leah had the distinct feeling that there was another presence in this room. It was as if that soft, marble skin had a power of its own. Leah shivered.

'Not being plagued by the financial worries of most men,' Minucius was saying, 'I have devoted a good deal of my life to travel.' He indicated the image. 'I discovered her on Cyprus. She was in a temple at Paphos, overlooking the sea. When I saw her, I had to have her!'

'How did you get her?' Leah asked.

'Like one gets most things in this world – with money. The priests – those holy, mercenary men – held out for a huge amount. I paid it. I was in love. I suppose that is why I never married.'

'You have been in love all that time?'

'With all my heart.' Then his tone changed. 'Stand beside her!' Leah moved closer to the statue.

'Take off that ridiculous drapery.'

Obediently Leah removed the loose toga with which he had covered her, and allowed it to slip to the floor.

She waited for him to say something, but he did not. He stood there wordlessly, drinking in the sight of the two naked female figures.

Leah found her own eyes drawn towards the Goddess. The marble face was as calm as ever, but Leah felt a rising resentment. Her resemblance to the statue may have been what attracted Minucius, but now Leah was irked at the idea that she should share this man's adoration with a piece of stone.

But as Leah continued to contemplate her marble counterpart, she felt her anger slip away and the vague fear returning. The tangible presence of this other female was disturbing and very real.

Then Minucius was beside her, but paying no attention to her. His gaze was fixed on Aphrodite. He reached out and caressed the statue's breasts, then ran his hands down the marble flanks and buttocks.

At last he turned to Leah and touched her in the same fashion. Her anxiety increased. This man had adored and worshipped Aphrodite. Now he would love her, Leah knew. She could sense his passion rising. Leah wondered if she could measure up to a goddess. Would he experience the same ecstasy with a mere mortal?

The water was tepid, neither too warm nor too cold. Leah could barely combat the drowsiness which was stealing through her limbs.

Indolently she ran her hands over her wet breasts, down her flanks. He had been pleased with her body, that was certain. He had not left her until the early morning. And Leah had not slept the entire night. Smugly she reflected that even in a contest with a Goddess, she seemed to have come off the better. Leah was becoming more and more aware of the sexual power she could exert. To see a man aroused to a fever pitch of desire for her, this gave her supreme joy and satisfaction. And she herself enjoyed the physical delight of mating. Only now that she had left her father and embraced life had she discovered the true sensuality of her being. The memory of Ben Hur's masculinity came to her. How she wished she could have enjoyed this physical side of her nature with him . . .

The female servant entered with a jug and a clean tunic and placed them on a stool by the bath. She took a cloth from under her arm.

'If you please,' said Teuta, 'I will dry you.'

Lazily, Leah hauled herself from the pool and sprawled on the warm marble floor. 'Thank you – but I think I'll just lie here and go to sleep,' she murmured. 'When I wake up, I will be dry.'

'Do not fall asleep,' Teuta warned.

'Why not?'

'The master will soon be sending for you to give you your money.'

'What money?'

'The money for your favours. What else?'

Leah sat up indignantly.

'I am not a whore!'

Teuta smiled sardonically. 'That's what they all say. But when morning comes – they take their money and go their way.'

Leah chose to ignore the comment. 'Does Minucius have lots of women?'

The servant laughed coarsely. 'He is like a goat! He must have a woman every night – but he cannot stand the sight of them in the morning.'

Leah experienced a flash of doubt, but it was gone, almost as soon as it had come. However many harlots he bedded, Leah knew that she was not like the others. If he had merely thought of her as a common prostitute, would he have come to the theatre repeatedly to admire her beauty from a distance? And, furthermore, Leah was certain that he had compared none of the whores to his prized Aphrodite. But the most telling indication of all had been Minucius' performance the previous night ...

A boy entered the bathing room, paying no particular attention to Leah's nudity. He approached her and bowed politely.

'My master wishes to see you in the tablinium immediately,' he announced.

Without waiting for Leah's reply, the boy trotted out of the room again. Leah glanced at Teuta, who grinned, holding up the towel.

Leah permitted herself to be dried, and soon was being helped into the fresh tunic. Then she sat on the stool and laced the shoes which Teuta had also brought. Finally she rose resolutely.

'I'll show you the way,' Teuta offered.

Head high, Leah followed the older woman. She was certain that Minucius was not going to send her away – no matter what Teuta had said.

At the end of the hall, they stopped at a doorway. Teuta pulled back the hanging and stood aside. Leah entered the room and found herself facing not only Minucius, but Paris as well. The actor's brow was dark with rage.

Minucius spoke first. 'Your pantomime friend has come to take you back. The choice is yours. I certainly do not wish to keep you here against your will.'

Leah hesitated, her glance going from one man to the other. She was startled, not only by Paris' presence but by Minucius' attitude. Suddenly her confidence was gone. If she had made such a vivid impression on him, would he now so casually allow her to walk out of his life?

'Do you *want* me to go?' she asked Minucius finally.

'No,' he replied. 'But to force an unwilling person to stay would hardly be worth the effort.'

Unexpectedly Paris lunged forward and seized Leah by the arm. 'You little parasite!' he snarled. 'You'll spread your legs for a crumb of bread, won't you? Now come along!'

Leah jerked her arm free. 'No! I am staying here!'

Paris' face grew purple with fury. He seemed on the verge of striking her.

'You are a fool!' he spat. 'You think you will have a life of ease here with him!' He made a deprecating gesture towards Minucius. 'How long do you think it will last? I'll tell you – as long as it takes him to find another pair of legs he can spread. And then where will you be? In the street, looking for Paris. But it will be too late. Paris will have somebody else.'

She bit her lip. The actor's words had made her afraid. Minucius might tire of her ... And no doubt Paris, being a man of capricious affections, would indeed find another love.

Nevertheless, she had to choose. Even though she knew little of Minucius, she knew enough to realize that he was infinitely preferable to Paris.

'I will stay here,' she said.

Paris grabbed her arm again, twisting it cruelly. 'I am not leaving this house without you!'

Suddenly Minucius was on him, holding him by the throat. He held the actor thus for an instant, then tossed him contemptuously against the wall.

'She has chosen,' said Minucius. 'Now get out of here!'

Paris started towards Minucius, as if to attack. The older man stood there stolidly, awaiting the assault. His stance seemed to discourage the actor, who retreated a few steps. Paris avoided Minucius' eyes and glowered at Leah instead.

'You'll be sorry,' he warned her. 'You'll be sorry ...'

Then Paris turned and left the room, with Minucius following closely.

Leah's mind was in a turmoil. She could only hope that Paris' insults had done nothing to lower Minucius' opinion of her. She tried to collect her thoughts, but before she could, her new lover had returned.

The Equestrian deliberately closed the curtain and faced her. 'I am curious,' he said. 'Why did you decide to stay with me?'

Leah feigned surprise. 'Isn't that obvious?'

'Not to me.'

'Why does a woman usually stay with a man?'

He smiled cynically. 'I would like to think that it is because I am overwhelmingly, irresistibly attractive to you. But I know better than that.'

Leah studied him. His manner was off-hand and careless. Underneath it, however, she sensed his need. She had not been long in the world of men, but was there not a note of pleading in his voice?

'You *are* attractive to me,' Leah said earnestly. 'That is why I want to be with you. Indeed it is.'

'Then why did you hesitate? For a moment, you were on the verge of going with that hairless pantomime.'

Leah was taken aback. She had not realized her indecision had been so apparent. Now she must reassure him.

'He took some jewellery from me,' she explained. 'I wanted to go and get it back.'

He laughed. His relief was obvious. 'Is that all? Forget it! Whatever baubles they were – I will give you more and better!'

Leah felt triumph surge within her. She had not judged wrongly. Obviously she supplied something which had been lacking in his life, and she had caught a glimpse of how weak and vulnerable a man could be – even one so wealthy, powerful and wise in the ways of the world as Minucius.

Truly she had discovered a great secret. And now that she had the key to it she felt she could conquer the world.

The stuffy little attic was dim, but the object in Joseph's hands seemed to glow with a light of its own. It was the silver chalice. He lifted it in both hands as if to drink, but paused with the cup halfway to his lips. He studied its shimmering silver surface, and the palms of his hands savoured its smoothness.

Once again the living warmth flowed through his wrists and arms, and filled his entire being. He forgot the stiffness of his joints, the bruises he had suffered in the riot at the theatre. Light began to flood the room. It was not the morning sun. It was the effulgence of his reanimated spirit – it was the dawn of a new age! Suddenly the air was filled with glorious music. The light directly above him grew dazzlingly bright. But Joseph did not shield his eyes, for there, immediately before him, a new presence was taking shape.

Then something began to intrude on the fringe of his ecstasy. Loud voices and footsteps were coming from the shop below, followed by the wail of Urgulania's infant. He lowered his arms, placing the vessel on the cot beside him. Carefully he wrapped it in its protective cloth, then secreted it in his bag. Regretfully, he took up his cloak, opened the trap-door and descended the ladder.

Waiting in the room below was Peter, with Urgulania by his side, holding the baby. Peter's face was still distressingly swollen from the encounter at the theatre.

'I have news,' he boomed, as Silas and Barnabas entered.

'What is going on?' Silas croaked.

'Peter has news,' Urgulania informed him.

They waited expectantly as Peter paused to fondle his son, a tiny bundle in its mother's arms. The child was undersized and frail. Joseph knew that both Peter and Urgulania were worried about its health. Now Peter was trying to entice it with the wooden doll he had made. But the infant paid no attention. At last Peter put the toy on the table and again faced Joseph.

'You know how I am,' he announced. 'I never give up. I went there again.'

'Where?' demanded Barnabas.

'Where do you think? To see Joseph's daughter.'

'You saw Leah?' Joseph wondered.

'No. All I saw was that actor Paris. She had gone.'

'That is not much news,' Silas wheezed.

'I have not finished,' Peter continued. 'I found out where she is. That actor fellow did not want to tell me – but I persuaded him.'

Joseph eyed him. 'You used violence?'

Peter flushed, suddenly aware of all the eyes on him. 'I – I – well, not exactly. I merely encouraged him. A bit ... Actually, I used love. I made him realize I would love to know where she is!' Peter shrugged. 'He finally told me.'

'Never mind all that!' Barnabas exclaimed. 'Where is she?'

Peter started to reply, but Joseph spoke first.

'It does not matter where she is,' the old man said quietly.

The others gazed at him in astonishment.

'You don't want to know?' Peter asked incredulously.

'No.'

'But she is your daughter! Surely –'

Joseph held up a hand for silence. 'I have lost her. It was not her fault. It was mine.'

Peter shook his head in puzzlement. 'Certainly that cannot be true ...'

'It *is* true! You said as much yourself, Peter. How can I blame Leah for not knowing the truth? I kept it hidden from her.' He looked round at all of them. 'We can do no more. She must find her own way back. It must be her decision ... I only hope I'll be here when she returns.'

Leah sprawled on her stomach, her eyes closed with ecstasy. The sun on her bare back would have been delicious by itself, but enhanced by the stimulating strokes of the strigil, it was sheer bliss.

'Turn over,' the Illyrian woman commanded.

Leah did so shielding her eyes against the afternoon sunlight which flooded through the atrium roof. She positioned herself on the mat to take full advantage of the slanting rays of heaven-sent warmth.

Now Teuta kneaded the soothing, sweet-smelling unguent into Leah's flesh. She began with Leah's face, then worked all the way down to her thighs and legs. When this was done, Teuta scooped handfuls of water from the atrium pool, and sprinkled it in a refreshing and cooling shower all over Leah's body. Then the Illyrian picked up the strigil and, with deft movements, started to scrape off the mixture of oil and water, leaving the skin glossy and glowing.

Leah felt like purring. She had been only a few weeks in residence at Minucius' house, but already it seemed as if she had lived there forever. Minucius lay with her ardently every night, and sometimes in the afternoons as well. When Minucius' passion was slaked, he left her to her own devices, and her every need or whim was immediately satisfied.

Rhythmically, the motion of the strigil approached the triangle of hair between her legs. As the bronze instrument reached the sensitive area, its motions became lighter and more delicate. Leah's thighs tingled with awakened desire. She spread them slightly, a little moan escaping her lips.

The sunlit atrium vanished. Leah was transported, as she had been on so many occasions, back to that cold dark floor of the Temple of Cybele. The anonymous bearded face was close to her, panting with the exertions of his brutal fornication, as the cruel thrusts of his hard organ brought her to the edge of a shattering climax.

The insidious movement of the strigil stopped. Leah groaned with disappointment.

Teuta massaged Leah's abdomen with her hands. But the movement of her fingers was probing, curious. Leah opened her eyes with a frown.

'If I were you,' the servant woman suggested suddenly, 'I would cease drinking that chilled wine with your supper.'

Leah was astonished. 'Why do you say that?'

'It is not good for the one inside you.' Teuta tapped Leah's stomach. 'It will increase your nausea – which is bad when one is pregnant.'

Leah sat up abruptly. 'I am not pregnant!'

The older woman laughed. 'Promiscuity should be practised with great care – like anything else.'

'I have never been promiscuous in my life!' Leah exclaimed indignantly.

'You silly child! You need not play the modest maid with me. There is nothing wrong with being promiscuous. Rut with the Fourth Legion if you like, provided – as I have said – you do it with care.'

'What do you mean – do it with care?'

Teuta did not answer immediately. She rose, making her way over to a flower box, by the door. Bending down, she picked something from the soil, and showed Leah a small, smooth, oval-shaped stone.

'Before you let a man mount you,' said Teuta, 'insert this in your sheath. But be sure to say a prayer to Hebe, or have a sorcerer cast a spell on it first. Then, as long as the stone remains within you, no man's seed will ever sprout there.' She tossed the pebble in the pool with a splash. 'But it is too late now – seeing that there is already a loaf in your oven.'

Teuta drew up her stola and squatted on her heels. She lowered her voice confidentially. 'Now you must find a way to get rid of it.'

'How?'

Again Teuta laughed. 'So you admit you are pregnant!'

Finally Leah nodded.

Teuta regarded her penetratingly. 'Well – do you want me to tell you, or not?'

'Please . . .' said Leah in a small voice.

'First, you must make an offering to Hecate. If the Goddess

favours you, that may be enough. If not, more may be required ...'

'More?'

'The surest way would be to have someone insert something like this.' She held up the strigil. 'After enough scraping, they might extract the seed. It is the surest way, as I have said, but it is also the most dangerous. A terrible sickness sometimes results. You can swell and burst inside.'

Leah shuddered. 'What other ways are there?'

'Put yourself in the way of a fright. Sometimes that can cause a woman to miscarry. Jumping, too! Jump from a table often. The shock is good. Sometimes it jars the seed loose. And one can try herbs. Some are very effective. Raw onions, followed by snail's heads without sauce, are particularly good.'

Leah was overcome by revulsion at the idea of abusing her body in any of the ways Teuta had suggested. There was *life* inside her! Strangely she thought of her father. She could visualize the joy on his face at the sight of his grandchild. And the ghost of her mother would be watching too. Leah had severed the bond with her kin, but that child within her still carried their blood in its veins.

'No!' Leah burst out. 'I will *keep* the child.'

'Any animal clings to its young. But you must put aside the natural feeling. No man will want to keep you with a brat tagging along.'

'I don't care! I'll have the child!'

'You are only making it harder for yourself. What if, in the end, you are forced to put the child out to die?'

'I'll never do that!' Leah exclaimed. 'Never!'

She got to her feet, and donned her tunic.

'Where are you going?' Teuta wondered.

'To Minucius.'

'What for?'

'I'll face him now. Tell him the truth.'

The Illyrian woman raised a sardonic eyebrow. 'And what do you think he will say?'

Leah stared at her defiantly. 'Not what *you* think!'

Teuta sighed. 'You know nothing of men.'

'I know that this man cannot get enough of me,' said Leah proudly. Defiantly she left the atrium.

With determination, Leah strode down the narrow hall. She knew exactly where to find him. When she came to the curtained entrance, she paused, mustering her courage, then pulled the hanging aside.

Sure enough, there sat Minucius, reading, his lips moving almost imperceptibly, as he intoned the words softly to himself. In the afternoons, he often came to the shrine to read, or to contemplate, for he liked the company of the goddess and the scent of the perfumed tapers.

Now he looked up and smiled when he saw Leah.

'Come in.'

She moved into the room cautiously. 'I hope I am not intruding ...'

'How could you?' He gestured blandly towards Aphrodite. 'You are already here ...'

Leah felt a flash of resentment. She hated being constantly compared to that piece of sensuously sculpted marble.

'There is something I must tell you ...'

Minucius rolled up his papyrus and regarded her questioningly.

Leah continued. 'Minucius ... I did not say this earlier, because of my deep fondness and affection for you.'

'Then perhaps it should remain unsaid.'

'No. I must tell you the truth. I am with child.'

'Is it the actor's?'

'Does it matter?'

'No,' said Minucius, rising from the chair. 'But what *does* matter is your attempt at deception. You claim to have withheld this confession because of your esteem for me. If you really regarded me so highly, you would have told me earlier. You have only told me now because it will soon be obvious. All you're afraid of is losing your secure little nest here. You care about nothing else.'

Leah could not restrain her anger. 'You forced me to come here!' she shouted. 'You were desperate to have me! I was the only woman in the world as beautiful as that thing!' She indicated the image of Aphrodite.

'I detect false modesty. You really mean you are *more* beautiful.'

'I'm at least alive!'

Minucius controlled his rage with an obvious effort. 'Don't rate yourself too highly. In most ways, even this statue is superior to you. She is neither vain nor selfish nor greedy. Nor is she deceitful.'

'If she is so wonderful,' Leah cried, 'why do you need me? Sleep with her!'

'That's all you understand. You think that hole between your legs entitles you to anything.'

Blindly Leah flew at him, scratching wildly at his face. He staggered back, clutching his bleeding cheek. For an instant she stood still, panting with impotent fury. His unapproachable, indefinable superiority drove her mad, and worse was his insinuation that there were virtues she did not have or understand – virtues which were somehow inherent in the despicable piece of marble.

Suddenly she snatched up one of the iron taper stands. With all her strength she swung it, smashing it into the face of Aphrodite, knocking off the nose of the statue. Minucius was too paralysed with horror to move as she inflicted yet another blow, defacing the beautiful marble cheeks. Then, recovering his wits, the big man moved with frightening speed, seizing the stand as she raised it again, tearing it out of her hand.

Leah turned her fury on him again, but Minucius was far too powerful. He pinned her hands together, and dealt her several stunning slaps in the face. Then he tossed her aside.

'Get out!' he gasped in a choked voice. 'Get out now! I want you out of this house! If I see your face again – I'll kill you.'

His white, contorted face sent a chill through her. She had never seen an anger like this before. In sudden terror she fled.

CHAPTER THIRTEEN

Leah opened her swollen eyes. With difficulty she struggled to her feet, leaning against one of the great temple columns. Her body ached unmercifully, and her stomach knotted with hunger. At least she was not cold, for she had wrapped herself in the cloak she had brought with her. It was the only thing she had had time to seize before running out of the house.

What could she do? Where could she go? Since she fled from Minucius yesterday, she had eaten nothing but some fruit she had stolen from a street stall. With the other life inside her, craving for food was stronger than ever. And she must find shelter too. After a day of aimless wandering, she had crept on to the portico of this temple to seek rest, but she could not endure another such night, huddled on the cold hard stone.

Once again she thought of going back to Paris and humbling herself, but, as she had before, she put the idea from her mind. Surely – somewhere in the great city – there must be a better way for her to live! She would *not* give up yet. She would allot herself the remainder of today at least, in order to find some refuge, hunger or no hunger.

Resolutely, she wrapped her cloak more tightly about her body, and started down the steps. Reaching the bottom, she scanned the area.

Before her lay a grassy field, contrasting sharply with the city sprawling all round it. She had heard her father's friends call this place the Field of Mars, and in some awe they had pointed out the great bath-house which was being constructed not far from the temple. The baths, to be opened to the public, were paid for with funds donated by the Emperor and were to be named after him.

Leah speculated on what life must be like in the court of Rome. She tried to visualize the stupendous state occasions, the sumptuous banquets, and other wondrous pleasures, all of which, she was certain, must be far beyond the luxuries she had known with Minucius.

She forced her mind back to her predicament. Perhaps she could go to the Vicus of the Clothmakers and find some employment there. After all, she had learned to weave as a child. If that failed, she would have to think of another plan.

She set out across the Field of Mars. It was not a long walk and soon she was nearing the Flaminian Way. To her astonishment, it was teeming with people, all pushing and jostling their way towards the centre of the city.

Leah stopped by the road. It was extraordinary to see such a multitude at the break of dawn. And, even more surprisingly, it was not the ordinary, sullen mob – the people were in a holiday mood, some singing, most of them drunk.

A rotund man, carrying a jug, stopped in front of her, appraising her with his satyr eyes.

'My little asparagus,' he sang, 'have a drink.' He thrust the jug at her.

Without hesitation, Leah gulped the thick, sweet liquid, desperate to still the gnawing hunger pains.

'Hold on,' the man protested, snatching the jug away. 'I said have a drink, not the whole lot! You can drink more when we get there.'

'Get where?' The wine sang through her blood, and already her head was spinning.

'You don't know what's going on?' her companion asked incredulously.

She shook her head.

'Everybody is going to the Theatre of Marcellus.'

'Oh,' said Leah, snatching the jug again and taking another drink, 'a pantomime ...'

The stranger laughed uproariously. 'A pantomime! What distant land have you sailed in from?'

'You said it was a theatre.'

'So it is. But today the games are being held there. The Praetor Bibulus is putting on the show, and he's got the best fighters in the Empire – some of them new, from Africa. It will be standing room only, my little asparagus. And Bibulus always furnishes the tastiest food.'

'Food!' Leah exclaimed. 'Is it free?'

'It had better be – if Bibulus wants to be re-elected Praetor next year!'

'Oh!' Leah moaned. 'I am famished! Let's go!'

He squeezed her arm affectionately. 'We're on our way.'

His hands began to rove over her body, but Leah did not care. All she wanted was food.

'Take your hands off my daughter!' a deep but feminine voice boomed suddenly from right behind them.

Startled, Leah and her companion both turned. A big woman was pushing her way towards them. She was middle-aged, fat, with enormous breasts, but there was a solidity about her shoulders which hinted at great strength. In spite of the cool morning air, she was perspiring heavily, her thick make-up running in streaks.

In an instant she was beside them, knocking the man's hand away from Leah. 'You monster!' she exclaimed. 'Trying to billy-goat my little girl, are you? She's just a baby. Get on your way, or I'll break every bone in your body!'

The man obviously had no desire to press matters with so big an opponent. He glared at the big woman, but retreated into the crowd.

The woman favoured Leah with a toothy grin. 'That's the last of him!'

'Why did you say I was your daughter?' Leah murmured.

'Best way to get rid of him. I saw the way he touched you. I've been following you. It was obvious what he had in mind. The city is full of creatures like him. Abduct some child ... When they've finished with her, she's dead in a gutter.'

'I just wanted something to eat,' Leah muttered.

The woman stared at her with apparent concern. 'You are hungry?'

Leah nodded.

'I'll see that you get a meal.' Without waiting for a reply, the woman took Leah by the arm and led her along with the crowd.

'How long since you've had any food?' Leah's benefactress inquired with concern.

'Nearly two days ...'

'We'll be there very soon.' She appraised Leah knowingly. 'Are you running away from something?'

'What makes you say that?'

'Girls of your age who have not eaten for two days are usually running.'

Leah nodded.

'Don't you worry, child. You are all right now. I'll take good care of you. My name is Calpurnia. I own a guest house – an inn near the Milvian Bridge. You can stay there.'

'Thank you,' said Leah. 'You are very kind.'

Calpurnia shrugged self-deprecatingly. 'I like to help young girls in trouble. I'm always taking them in off the streets. Nothing grieves me more than to see some innocent child led astray.'

Leah glanced covertly at her companion. The woman did not look like a doer of good deeds. But Leah was too faint to waste time on speculation.

It was some distance to the Capitoline Hill, and by the time they reached it Leah was exhausted. They followed the crowd off the main road, past the great gleaming Temple of Jupiter, until they reached the banks of the Tiber, where the greyish bulk of the Theatre of Marcellus rose above the neighbouring tenements. Leah could make out the gaily coloured awnings which were stretched about it to ward off the sun. The arched entrances on the lowest level had been thrown open, and the multitude was funnelling its way in through the gates.

There was a solid wall of humanity choking the entrance. But Calpurnia hunched her shoulders and elbowed her way through the press, with Leah following in her broad wake.

The light in the theatre was much softer, filtering through the muslin canopy above, filling the arena with multicoloured rays.

Calpurnia led the way up the steps into the seats. But she did not go far. When she had mounted to the fifth level, she started along the tier. Leah knew that in all theatres or circuses in Rome the best seats were reserved for senators and equestrians. She was certain, however, that Calpurnia was not from the upper reaches of society. Yet here she was, advancing with perfect confidence towards a whole flock of purple-striped togas already filling the choice seats nearest to the sand.

As they passed an aisle, which bisected the rows of seats, Leah noticed two gaily painted women loitering there, calling out familiar greetings to the men who passed. One of them noticed Calpurnia approaching and nudged her companion. Both waved. Calpurnia saw them, but pointedly made no acknowledgement.

'The lowest of the low,' she whispered to Leah. 'Never associate with that sort of riff-raff.'

The two ladies of the morning gave Leah a cold professional appraisal as she passed, and one whispered something to the other. The words were not audible, but doubtless they were not complimentary.

Calpurnia guided her to the section where the purple-striped togas were congregating, most of them having already taken their places on the stone benches. To Leah's surprise, some of the gentry recognized Calpurnia and called to her courteously by name. The big woman acknowledged the greetings, smiling at all of them and putting her arm round Leah as she advanced. Four or five aristocrats rose, offering their seats.

'Take mine, Calpurnia,' invited an elderly gentleman, who wore the toga of a senator.

'There is more room over here,' called another.

Another man patted Leah's cheek. 'What have we here, Calpurnia?' he wondered. 'A new girl?'

'Don't touch,' said Calpurnia with a wink. 'She bruises easily.'

'Indeed!' the man exclaimed, with a gleam of interest in his eyes.

Leah forced herself to smile but vowed inwardly to part company with Calpurnia and her friends as soon as possible. She would wait for only one thing, the promised meal.

'Calpurnia! Over here!' a voice called from one side.

Everyone turned. The voice came from an enclosure, in the middle of the front row. It was a temporary wooden structure, draped on all four sides with purple hangings. The sole occupant was a florid, heavy-set man. He waved at them, and mopped his brow with the hem of his toga.

'We'll sit there!' Calpurnia exclaimed. 'That's Bibulus, the Praetor.'

They made their way down to the place of honour. Bibulus opened a gate in the box and stood aside for them to enter. With great deference, he indicated seats for them.

'It promised to be a lonely day, sitting here all by myself,' said Bibulus. 'But I have been saved by your arrival, Calpurnia. And I cannot imagine any company I would like better.' He kissed Calpurnia soundly on both cheeks. But the entire time, his eyes were on Leah, appraising her thoroughly.

'Who is your little friend?' Bibulus asked, when Calpurnia had taken her seat. 'Is she staying at your house?'

'She's just moving in,' Calpurnia replied. The stout woman glanced round the arena admiringly. 'What a crowd you have!'

'These people haven't come for nothing,' the Praetor asserted, turning to Leah with a smile. 'I brought the fighters all the way from Carthage. Wait until you see them, my child. I'll wager it will be the thrill of your life!'

'She didn't come here to see your gladiators, Bibulus,' Calpurnia said. 'She's hungry.'

Bibulus looked dismayed. 'Indeed! Well – we cannot allow that. I'll start things immediately.'

The Praetor moved to the front of his box and raised both his arms high.

Immediately, from archways leading under the seats, purple-coated trumpeters emerged. As one, they raised their long instruments to their lips, and split the air with a brief, shrill fanfare. Instantly the entire place was silent. All heads turned expectantly to the Praetor's box.

'Welcome! Welcome! I hope you enjoy the festivities today!' Bibulus shouted, his voice echoing round the theatre. 'I only ask you to remember one thing – Bibulus never forgets you and prays that you never forget him!'

A thunderous cheer burst from the spectators. Bibulus acknowledged it by clasping his hands above his head, but it was a few moments before the applause subsided.

Then came the clash of cymbals and the steady beat of drums. A gate at the far end of the theatre opened, and a fantastic sight met Leah's eyes. An elephant decked out in purple plumes led a parade into the arena. First came the musicians, sounding out a stirring rhythm on trumpets, drums, portable water organs and pipes. Then came soldiers dressed in ceremonial garb, followed by the gladiators themselves. Some wore no armour, but were practically naked, each bearing only a large net and a sharp trident. Others were encased in heavy helmets and breastplates, carrying long rectangular shields, but were equipped with javelins in addition to swords. Far outnumbering the small group of gladiators, a large concourse of spear-bearing guards brought up the rear.

Now came another plumed elephant, followed by strutting ostriches, each one dyed a different colour. Behind the birds, cages of snarling wild beasts were wheeled into the theatre. There were lions, tigers, black panthers, and many other creatures which Leah did not recognize.

While this was going on, attendants in purple tunics were making their way down the aisles, distributing food, sweets, and little gifts from great baskets. As one of these men approached the Praetor's box, Bibulus beckoned to him. Obediently the youth came over.

'Leave the basket,' Bibulus commanded.

The attendant bowed and placed the pannier on the floor of the box. Bibulus lifted the cloth cover and indicated that Leah should help herself. It contained cakes filled with raisins, nuts and dried fruit. There were cooked thrushes wrapped in olive leaves and onions, dormice in oil, salted fish, and glazed rose petals.

Salivating with hunger, Leah stuffed the delicacies into her mouth, not caring whether she mixed the sweet with the piquant.

Bibulus watched her with a smile. 'Your girls are always hungry,' he commented to Calpurnia.

'That's because they're lusty and full of life,' she replied.

Leah winced. She would show them how 'full of life' she was when the time came to make her escape.

Continuing to wolf the food, she considered ways of slipping out. It would not be easy, for the box was the most prominent place in the theatre. If she excused herself to visit the latrine, would Calpurnia insist on accompanying her?

She glanced at the arena. Two unarmoured gladiators advanced on to the sand and began tossing blunted spears at each other, missing by ridiculously wide margins. The musicians, who had stationed themselves on either side of the arena, struck up a jerky rhythm, which accompanied the antics of the two clowns. Finally, when they had thrown all of their spears, they drew wooden swords and charged at each other with mock menace. They feinted, thrust, ducked, danced and ended up chasing each other in circles. The audience roared with laughter.

Leah laughed too. It had been a long time since she'd had anything to laugh about. It was an enjoyable sensation. Suddenly she decided to stay and see the spectacle. She could always make her escape later. In fact, it might be easier then. With the mob funnelling through the exits, it would be a simple matter to disappear into the sea of people.

The trumpets blasted once more. The clowns gathered up their wooden weapons and ran off. An expectant silence fell over the theatre. Now the first combatants appeared from opposite tunnels. Armed guards filed in and ringed the sand.

One of the gladiators, Leah knew, would die. The very thought filled her with horror. Condemned criminals, slaves they might be, but they were human, and she had never seen anyone killed. Again she was seized by a desire to flee. Yet fascination held her rooted to the spot.

Attendants took the gladiators' swords, carried them to the Praetor's box and presented them to Bibulus, who ceremoniously inspected them. The shining cruel blades were only a few feet from Leah's face. She gazed at them with fear and revulsion.

Finally the swords were returned to the gladiators. A cheer went up from the crowd.

At another fanfare from the trumpets, the fighters took their positions, confronting each other in the middle of the sand.

The Praetor stepped to the front of his box. 'No mercy will be shown to any man who shrinks from the blade,' he announced. 'So fight bravely! Now let the combat begin!'

Raising their swords, the gladiators began to circle each other warily. Neither opponent made a move towards the other, each searching for an opening. The crowd was quiet, and the only sound was the inappropriately cheerful tune struck up by the musicians.

Suddenly one of the gladiators lunged. The other was ready, raising his shield to parry the blow. There was a metallic clang, as the sword-point struck the boss.

Leah tore her eyes away, looking up at the coloured awnings where the sun filtered through. She was determined not to watch the savage display. Resolutely, she examined the patterns in the muslin stretched above. But she could not shut out the sounds, and she shuddered every time she heard the clash of metal.

Irresistibly, her eyes were drawn back to the arena. The fighters were close together, stabbing brutally at each other, blocking the blows dexterously with their shields. The crowd was beginning to come alive, cheering the combatants on, some starting up a stamping rhythm with their feet. Leah shut her eyes tightly, clenching her fists. She knew that if she saw blood drawn, she would be sick, yet the suspense of the combat was unbearable.

There was a sudden shriek of excitement from the spectators. The din pierced her whole being, reverberating in her head. She had to open her eyes.

One of the fighters was staggering; his shield lay on the ground, and a crimson stain was flowing down his arm.

Leah was amazed. She felt not the slightest sign of nausea! On the contrary – the sight was compelling, thrilling. She could not look away. The injured man was retreating before his advancing opponent!

Then, with a motion so deft it was almost imperceptible, the wounded man scooped up a handful of sand, and hurled it full into the visor of his oncoming enemy, who paused, shaking his head. Taking swift advantage, the wounded man aimed a powerful thrust at the other gladiator's midriff, just missing, as the other sidestepped at the last moment. The wounded fighter stumbled forward with the impetus of his charge, but was able to retrieve his shield, and turned once again to face his enemy. The crowd went mad.

The combatants exchanged blows furiously. One of the wounded gladiator's thrusts found its target, and his enemy's neck spurted blood. Now both fighters were covered with red stains. Leah was hypnotized. Her father and others had often spoken of the beastly addiction of the Roman mob to this blood sport. But now that she was witnessing it, Leah herself was irresistibly caught up in its macabre spell.

The bodies of the fighters glistened with blood from head to foot, and the sand was stained red as well. Leah wondered how much longer these men would be able to stand. Almost as the thought occurred to her, there was another thunderous outburst from the spectators. One of the fighters was on his knees. It was the man who was first wounded. The combat was brought to a rapid conclusion, with the stricken man raising his shield in a pathetic last attempt at defence. But his enemy ran at him, and with all his force drove his sword right through the vanquished gladiator's breastplate, sinking it deep into his chest. A torrent of blood gushed out, as the victim's head bowed over slowly in death.

The audience were on their feet, applauding, screaming, some even throwing things on to the sand. Leah rose too, shouting along with the others.

Callously the victorious gladiator placed a foot on his defeated enemy, and, with a heave, withdrew his sword. The dead man pitched limply backwards, as the victor raised his bloody weapon in triumph, and began to strut up and down, acknowledging the cheers. He removed his helmet, revealing an ugly pale face. Women were leaning over the barrier, throwing kisses at the victor. A few actually swooned with excitement.

'Now there is a man!' Calpurnia exclaimed.

'I hope he hasn't lost too much blood,' said Bibulus. 'I'd like to fight him again. I'll speak to the Lanista about it.'

The cheering subsided, and the gladiator stumbled off towards the iron barrier of the tunnel whence he had emerged. His gait did not augur well for his fighting again in the near future.

'Are you enjoying yourself?' Bibulus asked Leah.

She did not answer, for her attention was taken by an odd movement on the sand below. From one of the tunnels emerged a little old man, with a long white beard. In his thickly gloved hands he gripped a red-hot, glowing iron. As he approached the dead body in the centre of the arena, the ancient one did a ridiculous, capering little dance. Madly he pranced circles round the corpse, kicking up his heels, jumping high in the air, brandishing his hot iron right and left. The audience roared with laughter.

'Who is that?' Leah whispered to Bibulus.

'Charon, the boatman of the underworld,' the Praetor said with an indulgent smile. 'He ferries dead souls across Styx, into that land of shadows from which none returns.'

Bibulus laughed as Charon made a particularly outlandish leap. The Praetor nudged Leah. 'Now watch him ... He's come to claim another one.'

The old man's circles grew narrower and narrower. Suddenly he darted forward, pressing his hot iron to the leg of the corpse. He held it there, until the hiss was audible from where Leah was sitting and the smoke rose from the burning skin. Charon turned, waving the iron in the air again, dancing up and down in triumph.

'That settles it,' said Bibulus with satisfaction. 'He's dead all right.'

Charon made several mock forays at the spectators in the front rows, menacing them with his iron, then he scuttled back to the tunnel from which he had appeared. Immediately a stretcher was carried into the arena by four bearers. They wore costumes as well – little wings on their caps and shoes, which Leah recognized instantly as symbols of the god Mercury. Dumping the corpse on to the stretcher, the 'Mercuries' hoisted their burden up, and made a hasty exit. Meanwhile, other attendants had come out. Some raked away the bloodstained spots, and others sprinkled the area with fresh sand.

Trumpeters stepped forward, and blasted another fanfare. Two fresh fighters appeared. Like the first combatants, they approached the box and began the ritual of sword inspection. One of the gladiators caught Leah's attention. He was a tall, lean man. His helmet bore a distinctive red crest. His limbs had the shiny hardness of ivory and the suppleness of his stance suggested deadly swiftness. He did not look like most gladiators; he was of lighter build. He seemed somewhat older than the other fighters. In fact, there was something familiar about him.

Her heart jumped. It was incredible! Could it be Judah Ben Hur? But an Equestrian like Judah would have no reason on earth to sell himself into the arena. And had not Peter said that Ben Hur had left Italy?

As the fighters took their positions, other memories crowded in on her. When still a child, Leah had heard whispered comments that her father's great friend, the Prince of Hur, had not only been in the Circus but the arena as well. Of course, it was not the sort of thing people talked about openly ...

Bibulus, standing in the front of the box, raised both his hands. 'Let the combat begin!' he shouted.

The gladiators advanced cautiously, testing each other with the ritualistic thrusts and feints which seemed to begin every fight.

Then suddenly the tall man moved, appearing to attack from two sides at once. His blade glittering like a lambent flame, the tall fighter bewildered his enemy, driving him against the barrier which bordered the arena. The one-sided contest was over before Leah could draw another breath. She did not see how it happened, but suddenly the overpowered gladiator pitched to the sand, mortally wounded. His lean opponent turned to receive the acclaim of the crowd. The audience was stunned. It was a moment before a single voice was heard. Only when the victor began his morbid strut round the sand did the shattering applause erupt from the onlookers.

But, despite the encouragement of the crowd, the gladiator did not remove his red-crested helmet. He completed the circuit of the arena and ran towards the portcullis.

CHAPTER FOURTEEN

Leah could hardly sit still for the rest of the spectacle. She was determined to learn the identity of the mysterious gladiator. And the key to that knowledge was Bibulus. But it was the Praetor's duty to preside over the fights, and she dared not disturb him until they were over.

She was forced to remain here in the box, an unwilling witness to the bizarre contests which followed. There were armoured men fighting naked opponents equipped only with nets and spears. Horsemen fought gladiators on foot. Fighters in chariots battled others mounted on camels. In an extravaganza of blood and slaughter, crazed wild beasts were released into the arena – no match, however, for a skilled opponent, who slew the animals deftly with a single spear thrust each.

Finally the bloodbath was ended.

The equestrians and senators were on their feet, lining up to offer congratulations to Bibulus on the success of his games. After what seemed an age, the formalities were over. Bibulus turned to Calpurnia, but Leah caught him by the arm.

'Excuse me, Renowned Sir,' Leah asked, trying to suppress her eagerness. 'The second contest. The gladiator with the red-topped helmet ... Who is he?'

He laughed. 'You're like all the other ladies of Rome. You love a winner.'

'It has nothing to do with that. There's something about him. I think I know him.'

'I have no idea who he is,' Bibulus replied. 'But the Lanista can tell us. I'll –'

'Who is the Lanista this time?' Calpurnia interrupted.

'Crescens, from Massilia.'

'He's an old friend!' Calpurnia exclaimed.

Bibulus turned back to Leah. 'Come along down to the pit. We'll ask Crescens about your gladiator.'

Waving to the senators and equestrians still clustering nearby, Bibulus led the two women down to the path behind the barrier and the first row of seats. They followed him to a stairway behind the theatre, and descended into a dark passage.

They emerged into a long and low room without windows lit by torches. It was bustling with activity; half-naked attendants running to and fro, carrying towels, strigils and many other implements. Stationed at intervals against the walls were the ubiquitous armed guards.

In a cage at the far end of the room, the gladiators were confined, stripped of their weapons and armour, wearing only loincloths. Leah could recognize several of the victors of the day. Nearly all had fresh wounds and were disfigured by a multitude of old scars. They resembled wild beasts behind those bars. But the man she was looking for was nowhere to be seen.

A few gladiators were being taken out of the cage, and led to the tables, where the attendants ministered to their hurts, or massaged them.

'I give the fighters only the best,' said Bibulus. 'I had to get permission from the City Prefect to use the theatre. Normally this is an actors' changing room. Of course I had to make some alterations to it, but it is much better than the pens where they keep gladiators in the Circus.'

'It cost you a lot of money, I'll wager,' Calpurnia observed.

Bibulus smiled. 'It also brings me great rewards.'

'Most of all popularity,' Calpurnia added, nudging the Praetor.

At that moment, a plump little man of middle age wearing a tunic hurried up, and bowed to Bibulus.

'Renowned Sir! Welcome!'

'Well done, Crescens!' Bibulus exclaimed warmly. 'The fighters were superb. It was a demanding audience, but you satisfied them.'

'Your words make me very happy, Renowned Sir.'

'This will make you even happier,' replied Bibulus, handing a money bag to the Lanista.

'My thanks,' said Crescens.

Now, for the first time, the Lanista seemed to notice Leah.

'What a little hazel blossom!' he exclaimed.

'As fresh as the morning dew,' Calpurnia agreed, winking lasciviously.

Leah fought down a hot flush of anger.

She turned to Bibulus. 'I don't see the fighter who wore the red crest.'

'Deadly, isn't he?' Crescens said proudly. 'Faster than a blue lamprey!'

'Who is he?' Bibulus demanded.

Crescens shrugged. 'Who knows? I haven't had him long. Like all the others – he doesn't talk about his past. But we call him "the Fish".' He pointed. 'He's on that table at the far end. Go over and have a look at him. It isn't every day he meets a praetor.'

Bibulus led Leah towards the table.

'I bring a lot of women down here,' Bibulus confided in a whisper. 'You'd be amazed how many of them like to consort with gladiators. Noblewomen too. Of course, most of them won't admit it. But given the opportunity – there isn't one who will say no!'

As the Praetor led her among the massage tables, Leah caught sight of the lean fighter. But he was lying on his stomach. Her pulse quickened...

Leah pointed. 'That's the one.'

They moved over to the man.

'Turn him over,' Bibulus ordered the trainer.

The attendant prodded the naked man with a strigil. 'Over, Fish!'

The Fish obeyed. Leah was sick with disappointment. She realized why the man never took off his helmet. He was horribly disfigured, missing both an eye and an ear.

'I – I don't know him.'

Bibulus laughed obscenely. 'I never thought you did ... Enjoy yourself.'

He patted her arm and hurried away.

For a moment she stood there, surrendering to her despair. With a hideous grin, Fish swung to a sitting position. He pointed to his genitals.

Leah backed away, shaking her head. 'No! No! It's a mistake.'

What was left of the Fish's mouth twisted scornfully. 'You'll love it.'

He started up, but the trainer took him by the arm and pushed him back.

'You heard her say no. She's the Praetor's woman.' He emphasized his point with the strigil, jabbing the Fish in the side.

Sullenly the gladiator reclined on the table again. Clearly he was intimately acquainted with the penalties for rebellion.

Leah hurried away from the tables. Bibulus was nowhere to be seen. There was no sign of Calpurnia either. Leah was filled with relief. She would no longer have to worry about extricating herself from the old bitch's unpleasant society.

'Where are you going?' inquired Crescens, intercepting her.

'To find Bibulus.'

'Oh, no, you're not. You're staying with me.'

Leah stared at him incredulously.

'I just purchased you from Calpurnia,' Crescens stated. 'Paid a pretty price too ... But I think it was worth it.'

He patted her cheek. 'We will get along – you and I. Like my fighters, you have no choice but to do what I tell you. If you do it well, I will reward you.'

Leah controlled her panic. If she made any protest, Crescens would only guard her more closely ...

She mustered a smile and shrugged. 'You will not hurt me?'

He squeezed her breast. 'Not unless you want me to ...'

Leah shook her head emphatically. 'I don't like being hurt! But I'll please you ...'

'I am certain you will! Come ...' The Lanista led her away. As they passed the massage tables, Leah noticed that the Fish was being conducted back to the cage and locked in. Crescens indicated a pile of straw. 'Sit here. I'll be right back. I'll get some wine.'

Glancing towards the stairs, Leah measured the distance. It was much too far. Her eyes returned to the Lanista. He was talking to one of the attendants.

Leah noticed a side door nearby. Hope surged within her. Could there be another way out?

Her eyes flashed to the Trainer. He was still facing away from her. She darted over and tested the door. It was unlocked. Stealthily she opened it and slipped through.

Leah blinked. This room was flooded with light which poured through a grating in the ceiling directly open to the sky. A dreadful stench filled the chamber. It was so overpowering that Leah nearly choked. As her eyes became accustomed to the brightness, she caught her breath with horror. The room was filled with the victims of the day's slaughter. There were piles of corpses spotted with congealed blood, some bloating already and swarming with flies.

She choked, but forced her eyes to search the place. There was only one door – the one through which she had entered. Desperately she looked up at the grating. The bars were close together and far too high for her to reach. She was trapped!

Something on a wooden table in the centre of the room caught her eye. It was fluffy and white, resting on a greyish pile of cloth. The mask, wig, and long ragged cloak of Charon! In a bucket under the table was the iron he had to test the corpses.

Leah darted forward, and seized the mask by its voluminous white beard. She pulled it over her head, then picked up the cloak and wrapped it round her, making sure her gown was concealed under its folds. Now she flung herself to the door, opened it a crack and stepped out.

In the flickering light of the torches, she could not see Crescens anywhere. Her blood racing, she started for the arched entrance, forcing herself not to move hastily. Then Crescens appeared, holding an amphora. His eyes swept the room, searching for her. He looked right at her without recognition. It was going to work. She increased her pace slightly.

'Stop!' Crescens shouted suddenly, charging forward. Two attendants dropped their towels and joined the chase.

The entrance was not far now.

Tearing off the heavy mask, and hitching up the clumsy robes, she sprinted for the stairs. Crescens was right behind her. Lunging forward, he stumbled. One of the attendants grabbed hold of her cloak. But she flung the garment from her shoulders, leaving the man holding it. In a moment she was through the doorway and plunging into the fresh air.

Once through the theatre gate, she fled along the street, diving into the first alley she saw. She could smell the river nearby.

It was not long before she reached the refuse-strewn bank. She paused, gulping the air into her aching lungs. A bridge led to an island in mid-stream, where a temple rose from the waters like some strange gilded ship. She wondered if she should seek sanctuary there, but dismissed the idea immediately. If sanctuary were denied to her, she would certainly be trapped, with no place to go.

Again Leah took to her heels. She sloshed along the muddy bank, climbing over wooden jetties, until she came to tidal flats, which flanked a wider section of the river. Here a barge was beached, unloading cattle. Leah guessed that the herd would be driven inland to the great cattle market, not far from the Forum.

She halted, surveying the banks and listening. There was no sign or sound of pursuit. A row of sheds nearby offered some cover. Moving behind them, Leah sat down wearily on a pile of wood. It was time to assess her situation. Things looked bleak indeed. The best plan was still the one she had this morning. It was the only one, in fact.

'There's no work here!'

Leah tried to smile politely. 'Then please tell me if –'

The woman banged the shutter in her face. Leah pounded on it, but it remained closed.

She turned away, huddling into her cloak against the night rain. The Vicus of the Clothmakers was obviously not going to receive her with open arms.

She considered trying another shop. True, they were all closed – but there was no question of waiting until the next day. She had to find a refuge now.

Smoke was rising from behind the shabby buildings. Her nose caught the odour of cooking meat. She was hungry again.

She started to cross the alley, but a figure carrying a staff materialized from the darkness, blocking her way.

'What do you want?' he demanded.

'Who are you?'

'The Magistrate of the Clothmakers. Now – state your business!'

'I am looking for work.'

'No work here.'

'Surely someone needs an apprentice?'

'No. And we don't allow beggars here either.'

Leah started to speak, but he raised his staff threateningly.

'Be off!'

She retreated hastily, halting only when she reached the end of the alley. There was the inevitable shrine, housing the Lares of the Clothmakers. She shot a look back into the Vicus. The Magistrate was still standing there, watching her. Leah stepped closer to the shrine and spat contemptuously on the grotesque little images of the deities, then fled into the street.

Only when she was certain that the Magistrate was not pursuing her did she stop running. She paused to regain her breath.

Once again, she thought of going back to Paris. The idea was no longer so repugnant. If she were to regard Paris as merely a temporary expedient perhaps a sojourn with him might be bearable. Forcing her throbbing legs to move, Leah pushed onwards.

Leah tramped on and on, through the miry labyrinth of the city. She wondered if she was getting lost. But no – there was the theatre ahead. Passing its barred gate, Leah crossed the street beyond to the lodgings where she had once lived with Paris.

The building was tall and narrow. Paris' rooms were on the top floor, where the price was lower because the fire hazard was greater. But Paris had always insisted that he did not mind living dangerously, provided it cost less to do so.

Leah forced her weary legs up the rickety stairs. At last she reached the top and staggered to Paris' door. She rapped. There was no response. Once again she tried. This time Paris opened it. He stood there, unabashedly naked.

'What a surprise! What do *you* want?'

'Please, may I come in?'

'Why should I let you in?'

'Is it not possible for me to talk to you?'

He grinned. 'Anything is possible.'

He stood aside for Leah to enter. The rooms, which had been somewhat drab during her brief interlude with Paris, had undergone a remarkable transformation. The walls were painted with gay colours and pictures. New shutters covered the windows.

Flowers were everywhere, filling the chambers with a welcome scent. But what caught Leah's attention in particular was the stand for tapers. It was carved to resemble a huge phallus, and held the lights in metal brackets set at intervals along its length.

'Do you like it?' Paris asked.

'It suits you.'

He indicated a couch in the corner. 'Recline, Leah. I will bring you some wine.'

Wonderingly, Leah sagged on to the couch. She watched Paris as he took goblets from a cupboard and filled them. She had not expected this sort of reception. Paris was a man of many whims, but she had never seen him so gracious and polite. It was almost as if there had never been a rift between them.

The actor brought the wine to her. She sipped the cool liquid. Paris pulled a curved chair next to the couch and sat down.

'You're a little pale,' he observed. 'You look as though you've been bled by a Chaldean surgeon. The wine will do you good.'

Leah drank some more. 'I have had a terrible time.'

Paris held up a hand. 'Do not tell me. There is no need.'

'How kind you are!'

'It is not kindness. It is merely that I don't enjoy listening to other people's troubles.'

'I think it *is* kindness,' Leah insisted. 'And I don't deserve it.'

'You certainly don't,' Paris agreed.

There was a moment without words. Leah sighed. 'I am very sorry indeed for the way I treated you ... I can only say I've learned a lesson.'

'Never mind that,' said Paris amiably. He slouched back in his chair, spreading his legs. 'We all make mistakes. We cannot let them get in our way.'

'You hold no grudge against me?'

He shook his head.

'Then perhaps you will let me come back and make amends for the past?'

'You *want* to come back?'

She nodded.

'Forgive me. I must adjust to this. The last time I saw you – you had no use for me.'

'I was wrong. I did not know my real feelings.'

Paris regarded her solemnly. 'Do you know them now?'

'Yes, I want to be with you.'

'Are you sure?'

'Quite sure.'

Paris continued to look at her steadily. Leah had been prepared for a burst of recrimination and scorn, not this seemingly sincere consideration.

Paris spoke again. 'What happened to Minucius?'

'I left him.'

'I'll wager he did not like that!'

'No, he didn't.'

'Did he make a great fuss?'

Leah finished her wine and nodded. 'It was awful.'

'He probably shouted and screamed. Invoked the very Gods to keep you.'

'He did not do that. But he did beg me to stay.'

'On his knees no doubt. When did you make the big decision to leave him?'

'It has taken time. I ... I gradually realized where my true feelings were.'

He chuckled. 'Now, Leah, if there is going to be any future for you and me, it must be based on the truth.'

'I have told you the truth.'

A sly little smile twitched the corners of his mouth. 'I must know for myself ... I have it! We will go to Minucius – you and I. Well face him, and hear it from his own lips.'

'No!' said Leah hastily. 'You must understand. I have my pride. We quarrelled, we ... we ... agreed that I should go –'

'He kicked you out,' Paris interrupted flatly.

She fought down an urge to strike him. The effort made her tremble.

'Say it. He kicked you out.'

'All right – he kicked me out.'

'There now,' Paris said affably, 'was that so hard to admit?'

'No. But I *was* telling the truth about my feelings for you, Paris. I mean that. Really.'

'Of course you do! I would never doubt that for a moment.'

Getting to his feet, Paris came over and sprawled on the couch beside her. 'Do you remember how you used to restore my spirits after a wearying performance?'

Leah nodded.

'Today's performance was particularly arduous ...'

Leah put down her cup. She did not feel like doing what Paris wanted. Never in her life had she felt less like it. But she knew she had to.

Slowly she went down on her knees. She reached out gingerly.

'Not that way,' said Paris.

With loathing she bent her head, not wanting to open her mouth.

Paris began to giggle, softly at first, then louder and louder, until his whole body shook with spasms of laughter. Leah felt the full force of her humiliation. Paris was not even looking at her. Still convulsed with laughter, he was gazing across the room.

Leah turned. A heavily made-up figure, wearing a long diaphanous robe, was standing in the doorway to the bedroom. The gown was expensive and exquisitely feminine, and it was a moment before she realized that a boy was wearing it.

'I was dreaming of goldfish,' the youth pouted in shrill tones, 'thousands of them. And then all this chatter woke me up. That would be bad enough – but now I find you like this, Paris!'

'An old friend just dropped in to say hello,' Paris replied. 'Now be a good boy, Giton, and go back to bed.'

Tears sprang into Giton's eyes. 'You're cruel! You expect me to lie still in the next room while you let her do that to you?' He started to sob.

Paris pushed Leah away, and rose. 'Don't be silly.'

'I *will* be silly!' Giton wailed. 'I'll be silly until you send this cow away!'

Paris guffawed. 'I needed a little stimulation, but you were asleep. I was considering waking you when this gift from the Gods flew in. But don't worry – she's going.'

Leah got to her feet. 'You were lying about taking me back. You did not mean to at all, did you?'

The hairless man looked aggrieved. 'How could I?' His eyes flickered to Giton. 'My bed is already occupied.'

Hot tears flowed down Leah's cheeks. She could think of no

way to strike back at him, and her impotence frustrated her beyond words.

Paris made a gesture of disgust. 'Tears! Always a woman's last resort. I am surrounded by weeping women!' The actor rounded on Giton. 'And you are no better than she is!'

Giton flinched and began to cry again. 'How dare you call me a woman! I hate women!'

Paris laughed. 'I must find a way to pantomime this for my next show. It will make a fortune.'

Suddenly his mood changed. Striding to Leah, he took her by the arm and squeezed it cruelly. I've had enough for one night. Now get out!'

She shook off his hand with spirit. 'I'll go! I should never have come.'

She started for the door, but something caught her eye. It was the pair of jewelled earrings Giton was wearing.

Speechless with fury, she advanced on the boy. 'Those are *my* earrings you've got! Give them to me!'

Giton blanched. 'Your earrings? They're mine.'

'You little catamite!' Leah hissed. 'Give them to me – or I'll kill you!'

'They're mine!' Giton screamed. '*He* gave them to me!' The youth turned on Paris. 'You said you bought them for *me*!' Yet again Giton burst into tears. 'You lied to me!'

Paris rolled his eyes heavenwards. 'By the white bull of Europa!'

'Give me my earrings!' Leah shouted. 'And the rest of my jewellery!'

She moved even closer to Giton, who backed away.

'I won't! I won't! I won't!' he shrieked. 'You stay away from me!'

Leah lunged at him. But he pushed her off and darted towards the bedroom door. She caught him, tearing his gown.

'Paris!' the youth cried. 'Help me!'

Out of the corner of her eye, Leah glanced towards the actor. He was not intervening. Grinning, clearly preparing to enjoy a show, he sat down at the table and poured himself some wine. Let him have his show, Leah thought grimly.

Leah renewed her assault, groping for Giton's ears. Viciously

Giton scratched at her, but Leah did not care. Her hands dug into his neck. He spat in her face, and his fists flailed at her head. He was thin, but wiry and surprisingly strong. Leah was stunned by the buffeting blows. Shaking her head to clear it, she attacked again, striking out as well.

They stood there, exchanging furious punches. Leah's anger was goaded even more by the sound of Paris' laughter. Leaning back in his chair, the actor was bellowing with mirth, slopping wine on the floor.

Leah had been distracted for just an instant, but it was enough to give Giton an opening. He was on her, filling her nostrils with the scent of his cloying perfume. He seized her hair, and began to jerk it so savagely Leah thought he would pull it out. She retaliated, tugging his hair furiously. He screamed. The two rolled on the floor, gouging and tearing at each other. With all her strength, Leah jammed her knee into his groin. Gasping, he released his hold on her.

She grabbed an earring and wrenched it violently away, tearing it right through the flesh of Giton's ear-lobe. Panting with rage, Giton clawed at her fist. Inexorably, he forced her hand open, prised out the earring, and tossed it across the room out of Leah's reach. Now he turned on her, and, with redoubled strength, began to beat her. She staggered back, falling into the phallus-shaped taper stand, overturning it with a deafening crash. The hot taper wax splattered all over the floor. Flames shot up in several places.

Paris leaped to his feet in alarm. Squealing with panic, Giton took up the amphora and emptied its contents on to the blaze. The heavy resinous wine was only added fuel, the flames leaped even higher.

'You idiot!' Paris shouted.

He darted into the other room and reappeared with a blanket, which he threw on to the fire. Then he jumped on it, trampling out the flames. Only when he was sure that they were extinguished did he stop.

The room was silent. All stood motionless for a moment, regaining their breath. Paris' angry eyes surveyed the damage. Abruptly he moved to a leather bag in the corner and reached inside it. When he turned, there was a dagger in his hand. His face was expressionless, but one look at him told Leah that it would be death to remain in this room any longer.

She darted to the door, pulling it open, hurrying out onto the dark hall beyond.

Risking a fall, she clattered down the unlit stairs, until she reached the bottom floor and plunged out into the street.

She started across to the other side, but leaped back just in time to avoid a cart trundling by. Leah tried to regain her balance, but strangely she could not. Her head was swimming. She sank to her knees. For the first time in many hours she thought of the child in her belly. Experimentally she touched her abdomen, then felt between her legs. All seemed well.

In despair Leah got to her feet. She stood in the protection of a doorway as the traffic clattered past.

Just then she became aware of a figure approaching from across the street. Indeed peril had come sooner than she thought! She steeled herself to face the newcomer, but then she gasped with surprise.

Minucius stopped in front of her, his eyes full of compassion.

'I am glad I found you,' he said quietly. 'I waited here last night. You did not come. I've been back several times. I had a feeling you would end up seeking out Paris.'

She hesitated. What should she say to him? She knew her pride would not help her now. It was his sympathy that she needed.

'Paris would not have me,' she said brokenly.

Gently he touched her shoulder. 'I am sorry for what happened between us. I lost my temper. I want you to come back.'

'I too am sorry,' said Leah. 'I broke your beautiful Aphrodite. I know you prized her.'

'Perhaps it was for the best.' He smiled. 'Now there is only one of you.'

She regarded him covertly. It was true. Her rival was gone now. He must want her desperately. And she would see to it that his want became a narcotic he could not live without! She would be dutiful, loving, and kind. She would make him happy as no other woman could. But one day, perhaps one day, she would make him pay for the agony she had suffered since he had sent her away. And if that chance ever came, she would show no mercy.

'The sight of you, Minucius, is the gladdest thing which has ever happened to me,' Leah said. 'From now on I will worship you.'

He cupped her face in his hands and held it up so he could see it. 'I am glad there is only one of you.'

BOOK THREE

BRITANNIA

CHAPTER FIFTEEN

He placed the magic spear against the stone plinth of the altar. Then he lifted the bronze bowl with its marvellously incised designs, examined it carefully to make sure there was nothing impure on its surface, and placed it too on the altar. Flinging back his cowl, he lifted his blue-tinted face, staring at the leaves of the sacred oak, sniffing the fragrance of its acorns. Standing thus, he breathed a silent prayer to Lugh of the Long Arm to prosper his cause. There were many deities of war, but in this phase of the moon Lugh was pre-eminent, and all quailed before his magic spear.

Turning, Dumnorix heaped acorns on the fire until it smoked furiously, hissing and crackling.

He hoped the ancient knowledge of the Necromancers would guide him as unfailingly as ever.

Peering through the thick smoke, Dumnorix surveyed the village, with its round huts perched on their wooden stilts among the trees. The Silures and the Ordovices had been steadfast in their resistance to the Romans, and Dumnorix was determined to keep their spirit strong until the invaders were driven away. The Druid breathed yet another invocation. 'Fill me with power, O peerless Lugh! Make my tongue nimble. Send my words with the speed of an adder.'

Dumnorix had come a long way from the foggy island of Mona, where he and his fellow priests ruled Britain. There were other Druids like him, Dumnorix knew, who were out among the villages and clans, strengthening the will of the warriors to fight. For should the Emperor in that distant place they called Rome be the victor, the Druids' day would be over, and there would be no one to lead the Britons on their final journey beyond the land of the living.

The sorcerer stiffened. They were coming. He could see the chiefs in their robes of squirrel skin descending the ladder from the long house, leading their guest towards the hill. The Druid's lips tightened. He must resist the blandishment of this newcomer, whatever message the fellow brought from his Queen.

Now the procession was toiling up the slope towards the Druid waiting on the summit. Soon they had arrived at the fire. All of them bowed reverently before the ground where the Priest was standing; then, one by one, each moved over to the plinth and kissed its flinty surface. When the ritual was completed, all took their seats on the ground. Dumnorix allowed his eyes to survey them.

'I will listen,' said the Druid finally.

Cimber, the bard, got to his feet and spoke. 'O, messenger from the Sacred Grove of Mona, the mighty Boudicca, Queen of the Iceni, has sent her ambassador with words for us all to hear.'

'I have said that I will listen,' Dumnorix repeated.

As Cimber sat down, the ambassador rose. He was a man of princely bearing, with the supple movements of a warrior. Brushing aside his mane of golden hair, the newcomer took off his cloak, revealing the twisted gold torque which circled his neck.

'Wise Druid,' he said. 'There is no need for me to sing the praises of my Queen or the mighty tribe she rules. I have brought sumptuous gifts from her, tokens of her esteem and friendship for you.'

'Bought with Roman gold!' Dumnorix spat.

Ignoring the comment, the warrior continued impassively. 'I have come on a mission of peace. My Queen lives in friendship with the Romans, and her people are prospering. She is distressed that her kinsmen in the west are still shedding their blood to no avail. Rome has brought peace to the whole world, and my Queen desires that you should allow them to bring it to you as well. Cease this futile fight! Yield to the Romans! Their demands will not be hard.'

When his speech was concluded, the impressive stranger resumed his seat.

Narrowly Dumnorix appraised the reactions of the chiefs, and he did not like what he saw. Clearly the oily words had impressed them. They were nodding to themselves, muttering to each other.

Finally Cimber got to his feet and faced the Druid. 'Sacred Messenger, you have heard the words of the Queen. Shall we follow them? We need your counsel.'

Dumnorix replied with contempt. 'What you have heard is not a message from the Queen, but from her master, the Roman Governor. What this self-seeking Queen calls friendship with the Romans is another word for slavery. She hopes that by persuading us to yield to the same slavery, the Romans will lighten the yoke on her people. She rules a great and populous nation, but it is inhabited by warriors with the souls of mice!'

Ashen-faced, Cimber licked his lips. 'Surely you would not send such a message to Boudicca,' he muttered.

'Druid, I beg you to use caution,' the ambassador added. 'Do not antagonize her with such harsh words. Boudicca is a proud Queen.'

Dumnorix's glare raked the group in front of him. 'You asked for my counsel. You have heard it. The decision is yours.'

He continued to fix them with his burning gaze, but they avoided his eyes, shifting uncomfortably. Silence fell over the group.

Cimber turned to his fellows. 'What message shall we send to Boudicca?' he asked.

Dumnorix could sense the doubts. The Druid knew that any further delay would be fatal. The fears of these leaders would infect the fighting men. Dumnorix knew that the warriors would die for him if he asked them to, and he did not want anything to weaken their spirit. Somehow the fanatic will to keep fighting must be reinstilled in the chiefs – here and now.

'We must not be hasty,' one of the elders was saying.

'Sometimes it takes the most valour to admit it is time to make peace,' said another.

'Let us consult the Gods,' Cimber proposed.

Immediately the others seized on this, expressing their assent vociferously.

Cimber turned back to the Druid. 'Shall I fetch an animal so that we may consult its entrails?'

'No need,' the Druid replied. 'We have a victim here ...'

With a lightning-like motion, Dumnorix drew a long dagger from under his cloak, leaped on the ambassador and plunged the weapon into his heart.

The tall warrior of the Iceni, transfixed, tried to stagger to his feet, but he only swayed, his eyes bulging hideously, then he pitched to the ground. Deliberately the Druid turned the dying man over and extracted the dagger.

Before the eyes of the stunned chiefs, Dumnorix took the bronze bowl from the altar, filled it with the ambassador's blood and poured a libation on the plinth. The warrior, not yet dead, coughed a feeble curse, but Dumnorix paid no heed. Ripping aside the man's garment, he split his stomach open with a slashing sweep of the knife. Immediately the Druid plunged his hand into the wound and pulled out the bleeding intestines. Holding the steaming entrails high, he peered at them.

'The augury is clear,' he announced. 'The war must continue! The Romans must be slain and driven from this land!'

He glared at the assembled chiefs, challenging them to meet his eyes. Then, savagely, he hurled the torn entrails into the face of the expiring victim.

It was a miracle, thought Ben Hur. It happened every afternoon, when the day's march was concluded, but the wonder of it always remained.

The column would halt on the chosen site for the camp. In a preordained plan which had become second nature to them, the Roman legionaries would spread out and set about their assigned tasks. Before the sun even touched the hills, the landscape would be transformed into a little city, a grid of streets separating the neat rows of tents. In the centre, the commander's tent would preside over the headquarters, supply depots and all-important shrines, the whole settlement enclosed by a deep ditch and palisaded rampart, forming a perfect square.

No Roman army ever passed the night without such protection. It was an ironclad rule. By the time the morning's sun rose over the eastern horizon, the city would have vanished, leaving only the hastily refilled ditches and disturbed ground as evidence of its existence. The Legion would be on the march again.

Now it was the end of yet another day. The green Silurian Hills echoed with the shouts of the men as they drove the wagons and mules into the enclosure. Surveyors stood at the four corners they had laid out, holding white flags, while the rest of the Legion deployed, century by century, to its assigned area. At the blast of a trumpet, each man stuck the two stakes he carried into the ground, leaned his shield against them, and from this, made a pyramid of his helmet, pack and javelins. Another trumpet call, and they attacked the earth with spades. Those who were not digging were measuring out the streets or unloading the sausage-shaped tent rolls from the mules.

Ben Hur's glance went to the distant high ground, where the sun glinted on the helmets of the scouts. Between these outposts and the men at work, the cavalry circled restlessly, ready to swoop down on any point threatened by a surprise attack. And, if the need were pressing, the camp builders could easily drop their spades, seize their weapons, and take battle positions under the officers who supervised their work.

As the shovels of the legionaires bit into the earth, Ben Hur reflected on his predicament. Every day he had sought for a chance to desert and make his way to Otho in Spain. Only there, under Otho's protection, could he dare send a message to Joseph and Leah, telling them of his fate.

He had been two months now in this misty land, and the Twentieth Legion was already halfway to the west coast. Isolated in this remote country, enduring the rigours of military life, Ben Hur found himself longing more and more for a peaceful existence with a young wife, who would bring him companionship and perhaps even a family.

But there was no room for bitterness. He was thankful for whatever blessings he had received. At least he had managed to avoid detection. His years as a gladiator had enabled him to acquit himself well in the few skirmishes they had experienced. He only hoped his luck could last.

Gradually he became aware that the men were muttering, throwing sidelong glances at him. Then Ben Hur realized what was disturbing them. It was the soldier Paetus. He had been limping for days, and it was hard enough for him to accomplish the marches, especially since it was his duty as Optio to set the pace for the others. Ben Hur cursed himself. He should have remembered to exempt Paetus from ditch digging. The men were quick to notice anything they thought was unfair and to show their resentment.

'Paetus!' Ben Hur called.

The Optio impaled his spade in the earth and turned to face his superior. 'Yes, Centurion . . .'

'Stop digging and sit down. You've got a bad leg.'

The man shook his head. 'I can dig.'

'I said – sit down!'

'Yes, Centurion.' Paetus took up his shovel, returned to the spot where his equipment was piled, and squatted beside the neat pyramid. Ben Hur watched him. He knew that the leg must be very painful, but Paetus stoically revealed no sign of discomfort.

How fortunate he was, Ben Hur thought, that he did not have to do what they did. He found the daily marches gruelling indeed, but he did not have to carry the pack or the equipment of the common legionary. In addition to the two stakes used in making camp, each soldier bore the burden of entrenching tools, cooking materials, and blankets. Furthermore, being a Centurion, Ben Hur wore a coat of mail studded with embossed metal discs, which was much lighter and more comfortable than the flexible, segmented breastplates recently introduced to the legionaries. Everything was relative, he mused. Although he longed to be free and away from this hard life, his lot as a Centurion must seem enviable indeed to these common soldiers.

When the men had completed the ditch, they clambered up the mound of spoil behind it, and planted their stakes, creating their section of the palisade. Once this was done, they recrossed the ditch and formed up in front of it, waiting for the Centurion's dismissal.

Ben Hur strode along the rank, making a cursory check of his century and their work. He was about to give the word which would send them to their tents when the jingle of harness distracted him.

It was none other than the great General himself, flanked on either side by a dozen aides and standard-bearers, all mounted. And Suetonius Paulinus, Commander-in-Chief of the Province of Britain, was an awe-inspiring sight – as much to his own soldiers as to any enemy. He was bare-headed, his white hair close-cropped, and he rode on a white horse which looked almost as strong as he. The General was well into his sixties, but men remarked that he seemed to grow tougher and harder with each passing year.

Suetonius was blunt and direct, a man who preferred confrontation to diplomacy. In characteristic fashion he was determined to crush the resistance of the Britons. For weeks he had tried to entice the enemy into a pitched battle, but so far they had evaded him. It had not improved his temper.

Ben Hur's contact with the General had been strictly limited. In the skirmishes they had fought, orders had come down from Suetonius through the tribunes, or were relayed by trumpet signals from cohort to cohort. On the few occasions when the legion had been paraded, Ben Hur had received no more attention than any other Centurion.

Eyeing the progress of the General and his staff, Ben Hur waited for them to halt and dismount, but they did not. Instead, they continued to canter closer and closer. Ben Hur drew a deep breath. Perhaps it was his turn this evening.

When each day's march was concluded, and the camp all laid out, it was Suetonius' habit to make sudden spot checks of the fortifications. Most commanders would rely on the reports of their tribunes, but not Suetonius. Of course, it would be impossible to check the entire perimeter designed to house a whole legion and its equipment, so Suetonius resorted to random inspections of the work according to century. Thus each Centurion would have to make sure his men had done their work properly, never being certain when his unit would come under the eye of the General.

Lifting his hand, Suetonius reined his horse to a halt directly in front of Ben Hur, and the entire staff did likewise. Suetonius did not bother to look at the Centurion. His experienced eye ranged up and down the line of men deployed in front of the ditch. Then, lightly, he swung off his horse. Immediately Ben Hur clenched his fist in salute. Perfunctorily Suetonius returned the gesture, his glance disposing of the Centurion like a sword slash.

'Severus, isn't it?' he asked.

'Gaius Severus – Third Century – First Cohort – Twentieth Legion,' Ben Hur rapped out with precision.

The General nodded, then walked past Ben Hur, striding along the line of legionaries. He stopped in front of Paetus, who immediately saluted respectfully.

'Paetus,' said Suetonius. 'Flavius Paetus. Two years' service in Britain. Wounded in the leg at Chalk Hill. If I remember rightly, you held the cohort together.'

'The August General honours me,' Paetus replied, clearly moved by being singled out for praise.

With no more words, Suetonius moved past the soldiers and jumped into the ditch. In one sweeping glance he appraised its contours, the angle of the rampart, and the way the stakes were placed. Then, with equal ease, he vaulted out again.

He strode back to Ben Hur. 'Report to me immediately your men have retired,' he ordered.

Suetonius leaped on to his horse, kicking the beast to a gallop. His suite followed with a great thunder of hooves and clattering of armour, weapons, and accoutrements.

Ben Hur wondered why the General wanted to speak to him. All was not well ... He felt a wild impulse to flee, but suppressed it. That would be sheer folly.

He gave the curt signal of dismissal. The soldiers broke ranks and filed off towards the main gate of the camp.

The night was still. Illuminated only here and there by guttering torches, the lines of goatskin tents resembled hundreds of great sleeping animals. The only movements were the rhythmic metallic glints at intervals along the ramparts, where the soldiers on guard duty ceaselessly peered into the hostile darkness beyond the camp.

Ben Hur left the tents which housed the Third Century of the First Cohort, and turned on to the Via Quintana until he reached the Via Praetoria. A cohort away, this street intersected with the Via Principalis, where lay the larger tents comprising the headquarters of the commander and his staff. Ben Hur reflected ironically on the confusion of the city of Rome at the centre of the Empire, contrasted with the orderliness of a camp on the far-flung borders.

The guards stationed in front of the headquarters nodded, and Ben Hur knew that he was expected. He turned down a narrow avenue until he reached the Commander's tent, at the entrance of which another sentry was posted. Ben Hur halted just outside.

'The General is not here, Centurion,' said the sentry.

'Where is he?'

The man indicated the adjoining tent. 'In the Treasury. He will be back in a moment.'

Ben Hur started for the other tent.

'I wouldn't go in there, if I were you, Centurion,' the soldier cautioned.

Ben Hur turned back with a smile. 'The General said "Report to me immediately your men have retired." An order must be obeyed. Just remember that, soldier.'

Moving to the Treasury, Ben Hur pulled aside the flap and entered.

The place was lighted by torches impaled in the earth.

In one corner of the tent, bags were placed in orderly rows. They contained the regular accounts filed by each Centurion of the Legion. Adjoining these were chests containing money, used for paying the soldiers and other purposes.

In the very centre was a shrine, dominated by the proud golden Eagle of the Legion, high on its pole. The bird was ferocious, its wings outstretched, gripping a thunderbolt in its talons. Surrounded by subsidiary standards and insignias, it seemed to command everything in the tent, including the General, who stood before it.

Suetonius' eyes were closed in concentration, and his lips moved silently, invoking the spirit of the Legion which resided in the Eagle. The prayer concluded, he took up a silver flask, and ceremoniously poured a libation in front of the portable altar. This done, he replaced the flask and turned to find himself facing Ben Hur, who saluted.

'You are prompt, Severus.' He appraised Ben Hur closely. 'You seem surprised. Is it because you find me here?'

'The worship of the Eagle is practised by common soldiers – not generals.'

'I was once a common soldier – but I am no common general!' Suetonius laughed at his own pun, then went on. 'Highly placed men despise the Gods of the ranks, but I don't give a fig for highly placed men. It is the common soldiers who do the fighting and the dying. *They* suffer the wounds. I think *they* know which Gods to worship!' He glanced back at the great golden bird which glittered in the torchlight. 'The hopes and faith of the soldiers have been vested in that Eagle ever since it was given to the Legion by the Deified Augustus. That is why I know it will always guide me well.'

'As it did in Mauretania ...'

'You know about that part of my career!' Suetonius exclaimed, not unpleased.

'You won Mauretania for the Empire. You were the first Roman to cross the Atlas Mountains. You wrote a book about it.'

'You read my book?'

'I did. And it was enthralling indeed – the work of a man who lived what he was writing about.'

'You are not like most Centurions, Severus. They do not spend their time reading. Do you have a library?'

'Once I did ...' Ben Hur replied carefully. 'Not many books, but the best quality.'

Suetonius did not reply. He regarded Ben Hur thoughtfully for an instant. Then he beckoned and led the way out of the Treasury.

Ben Hur followed him across the darkened avenue. The two men passed the sentry, entering the commander's quarters.

Once inside, Suetonius drew closed the tent flaps.

'Why do you call yourself Severus?' he demanded bluntly.

The words struck Ben Hur like a thunderbolt. 'I – I do not understand ...'

'I think you do. *Who* are you?'

The General's question took Ben Hur by surprise. He found himself at a loss for a reply.

'Were you satisfied with your men's work, pitching camp this afternoon?' Suetonius barked.

'I suppose so ... Yes.'

'Yet you allowed them to dig a ditch six feet deep. Regulations call for seven. No one who has been sixteen years in the Praetorians would make an error like that!'

Ben Hur was silent.

'What is your game?' Suetonius persisted.

'My game, as you call it, General, is to be a good soldier – and to serve you well.'

'You are running from Nero, aren't you?'

Ben Hur's eyes met the General boldly. 'Why do you say that?'

'It is not hard to guess. Nero is a madman. Rome is full of plots against him. I hope one of them succeeds. But even though I despise the Emperor, I refuse to make politics my business. The day soldiers start doing that is the day of disaster for Rome. My job is to keep the army strong and great, so that when Nero is gone, the Empire will still be there. You spoke about being a good soldier and serving me well.'

'That's right.'

'Do that – and you have nothing to fear.'

Ben Hur took a deep breath. 'General ...'

Suetonius held up his hand. 'No more talk ... Just remember one thing – in future dig your ditches seven feet deep. Six feet is for a grave.'

Ben Hur saluted and strode from the General's tent. Making his way through the headquarters block, he reached the Via Principalis and stopped.

He looked up at the sky. There were times, Ben Hur had often thought, when it seemed as though some mysterious force had intervened in his life and radically altered its course for some incomprehensible purpose. So it was now.

In the past, Ben Hur had always looked on the Roman army as a ruthless, all-conquering military force. But now that he had seen it from the inside, he realized it was far more than that. It was a superbly organized machine for war, but it was also an agent for peace. When there were no enemies to fight, the soldiers created aqueducts, roads, cities. Indeed, hardly any time ever seemed to pass when the soldiers were not striving to complete some feat of engineering or construction, be it for war or peace. No matter how incompetent the ruler in the Capitol might be, the army continued its tasks as efficiently as ever.

Ben Hur had been two people already. Was he now to become a third? If the General's good will persisted, might there not be a safe and obscure retirement ahead as Gaius Severus, with a pension from the Legion, as one of those many founders of Romanism in a distant province?

It would mean giving up his hopes of settling down with Leah, but perhaps that would be for the best. Even under the most fortunate of circumstances, it would be a long time before he would be with her again. And, should they marry, would it be fair to Leah? After all, Ben Hur was a wanted man. Could he ask her to share a hunted existence?

The shriek of a wounded man cut into his sleep like a knife. Ben Hur tried to shake the fog from his head. Struggling to a sitting position, he groped for his armour. The surrounding gloom was filled with men donning their helmets, seizing shields and javelins. He felt hands on his neck. It was Paetus, holding out Ben Hur's coat of mail. Immediately Ben Hur wriggled into it. Snatching his helmet and shield, Ben Hur hurried out after the others.

'Form up,' he shouted, as he emerged into the cold night air.

The order was hardly necessary. The century obeyed with the mechanical precision created by endless drill, falling into their square battle order just in front of the tent.

Ben Hur glanced about, surveying the situation. The scene was lighted by scores of firebrands, which had been hurled into the camp and were now strewn about everywhere. A few tents were blazing furiously. The ramparts were filled with thousands of struggling men, their weapons glinting eerily in the firelight. Obviously the barbarians were assaulting the camp in great force, relying on surprise and darkness to give them their chief advantage.

With dismay Ben Hur noticed a large group of men locked in combat near the Via Quintana. Clearly a body of the enemy had penetrated the defences, and were now only held back by a dangerously small group of Romans.

Turning to his waiting men, Ben Hur pointed with his sword. 'That way! Quickly!'

Immediately the legionaries advanced at a trot, poising their javelins for the throw.

'No javelins,' Ben Hur commanded. 'We might hit our own men. Use your swords only.'

Obediently the men dropped their throwing spears. There was a swishing, rasping sound as they all drew their swords. The trot became a run as they charged to the attack. Ben Hur followed, and the Romans crashed into the mass of Britons from behind. The legionaries struck first with their shield bosses, to knock the fair-haired warriors off balance, then each Roman thrust with his sword. Taken by surprise, many of the Britons fell, some screaming with agony. But the second rank of Celts turned to face their new opponents, stabbing with spears, slashing out with their long swords. Ben Hur watched his men closely, waiting to see where he would be most needed. But the legionaries were holding their own. Encouraged by the shouts of Paetus, who stood behind them near Ben Hur, the Romans pressed in close to their enemies. The Britons found their longer, clumsier weapons of little use at such close quarters.

Signalling for Paetus to take the left of the line, Ben Hur took the right, joining the struggle only to find himself facing a blood-maddened Briton. The man's great sword was raised high for a blow which woud have split Ben Hur in two, had it ever landed. But Ben Hur lunged in close to his enemy, knocking the Briton's shield aside with his own, stabbing into the other man's stomach.

He pressed forward, ready to meet the next opponent, but the intruders, attacked on two sides, were backing up hastily to the nearest rampart. The two groups of Romans joined ranks and followed. Ben Hur noticed that Paetus, in spite of his lame leg, was up with the leaders. In an instant, the Britons reached the ramparts, clambered over, and retreated to their fellows on the other side.

Behind the palisade, Ben Hur braced himself, waiting for the renewed assault which must surely come. But to his amazement, the enemy withdrew. He looked round. As far as he could see, along the entire length of the rampart, the Britons were melting back into the darkness, and the Romans were straightening up, wearily lowering their weapons.

The sonorous blast of a horn was heard. He looked off towards a grove of oaks from which the sound had come. Illuminated by the flames of torches, a strange procession was approaching the camp.

Ben Hur noted with some surprise that they were unarmed. They flanked an outlandish figure in a long black cloak. This man, obviously a leader of some sort, was middle-aged, gaunt, and wore his hair close cropped. When the procession came to a halt about one hundred paces from the main gate, Ben Hur perceived that the black-clad dignitary had coloured his face blue with woad.

Feeling someone squeeze his arm, Ben Hur turned. It was Paetus. The Optio was looking with distilled malevolence at the Druid. Paetus had always been the most stoic of soldiers. This was the first time he had ever shown any emotion.

'It is Dumnorix!' Paetus hissed. 'I recognize him! Many a time I have seen him – on hilltops – staring at us from the forests – urging his warriors to attack. With magic he drives them. Until they will hurl themselves on the very points of our swords. Nothing stops them – except death!'

Ben Hur's eyes went back to the Druid, who was speaking to one of his warriors. The man trotted forward, daring to come very close to the gate of the camp, where he waited.

An instant later a Roman Tribune emerged from the T-shaped opening. It was Julius Agricola. Ben Hur knew Agricola was already a veteran of several years' service in Britain. An aristocratic career officer, Agricola had achieved advancement because of his remarkable facility at picking up barbarian languages.

An interval passed, while Agricola conversed with the Briton; then each man returned to his own side.

When Agricola had re-entered the camp, there was a stir near the gate. Ben Hur could see that every Roman head was craned in the direction of the blue-faced Druid.

'I wonder what that whelp of a demon is up to,' Paetus growled.

'A truce, no doubt,' Ben Hur surmised.

'Not him!' Paetus exclaimed. 'More likely he's asking our surrender.'

'No!' another soldier cried. 'Look what he has in his hand ...'

Ben Hur strained his eyes into the darkness, and could just make out what appeared to be a bunch of leaves held by the Druid.

'An acorn branch!' Paetus whispered incredulously. 'Then it *is* peace he wants!'

Now a great commotion was heard. Once again Agricola appeared in front of the camp gate. But with him was Suetonius. They were followed by six legionaires without swords, who were, however, wearing armour and carrying their shields.

The Romans approached the Druid and his men, halting only a

few feet away from Dumnorix, who stepped forward, holding up the oak branch. An animated conversation ensued, with Agricola translating, but Ben Hur could not make out any of the words. He watched with avid interest, for he knew that Suetonius had been able to establish good relations with the tribes of the south-east. Would he be able to make peace with this Druid too?

It happened so fast Ben Hur hardly saw it. Dumnorix vehemently threw the oak branch away, whipping a dagger from his cloak. The six Britons leaped forward, thrusting their torches into the faces of the Roman escort. Suetonius knocked the Priest's arm away, but the Druid renewed the attack, slashing at the General viciously. In the meantime, the Roman soldiers, although unarmed, were able to beat off their assailants, and ran forward, covering Suetonius protectively with their shields.

Ben Hur could see no more, for the clearing in front of the camp was suddenly filled with screaming enemy warriors. They materialized from the woods, behind rocks, ditches and culverts. The very ground seemed to sprout them. A large body made for the struggling figures near the gate, but the vast majority launched themselves towards the ramparts.

The shouted orders of the tribunes echoed from the hills, but they were not needed. At the first sight of the treachery, the normally disciplined soldiers had left their posts and were already plunging across open ground to the rescue of their commander.

Now Ben Hur leaped over the palisade as well, followed by all his men. He tried to scramble up the opposite face of the ditch, but already the enemy was there above him, their long blades hacking downwards with awful force. Ben Hur felt himself being pressed back by sheer force of numbers and the necessity of having to fight uphill.

A shadowy Briton, who grasped a spear with both hands, drove the weapon down at Ben Hur's face. He lurched aside to avoid the blow, but the point lodged under the cheek guard of his helmet. Ben Hur thrust upward as hard as he could, and his sword sank into the abdomen of his adversary. The Briton went down, but Ben Hur was assailed by a storm of blows. He cowered behind his long, semi-cylindrical shield, still trying to free the spear from his cheek guard. The double edged point was biting into his flesh, but his involuntary cry of pain was drowned in the din of shouting men and clashing arms on every side.

He was about to tear off his helmet in a desperate attempt to free himself from the instrument of torture when he saw an apparition out of the corner of his eye. It was a skin-clad warrior, with his upraised axe aimed right at Ben Hur's head. Ben Hur wriggled desperately, trying to retreat, but the press of his own men behind him held him where he was.

He blinked. The awful blade had not moved. It was an instant before he realized that the barbarian had no head. The axe slipped from the dead man's fingers, and the decapitated trunk pitched forward. Paetus was standing on the edge of the ditch grinning down at Ben Hur, his sword dripping blood. He beckoned for Ben Hur to climb up.

With huge relief, Ben Hur hurled his helmet off, freeing himself of the spear, then clambered out. He looked round. The men of his century had emerged from the ditch also and were forming up, waiting for his orders. Waving towards the main gate with his sword, Ben Hur started for it. The legionaries followed. Even in the darkness of the night it was obvious that the struggle was the most intense in that area.

Just then his way was blocked by a grotesque figure in a black robe. It was Dumnorix! With an atavistic growl, Ben Hur lunged for him. But the magician sidestepped as nimbly as a dancer. For an instant, the Druid stood there. A croaking sound came from him, like the cry of a raven. Then he was gone. Dumnorix had vanished like a wisp of smoke blown away by a breeze. But his place was taken by a fresh horde of tribesmen, bristling with weapons.

The Romans, however, were now on level ground, and it was easy for them to fall into their customary battle order. Holding their oblong shields firmly in front of them, their sword arms drawn back ready to thrust under the long blades of their enemies, the Romans rushed forward, heads lowered. They crashed into the Britons, who wavered under the shock, but managed to hold their ground, though many fell under the stabbing swords. As was their custom, the Romans fought with full intensity for only a few moments. Then, at a trumpet signal from one of the Optiones, the first line fell back in an orderly fashion, to be instantly replaced by a fresh second line, who ran into the fray with similar intensity. They too fought only for a short time, and, at another trumpet call, were replaced by the third rank.

Ben Hur, coming up on the right, surveyed the confused and rapidly tiring mob of Britons, who fought all at once in a single line. He could see that inevitably, in spite of their superior numbers, they would crumble under the terrible onslaught of the Romans. The legionaries performed their manoeuvres with precision and skill, fighting as though their weapons were part of them.

It happened before he expected. The enemy was broken, fleeing in a disorganized mass towards the woods. Ben Hur looked towards the main gate of the camp. The Britons were withdrawing on all sides. Sections of the Roman army were linking up everywhere now, forming a protective wedge, awaiting any renewed attack.

Ben Hur knew there would be no pursuit of the enemy. For one thing, the horses of the cavalry were still stabled in the camp. And even if the cavalry were available, no Roman commander worth his salt would send them galloping off into the darkness of night, to cross unfamiliar terrain and to be cut off from their fellows. The Romans would wait until a time and place of their own choosing to fight the decisive battle, as was their normal strategy.

Yet again Ben Hur surveyed the scene of the carnage. Bodies were everywhere. Most were Britons, but there was a disturbingly large number of Romans as well. The Twentieth Legion had suffered badly this night.

A sudden cheer from the ranks distracted him. Torches had being lighted round the area where the wounded were being brought. A man with a bandaged arm left the ring of light and approached the soldiers. It was Suetonius.

Bareheaded as usual, the General halted directly in front of the army, still drawn up in battle order. Their cheers grew louder.

Suetonius held up a hand for silence. In a moment, the acclaim of his men died down.

'My comrades,' the General shouted, 'you fought like demons

tonight! You slaughtered these barbarians in true Roman style!'

Another cheer erupted from the ranks, and yet again the General had to hold up his hand for quiet. 'They have killed some of us as well. But I promise you – we will pay them back tenfold! As for that blue-faced sorcerer who leads them – and who nearly did for me tonight – I hardly need tell you what I'll do to him if I catch him.'

Suetonius paused, noticing something on the ground. He stooped and picked it up. It was the acorn branch which Dumnorix had brandished as a token of peace.

An angry mutter rose from the soldiers, building into a threatening roar.

'I'll tell you one thing,' Suetonius bellowed. 'I won't give *this* to him!' He waved the oak branch. 'I'll stuff it down his throat after I've crucified him!'

The army roared its approval.

Ben Hur wondered if the General would ever make good his threat. He recalled how nimbly the Druid had leaped away from his sword, and then inexplicably vanished. It had been uncanny. And even now he could hear the strange cry the magician had uttered. He had a premonition he would hear that cry again.

CHAPTER SIXTEEN

The numbing weariness hung like heavy weights on his limbs. He had not thought of his age much recently, but tonight he had been forcibly reminded of it. Suetonius, Ben Hur had noted with envy, though even older and slightly wounded as well, had shown no sign of flagging energy and at this very moment was in his tent engaged in a wild wassail with his officers.

Ben Hur glanced towards the ramparts. The guards were at their usual posts, their armour glinting dully in the grey light which was beginning to appear in the east. It was hard to believe they had been fighting for their lives only a short time ago.

When the camp had been put in order, the men had filed to the shrine, one cohort at a time. There they had given thanks to the gold Eagle of the Legion for bringing them victory. It was expected that a Centurion would join in the rite, but that was not the only reason Ben Hur had made his offering along with the others. The Eagle's spirit was palpably present, an emanation compounded of the concerted belief of all the fighting men who had followed the great bird.

The act of worship completed, Ben Hur had done his duty. He had visited the tents of his century, one by one, congratulating his men, trying to maintain the rapport which was indispensable to his function. Each tent was meant to house eight soldiers, though after this night's action many held less. But the legionaries were not bemoaning their losses. They were celebrating, not a man of them asleep. They were all tired, gaunt and hollow-eyed, but the fever pitch of victory still sustained them. Ben Hur had exhorted them to seek rest, but his pleas had fallen on deaf ears. The men must have consumed at least a week's ration of sour red wine, ignoring the abstemious week which would certainly follow.

More than anything, Ben Hur wanted to stretch out in his tent and close his eyes. But one more duty remained. He headed for the tent next to his own, which was alive with ribald laughter.

Pushing aside the flap, he entered. The interior was illuminated by oil lamps. Rumpled blankets were strewn all over the earthen floor. All eight men had survived and were addressing themselves with gusto to skins of wine, shouting, laughing, boasting. These were the leading men of the century. There were five Optiones, including Paetus, two standard-bearers and a signaller named Longinus.

'Centurion!' yelled one of the standard-bearers. 'Have a drink!'

The man hoisted a huge, full skin of wine from the ground and lurched forward. Ben Hur waved him away, then crossed to Paetus, tapping the Optio on the shoulder. Paetus turned, blinking, trying to concentrate on his officer.

'Paetus,' said Ben Hur solemnly, in a voice for all to hear. 'I could not let the night pass without thanking you.'

'For what?' Paetus demanded.

'For saving my life.'

'Oh, that!' The Optio laughed, seizing a skin and taking a deep drink. Then, wiping his lips, he fixed Ben Hur again with bleary eyes. 'You should not thank me. It was just an impulse. I obeyed it without thinking.'

'And if you had thought,' Ben Hur wondered, 'what would you have done?'

'I might not have been so hasty. If I had let that barbarian split you in two, I might be a Centurion by now.'

The Optiones shouted with laughter.

'Have some,' the standard-bearer insisted again, shoving the wine skin into Ben Hur's hands.

'Come on, Centurion!' another called out. 'Join the celebration.'

'That's right,' Longinus chimed in. 'It would be an offence to the Gods for any throats to be dry tonight!'

Ben Hur did not want to offend any Gods, but neither did he enjoy getting drunk. And tonight, of all nights, it was the last thing he wanted to experience. He pushed the skin away. 'I'll be thinking of you men on the march tomorrow, when you are trying to hold up your aching heads as well as your packs.'

'Forget tomorrow,' Paetus urged. 'We won't need to be alert. Those barbarians won't be back. Not after the lesson we taught them.'

'You are more confident than I am. Defeat will never stop them. They are driven by something we do not understand.'

'Let them come,' Paetus slurred. 'We'll give them the other side of our swords!'

'You'll have the opportunity,' Ben Hur assured him. 'They'll continue their attacks. It does not matter to them how many men they lose. They have thousands more to call on. As for us – our numbers are limited. Hundreds of Romans were killed tonight. We dare not lose many more.'

'The Centurion is right,' a voice said.

They all glanced in the direction of the speaker. It was Longinus. The Signaller continued. 'Seventeen years ago, when Claudius was still Emperor, I joined the Legion. I had only been here a few days when I experienced my first battle. I have never seen one as big since. We fought the combined tribes, both Ordovices and Silures, under their greatest leader, Caratacus. We won a crushing victory. Caratacus fled, but was later captured. The tribes seemed to be smashed. The war should have been over. That was sixteen years ago. We're *still* here, fighting that same enemy!'

A cloud of gloom settled over the whole group. 'I worked on a farm near Tarentum,' said one of the Optiones finally. 'I joined the Legion because I hoped one day to use my discharge pay to buy a farm of my own and have a family. But I fear that I will never see Tarentum again. I'll end up here in Britain with some crow picking out my eyes.'

'Shut up!' Paetus growled impatiently. He snatched a wine skin from a comrade and took another drink. 'You're forgetting something. The Eagle. It has led the Romans to the ends of the earth and back again. As long as it is up there, showing us the way, nothing can stop us!'

Ben Hur wiped the sweat from his brow. Someone had told him once that it never got hot in Britain. He could not remember who it was. But he wished with all his heart the person were here now, marching with the Legion on this humid August day.

The soldiers kept up a steady, brisk pace in time to the beat of the drums. Ben Hur emphasized the rhythm, swinging his vine staff. His glance travelled along the impressive column, which curved like a giant snake down the sloping, hilly terrain. Each man carried his pack suspended from a pole with one hand and a pair of javelins with the other. All were bareheaded, their helmets hanging on straps from their right shoulders.

Suetonius' soldiers were ready for battle. The General was dangling the bait. But Ben Hur was certain that the Druids would think twice before assaulting this formidable column.

In the distance, in the lead, gleamed the armour of cavalry and scouts. Next came the vanguard of two cohorts and a detachment of auxiliaries, blunt-headed Germans from beyond the Rhine. Not far in front of Ben Hur was the General himself, mounted on his stallion, surrounded by his staff. Immediately behind Suetonius marched the Legion's standard-bearers. Most prominent and honoured of these was the one wearing a bearskin head-dress, who proudly bore the golden Eagle. Following this group came the First Cohort, of which Ben Hur's century occupied the third position from the lead. Behind the First Cohort marched two more cohorts and auxiliaries. Additional cavalry brought up the rear, surrounding the wagons and the pack animals which carried the supplies and artillery.

Ben Hur had seen this sight many times now, but he never failed to be impressed by it. His eyes lifted and gazed at the golden Eagle, seemingly on fire in the sunlight, the thunderbolt in its talons flashing.

He glanced back at his century. Every man of them, he realized, must have a terrible hangover – especially in this heat. But none showed it, each enduring his private misery like the practising stoic he was. Ben Hur noticed Paetus' bloodshot eyes flickering in his direction, almost as if challenging the Centurion to find fault with the pace he was setting.

An order from Suetonius caused Ben Hur to look forward. The Legion was approaching a wood. Tribunes were galloping off to the cavalry at the front and rear of the column.

When the General's orders reached the horsemen, they dismounted and led their beasts back to the main body of the Legion. The light-armed auxiliaries fanned out on all sides, forming a protective screen to guard against surprise. Only now did the column risk taking the path which led into the woods.

Ben Hur knew that the formation Suetonius had adopted was a classic one, employed by all Roman armies since the days of Augustus. In those times, three legions commanded by General Varus had suffered a fearful disaster in the wilds of Germany, marching into just such a forest. Varus, an impetuous and headstrong man, had been seeking for months to crush his elusive enemies in battle. Knowing this, the Germans had enticed him into the trees, and then, as the Romans stumbled along lost, picked them off one by one until they were slaughtered to the last man.

A movement overhead interrupted his morbid reflections. It was a bird, circling high. At first he thought it was a hawk, but then he recognized it as an eagle. Suddenly it plummeted, making straight for the standard right in front of Ben Hur. Silently it soared just above its gleaming effigy, as if fraternizing with its fellow.

Some of the soldiers saw it and broke into shouts. Others lifted their eyes in the same direction. Soon the whole column was cheering loudly, acclaiming this auspicious omen. Suetonius glanced up as well. He grinned at the soldiers, raising his clenched fist in salute.

A moment later, with powerful strokes of its great pinions the eagle winged rapidly away. All along the ranks the men were chattering excitedly. The Centurions cursed, trying to silence them.

Soon they were under a thick canopy of trees, which shut out the sky completely. As they marched, the ranks fell silent. Their ebullience seemed to be submerged in the forbidding gloom of the forest.

Instinctively Ben Hur lifted his gaze to the Eagle of the Legion. Even its brilliance seemed to be dulled. Then he caught his breath sharply. A dark shadow was moving through the branches just above the standard. With a thrill he realized it was the live eagle, ghosting silently through the trees, accompanying its golden comrade.

A quick appraisal of the troops told Ben Hur that none of the others had spotted it. It would be wiser, he decided immediately, not to call attention to it. In the fastness of this forest, it was far more important for the legionaries to concentrate on keeping their formation.

In fascination Ben Hur watched the movements of the bird. With an uncanny sense of direction it glided along, evading branches and leaves, as if guided by some supernatural hand.

The regal bird's wings moved with sudden urgency. It shot forward silently, disappearing among the trees ahead.

For a few moments, he searched for it in vain. Then his eyes caught something else – a dark shape, crouched on a branch which overhung the advancing column. It was a man clad in skins which blended marvellously with the surrounding trees. The apparition was grasping a spear poised to hurl straight down at the approaching Roman General.

Ben Hur tossed away his vine staff and shield, dashing forward. He knocked aside the startled standard-bearer and leaped on the General from behind, pulling him from his horse – just as the assassin's spear grazed the saddle, thudding into the earth right next to the rearing animal.

In a flash Ben Hur was on his feet again, snatching a javelin from the nearest soldier, looking up.

Like a squirrel, the Briton leaped from his perch to an adjoining tree. With all his strength, Ben Hur hurled the weapon. It sailed upwards, impaling the barbarian's thigh. The Briton did not even cry out. Savagely he tore the iron point from his own flesh, tossing the spear down. Then, as if he had suffered no hurt at all, he resumed his swinging flight from tree to tree.

By now the Syrian archers who comprised one of the auxiliary cohorts had strung their bows, and were sending shafts hissing after the assailant. But to no avail. The Briton had long since disappeared.

Trumpet signals and shouted orders from the Tribunes called the Legion to a halt. The men grounded their packs and arms, waiting. A buzz of speculation began to travel through the ranks. But almost instantly it was silenced by the harsh reproofs of the Centurions.

Ben Hur walked back to the General. Suetonius was on his feet, dusting off his ornate, shining cuirass. He grinned at Ben Hur.

'It seems I must express my gratitude,' Suetonius said.

'I know the whole Legion rejoices that you are unhurt,' Ben Hur replied. 'I only regret the javelin did not kill the barbarian.'

'I'm glad it did not kill him ...'

Ben Hur frowned. 'Why?'

'Think of the nice big trail of blood he's leaving.'

'The German scouts?'

The General nodded. 'They'll track him down. At the worst, they'll kill him. At best – he might lead us to the nest where these Druids roost. How I have dreamed of finding it, Severus! If we can only crush the Druids – we'll stamp out the very root of resistance!'

Ben Hur nodded, saluted, then turned to resume his post.

'Severus. How did you know he was up there?'

Ben Hur paused with a smile. 'Something made me look in the right direction. Perhaps it was the God you worship ...'

A nasal snorting from the depths of the bracken told the beaters that their quarry was still there. The warriors were dressed as if for battle, baggy trousers laced tightly up to the knees, their long, blond hair carefully braided. They carried bronze-coated shields and heavy broadswords.

Suddenly the grunting became a vicious whistle. There was a stirring in the shrubbery, and the great boar's head emerged, low to the ground. The muscles in the beast's shoulders twitched, ready for its charge. The beaters lifted their swords, striking their shields with the flat of the blades. The clanging resounded through the woods, and the animal drew back into the thicket, bellowing furiously.

Not far off, under a spreading oak, the royal party waited. Tasgetius, the ancient Councellor, regarded the slim woman beside him with a smile. He was proud of his niece. After all, the Queen was in middle life; it would have been understandable if she had remained by the comfort of her hearth while the hunters provided the meat for the great feast. But Boudicca had insisted on being present.

Tasgetius breathed a silent prayer of thanks to the Divine Cernunnus. The God had blessed them, for the beaters had run the boar to earth early in the day. Boudicca could return to her dwelling, rest and restore her strength for the night which was to come. She would need all her wits about her.

He moved closer to Boudicca, pointing down the path towards the thicket where the cornered boar growled its defiance.

'This monster will do nicely,' said Tasgetius. 'If we hunted all day, we would not find a bigger one. I think you should retire, my Queen.'

There was a hint of reproach in Boudicca's eyes. 'Retire?' she asked.

'You have blessed the occasion with your presence. Now I will call in the hunters for the kill.'

'I will kill the beast.'

Tasgetius blinked with astonishment. 'You? But –'

'Yes!' Boudicca insisted. 'Catus Decianus is the Roman Procurator, the emissary of a great Emperor. For such guests our ancient Kings always slew the game with their own hands.'

'This custom has not been practised for generations,' Tasgetius reminded her.

'It is time we returned to the old ways,' the Queen replied haughtily. 'The strength and pride of the Iceni must be restored. I will set an example. If I do, those who accuse me of being weak will have to find new slanders. I will be taken more seriously.' She smiled. 'At least by the boar. Now give me the spear.'

Another elderly man stepped forward. Segovax, like his brother

Tasgetius, wore his white hair long, and was clean shaven but for the enormous moustaches which drooped well below his chin. His thin, veined fingers anxiously rubbed the gold torque which encircled his neck. 'You should not attempt this,' he admonished Boudicca. 'You might be killed.'

'In that case, Uncle,' said Boudicca, 'either you or Tasgetius will have to kill the boar. And whoever does will rule in my place.'

The two old men stared at each other with resignation. Boudicca held out her hand. 'May I have the spear?'

Tasgetius shrugged, then beckoned to a tall young warrior.

The youth came forward, offering the weapon to the Queen. She took it, hefting it experimentally. Mounted on the heavy oaken staff was a wicked-looking blade nearly as long as a short sword. Immediately below the head of the spear was a crossbar, so that the weapon could not penetrate deeply enough to prevent its being withdrawn.

Grasping it tightly in her slim hand, the Queen stepped out alone on to the forest path.

As Boudicca moved towards the thicket where the beaters held the boar at bay, Tasgetius watched anxiously. To look at, his niece was an unprepossessing woman. She was small and not particularly attractive. At first glance, one would suppose she was a wife and mother who had raised her children and settled down to enjoy her latter years in peace. And that was exactly what Boudicca had been – until a few years ago, when the course of events brought out an unknown side of her character.

Her husband, King Prasutagus, one of the first to establish friendly relations with the occupying Romans, had died suddenly. He had left the rule of the Iceni jointly to his wife and his allies. Everyone expected that the Romans would take over and that Boudicca would be pushed back into oblivion. But instead, while pursuing her husband's policy of good relations with the Romans, she had asserted herself as ruler of the Iceni with great determination, showing fairness and wisdom in all her dealings.

Tasgetius caught his breath anxiously. Boudicca had halted about thirty paces from the thicket. The old man's lips moved in a silent prayer for her success.

Carefully she selected her position, then took up her stance, gripping the spear with both hands. The movement, the weight of the weapon, revived long-dormant memories. As an adolescent, she had accompanied her father on many hunts. That worthy chieftain had been determined that his daughter would be just as knowledgeable about weapons as childbearing. She had learned to hit the boar exactly right, killing with one thrust. She wet her lips, wondering if she could still do it.

Boudicca lifted her left hand in a swift gesture, signalling that she was ready.

Warily the beaters advanced on the thicket, rattling their shields with their swords, until the forest reverberated with the din.

There was a heavy thrashing in the bushes. With a roar of anger, the boar broke cover. Almost on its belly, the creature crept towards one group of beaters. More violently than ever they pounded their shields, coming inexorably closer to the boar.

Snarling, the beast retreated into the brush again, only to emerge on the other side and to be similarly driven back. In a panic, it darted to and fro, and was repelled each time. Finally the crazed animal stopped, slavering pendants of saliva dripping from its jaws. The only escape was towards the lone hunter who waited silently.

Without warning, the boar swung round. Lowering its tusks, it charged full speed at Boudicca.

Grimly she held her ground as the monster hurtled towards her. She remembered her father's advice. Never watch the tusks! Keep the eye fixed on the hump just behind the shoulder . . .

Boudicca did so, concentrating, until all she could see was that dun-coloured circle of fur. She waited until she could almost feel the tearing impact of the tusks. Then, with every vestige of strength in her body, she lifted the heavy weapon and drove it at the oncoming spot. The blade sank in easily up to the crossbar, and she knew even before the creature shrieked in agony that she had struck the heart.

A shout of triumph broke from the bearers and the royal party. The Queen was surrounded, all the warriors and counsellors congratulating her on the kill. Both the aged uncles embraced her in turn. Tasgetius was weeping.

Boudicca savoured a glow of satisfaction. Well she knew that the tale of this hunt would be flying through the settlement the moment they returned. And in a few short weeks the Queen's exploit, transformed into epic verse, would be added to the songs of the bards in every village in the land. Truly the ancient way was the path to the hearts of the people!

Soon the boar was ready for its journey to Boudicca's citadel. The animal's feet were trussed over a stout wooden pole, which two of the men hoisted on to their shoulders.

Laughing and shouting, the procession started off. Boudicca took the lead, revelling in the sounds of the forest and the springy softness of the turf under her feet.

The Queen found herself wishing she had brought her daughters on the hunt. She had considered it, but finally decided against it. Instinctively she had felt that Brigantia and Sulevia would not take kindly to such a suggestion.

Times were changing, and Roman ways were gradually creeping in everywhere. Unlike Boudicca's ancestors, the Romans did not train their women in the same skills as men. Fighting and hunting were not the pastimes of well-bred Roman ladies.

Sulevia and Brigantia had become more like Romans than Iceni princesses. As a conscientious mother, she had discouraged this, but she knew that to some degree it was inevitable.

A strange smell, wafting through the trees, abruptly recalled Boudicca to her immediate surroundings. It was the sharp, pungent odour of burning acorns. The warriors smelled it too, glancing at each other questioningly, slowing their pace. Then the party rounded a bend in the track and came to a ragged halt.

A mysterious black-robed figure sat by a fire which blazed on the path ahead. His face was hidden in the shadows of his deep cowl. At the sight of the hunters, he rose and drew back his hood, revealing his hawk-like face, stained with woad.

Boudicca heard the gasp of terror behind her. She glanced at her retinue. All, including her uncles, regarded the Sorcerer with dread. They seemed on the verge of flight.

'Wait here,' she told them, hoping that the sound of her voice would reassure them.

She turned and approached the Druid, who awaited her impassively. Boudicca halted not far away from him. Deliberately the Priest lifted his robe, revealing his bare feet. He stepped forward on to the fire, treading on the red-hot embers until they went out.

He showed no sign of pain. When he had finished, he regarded Boudicca thoughtfully.

'Why have you ignored my messengers?' the Druid demanded.

'Because I knew what you wanted,' Boudicca replied, 'but I have sent a messenger of my own, an ambassador of peace to the other tribes.'

Dumnorix shook his head sadly. 'That was a serious mistake. The tribes lust for Roman blood – they believe in their own destiny. Your spineless words might rouse them to violence.' He paused, then added silkily, 'I hope no harm comes to this ambassador of yours ...'

The Sorcerer picked up some charcoal, rubbing it thoughtfully into his hands and hair. 'You have turned your back on your ancient allegiance to the Druids ... Why?'

'Because you are mad! You will sacrifice anything to fight the Romans. I too love the old ways. But not so much that I would destroy my people.'

'If you really cared for your people, you would be at war with the Romans too.'

Boudicca shook her head. 'I will never make war unless I can win more by victory than I might lose by defeat.'

A croaking chuckle bubbled up from the Druid.

'Peace!' he sneered. 'The Romans steal your crops! They drain your wealth, cripple you with taxes! They humble your nation! That is the peace of slaves.'

Boudicca felt anger blaze inside her. Since childhood, she had been imbued with respect and fear for this priestly order, but that was gone now. 'Who are you to censure me, you blue-painted demon!' she shouted. 'I see what *your* way has brought – nothing but death and defeat!'

'We are standing close to each other ... There is no need to shout. Just answer one question honestly. If you could go back to the life of your ancestors before the Romans came, with all the land and wealth once again in the possession of your people ... would you not prefer that?'

'If all rivers flowed milk, we would not need cows.'

Dumnorix made an impatient gesture. 'What I am talking of is possible ...'

'Your words come easily, but they are like the wings of death.'

'You must listen,' the Druid insisted.

Boudicca shrugged, waiting for him to continue.

'The Romans have discovered our most cherished secret,' he said softly, 'our Sanctuary on the Island of Mona. They are on their way to attack it. I prayed this would never happen! But it has, and now I realize it is a divinely ordained sign. Do you –'

'My patience wears thin and your breath stinks!' Boudicca snapped. 'Say what you came to say, and be done with it!'

'We can turn this to our advantage,' Dumnorix insisted. 'The Roman General has taken the strength of his armies to Mona with him. If all the nations of the Britons rise now, together we can overwhelm the remnants of the enemy which remain.'

'And what will happen when the Roman comes back from Mona?'

'His reinforcements and supplies will be gone. He will be outnumbered in a hostile land, unable to replenish his strength. We will destroy him! The Iceni are the most populous tribe in Britain. Will you lead us?'

'Not one step!' Boudicca replied firmly.

'That is your final word?'

'It is.'

'You will change your mind. When you do, you will find me.'

Without answering Boudicca turned her back on the Druid and rejoined the hunting party.

Dumnorix watched them go. Contempt soaked through his spirit, staining it with hatred. How he despised people who sought the easy way – the safe way – as Boudicca was now doing. But there never *was* an easy way. In the end, suffering and hardship would always come. It was better to seek it out, embrace it, and never live apart from it.

Even as a child, Dumnorix had known that embrace. Boys chosen for the Priesthood of the Necromancers were taught to endure pain by having hot irons laid on their bare flesh. Dumnorix still bore those brand-marks and took pride in them. At the age of ten, with no ability to swim, he had been flung into a deep, icy pool and left to save himself. On far-off Mona, where he had learned the arcane secrets of the sorcerers, flagellation had been a daily ritual.

He had found the supreme joy of his life when he had gone out into Britain, his face now wearing the woad, and experienced the shrinking fear and awe with which the tribesmen regarded his magic. To this day, he lived only for the ultimate fulfilment which this power gave him.

Yet this very power was now threatened by the Romans. At all costs, they must be stopped. And if this weak-kneed Queen continued to help them, she too must be removed.

CHAPTER SEVENTEEN

It was mid-day when the hunting party reached the citadel. They mounted the slope towards the earthwork ramparts, the bearers sweating under the load of the heavy carcass.

Passing the cattle grazing on the hillside, they reached the timber gates, which stood open, as they always did during the daytime. Even before the hunters entered, Boudicca could hear the babble of excited voices coming from the common ground in the centre of the settlement.

Within, a festive sight met her eyes. Right by the well, which stood between the circular dwellings on their stilts, a wagon of many colours was stopped. Clustered round it were the people of Boudicca's clan, eagerly examining the wares displayed in front of them. Nearby, watching over his goods, and occasionally making a sale, stood a stocky, grey-headed figure. Boudicca knew him only too well. It was Milo, the Roman trader.

Milo smiled when he saw the royal party approaching. Putting down a sample of cloth which he was showing to one of the women, he went to meet the Queen.

Boudicca made a sign, and her retainers halted. With obvious relief, the bearers set their burden on the ground. The trader bowed.

'A lovely day, great Queen,' Milo rasped in his throaty voice. 'I looked for you earlier, but I did not find you.' He surveyed the boar admiringly. 'I see you've been hunting.'

'Hunting instils reverence for the Gods,' Boudicca replied. 'It reminds us how mortal we are.'

'That is the one thing I do *not* want to be reminded of!' He pointed to the boar. 'Who stuck this overgrown pig?'

'I did.'

The trader's eyebrows went up. 'It took a lot of stomach to face up to a beast like that.'

'I've killed bigger ones.'

'That's what I like about you Briton women. You're strong and lusty, by Jupiter!'

She caught the look her uncles gave each other. They did not approve of Milo's familiarity with their Queen. But, of course, as they grew older, they approved of less and less.

Boudicca waved Milo away. 'Go back to your trading, Roman.'

'I will – before your people rob me blind. Perhaps you'll grant me an audience later.'

'Perhaps,' she said with a smile.

Milo bowed and was off.

Tasgetius and Segovax sucked their teeth, and wagged their heads.

'That insolent spawn of a whore –' Segovax began.

The Queen held up her hand for silence. 'He means no harm. It is only his way ...' She turned to the bearers. 'Take the animal. Dress it, and prepare it for the evening.'

Beckoning for her uncles to follow, Boudicca started for the Long House, which lay at the end of the common ground.

As she went, Boudicca cast another glance towards Milo. He had unsealed two earthenware jars of spices and was holding them out seductively for the Iceni men and women to sniff.

Boudicca remembered that he had been standing exactly thus when she had first laid eyes on him four years ago. How she had resented and hated him then! A symbol of the Roman conqueror. An ex-legionary himself, Milo had been plying his trade up and down the Iceni lands. Boudicca, new to power, and fearful of antagonizing the Romans, had not dared to forbid Milo access to her country, but she had steadfastly avoided all personal contact with him.

Then, the year before last, the harvest had been very poor, and grain stocks not sufficient to last the winter. In that dark season, it looked as if her people would starve. But Milo's coloured wagon had appeared one blustery day, laden with casks of salted meats, fish and other preserved food, for which he had refused any payment.

Her uncles had insisted that the Roman had an ulterior motive, seeking only to buy their good will and thus ensure himself greater profits in times to come. But Boudicca thought otherwise. She had consulted a seer. He had sacrificed an animal. The shape of its entrails confirmed the Roman's sincerity. From that time on, her relations with Milo had improved and grown steadily into a warm friendship.

Reaching the Long House, Boudicca mounted the steps. Tasgetius and Segovax followed, breathing heavily.

As usual, she paused near the entrance to allow her eyes to adjust to the dimness within. She was always gladdened by the familiar odour of her home, a strange mixture of the pleasantly musky skins which draped the walls and windows and the sweet-smelling, fresh rushes strewn on the floor.

The great communal bed dominated the room, and, as always, seemed to offer an invitation to rest and reflect. But all thought of repose vanished when her eyes became accustomed to the darkness.

Two figures were waiting in the shadows on the far side of the bed. They were her daughters, but hardly recognizable. The light Tyrian silk of their long Roman stolas left one shoulder bare, accenting the shapely, nubile figures. Their hair was piled high, in elaborate, stylized coiffures which reminded the Queen of herons' nests. But worst of all – their faces! Their cheeks were painted such a stark white it seemed as though they had been drained of every drop of blood. Their lips were the colour of rotten-ripe cherries, and their eyelids daubed purple.

'If this is some new jest, acquaint me with the humour of it,' Boudicca commanded sharply.

'It is no jest,' said Sulevia, whirling round to display her tall, slender figure, 'it is the new style.'

The other, Brigantia, regarded her mother with a winning smile. 'I hope you like our new clothes.'

Boudicca studied them with distaste. 'Is that what you are wearing? Clothes? And what have you done to your hair?'

'It took all morning to prepare,' Brigantia replied, patting her curls.

'When we were in Londinium for the great market, all the Roman women were wearing their hair up,' Sulevia added. 'The Aedile's wife had hers plaited exactly like mine.'

'Milo says they wear it even higher in Rome,' her sister asserted. 'Sprinkled with gold dust.'

'Milo!' Boudicca exclaimed. 'You got these gaudy rags and face-paints from him!'

'I have warned you about that Roman,' Tasgetius' sepulchral voice intoned from behind her.

The Queen rounded on her uncles. 'Be quiet! Both of you! Let *me* deal with this.' She faced her daughters again. 'Take off those ludicrous things!'

'We were going to wear them tonight!' Brigantia protested.

'Yes,' Sulevia added. 'As a compliment to the new Procurator. Surely he will appreciate our greeting him dressed as his own countrywomen do.'

Boudicca surveyed her daughters sardonically. 'You really think that will make a good impression?'

'But of course,' the taller girl insisted. 'How can it do otherwise?'

'You silly creatures!' Boudicca cried. 'Our guest is an important magistrate. He lives his daily life among the richest Romans. No matter how closely you try to imitate their clothes and paint – to him you will never be anything more than figures of fun. You will look like Iceni trying to be Romans. Be Iceni, because that is what you are. *That* will earn his respect more than anything else!'

Brigantia regarded the Queen reproachfully. 'Mother ... You are *so* old-fashioned!'

Boudicca appraised the girl. Though Brigantia was shorter and sturdier than her older sister, the Queen was well aware that she would be no less attractive to men. Sometimes the sight of her daughter's round, innocent face filled Boudicca with apprehension. The new world which was engulfing Britain seemed to be teeming with unscrupulous people, only too ready to take advantage of such a child.

'Go from my sight!' Boudicca said gruffly. 'Do not come back until you have put on proper clothes and washed your faces.'

Once again Brigantia started to protest, but Sulevia, with a look at her mother's flashing eyes, took her sister by the arm, pulling her away.

With an odd mixture of amusement and irritation, Boudicca watched them retreat from the Long House. Finally she sat down heavily on the gigantic bed.

'Was there need to be so harsh?' Tasgetius inquired tentatively.

The Queen regarded her uncles with exasperation. With their sad, reproachful eyes, exaggerated by their long, drooping moustaches, they looked exactly like ageing hounds who could no longer run with the rest of the pack.

'Do you really think I was too harsh?'

'Frankly, yes,' Tasgetius replied. 'One must not expect too much from girls so young.'

'The green sapling bends with every breeze,' Segovax added sagely. 'Blame the wind, not the twig.'

'If you must be harsh,' Tasgetius continued, 'be harsh with that Roman trader. He comes here ... dangles his gaudy wares in front of impressionable girls ... What do you expect? Not only does he pervert our young, he shows no respect to you, as a Queen.'

At that moment, the skin curtain which covered the entrance was pulled aside. Milo stood there, grinning at the two elderly men. 'I believe I heard my name mentioned ...'

'You did indeed,' Boudicca laughed. 'We were discussing the corrupting influence of your trade on the morals of our young people.'

With dignity, Tasgetius and Segovax withdrew, bestowing disdainful looks on Milo as they passed.

'I know my friends when I see them,' the Roman observed wryly.

'They have a point, Milo. What do you mean by selling my girls vulgar clothes and stinking ointments? Surely you know better than that.'

Milo's eyes twinkled. 'You should have seen their faces when they laid eyes on those silks! I could not resist them. So I gave them the garments – and I threw in some cosmetics too.'

'You *gave* them?'

The trader nodded. 'And I have a gift for you as well.'

Before the amazed Queen could speak, Milo handed her a bag of squirrel skin.

'Open it,' he said.

She loosened the string and extracted an ivory figurine. The surpassing loveliness of its contours took her breath away. 'I have never seen anything like it,' she murmured.

'It is an ancient image of Isis – from Egypt. May she bless your days, Boudicca.'

'You still have not told me the reason for the gift.'

'Must one always have a reason for everything? You Iceni are so suspicious!'

'It is the curse of our race. Now, out with it, Milo – why the generosity?'

He shrugged. 'Why does one usually give a gift? Because of regard and esteem for another person.'

Boudicca smiled at him warmly. 'Thank you, Milo.' Her fingers stroked the delicate ivory of the statuette. 'I shall cherish it.'

He took the figurine and fastened a leather thong to a ring on its back, then he looped it over the Queen's head. For an instant their eyes met in silent affirmation of their friendship.

'I have a present for your uncles too,' he said jovially.

'Surely not!' she exclaimed. 'You know how they dislike you.'

'That is why they will like my gift.'

'What is it?'

'My absence. This is my last visit.'

'Why?'

'I'm retiring. I've been wandering all my life. I've been a soldier, sailor and merchant. The time has come for me to put down roots before I get too old. So I will buy a little piece of land somewhere.'

'We'll miss you, Milo.'

'Paths which have crossed as often as ours may cross again.'

'We must ensure that they do.'

Milo bowed, and when he spoke again, it was in his usual bantering tone. 'And now, O great Queen, it is time for me to take my leave.'

'So be it. May your Gods go with you ...'

Milo snorted derisively. 'They have not displayed much interest in my travels so far. But I certainly hope you are right!'

With a jaunty salute, Milo strode to the door and disappeared.

Her hand went to the image round her neck. She held it up and studied its ivory face. She fancied that it looked sad, as Milo had for an instant. Boudicca felt pity for Milo. He *was* a wanderer. And now, belatedly, he was trying to settle down. She hoped with all her heart he would succeed.

The sun was sinking towards the western hills, but the gates to the citadel were still open. Normally they would be closed well before sundown, the watch posted round the palisade, the animals herded from their grazing in the ditches into the safety of the village. It was ancient custom, however, to leave the gates open all night when an important guest was to be received. This was the highest sign of welcome and hospitality, and Boudicca was determined to impress Catus Decianus with her friendship for Rome.

She hoped that her posture was regal, sitting here on the dais of pelts in front of the Long House, shaded by bullhide awnings lashed to poles set in the earth.

The smell of the roasting meat assailed her nostrils. The common ground was filled with cooking carcasses, mostly sheep, but also a few rabbits. On the spit nearest her seat was the huge carcass of the boar she had slain. Its flesh would be reserved for her, the uncles, her daughters, the Procurator and his staff. She was ravenously hungry and eager for the banquet to begin.

Boudicca's seat of state was positioned at the summit of the hill. Over the conical roofs of the Iceni dwellings within the ramparts, she had a clear view into the valley below. But so far there had been no sign of her awaited guest's approach.

'The messenger said the Procurator would be here before sunset,' Tasgetius murmured for the tenth time.

She smiled at the uncles, who shared the dais on the right-hand side.

'He'll be here,' she insisted.

Her eyes moved to her left, where Brigantia and Sulevia sat. Their faces were scrubbed clean, and they wore gowns of sheepskin trimmed with rabbit's fur. Boudicca felt a surge of motherly pride. At last they presented an image befitting the princesses of such a renowned tribe. Soon it would be time to select good husbands for them.

At that moment, a young warrior dashed into the canopied enclosure.

'They are here!' he gasped. 'Many soldiers.'

As one, the Queen, Tasgetius, Segovax and the two girls stood up, shading their eyes against the rays of the setting sun.

Not far away, at the base of the hill a cavalcade of mounted men was starting to ascend the slope towards the settlement. There were at least a hundred of them, their weapons and armour glinting ominously. The column was accompanied by a score of pack animals.

'It seems he has come ready to do battle, not to enjoy hospitality,' Segovax observed.

'The escort is only a precaution,' said Boudicca. 'It is a long journey from Londinium.'

'Through friendly country, ruled by you,' Segovax reminded her. 'I think he does not trust you.'

'Not trust me!' she exclaimed. 'If that were true, all he had to do was to summon me to Londinium. But Decianus has chosen to come all the way out here to pay his respects to me. Surely that means something!'

Soon the horsemen were riding through the open gate. On reaching the centre of the settlement, they dismounted. Boudicca noted how they spread out, each Roman taking a position, as if it were a military exercise. One of them, a balding, heavy-set man of middle age, remained on his horse, appraising the layout of the citadel. Finally his attention settled on the royal dais, and he too dismounted. He whispered a brief word to the officers who flanked him, then started forward. A half-dozen of his staff accompanied him. Two were in the uniforms of military tribunes, while the others wore civilian tunics and cloaks.

The balding dignitary halted only a few feet away from the Queen, his officers remaining respectfully behind him.

With a little bow, the Roman spoke. 'Do I have the honour of addressing Boudicca, Queen of Iceni?'

'I am she,' Boudicca replied. 'You are Catus Decianus, the Procurator?'

'I am. I bring you greetings from Caesar Augustus Nero, as his sole representative in this province.'

'I am grateful,' Boudicca replied. 'When you next communicate with the Emperor, convey my respects to him. Assure him of the continued allegiance of the Iceni nation.'

'I shall do so. In fact, I shall be sending dispatches as soon as I return to Londinium. So perhaps we should get our talks underway. There is much to discuss ...'

'Surely you and your men will eat first. We have prepared a great feast.'

Decianus surveyed the roasting boar, sniffing the aroma appreciatively. 'Very well ... I'll confess we did not expect such a warm welcome. I am certain my men will prefer fresh meat to their rations.'

He stepped over to a tribune and muttered instructions; then all the Romans moved away.

There was something in Decianus' manner she did not like. He had spoken of "talks" as if there were something at issue between them. As far as Boudicca knew, the Procurator's visit ought to be a pure formality. The Iceni had a treaty with the Romans, and in the past it had been enough merely to affirm their allegiance.

Leaving their horses for Boudicca's grooms to herd into the stables, the Romans moved over to the banquet area, the whole crowd of them finding seats by the fires.

Boudicca rose and clapped her hands sharply. Immediately four Iceni youths ran forward, taking the pelts from the dais, and spreading them round the fire where the boar was cooking. Then they trotted off towards the Romans.

Nodding to her uncles and her daughters, Boudicca took her seat for the feast. The old men and the princesses did likewise, eyeing the boar hungrily. A moment later, the youths reappeared, leading the Roman officers, indicating they should sit with the Queen.

Boudicca introduced her family to the Romans. Decianus, in turn, presented his two Tribunes, Macer and Victorinus. They were young for such high rank but, apart from that, seemed to be typical Roman officers, hard-faced, implacable, cold-eyed.

She noted that the Procurator did not bother to introduce the rest of his staff. Their civilian clothes seemed somewhat out of place in this military group. None of them had Equestrian rings. Boudicca concluded that they must be of lower social status. Perhaps the Procurator had brought them along for some sort of clerical duty.

When young women approached, bearing bowls of warm water, Boudicca beckoned to the Roman officers.

'It is our custom,' she announced, 'to bathe the feet of all honoured guests, as a gesture of welcome. But since there are so many of you, our Gods will be satisfied if we confine the ceremony to the commander and the Tribunes.'

'Curious,' Decianus grunted. 'Some of the Semitic tribes practise the same ritual.'

While half a dozen young Iceni girls performed the ceremony,

Boudicca eyed the newcomers. Every one of them was wearing sword and dagger. The Iceni did not permit weapons at meal times. However, in view of the Romans' military traditions, she decided that it might be politic to ignore the matter.

When the formalities were concluded, and all had taken their places, Boudicca studied the Procurator's plump face keenly. It gave no hint of his intentions. With an inward curse, Boudicca realized that by asking him, she would only reveal her own anxiety. She would have to remain silent.

Women hacked off great chunks of the roast boar and served the group round the fire. The Procurator clearly had only one thing on his mind at the moment – satisfying his appetite. Without waiting for the smoking meat to cool, he stuffed it into his mouth greedily, licking his fingers.

At that moment a serving woman approached, bearing a large amphora and goblets.

'Would the Distinguished Procurator care for wine?' Boudicca inquired, trying to sound casual.

Decianus' eyes widened with surprise. 'Wine! I thought you Britons only drank milk.'

Boudicca nodded. 'That is still the custom for most of us, even today. But I also know Romans prefer wine. You will find this a good Falernian ...'

Decianus was clearly delighted. The serving woman filled cups and handed them to the Romans. The Procurator sniffed the liquid and took a sip. He sighed. 'Queen Boudicca – indeed you are a most thoughtful hostess. I will not forget this kindness.'

Boudicca glanced at Brigantia and Sulevia. They were not eating. Normally they had robust appetites, but tonight they seemed uncomfortable. Boudicca looked across the fire and realized the cause of the uneasiness. Macer and Victorinus were staring at the maidens in a manner which was not hard to interpret. Boudicca's lips tightened. She resolved to send her daughters to the Long House the moment the meal was over.

Suddenly Brigantia leaped to her feet, snatched Macer's cup and dashed its contents over both Tribunes.

'Ugly vultures!' she snarled in the Icenian tongue. 'You look at me like that again – I'll kill you!'

Boudicca jumped up and pulled her daughter away.

'Brigantia! What are you doing? They are guests.'

Brigantia's eyes flashed. 'I don't care who they are! They look at me like a paid woman!'

'Sit down!' the Queen ordered sharply.

Her cheeks still flushed, Brigantia resumed her seat.

Boudicca turned apologetically to the Procurator.

'You must excuse my daughter.'

But Decianus only laughed good-naturedly.

'Do not chide your daughter,' he said. 'My officers are to blame. They've been too long without women.' He turned to the Tribunes with mock severity. 'Keep your eyes on your food!'

Macer and Victorinus glanced sullenly at their commander, then returned to their meat, saying nothing. But they did not look at the girls again.

Hastily Boudicca beckoned to the serving woman, who poured the Romans more wine. With gusto, Decianus drained his cup.

'What a feast! I shall be most reluctant to leave here.'

'The Iceni are renowned for their hospitality.' She smiled with studied politeness. 'Stay as long as you wish.'

'Unfortunately I cannot. I must return to Londinium the moment my business with you is concluded.'

Boudicca could restrain her anxiety no longer.

'What "business" do you refer to, Procurator?' the Queen demanded.

Stuffing another piece of the meat into his mouth, he wiped his hands on his tunic. 'I have come to collect the loan repayment you people owe.'

Boudicca was astounded. 'Loan repayment! We have received loans from nobody. Certainly not the Romans!'

'No? What about the money the Emperor Claudius loaned you?'

'That was a gift! To celebrate the signing of our treaty of friendship.'

'Not according to my superiors,' Decianus insisted. 'And, according to them, you can well afford to pay. They say your husband left a large treasure when he died.'

Boudicca glanced at her uncles. Segovax and Tasgetius were expressionless, but she knew what they were thinking.

'We have been loyal allies of Rome,' she said, trying to keep her voice moderate. 'Certainly Rome will not repay our loyalty by extorting gold from us!'

'It was a loan,' Decianus repeated. 'If you thought otherwise – you made a mistake.'

'This is outrageous!'

The banquet ceased. Both Romans and Iceni were getting to their feet, staring in the direction of the altercation. With an effort, Boudicca remained seated, for she knew that if she rose, it would signal the end of the festivities.

'I am not accustomed to being shouted at,' Decianus said ominously. He added sarcastically, 'Even by a Queen.'

'I would not be much of a Queen if I did not object to injustice!'

'Injustice! We have been indulgence itself! We would have been content to forget about repayment of the loan. But we are fighting an expensive war with the tribes of the west, to ensure the continued existence of the peace and prosperity you Iceni are now enjoying. It is only fair that you share some of the burden.'

'You talk of fairness! Then let us start with honesty. Do not give me these shameful lies about loans! If the great and mighty Romans need help, ask for it! I will send warriors!'

The Procurator regarded her with thinly disguised contempt. 'I fear we would have no use for them. I have orders to collect only money.'

Boudicca was aware of the resentful murmur from her people. She got to her feet. The Procurator did likewise.

'Roman,' she said harshly, 'I will not give you a piece of worthless lead!'

Decianus made a signal. She could see the Roman soldiers, grey shapes in the twilight, leaving the feasting area and taking up their arms.

Boudicca was not intimidated. 'The Iceni warriors in this citadel are few. No doubt your escort outnumbers us. But very near here there are hundreds of other forts similar to this one. Some of them are just over the next hill. I have only to send word – and by dawn I can have ten thousand fighters at my back!'

Decianus smiled unpleasantly. 'I will be finished long before dawn. Now – the gold your husband left – bring it out!'

'There is not enough gold in this citadel to pay for the disaster you will bring down on yourself – if you do not leave immediately.'

Decianus regarded her with mock surprise. 'You threaten the envoy of Caesar?'

'If Caesar himself were here, I would say the same thing.'

'No doubt. I would expect nothing less from a barbarian.'

The word 'barbarian' stung Boudicca to the core. With the back of her hand, she struck him across the mouth.

The Procurator staggered backwards. He touched his lip, then looked at the blood on his fingers.

'You need instruction ...' he hissed. He turned, shouting. 'Victorinus!'

The Tribune stepped forward, awaiting the Procurator's orders.

Decianus pointed at Boudicca. 'Give her ten lashes!'

Victorinus started towards her, but Segovax interposed himself. 'She's the Queen of the Iceni!' the old man gasped, his voice trembling with indignation. 'You shall not touch her!'

Tasgestius joined his brother. But Victorinus pushed the uncles aside and beckoned to Macer. The Tribunes dragged Boudicca towards one of the poles supporting the canopy. But then they were hit by two furies.

The princesses attacked, tearing and scratching. For a moment the astounded Romans endured the assault until a group of soldiers hurried up and jerked the young women away. Then the Tribunes thrust the Queen into the arms of two cavalrymen.

All around the clearing, the angry Britons pushed forward, but they were blocked by Roman swords. A Decurion stepped forward, shouting, 'Do not come any closer! Or you will all be killed.'

Boudicca saw her people hesitate. They were few, and their weapons lay useless in their houses. She prayed that they would do nothing foolish.

She groaned inwardly when one of her warriors rushed at the Romans, his dagger drawn. He was cut down instantly. The other Iceni fell back. The cavalrymen drove them towards the huts.

Decianus turned to Victorinus and Macer. 'Get on with it ... I said give her ten lashes!'

The Tribunes nodded to the soldiers, who tied Boudicca's hands to the post. Brigantia and Sulevia suddenly tore free of their captors, but were seized by the two Tribunes, who pinioned the sobbing girls' arms.

The Procurator smiled cruelly. 'If you want to amuse yourselves with them – do so. Perhaps then you will cease your complaints that I allow you no women!'

The Tribunes did nothing for a moment, as if astonished by their commander's sudden generosity. Then Macer tore the sheepskin garment from Sulevia, exposing her body. At the same time, Victorinus threw Brigantia to the ground and held her there, despite her struggles.

Boudicca could not cry out. A giant's hand seemed to squeeze her throat, choking her, as she watched the Romans rape her daughters. The whip struck her, but she did not feel it.

She was hardly aware when the blows of the whip had ceased. Decianus was standing before her. 'Where is the gold?' he demanded.

Boudicca spat full into his face.

The Procurator wiped away the saliva. 'Cut her free,' he ordered surprisingly.

An officer moved to obey.

'Perhaps we will keep your daughters a little longer,' the Procurator suggested. 'The rest of my men would like a chance at them. It is up to you ...'

'No!' she gasped. 'Let them go!' With a shuddering sob, she looked at the Roman with hate-filled eyes. 'Take your gold! I'll give you everything I have! But you must let them go first!'

CHAPTER EIGHTEEN

'Do you have any trouble with mice?' Milo asked.

'Never,' Ulpian assured him. 'I keep four cats, and they are included in the price.'

Milo tried not to appear too eager as he surveyed the stout little house. A display of enthusiasm could only undermine his bargaining position. True, this was exactly the sort of place he was looking for, but four hundred sesterces was just too much money. Experienced trader that he was, it was not hard for Milo to frown sceptically. The stocky owner watched him with obvious anxiety.

Experimentally, Milo trod on the pounded clay floor. Then he stepped over and rubbed the coat of whitewash covering the walls of wattle and daub. Kneeling, he inspected one of the timber supports where it was sunk into the ground. As he thought, there was no sign of rot. He was sure the house was in good condition, but nevertheless he checked the shutters.

'Loose,' he commented.

'I'll fix it,' Ulpian promised. 'Three hundred and eighty sesterces and the house is yours.'

'Why are you selling?' Milo asked suspiciously.

'My wife inherited some property just outside Londinium.'

'Why don't you sell that and keep this?'

'Because I can make a fortune from her land. Londinium is growing so fast that my wife's property is almost in the town now. I'll build some shops on it.'

Thoughtfully, Milo gazed up at the rafters of the roof 'I don't know ...'

'Come outside with me. I'll show you something.'

Ulpian moved over and took a javelin from a hook on the wall. 'I carried this in the Ninth Hispania ...' he smiled. 'It's a little rusty now.'

'Ninth Hispania, were you? I was in the Fourteenth Gemina.'

'Indeed! One of the best legions – the Fourteenth.'

Ulpian led the way to the low doorway. Milo followed him out into the substantial garden. It was a long strip of land stretching behind the house, separated from the neighbouring dwellings by wattle fences.

After walking a short distance, Ulpian stopped, indicating the soil at his feet. 'Watch this ...'

He placed the point of the javelin on the ground, then, revealing surprising strength for a man of his years, he gripped the shaft with both hands and drove the spear deep into the earth. It sank in fully halfway. Ulpian regarded Milo triumphantly. 'Topsoil ... And there's more even farther down. You could grow anything here ...'

Milo gave the property one more searching look, then faced the owner. 'Three hundred and fifty.'

'Done.'

Milo offered his arm, and Ulpian took it, clasping it up to the elbow.

'Let's have some wine and celebrate our agreement,' Ulpian proposed.

'A brilliant idea.'

'Crassus, my old Decurion, runs a wine shop at the end of the street. None of that stuff the Britons brew. This is shipped in from Rome!'

Leaving the javelin embedded in the earth, Ulpian walked back to the house. Milo entered behind him. The two old soldiers crossed the large room, Milo taking a proprietary look as they went.

Coming out of another door, they stepped into the street. A cold wind was blowing in from the sea, which was not far off. Milo glanced up and down the unpaved road. Camulodunum was a new settlement, and quite undeveloped, but it was expanding fast. He surveyed the rows of similar wattle houses, all overshadowed by the grey colonnaded front of the huge Temple of Claudius on high ground at the far end of the street. As yet, this was the only monumental stone building in the area. But it was a sign that Britain was becoming less of an outpost and more of a civilized part of the Empire. Milo decided that he could be happy in this place.

A short walk brought them to a house somewhat larger than the others. They entered.

Inside, it was quite similar to the dwelling which Milo had just purchased. Squatting on the clay floor, several old veterans were playing knuckle bones. There were other men, seated on wooden benches which flanked tables in one corner of the room, drinking quietly or dozing.

Crassus, an amazingly scarred man, limped forward and was introduced to Milo. Learning that Milo was about to become one of his neighbours, Crassus grinned, revealing his two remaining teeth. 'I'll let you have a pot of Falernian as my dedication to your hearth. No charge! But I want your word that you'll always bring your business to me if anyone else opens a drinking place in Camulodunum. And that is bound to happen.'

Milo duly made the promise, and Ulpian ushered him to one of the tables. Both men sat down with a sigh. A few other veterans came over to join them and were presented to Milo. A moment later, Crassus brought the jug of wine. Producing some cups from the pocket of his leather apron, he wiped them, and placed them on the table next to the jug. Soon Milo was sipping the wine, undiluted like a true legionary, enjoying the sensation of warmth creeping through his limbs.

'I have told you all about my plans,' Ulpian said. 'Now tell me what you have in mind – once you have settled in the house.'

'I'll cultivate the garden. Perhaps open a little shop. But most of all – I want to find a wife and plant some seed of another kind. Somehow I don't fancy the idea of departing this world without leaving someone behind me.'

'That will be a more difficult task than you think,' one of the men said.

Another nodded his agreement. 'Not too many Roman women in this land.'

'What is wrong with Briton women?' Milo wondered.

'Nothing,' said Ulpian. 'But you know how it is – one tends to go with one's own kind ...'

Milo made a scornful gesture. 'I'm not so choosy. Look what happened in Gaul. Not much more than fifty years ago Romans and Gauls were like oil and water. Now no one can tell the difference any more.'

Ulpian was about to reply, but paused. All of the men heard it. It was a distant commotion outside – shouts, cries, the hubbub of a large group of people.

'Noisy town, this ...' Milo observed.

'Not at all,' said Ulpian. 'It is usually very quiet.' He listened. 'I wonder what is going on ...'

'I'll go and see,' Crassus announced. He wiped two more cups on his apron, put them down and went out.

Ulpian took a drink. 'We were talking about women ... I could never get used to these Briton females.'

'They are not to my taste either,' another agreed. 'They wear too many skins.'

Milo chuckled. 'But once you get those skins off them, they look just about the same as Roman women!'

He picked up his cup, but put it down again without drinking.

The noise was louder now, more strident. Obviously there were many people out there. Suddenly the din was punctuated by a scream.

The men gazed at each other in consternation, then Milo rose and started for the door. The others followed.

In the doorway, Milo stopped with amazement. People were running madly up and down the street. A formidable horde of blond, moustachioed warriors, with many sword-wielding women in their ranks as well, were causing destruction and mayhem on all sides. Some of the dwellings were already on fire.

The thunderous crash of falling masonry caught Milo's attention. Down the street, the great Temple itself was ablaze, huge tongues of flame licking evilly round its massive piers. Suddenly there was a booming roar and a shower of sparks as the wooden roof of the temple caught fire. In a second the whole structure was a fearsome inferno, the stones cracking in the heat.

Breathing hard, Crassus hurried up. 'The Iceni!' he cried. 'They've gone beserk! Thousands of them!'

'By the sword of Sulla!' swore an old soldier.

'Let's find arms!' Ulpian cried.

'That Queen of theirs is leading them!' Crassus shouted. 'She's killing everyone in her path! With my own eyes, I saw her murder Faustus!'

But the others were not listening. They had scattered and were running off in all directions. One seized a ceremonial sword hanging on Crassus' wall. Crassus, too, started away, but Milo took him by the arm. 'You are sure it was Boudicca you saw?'

The scarred veteran nodded.

Milo shook his head with disbelief. 'I know her! It cannot be true! She would *never* do this!'

Crassus wrenched his arm away. 'It's her, I tell you! I saw her down by the Temple! Now let's find weapons before we're all butchered!'

Milo ran as fast as he could towards the blazing Temple. He approached it rapidly, but had to halt about a hundred paces away. Even from this distance he could feel the ferocious heat.

Just to his left was the colossal statue of the Deified Claudius, which stood on the edge of the Temple precinct. Clustered round it was a crowd of Iceni warriors, heaving on ropes attached to the arms and legs of the imperial image.

With a shock, Milo recognized the figure who was directing them. Boudicca was gripping a heavy, cross-barred hunting spear. Behind their mother were Brigantia and Sulevia. Surprisingly both girls clutched swords, but in contrast to the Queen, they did not look warlike at all. They seemed to cower, gazing fearfully at the conflagration surrounding them.

The tall statue toppled. It canted over, hanging suspended for an instant. Then it smashed to the ground with an earth-shaking impact. Its bronze head flew off, bounced and rolled to a stop only a few feet from Milo.

Stunned, he stared down at the gargantuan face of Claudius. When he looked up, the Queen was before him, but there was no recognition in her eyes.

'Boudicca!' he cried. 'It's me! Milo! Your friend! Have you gone mad?'

Boudicca did not answer. She raised the spear, and with all her strength, drove it through Milo's body.

'Mother!' shrieked Brigantia.

Impaled on the weapon, Milo continued to gaze incredulously at the Queen. He was dead almost instantly.

With a savage wrench, she pulled the spear out of the body.

Sulevia broke into sobs. Brigantia threw down her sword and knelt beside the dead Roman. Wildly, she looked up at her mother. 'Why have you done this?'

'He was a Roman.'

'He was our friend!'

'We have no friends.'

Fiercely the Queen stepped closer to her daughter. 'Now take up your sword again. There is no turning back.'

The girl hesitated.

'Take it up!' Boudicca shouted.

Eyes downcast, Brigantia obeyed.

Boudicca's hand went to the ivory figurine which still hung round her neck. She ripped it off and flung it into the dead man's face.

*

Ben Hur stared at the heavily wooded island just across the narrow strait.

Paetus spoke dourly. 'They say the Druids can make it disappear. That is why no one has ever been able to capture the place.'

'Whoever tried to find it before,' Ben Hur replied, 'never had the services of Suetonius' German scouts.'

A few nights ago the Batavian trackers had come into camp with excited reports of how they had followed the wounded Briton and discovered the Isle of Mona. Instantly Suetonius had sent out messengers, ordering all available reinforcements to join them. The Twentieth had remained waiting in camp for five days, until the arrival of most of the Fourteenth Gemina. Only then did the Roman forces set out.

From the position his century occupied on the headland, Ben Hur surveyed the invasion force Suetonius had deployed for the crossing. To the left, barges were lined up on the pebble beach. The Legion's carpenters had spent the last day and night felling trees from the nearby forests, expertly cutting them into planks. Using a caulking made of tallow and hemp, they had fashioned a whole fleet of flat-bottomed vessels.

On the right waited the cavalry by their horses, knee-deep in water. They were stripped to their loincloths, their armour, clothing, packs and weapons tied into neat bundles and fastened to the backs of their animals.

Riding up and down the beach on his white charger, bareheaded as usual, was Suetonius, making the last-minute inspection of the whole impressive array. Suddenly the General waved his hand and galloped over to the central position where his staff waited under the protective wings of the golden Eagle.

A trumpet call shivered in the brisk morning air.

Ben Hur grinned at the soldiers. 'All right, you miserable scum.'

The men followed their Centurion down the beach towards the barges, as every other century was also doing. They took their pre-arranged places in the boat allotted to them, half of the detachment staying on the beach to push the craft into the water when the next signal came. He noted that the General, his staff, and the standard-bearers, in the adjoining boat, were already out in the channel.

According to tradition, a Roman general must always be first in the area of the greatest danger ...

A second trumpet call split the air. With a shout the soldiers pushed the barges into the water and clambered in, the rowers extending their oars. The cavalrymen urged their mounts into the strait, swimming alongside the beasts, none of them showing the slightest sign of discomfort, despite the chilling temperature of the water. Ben Hur did not envy their task.

The strait was no wider than a large river and the island loomed up rapidly. Not a sign of life or movement stirred along the beaches. Yet Ben Hur was certain that such a formidable invasion force could not have gone undetected on Mona.

In a short time the blunt prow of the landing craft grated on to the pebbles. Ben Hur did what was expected of a Centurion. He was the first man in the century to leap from the barge and splash through the shallows on to the hostile shore. He urged his men to follow, and when the boat had been dragged on to the beach, he lined his soldiers up in battle formation, making sure each was in his proper position. A quick look told him the rest of the Legion was doing the same all along the water's edge.

A thick white mist was descending over the beach, obliterating the strait. In a matter of moments, the island had disappeared! He could barely make out the faces of Paetus and the men surrounding him in the clammy gloom. The signaller cursed fervently, his voice sounding muffled in the fog.

'Shut up,' Ben Hur snarled.

The men fell silent. The whole beach was quiet, save the lapping of the water, the occasional jingle of harness or snort of a horse.

A trumpet call reverberated through the mist. It was the signal for the army to hold its position. Obviously Suetonius had decided to wait here on the beach for the fog to lift, rather than leading his legions into a strange and hostile land, when they could not see more than a few feet in front of them.

It was distinctly unpleasant to stand immobile. Ben Hur felt vulnerable, anticipating an attack which might come at any moment.

There was a glimmer of something in the fog. He strained his eyes into the murk, then saw it again. It was the Eagle of the Legion just to his left, reflecting something. Could it be sunlight?

The clammy vapour was definitely thinning. He glimpsed a patch of blue sky, and the rays of the sun were beginning to filter through. But strangely there was not a breath of wind.

Swiftly the fog was swept away, as if by an invisible hand. A gasp went up from the entire army.

The cliffs and headlands surrounding the landing area, deserted so shortly before, were now lined by crowds of black-robed men and women. Some, older than the others, their long, white hair hanging to their waists, were clearly the leaders. Their faces were stained blue with woad. One gaunt apparition raised his hands high, making a cabalistic sign. Then he emitted a long drawn-out, piercing shriek.

Immediately the horde of Druids moved their arms in unison, uttering a low, mysterious chant. As if ignited by the same supernatural hand which had made the fog vanish, enormous bonfires flared into life on the cliff.

The chilling wail was repeated. A long line of wild-eyed women, brandishing torches, filed down from the trees, screaming curses and imprecations. Now, from the woods behind the Druids, a host of warriors appeared, beating out the rhythm of the chant on their shields, using the flat sides of their long swords. When they joined the priests, they halted, and the whole multitude continued the incantation.

An icy dread filled Ben Hur's soul. The nightmarish depths of the Underworld, which lived so luridly in the stirring poetry of Virgil, were suddenly reincarnated here on the green shores of Mona.

Roman trumpets brayed the order to attack. But nothing happened.

The men stood like pillars of stone, frozen with terror.

Again the trumpets blasted. Still the soldiers remained rooted to the spot.

Ben Hur's eyes went to the Eagle of the Legion. The golden bird was not afraid. Its glow was as brilliant as ever, wings outstretched defiantly as it flung its magic against the Druids.

Obeying a sudden compulsion, Ben Hur leaped forward and snatched the image from the bemused standard-bearer. Shouting, holding the glittering effigy aloft, he ran towards the black-robed horde on the high ground. A cheer from behind him told him that the Roman forces were advancing at last. The Druids' spell was broken!

On the cliffs the multitude of Druids withdrew into the trees. In a moment the high ground was empty. Only the blazing bonfires bore witness to the fact that the black-clad priesthood had ever been there.

The legions advanced, toiling in two columns up the steep hillside. After an exhausting climb, they reached the summit where the spectral host had appeared. Here Suetonius called a halt. Gratefully the perspiring soldiers shed their packs, but remained in formation while they gained their breath. Ben Hur sought out the standard-bearer and returned the Eagle to him.

The soldier shook his head in bafflement. 'By the Lares of my grandmother ... Did I see those blue-faced demons, or were they ghosts? Centurion, why did they retreat like that?'

'Because they mean to fight us at a place more to their liking,' Ben Hur speculated.

'I think it is a trap,' the standard-bearer said direly.

'Perhaps. They fight with magic as well as swords.'

Just then Suetonius rode up.

'Tribune!' he bellowed.

Puzzled, Ben Hur did not answer.

'Severus!' the General shouted. 'I am talking to you!'

'But you said Tribune.'

'That's right. I've just made you Tribune.' The General's face cracked into a smile. 'What you did on the beach confirmed my suspicions about you. You have the instincts of a leader!'

Ben Hur groaned inwardly. It dawned on him how his seizing the Eagle must have appeared to Suetonius. But the appearance was a long way from the fact. As had so often happened at crucial moments in Ben Hur's life, some external force had inexplicably taken possession of him and impelled him to a deed utterly foreign to his nature. It always surprised him when such rashness was rewarded.

'Well,' demanded Suetonius, 'have you nothing to say?'

Ben Hur clenched his fist in salute. 'My gratitude, General.'

'That signaller of yours, Longinus. He's been here since Claudius' day. Turn your century over to him, and get yourself a mount.'

'Very well,' said Ben Hur. At least, he reflected ruefully, he would no longer have to walk . . .

'From now on,' Suetonius announced, 'you'll be my personal aide.'

The General swung his horse's head, and cantered away.

The march through the forest was too fast to be prudent, but Suetonius was determined on hot pursuit of the Druids. Only once had the Romans paused, when they had overtaken a sizeable group of stragglers. Suetonius had ordered them to be executed. The unfortunate captives had been butchered on the spot, then the column had resumed its rapid penetration of the woods.

When the legions emerged from the trees, the sun had barely passed its zenith. Before them lay meadowland. Beyond this rose a steep hill, shaped exactly like a bald man's pate. Crowning the summit were rings of ditches and earthworks. A long palisade circled the entire complex. The sunlight glinted on the points of many iron weapons within the stronghold.

Ordering a halt, the General dismounted and strode forward, appraising the citadel. He beckoned for his Tribunes, who joined him. There were ten – six from the Twentieth Legion, and four from the Fourteenth.

Suetonius pointed a triumphant finger at the hill fort.

'At last we've got the whole litter in one den! If we destroy them – the war's over! I want this hill invested at once! Every man who is not on guard duty will be on trenches or carpentry. You, Severus – see that four mantlets are built. I want them ready before the sun goes down . . .'

Ben Hur saluted and turned to begin the task of constructing the equipment for the long siege. Before he could give his first order, however, there came the sound of approaching horsemen. The other men heard it too. All heads were craning towards the forest, where presently two galloping riders appeared, cloaks billowing out behind them. In a moment they had reined to a sliding halt just before Suetonius and hurled themselves from their sweating horses. Ben Hur recognized them as soldiers from the detachment left to guard the beach.

'An urgent message, General!' one of the riders exclaimed. 'A disaster! The Iceni have risen! The Province is in arms. Boudicca is in the field with seventy thousand warriors!'

'You are sure of this?'

'Yes, General. Camulodunum has fallen! The veterans there massacred to a man! The courier told us the whole blood-crazed host is heading for Londinium!'

The General remained silent for a moment. Ben Hur could see the vein standing out on his forehead. He could read Suetonius' mind. The Romans had come within a hair's breadth of ending the war here on Mona. But now – all was ruined at one blow. The siege would have to be abandoned before it was even started. They would have to rush back to the mainland in an attempt to stamp out the revolt. Even if the Romans should succeed, the Druids would be given a vital reprieve. The war in the west would have to be fought all over again. It might last another twenty years.

'Arsehole of Mars!' Suetonius bellowed suddenly. 'May every Vestal Virgin be raped and the Senate drowned in a bowl of piss!'

He swung on Ben Hur as if to attack him. 'Sound the call to arms! We'll head back for the beach immediately!'

The day was bright, but not hot. Nevertheless, the entire Roman army was drenched with perspiration. Ben Hur, mounted now on a strong horse behind Suetonius, could survey the long column of doggedly plodding men.

For two days they had marched at rapid pace, covering no less than eighty Roman miles since regaining the mainland. It was the fastest march anyone had ever heard of, and the men showed it. But Suetonius was merciless. He drove them on, allowing only the most perfunctory rests. Relying on picking up reinforcements from the north, he was heading for Londinium at full speed.

Ben Hur let his horse drop back until he was riding parallel with his old century. They trudged along at the killing pace, the helmets hung on straps over their shoulders banging rhythmically against their chest-plates, adding irritation to torture. Many were gasping audibly. Ben Hur had known them only as stoic, tough men of war. Now the change was eloquent. Most seemed ready to drop. Longinus, the new Centurion, looked as though he would be quite willing to throw away his vine staff. Only Paetus' face was set in its usual unyielding lines. Seeing his former Centurion, the Optio raised his fist with the thumb between the two midfingers in the Latin gesture of contempt. But Ben Hur noticed that Paetus' limp was more pronounced than ever.

Urging his horse ahead, Ben Hur drew level with Suetonius.

'General . . .' Ben Hur began.

Suetonius glowered at him. 'What is it?'

'We must halt. The men won't stand much more of this.'

'I'll cross the Styx into Hades before I halt again.'

'You won't be alone. At this pace, the men will cross with you.'

Suetonius' dusty, sweat-stained face darkened, but he said nothing. He glanced up and down the column.

Ben Hur persisted. 'Do you expect them to fight in this condition?'

'Very well,' said the General gruffly. 'Call a halt. But it has to be brief.'

Ben Hur made a sign to the trumpeter, who sounded the welcome signal.

Many of the soldiers sagged with exhaustion as they staggered to a stop. Immediately the cavalry rode out on to the flanks to begin their tireless patrol, guarding against surprises.

Suetonius swung from his saddle, took a drink of water, then poured some on his head. He passed the flask to Ben Hur. As he drank, Ben Hur glanced covertly at Suetonius and felt a twinge of pity. Ever since receiving news of the revolt, Suetonius had become bitter and taciturn, hardly speaking a word to anyone.

The General stiffened. A rider was approaching, his red cloak proclaiming him as yet another courier. Ben Hur had grown to hate the sight of them, for each one bore worse tidings.

Galloping up, the newcomer jumped from his mount. Suetonius strode over to meet him. Ben Hur could not hear the man's report, but it was over in a moment. The messenger saluted and withdrew. Suetonius turned and walked back to Ben Hur. The vein on his forehead was throbbing again.

'Call the Tribunes,' he ordered testily.

Ben Hur moved to the trumpeter and repeated the order. The soldier raised his instrument and sounded the call.

One by one, the Tribunes hurried up. Suetonius waited until all ten of the officers were present.

'We've lost Cerialis,' Suetonius informed them. 'He tried to delay Boudicca. But the Ninth is only half-strength and the Britons are too many. Cerialis suffered bad losses. He was forced back behind the defences of Eboracum. He's still there – pinned down.'

The Tribunes greeted this unwelcome news with glum silence.

Suetonius continued. 'The only other force in Britain is the Second Augusta at Glevum under Postumus. They are severely under-strength as well, but they'll be better than nothing.'

'So what do you propose?' demanded Agricola haughtily.

'I'll tell you – if it is possible to tell you anything,' Suetonius replied with unnecessary rancour. 'Our forces will be in no condition for battle if we continue at this pace. Besides – I don't think the infantry will ever reach Londinium in time to stop Boudicca. So Severus and I will take a quarter of the cavalry and go on ahead.'

Ben Hur protested immediately. 'But that's only two hundred men!'

'I too can compute elementary sums,' snapped the General. 'It will be enough to strengthen the defences of Londinium. And perhaps, with the aid of the citizens, to defend it for a time.' Suetonius took another drink and continued. 'The rest of our forces – under the command of Agricola – will halt at Venonae to wait for Postumus and the Second. When junction is made with him, the combined army will head for Londinium to relieve me. Then we will have Boudicca between two fires.'

Agricola shook his head in disbelief. 'That will be like having an elephant between two fleas! She has seventy thousand warriors!'

'Are you questioning me?' snarled the General, his glare burning into the Tribune.

Agricola looked as if he would like to carry the matter further, but thought better of it. 'No, General.'

Suetonius scanned the group of tired faces. 'Any other helpful comments?'

When no one replied, Suetonius did not seem any less annoyed. 'Now,' he said grimly, 'does anyone of you know an exceptionally capable soldier? I need a man who can get through to Postumus with orders to advance to Venonae.'

'I know the man for you,' Ben Hur replied immediately. 'You recall Paetus?'

For the first time a twinkle appeared in the General's eyes. 'Paetus! Of course! Chalk Hill! He's a good man, Severus, but he's got a bad leg ...'

'I would rather have him with one leg than most men with two. He'll get through.'

CHAPTER NINETEEN

Ben Hur looked round with despair. He had wanted to find some sign of hope, but there was none. Certainly he did not relish the prospect of bringing Suetonius yet more bad news.

Reluctantly he nudged his horse into a trot, moving along the path by the Tamesis River. He noted the boats clustered on the banks and fishermen going about their daily work. Little did they imagine the fate in store for them and their bustling town of Londinium.

All of the new Roman settlements Ben Hur had seen were growing quickly, but Londinium was outstripping them all. Tangible signs of this were visible as Ben Hur approached the Forum, which was bordered on three sides by wooden porticoes. The fourth side of the square was occupied by a new basilica, with offices built behind it. And several large temples had just been completed, one to Isis, a deity from as distant a land as Egypt. He could only hope that Isis was a more powerful Goddess than anything the Druids could invoke.

Slowing his mount to a walk, he turned into the Forum. Not many people were abroad, but those civilians he encountered smiled warmly at him. When Suetonius' small cavalry detachment had ridden into Londinium, they had been greeted like saviours by the people, who had already heard of the atrocities committed by Boudicca at Camulodunum. This attitude of the townsfolk, Ben Hur reflected mordantly, was likely to change before the sun was down. For what he had to report would surely cause Suetonius to alter his strategy completely.

Taking the roadway which led round the great basilica, Ben Hur made for the administrative offices.

Suetonius had established his headquarters in the rooms allotted to the Procurator, and Ben Hur knew that the General attached great significance to the defence of this town. Because of its commercial importance, Londinium was the centre of the network of roads recently begun by the army. It was also becoming the seat of the provincial government. To lose Londinium to the rebels would be a serious blow indeed.

Ben Hur dismounted. One of the cavalry Decurions standing outside the office came to meet him.

'The General asked me to wait for you,' he said. 'He requests you to join him in the bath-house with the Procurator. I'll take your horse.'

Ben Hur smiled his thanks, and made his way towards a door where two more cavalrymen were posted as sentries. They raised clenched fists respectfully as Ben Hur approached. He returned the gesture, as they swung open the doors.

Suetonius was just climbing out of the warm bath and reaching for one of the soft towels piled on the slate floor.

'You are not getting out so soon?' Decianus protested, as he lounged back on the stone seat which surrounded the pool. 'I was hoping we could go to the steam room, have a sweat and return for another plunge.'

'Too much of that is enervating,' Suetonius grunted as he towelled his lean, spare frame. He caught sight of Ben Hur waiting in the doorway. 'Oh, Severus ... Join us.'

Decianus waved good-naturedly. 'Tribune! You look as if you could do with a little relaxation. Come on in.'

Such cheerfulness in the present situation irked Ben Hur, but he forced himself to smile politely. 'Thank you, Procurator, but I am afraid I have no time.'

'Well, Severus?' the General demanded, slipping into his tunic, and reaching for his boots. 'What is the result of your survey?'

Ben Hur took a deep breath. 'Londinium cannot be defended.'

Suetonius paused in his dressing. 'You are sure?'

Ben Hur nodded. 'There are no ditches or fortifications of any kind, and it would take too long to create them with the few men we have. Even if we could, there would not be enough soldiers to man them.'

Decianus rose from the bath, his ponderous belly glistening. 'You've got two hundred men! And my bodyguard – that's a hundred and eighty more!'

Ben Hur shook his head. 'We'd need five times that number for any sort of defence. The perimeter of the city is far too large.'

'There are the townspeople,' Decianus insisted. 'They'll fight. They'll be some help.'

'They will be more of a hindrance than a help.'

'In what way, Severus?' Suetonius asked.

'The young and able all fled after the news of Camulodunum. Most of those who are left are old or infirm, or small children.'

'What do you recommend?'

'Pull out as fast as possible – make for Venonae to join the others. By now Paetus should be back from Glevum with reinforcements.'

'No! You cannot!' Decianus howled. 'They say Boudicca is only twenty miles away. What about the civilians? Would you let them be slaughtered? In Camulodunum she did not leave anything alive – not the women, not the children – not even the dogs!'

'I have thought of the townsfolk,' Ben Hur replied. 'There are fishing boats on the river. We'll load the people aboard. They can sail to any part of Britain they choose – or even to Gaul.'

'Very good, Tribune ...' said Suetonius.

'This is an outrage!' shouted Decianus. 'Surely you will not let this city be burned! All the records of the province –'

'Piss on the records!' Suetonius snapped.

'Would you piss on the gold as well?' demanded Decianus.

Suetonius stared at him. 'What gold?'

'The money I have laboured to collect all year throughout the land. Taxes. Nero's gold.'

The General faced Decianus grimly. 'I would rather lose all the gold in the province than just *one* of my soldiers! You'd better get your people on those boats.'

The naked Procurator shivered. Suetonius turned his back on him and strode through the door. Ben Hur followed.

Emerging from the bath-house, Suetonius beckoned to the cavalrymen stationed outside. These soldiers mounted their horses and kept pace with the General as he set off on foot down the street. A brief walk brought them to the main gate of the city, not far from the Forum. Here the balance of Suetonius' force was bivouacked. A Prefect of Cavalry saluted as the General walked up.

'Saddle the horses,' Suetonius commanded. 'We are returning to Venonae.'

'The scouts have just come in,' the Prefect reported.

Suetonius was instantly alert. 'Is the road still clear?'

The officer nodded. 'But Boudicca's host is closer than we thought. Larger too.'

'We'll have to move quickly,' said Suetonius, turning to Ben Hur. 'Let's get down to the Tamesis immediately. We must see that the townspeople get aboard those boats.' He glanced at the Prefect. 'You come too. Bring some men with you.'

The Prefect saluted, and ran back to the other cavalrymen, who were clustered round their horses.

Thunder growled in the distance. Ben Hur glanced upwards at the darkening sky. 'A poor day for journeying by water ...'

Suetonius grinned bitterly. 'An even poorer day for having your throat cut!'

The Prefect returned with six mounted soldiers and two extra horses. Both Suetonius and Ben Hur vaulted on to the animals, and Suetonius led the way down the main street at a canter.

The rain came suddenly. It poured down in torrents mixed with large hailstones which clattered loudly on their armour. The paving on the road was still unfinished, and in a moment its dusty surface was turned into a sodden quagmire.

By the time they reached the river, there was already activity among the boats. A good number, filled with people, were under way.

Suetonius reined in, squinting through the driving rain. 'They're getting out!' he exclaimed. 'Decianus moved fast.' He glanced at Ben Hur with relief. 'It seems we won't be needed.'

Suetonius wheeled his horse. Ben Hur was about to do likewise, when something about the moving figures on the bank caught his attention. Even from this distance, he could detect the dull glint of armour –

'Wait!' Ben Hur called.

Suetonius halted impatiently. 'What is it, Tribune? We've got no time to waste!'

Ben Hur gestured towards the little fleet of boats. 'Those are *not* townspeople. It's the Procurator and his bodyguard. They are saving their own hides!'

Suetonius jerked his horse's head back in the direction of the river, glowering into the mist. There was a metallic swish as the General's sword appeared in his hand. With an angry twist of his whole body, Suetonius kicked his mount to a gallop.

Ben Hur and the other cavalrymen unsheathed their weapons also, urging their horses after the General.

They hurtled down on the fugitives, who were wading into the shallows. Aware of the danger, Decianus' men scrambled into the boats, hoisted out their oars and began to row frantically – just as the General's horse thundered into the water with a tremendous splash. Madly Suetonius slashed out with his sword, actually catching the stern of the last boat, slicing away a large chunk of wood. The rest of the General's party reined in beside him. There was nothing more they could do. The little flotilla had caught the tide and, aided by their oars, were rapidly moving away.

'Decianus!' bellowed the General.

Suetonius' voice echoed damply over the water, but there was no reply.

'Decianus!' he roared again. 'You can hear me! I know you can! Come back!'

A disembodied voice floated across the river. 'Not for a hundred thousand sesterces!'

'I order you to come back!' Suetonius yelled furiously.

'I'm afraid I must decline,' Decianus answered, his voice rapidly growing fainter.

Suetonius' face reddened. 'I'll have you brought to trial!'

'You'll have to survive to do that,' Decianus replied. 'But I don't give you very good odds ...'

Suetonius' eyes continued to blaze into the distance. Then his anger seemed to subside. In disgust he turned his horse's head, urging the beast up on to the river bank.

'Let's get on to Venonae,' he growled.

'Venonae!' Ben Hur exclaimed. 'What about the townsfolk here?'

The General shifted slightly in his saddle. 'What about them?'

'They have no means of escape now!'

'Do not tell me the obvious, Tribune. It is a fate not uncommon in warfare.'

'We can't just abandon them!'

The older man glowered at him. 'The people will be slaughtered – whether we go or stay. I don't believe in gallant gestures – particularly fatal ones.'

'General,' Ben Hur protested. 'I urge you to reconsider!'

'We're pulling out, Tribune! Now!'

There was a moment of silence.

'That's an order,' the General murmured implacably.

Ben Hur knew that he was right. Their few numbers could do nothing. And if they stayed here to die, their deaths would accomplish nothing either.

Numbly Ben Hur nodded. Suetonius wheeled his horse and the party moved off.

As they approached the city gate, the rain stopped as suddenly as it had come. A group of children burst out of a house and began frolicking in the puddles of the street.

Ben Hur looked away.

Grimly the Romans cantered up the slope. Ben Hur shot a quick look at Suetonius. The commander's face was hard and expressionless. But Ben Hur knew Suetonius was reaching the limits of his self-control. All the men were tired, but none bore the heavy load of responsibility which rested on the General's shoulders.

Suetonius could not endure retreat. Attack was his natural style. In his field tactics, audacity and surprise always took precedence over prudence. Yet, ever since he had withdrawn from Mona, he had done nothing but retreat. Abandoning Londinium had been both an agonizing personal decision and a humiliating experience for a soldier.

Only a short time ago, Fate had dealt him the most humiliating blow of all. Midway in their flight to Venonae, they had encountered a small party of Briton horsemen, not more than a hundred. It would have been an easy matter to annihilate them, but Suetonius could not afford the time to give battle. Apparently the Britons had been aware of this, for they had hung on the rear of the Roman column like ticks, picking off no fewer than eight Roman cavalrymen. All

Suetonius could do was grind his teeth in frustration and continue to flee from the inferior force.

The Romans crested the hill. There, at last, was the legionary camp at Venonae. The sight of it filled Ben Hur with relief. Extra ditches had been dug, and a second palisade built all round the perimeter. And somehow reassuring were the helmets of the Roman sentries, occupying their usual stations behind the ramparts.

Soon Suetonius' cavalrymen were sliding to a halt inside the enclosure. Agricola waited, saluting as Suetonius dismounted. The young Tribune's haughty face was almost as sour as his commander's.

'I have bad news, General,' Agricola said in clipped tones.

'Is there any other kind?' Suetonius snarled.

'Postumus and his men never arrived. And there's been no sign of Paetus either. We don't even know if he got through or not.'

'Shall I send another man?' Ben Hur asked.

The commander shook his head. 'Too late . . .' He turned back to Agricola. 'Call a staff meeting!'

The Tribune nodded and hurried away. Ben Hur followed the General to the Praetorium, and the two men entered the commander's tent.

Suetonius regarded Ben Hur stonily. Then, for the first time in days, his face seemed to soften. 'You know what this means, don't you, Severus?'

'We do not have Postumus' soldiers.'

Suetonius laughed harshly. 'They would not have made much difference. We would have been outnumbered seven to one instead of eight to one . . .' He opened the flap which covered the entrance to the tent so the Tribunes could enter. 'I swear by the Lares of my family – if I ever get out of this alive, I'll crucify every last Iceni on this island! I'll give the crows such a feast they'll die of overeating!'

'You think we shall get out of this alive?' Ben Hur wondered.

'You noticed I did not take any auspices when we returned.'

'Because you thought the omens would be bad?'

Suetonius glowered at him. 'We're beyond omens now. Whatever they are, I don't want to know!'

Agricola stooped and entered the tent, followed by the other

Tribunes. Respectfully they lined up in front of the commander and saluted.

'Sit down,' Suetonius advised. 'You'll need all the rest you can get.'

The Tribunes sprawled on the earth floor of the tent, while Suetonius perched on the edge of his cot.

'By now Londinium will have fallen,' the General said. 'The whole Iceni nation will be heading this way, after our blood.'

There was a silence.

'How is our food supply?' Suetonius asked.

'Good,' Agricola replied immediately. 'We can hold out – no matter how long the siege lasts.'

'Siege? You assume we'll just sit here while that she-wolf rages over the country?'

'What other course is there?' Agricola demanded. 'We're relatively safe here. I've strengthened the defences.'

'So I noticed,' said Suetonius sarcastically. 'You displayed commendable judgement. I would have done the same – had I not been bathing with the Procurator in Londinium.'

Agricola persisted angrily. 'Vulcan's forge! We'd be fools to venture out! Those barbarians know nothing of siege warfare. They can pen us in for ever – but they'll *never* take the camp.'

The vein in Suetonius' forehead was throbbing again.

Ben Hur intervened quickly. 'I do not think the Britons will stay out there for long.'

Suetonius rose from his cot. 'Really? Pray continue, Severus.'

'The scouts tell me the Britons were so eager to raise the full strength of their forces that they did not wait to get in their harvest. If they try to conduct a siege, they'll soon run out of provisions.'

The other Tribunes murmured their assent.

Suetonius regarded them scornfully. 'Food or no food, the Iceni will never abandon a siege. They dare not. After the atrocities they have committed – the butcheries of innocent children at Camulodunum, and no doubt Londinium by now – they know what will happen to them if they ever fall into our power again. There is only one thing they *can* do – keep fighting.'

'I suppose, then,' said Agricola wearily, 'in your vast reservoir of knowledge, you have some plan to defeat them in the field.'

'I can only say this. I have no intention of sitting here while they besiege me for the rest of my life. I mean to destroy them now, once and for all.'

Tensely the Romans waited in the pre-dawn light. They were in full armour and deployed ready to march. A tomb-like silence hung over the camp. Every eye strained towards the southern horizon, still obscured in the shadows of night.

Ben Hur strode along the line of wagons, inspecting the sausage-shaped tent rolls to be sure they were properly packed. Some of the tents had been left standing, preserving the illusion that the Romans were dug in, ready to stay for as long as necessary.

His eyes moved towards the palisade. It was still in place. Ben Hur knew that no one had filled in the ditches outside. To any observer, the camp would seem prepared to withstand a siege. It was essential to the General's audacious scheme that this illusion be maintained as long as possible.

Finally Ben Hur completed his examination of the wagons, then returned to Suetonius, who was waiting under the standards with his staff.

'The column is ready,' Ben Hur reported.

Suetonius nodded without taking his eyes off the horizon. Ben Hur stole a look at the other Tribunes. They were grim-faced, unhappy.

Panicked messengers had flogged their horses into the camp the day before, bearing confirmation of appalling massacres at Londinium and Verulamium. This had done nothing to increase anyone's confidence in Suetonius' reckless plan.

Now Ben Hur waited tensely with the others. The glow in the east was steadily increasing. Strangely he found himself wondering about Paetus. He wished the Optio were here. The sight of his stocky figure would be reassuring at a time like this. What had happened to him between here and Glevum? There could only be one answer ... Ben Hur tried to put the thought from his mind.

Just then the rim of the sun appeared over the horizon. In a moment it was a disc of fire, casting its ruby glow over the landscape.

Like a gigantic wave of lava, an amorphous mass was creeping down the hills to the south. It was shot through with flashes of red sunlight on metal – like a forest of moving lights. Boudicca's host had arrived.

An eternity seemed to pass. The Briton horde drew closer but still the Romans did not move.

Ben Hur felt the restiveness among his fellow Tribunes. Several of them were perspiring in spite of the cold air. Now the enemy was distinguishable as a myriad individual warriors, some on foot and others mounted.

'All right,' said Suetonius at last. 'Advance.'

Agricola made a sign to the trumpeters, who blasted out the order to the soldiers.

The column came alive, falling into marching formation, swinging down the Via Principalis towards the main gate. The legions took the left entrance, filing out into the broad plain before the camp.

When the entire Roman army had emerged from the defences, the staccato notes of the trumpets called the soldiers to a halt again. They grounded their shields and faced the oncoming enemy.

Ben Hur estimated that the vanguard of Boudicca's host was not more than a quarter of a mile away. Yet there were still others coming over the hills in the distance! As he watched, the front rank of the Iceni stopped. No doubt they were astonished to see the small Roman force emerge so unexpectedly from the safety of their ramparts and form up brazenly in the open to meet them.

A movement caught his attention. Three mounted figures detached themselves from the main body of the enemy host and began riding up and down the front rank. Even from this distance, Ben Hur could see that all three were women.

'Vulcan's forge!' the General swore softly. 'There she is.'

'Boudicca?' Ben Hur asked.

Suetonius nodded. 'And the princesses too ...'

'You know them?'

'I would hardly number them among my friends, but I did meet them once. When I first arrived in Londinium to take command, they were there with the other Briton leaders to greet me. They did not have swords in their hands then! They were offering peace and friendship!' The General glared at the bellicose women on the hillside. 'I'll give them peace! They'll be the first ones I nail on crosses when this is over!'

'When this is over, I hope we'll still be alive!' Agricola remarked soberly. 'I have never seen such a host in my life. Where is the end of it?'

'Up there,' Suetonius said, indicating the crest of the hills.

At last the rear guard of Boudicca's forces was visible. Ox-drawn wagons were crammed full of gesticulating people.

'Those carts are bearing the old, the infirm, the small children – and a goodly number of pregnant women,' said Suetonius. 'When the Iceni call everyone to arms, they mean *everyone*! No one is left at home. Those who cannot fight must at least watch the battle.'

Ben Hur appraised the hostile multitude. The truth of Suetonius' statement was apparent. In the enemy ranks there were nearly as many armed women as men.

Although he could not hear the words, Ben Hur knew that Boudicca, posturing her horse up and down before the horde, was exhorting her warriors, inflaming them with lust to kill. Every now and then, she paused, shaking her fist at the Romans, then continued her harangue.

'Like most women, she talks too much,' Suetonius said sardonically. 'Let's shut her up. Sound the retreat.'

At the trumpet signal, the legionaries formed into an orderly column, and began to march away from the enemy. The cavalry took up formation at the rear. Suetonius and his staff walked their mounts between the cavalry and infantry.

Ben Hur glanced back. Boudicca had ceased her harangue. The entire Briton host remained immobile. Obviously Suetonius' move had surprised them again. There could only be one explanation for an army which first offered battle, then retreated without striking a blow. Cowardice.

A thunderous roar of triumph burst from the ranks of the Iceni – as loud as anything Ben Hur had ever heard in the Circus Maximus. Then they began their pursuit, not advancing as a single unit like Romans, but in groups or as individuals. It took time, but when the entire multitude was finally underway, it resembled the surge of a great sea.

Ben Hur shot a look in the opposite direction, towards the wooded area which he knew was Suetonius' objective. The goal of the legions was a point where the ground rose slightly and the trees receded somewhat, leaving a crescent-shaped area of meadowland. Here the Romans could turn at bay, their flanks and rear protected by the dense woods. Ben Hur thought of the auxiliaries Suetonius had posted among those trees. In the darkness of night they had crept from the camp to take their positions. Ben Hur prayed that they would not be too cold to fight well when the time came ...

Uttering savage whoops, brandishing their weapons, clumps of Briton warriors were charging forward at a run, drawing recklessly ahead of the main horde.

At a trumpet signal, the Roman cavalry responded like an angry swarm of hornets, swooping on the advance groups of the enemy, impaling several on their lances. The venturesome Celtic warriors scattered in confusion.

The earth shook as the Briton horsemen galloped forward to protect their comrades. On one flank rode Boudicca and on the other, the princesses, urging their mounted fighters onward. The Roman cavalry did not wait for a confrontation with greater numbers. Hastily they wheeled, and sped away, rejoining the retreating legions.

Only a short distance from Ben Hur's position, the Briton horsemen reined in. Like the Romans, they were clearly not anxious to come up against the full strength of their enemies without the support of their main host.

Now Ben Hur, Agricola and the other Tribunes rode up and down the marching column, shouting orders. Immediately the legionaries increased their speed to double time. Yet still they kept formation.

Shortly they were climbing the gentle slope, reaching the meadowland which was Suetonius' chosen battleground. When they arrived at the crescent-shaped belt of trees, the trumpets sounded a halt. The Roman foot soldiers obeyed, facing the enemy. Screened by the cavalry, they deployed into the battle line.

Only when the manoeuvre was complete did the horsemen retire to the wings, exposing the infantry drawn up in their serried ranks. Suetonius and Ben Hur, accompanied by the other Tribunes, rode to their position immediately behind the first five ranks of the Roman lines. Suetonius threw a glance back at the few reserves which had been posted in the rear, ready to dash to any point where they might be needed. All along the line, the voices of the centurions were heard, encouraging the men.

Ben Hur gripped the reins of his horse tightly as the first wave of Britons broke into a run, charging up the gentle slope. The enormous numerical superiority of Boudicca's host was partially offset by the topography of the site Suetonius had chosen. Only a small portion of their forces could approach the Romans at one time, constrained by the thick trees bordering the meadow.

Nevertheless, the oncoming mass of Britons was a daunting sight, the men with their flowing moustaches and the women with their hair tightly braided under helmets of leather or bronze. They hurtled closer, bellowing curses and war cries. The Romans waited, an unwavering iron-clad line.

At the very last moment, when the Iceni were barely ten paces away, a shout went up from the centurions. Almost as one man, the legionaries hurled their javelins full into the faces of their enemies, killing or wounding many. Immediately the Romans followed with a charge of their own, rushing down the incline to meet their foes. The crash of the impact echoed among the hills, accompanied almost instantly by the screams of wounded men. The short swords of the Roman soldiers did deadly work, and many of the Iceni warriors were hampered by the javelins which had pierced their shields and were still hanging there. Soon the first line of Romans withdrew, and was replaced by the fresh second line.

Masses of the enemy warriors were coming up behind their fellows. The first rank of the Britons had been completely cut to pieces, but as fast as the Iceni were struck down, others replaced them. Despite this overwhelming onslaught, the Romans held fast. Then, when it seemed the Britons could advance no longer, the Queen and her two daughters rode into the very vortex of the fight, slashing out with their weapons. At the sight of them a cheer went up from the Britons, who threw themselves into the combat with new vigour, pushing forward, mindless of casualties.

Suetonius kicked his mount straight towards Boudicca. The rear ranks of the Romans opened to make way for him. Ben Hur beckoned to the other Tribunes, leading them after their commander.

Suddenly Ben Hur's horse bucked upwards with an agonized, screeching neigh. He had to drop his sword and cling to the animal's mane to avoid being thrown.

A spear had been driven into the creature's belly. As the stricken animal sank to the ground, Ben Hur leaped away to avoid being pinned under its weight, falling on his hands and knees. The Briton who had struck the blow did not bother to retrieve his spear. He drew his sword. Ben Hur tried to rise, but there was no time. Moustachioed lips drawn back in a snarl of hate, the warrior slashed downward viciously. Ben Hur rolled aside, and the long blade sliced into the soft earth. Before the Briton could extract the weapon, Ben Hur drew his dagger and plunged it upwards between the man's legs. Without a second look at his writhing enemy, Ben Hur scrambled to his feet and retrieved his own sword, his eyes searching for Suetonius among the struggling ranks. At last he caught a glimpse of him.

The General, still mounted, was fighting towards the Queen and her daughters, hacking his way through the Iceni ranks. Riding straight at Boudicca, he aimed a murderous cut at her head. But the taller of the Queen's daughters rushed forward, blocking Suetonius' blow with her shield. His face contorted with rage, the General swung again, this time at the girl instead, splitting her skull.

A groan rose from the Iceni clustered round the royal group. Scores of warriors thrust themselves between the Roman General and their Queen, bearing Boudicca and the remaining princess away. Suetonius was hotly assaulted on all sides. But the Tribunes quickly surrounded their commander, beating back the crazed Britons.

Ben Hur's glance swept the battlefield. The struggle seemed to be hanging in the balance. It was the Roman superiority in tactics against the enemy's overwhelming numbers.

He worked his way to the General's side. Seeing Ben Hur, Suetonius made a gesture towards the rear of the Roman ranks. Ben Hur knew what this meant. With a hasty salute, he hurried off.

Leaving the area of the battle, he passed the reserves and plunged into the thick woods behind the legions. Being careful to remain on the fringes of the trees, he skirted the meadow. He could still hear the sounds of combat. When the terrain began to slope downwards, he knew that he was nearing his goal.

Then he detected the flash of metal in the foliage ahead. A challenge rang out. Ben Hur halted.

'The Tiber has frozen,' he called softly.

'The sun will melt the ice,' a voice replied.

Bushes moved. A Decurion appeared, beckoning. He led the way to a clearing where the auxiliaries, about six hundred of them, lay crouched behind the foliage. Tensely each man gripped his small round shield and thrusting spear. They seemed alert and ready to attack, looking expectantly at the Tribune approaching them.

'You've had a cold night,' Ben Hur said to the Decurion.

The soldier nodded. 'No doubt it is warmer where you have come from?'

'It is.'

'My men could do with a bit of heat,' the Decurion stated with grim anticipation.

Ben Hur appraised the auxiliaries. These men, younger than the legionaries for the most part, and equipped differently, could be counted on to perform well in an emergency. Picked for their speed, carrying lighter armour and weapons, they were rarely used for frontal assaults, but more typically for missions like the one on which they were about to embark. None of them were Roman citizens, but Ben Hur knew that they were often given this privilege as a reward for valour in battle. No wonder they seemed so eager to fight.

'Let's move,' Ben Hur ordered. At a hand signal from the Decurion, the auxiliaries scrambled to their feet and followed Ben Hur through the trees.

Out in the meadow, not more than fifty paces away, the masses of Britons were still pressing uphill towards the Roman ranks.

Ben Hur waited only long enough to be sure that all the auxiliaries had fallen into position behind him. Then, unsheathing his sword, he nodded to the men and dashed out into the open.

Before the Britons were aware of what was happening, the auxiliaries were upon their flank, stabbing out with their long spears. In the first moment of the assault at least a score of the enemy fell. Such was the shock and speed of the attack that the auxiliaries were able to penetrate deeply into the Icenian horde.

The Iceni recovered swiftly. Their comrades, diverted from the main conflict, rushed to help them. Now Ben Hur and the auxiliaries stood a good chance of being cut off and surrounded.

Then came the welcome call of the Roman trumpet. At last Suetonius was committing his precious reserves to the battle. They joined the front line of the legions, just up the hill to Ben Hur's right. Backed by the fresh troops, the Roman line surged forward, concentrating their entire strength on this one point.

The Britons turned to meet the new threat behind them. Ben Hur waved the auxiliaries on, and they redoubled their assault. Pressed close together by the two-pronged attack, the Iceni were unable to wield their weapons. Many of them stumbled into each other.

Confusion spread like a swift poison through the Iceni host. Now the Romans were pressing into the enemy everywhere.

Another trumpet call rang out. Ben Hur threw a quick look at the opposite side of the meadow. The cavalry, which Suetonius had posted there, were galloping forward, cutting down any Britons in their way. But they did not engage the main host. Instead they circled wide, dashed down the hillside towards wagons which were waiting at the base of the slope. The Roman horsemen stormed among the vehicles, slaughtering the oxen. Then they wheeled their mounts and dashed through the wagons a second time, mercilessly cutting down the occupants.

The rout of the Britons became a panicked flight. At the base of the hill, the fleeing enemy were blocked by their own immobilized wagons. The Romans drove inexorably downhill into the swirling mass, and the space enclosed by the wagons became a scene of hideous carnage.

A terrified riderless horse zigzagged aimlessly towards the woods. Ben Hur snatched up the trailing bridle and comfortingly stroked the animal's neck. Then, taking a deep breath, he vaulted into the saddle. The horse reared for a moment, but soon quietened down.

Ben Hur scanned the area and caught a glimpse of the bareheaded figure of the General, still mounted, accompanied by his Tribunes. He was in the thick of the press just in front of the line of wagons.

Ben Hur nudged the horse and cantered downhill. By the time he reached Suetonius the battle was virtually over.

'The Iceni will never fight again,' the General said with grim satisfaction.

Bodies were strewn everywhere. A few pitiful survivors were throwing down their weapons and surrendering to the legionaries. On all sides the din of the conflict was dying down, and flocks of birds were already wheeling overhead.

The Senior Centurion strode up, blood pouring from a gash in his head. He halted by Suetonius' horse, but did not bother to salute. 'The wagons, General – shall I burn them?'

'No. We need the timber. Get some of your men started on making crosses. I want every prisoner crucified!'

Ben Hur drew a deep breath. He felt small pity for the Iceni, but the words brought back a painful memory. Once again he recalled the gentle carpenter's son who had suffered a criminal's death ...

A thunder of hooves brought his mind back to the present. It was Agricola, his mount in a lather.

'Well?' Suetonius demanded.

The Tribune shook his head. 'Boudicca has vanished! I could find no sign of her anywhere.'

Suetonius turned to Ben Hur. His eyes were hard and cruel like iron. 'This one I want! Even if I have to find her myself! Get the scouts, Severus!'

CHAPTER TWENTY

The deep forest was deathly quiet. Not even the birds seemed to sing. The little procession trudged mournfully along, as if carrying a body to its burial.

Boudicca led the way, the tight lines of her face showing no sign of the awful, numbing defeat which filled her soul. Brigantia, a smear of blood on her smooth girl's cheek, silently followed her mother. The princess still clutched a naked sword.

Raising her right hand listlessly, Boudicca signalled a halt. The two uncles and the escort of six warriors gathered round her.

'Why are we stopping?' Tasgetius demanded.

'The Romans cannot be far behind,' Segovax pointed out.

'That is why I must leave you.' She turned to her daughter. 'You must go with your great-uncles.'

Brigantia stared at her. 'I want to be with you! Why must we separate?'

'I will go to the other tribes. The resistance against the Romans must continue!'

'Let me go with you.'

'No.'

'Why not?'

'Our family must survive. If the Romans find us together, we shall all be destroyed.'

Brigantia regarded her mother stubbornly. 'If you die, I want to die too!'

'Don't be a fool!' Boudicca said angrily. 'We must look beyond ourselves. We must live for our people! It is their future we fight for.'

'I don't care,' said Brigantia defiantly. 'I could never leave you. Not now.' Suddenly the girl burst into tears, flinging the sword away. The sobs were somehow deadened in the gloomy forest. She gazed up pleadingly at the Queen, her eyes swollen with grief. 'Do not send me away!'

Abruptly Boudicca slapped her. There was a silence. Brigantia's weeping ceased.

'Go!' the Queen ordered.

'No!' Brigantia shouted back.

Tasgetius took her gently by the arm. 'Your mother is right. Obey her! Today you stopped being a child. Do not act like one ...'

Furiously she shook him off and faced Boudicca again. 'I will not leave you to the Romans!'

The Queen felt a bleak sense of pride as she met her daughter's eyes. The girl would make a great leader if only fate would spare her. Arguments, however, were clearly not going to work. Guile was necessary.

'My daughter, you act as though we were saying good-bye for ever. But that is not so. We will see each other soon – in only a few days.'

Brigantia looked puzzled. 'How can that be?'

'As soon as I have accomplished my mission, I will come to you.'

'You swear it?'

'I swear.'

'Then fix a time and place.'

'Very well,' said Boudicca, hating herself as she uttered the words. 'The Stone Ring. In ten days.'

The girl hesitated.

'Go!' Boudicca insisted. 'Hurry!'

'You will be there?'

'Yes! Now take up your sword, and be off!'

Still Brigantia did not move. Segovax picked up the sword and pushed it into the girl's hands.

'Come!' said Tasgetius.

The uncles drew Brigantia away, urging her down the trail. As she went, the girl turned, throwing a last pleading look at her mother.

Boudicca tore her eyes from Brigantia and faced the warriors who still waited by her side. 'Go with her,' she commanded. 'Guard her!'

Obediently the men shouldered their spears and set off after the girl and the old men.

Boudicca waited until they were out of sight. The scent which had first made her halt was still present. None of the others had noticed it, and Boudicca had been careful not to bring it to their attention. It was the smell of burning acorns, coming from the east.

Leaving the trail, she set out in that direction, moving purposefully through the bracken. As she tramped along steadily, the smell grew stronger and stronger.

Then she paused. She knew the fire was just ahead. She plunged forward into a clearing. There a sacred oak spread its gnarled tyranny over the earth. Under it, before the smouldering fire, sat the black-robed, cowled figure. He rose, drew back his hood, revealing the familiar blue-stained features.

'You have come ...' Dumnorix said.

She nodded. 'I fought the Romans as you wished. Now I have a service to ask of you.'

'We'll fight them again. The Romans have won a battle. Let them win a hundred. We will win the last.'

Boudicca stared at him incredulously. 'You are truly inhuman! You have no thought for life and death! You and your kind are doomed! The Romans cannot be stopped!'

Dumnorix laughed. 'All you see is the defeat of your own people. But I see beyond that. The Druids will still be here. Long after the Romans are driven away.'

Boudicca made a contemptuous gesture. 'What happens to the Druids means nothing to me.'

'Then why are you here?'

'I said – I have a service to ask of you.'

'What is it?'

'It is a terrible sin to take one's own life. Yet I do not want to live.'

He frowned. 'You are asking me to end your life?'

Boudicca unsheathed her dagger and offered it to him. 'Do not make me wait!'

Suetonius watched impassively as the Batavian scout turned the body over.

'What about the burial?' asked Ben Hur.

Suetonius scowled. 'Burial?'

'She was a Queen ...' Ben Hur kicked the mud of the forest trail. 'The earth is soft. It will not take long to dig a grave.'

'We'll leave the last rites to the crows!' the commander said flatly, starting away.

The Tribunes tramped after the General, pushing through the bracken until they reached the forest trail at the base of the hill. Here more scouts and cavalrymen waited, holding horses. Suetonius mounted, pointing to the shady depths ahead. 'Now for the others.'

'General,' said Agricola quickly. 'With your permission. The Queen is dead. Is there any point in going after a few stragglers?'

The General fixed him with an angry eye. 'Apparently I have not made my purpose clear. I want *every last Iceni*!'

Emphatically he wheeled his horse and waved the trackers on.

Ben Hur and Agricola exchanged a look. They were fortunate indeed to be fighting *with* the General and not against him.

The Romans rode in silence for a time. At last one of the scouts came padding back along the trail, holding up his hand urgently. Their quarry was ahead. At a sign from the General, they dismounted and noiselessly drew their swords. Now, cautiously, they followed the tracker down an ivy-covered slope. In a moment, the sound of a stream was heard.

Through the trees, the fugitives became visible. They had stopped on the bank and were clustered round one of their number, an old man. He appeared to have hurt his ankle, for a young woman was wrapping it tightly with a strip of leather.

Suetonius favoured Agricola with a sardonic smile. 'Running these "few stragglers" to earth has proved more worthwhile than you thought, Tribune,' he whispered. 'That female is Boudicca's daughter!'

The General beckoned with his sword and started forward at a half-crouch, but he trod on a dry trig which cracked like a whip.

'Take them!' Suetonius shouted, all attempt at concealment gone. He rushed forward. The other Romans dashed after him, crashing through the brush into the open.

The Briton warriors leaped to their feet, levelling spears to meet the attack. All the Celts lunged at Suetonius, prominent with his bare white head and elaborate cuirass.

Agricola shouted a warning, thrusting himself in front of Suetonius, as the other Romans rallied round their commander.

For a moment Ben Hur's vision was filled with nothing but flashing weapons and shouting faces. Then he was aware of a movement off to one side.

Boudicca's daughter was running away down the bank of the stream, and the two old men were making off rapidly in another direction. Instinctively Ben Hur went after the most valuable captive.

The young woman threw a look over her shoulder, then plunged into the bushes, disappearing from sight.

Ben Hur followed. Here the foliage was a green maze, branches and vines hanging everywhere. There was no sign of his quarry, but Ben Hur was not surprised. The thickness of the undergrowth would conceal anything more than a few feet away. At last he emerged into a clearing. No one was visible. His eyes probing the damp gloom, he advanced warily.

It was the sound which saved his life – a sharp intake of breath. Involuntarily he jumped aside just as a glittering blade whooshed past, only inches from his head.

The young woman stood there, eyes blazing. Ben Hur had not realized that she was armed. She raised the great broadsword, swinging another blow at him. Ben Hur retreated, holding his own weapon defensively in front of him. The adversaries circled each other. Again the Iceni's deadly blade swished through the air, and Ben Hur leaped away.

For once, the short Roman sword was no advantage. Without a

shield to block the slashes of his adversary, Ben Hur dared not move in close enough to use the stabbing blade properly. The Iceni girl seemed to sense this. In a sudden rush, she came at him, slashing with all her strength. Ben Hur darted to one side. Immediately she aimed another blow, and he had to leap away again.

He withdrew into the trees, but the woman followed him. Then, as she raised the weapon for another attack, she tripped over a dead branch, falling to her hands and knees. Instantly Ben Hur flung himself on her, seizing her sword hand, twisting the weapon away from her. She writhed like a rabid cat. It was all he could do to hold her, pinning her arms above her head, sitting astride her body. He stared down at the venomous little creature. Her eyes were pools of hatred. She muttered something, but Ben Hur could not understand the words. Then she spat in his face.

At last a crashing in the bushes told him the Romans were approaching.

'Over here!' he called.

Suetonius was the first to arrive. He strode over, staring down at the prostrate woman. 'Good work, Severus ...'

The scouts came up, followed by the cavalrymen. Two of the soldiers knelt either side of Ben Hur, gripping the girl's arms.

'Tie her!' Suetonius commanded.

Ben Hur rose, releasing her. Instantly she kicked out, catching one of the scouts in the shins. She struggled desperately, but four more Roman cavalrymen rushed to the aid of their fellows. In an instant they had her pinioned and helpless.

Ben Hur stared at her defiant face. Suddenly it no longer mattered that she had been trying to kill him only a moment before. Doubtless she wished all Romans dead. She had just witnessed the brutalities of battle. Her sister had been cut down before her eyes. Perhaps she had seen her mother die too.

'Put a halter on her,' Suetonius commanded. 'We'll nail Her Royal Highness on the highest cross of all!'

'General, with your permission,' Ben Hur found himself saying. 'Show mercy ...'

Suetonius glanced at him sharply. 'You heard my order.'

'Killing the girl will not solve anything.'

'I'm surprised at you, Severus. Would you seriously consider leaving Boudicca's heir alive – to raise more resistance? Besides – I mean to make an example which will never be forgotten!'

Ben Hur's glance went to the Iceni woman. They would tie her hands, then throw a noose round her waist, drawing it tight. They would force her to walk behind their horses to the site of her execution. If she resisted or faltered, she would be dragged.

Something seemed to take possession of him. Almost with a will of its own, his hand snatched up the sword from the ground, and pressed it against Suetonius' neck. 'Release her!' he heard himself saying.

No one moved or spoke. The silence in the clearing was deafening.

He cursed himself! He cursed his impulsiveness! His stupidity! God above – he was not this woman's champion, and he had no stomach for playing the part! She was a stranger. What did it matter if she died? Thousands had already been killed this day! How he wished she had been one of them!

'Get out of here!' Ben Hur bellowed at her.

She hesitated.

'Get out!' he shouted again.

Recovering her wits, the young woman dashed into the trees, disappearing immediately.

The Romans waited while the sounds of the body crashing through the brush grew fainter and fainter, then finally died away. But the tableau in the clearing remained the same.

Suetonius broke the silence. 'It seems to be an impasse, Severus. You can kill me now. But there are fourteen heavily armed men here. Do you think you can prevail against them?'

'I will not try. I will drop my sword if you give your word not to go after the Iceni woman.'

'You would take my word?'

'Yes.'

Suetonius laughed harshly. 'You are a dead man now, Severus – no matter what you do. You'll be brought to trial. There is only one possible penalty.'

'Do I have your pledge not to go after her?' Ben Hur demanded.

There was a moment of silence. Finally Suetonius nodded. 'You have my word.'

Ben Hur threw the weapon to the ground. Instantly fourteen swords hissed from their scabbards.

Suetonius watched thoughtfully as two of the cavalrymen sheathed their swords and began to tie Ben Hur's hands.

'Stop!' Suetonius ordered suddenly.

The cavalrymen paused obediently, but the others did not lower their swords.

'On reflection, Severus,' said the General, 'I owe you a life. Therefore, I will grant you yours. But in assaulting your commander, you have dishonoured the Legion and violated your oath. You can never be a soldier again. Now go.'

Ben Hur hesitated. He glanced at the other Tribunes. They too were amazed at the General's unexpected clemency.

'Go!' the Commander repeated.

Ben Hur bent over to retrieve his sword, but the General placed his foot on the hilt.

For an instant Ben Hur met Suetonius' cold eyes. Then, leaving the weapon, he made off into the trees.

He found himself on the rocky backbone of a line of hills. Before him stretched miles and miles of lonely forest. On one side the slope ran down into the green pasture land of a Celtic farm, bordered on its far side by still more forest.

An impulse made Ben Hur choose this way. Descending the hillside and crossing the grassland, he came to a gentle stream. He knelt and plunged his face into the still waters. For a while he remained on his knees, giving thanks for his deliverance. Now, refreshed, he resumed his journey until he reached the trees on the edge of the meadow.

Time passed, but he had no idea how long. He became aware that the trees were thicker, their great gnarled trunks covered with green moss. Yet the foliage overhead seemed thinner, for the light filtered down in green-gold rays. A feeling of intense drowsiness seized him. He tried to shake it off, still anxious to make progress, though he knew not where. But the torpor was insistent and grew stronger. He yearned for peace, if only for a few moments.

Finally he stopped and sank to the ground, resting his back against a mossy treetrunk. His weary eyes took in the idyllic beauty surrounding him. If he had to die, this would not be a bad place . . .

Then he was shaking his head to clear it. He had dozed . . .

Squatting on her haunches, not ten paces away, was the Iceni woman. Her large round eyes stared unblinkingly at him with no change of expression. For the first time he realized how comely she was. Her body was in the full bloom of youth, and her face still had the soft roundness of a child.

'What are you doing here?' Ben Hur demanded.

She replied, but the words were unintelligible. Ben Hur rose. 'Have you been following me?'

Again the girl spoke in her strange Celtic tongue. Ben Hur realized that she understood no Latin.

She got to her feet as well. She pointed towards the woods, and started away, beckoning to him.

He hesitated. Apparently he had won her friendship, but could not be sure. He remembered her hate-filled eyes as she leaped from behind the tree, swinging her sword at him . . .

She paused and beckoned again. Warily, he followed.

They tramped along steadily. For two days they had travelled through thick woods, interrupted only by rivers or rocky outcroppings. Ben Hur had never seen a land so heavily forested.

The girl had conveyed to him by constant repetition that her name was Brigantia. In spite of the language barrier they had managed to communicate through signs. Survival had been no difficulty. They were never far from fresh water, and Brigantia had proved to be skilled in the ways of the forest. She could trap small game and birds, she knew which plants were edible, and she cooked everything they ate. Ben Hur wondered if this was the way men had lived in the Golden Age described so lovingly by Greek and Latin poets. It made sense that long ago, before the invention of metals, weapons or private property, men must have lived in closer communion with nature, in a state of idyllic peace.

He peered ahead at Brigantia's attractive body as she toiled up a slope. He was close behind her, and suddenly they were clear of the trees, on the edge of a broad meadowland flooded with sunlight.

Before them rose strange and monstrous shapes; giant stones set upright in the ground to form a huge circle. Each stone was so large it would have taken many men to move it. Yet they had obviously been put here by men, for they were arranged in an elaborate pattern. Resting on top of many upright blocks were lintels of smaller size, creating massive, monolithic doorways.

Brigantia pointed to the place excitedly, chattering in her Iceni language. Then she beckoned for him to follow. As had become his habit in the last few days, he did so. But abruptly he halted. Other people were occupying the Stone Ring! They were about forty or fifty Iceni warriors, both men and women.

The princess impatiently urged him to hurry. He shook his head, indicating his Roman tunic. Other Iceni were not likely to give him a favourable reception.

Brigantia, however, took him by the arm and pulled. Ben Hur tried to extricate himself, but it was too late. The Iceni had noticed him. Picking up their spears, they moved forward threateningly. Among these warriors Ben Hur recognized the two elderly men who had been with the fugitives on the river bank.

Now the Princess ran to meet them, shouting loudly. The warriors lowered their spears, and a voluble conversation ensued. From time to time, some of the Iceni threw hostile looks at Ben Hur.

The two old men stroked their moustaches thoughtfully as they listened. Finally, they came over to Ben Hur. One of them spoke in halting Latin.

'I am Segovax,' he announced. He indicated the other man. 'This is my brother, Tasgetius.'

Segovax glanced at Brigantia, who joined them. Then he faced Ben Hur again. 'Our great-niece is very thankful for what you have done. And so are the rest of us. Tell us what you are called, so that we may thank you by name.'

'I am Gaius Severus, Tribune of the Twentieth Legion.'

Segovax and Tasgetius exchanged an uneasy look.

'It will be difficult for us to make our warriors look on a Roman Tribune as a friend,' Segovax muttered. 'However, I will try.'

'Perhaps I can help you,' Ben Hur suggested. 'I am Roman only by adoption. My real name is Judah Ben Hur. I was born in Judaea.'

The two uncles frowned.

'Judaea ...' Segovax said thoughtfully. 'I have never heard of that land ...'

'It is on the other side of the earth,' Ben Hur told him. 'Like you, the people of Judaea have fought the Romans for many years.'

Satisfied, Segovax nodded. He turned and addressed the other Iceni, who listened with rapt attention. Tasgetius added his own exhortations to his brother's. Ben Hur glanced at Brigantia. He thought he could detect new interest in her eyes.

Finally, when the uncles had finished their speech, they turned back to him.

Ben Hur pointed to the monoliths which surrounded them on all sides. 'This place where we are now,' he wondered. 'What is it?'

The old man spoke reverently. 'It was built by the Gods before time began. The Stone Ring is one of the holiest shrines in Britain. All the Iceni who have survived the battle will eventually come here.'

'How long will you remain here?'

'Until our Queen comes.'

'She will not come,' Ben Hur said quietly. 'She is dead.'

Both men were overcome with dismay. Tasgetius finally found words. 'Are you sure of this?'

Ben Hur nodded. 'I saw her body.'

Once again the uncles exchanged a look. Then they faced Brigantia and spoke to her soothingly.

She stiffened, choking out a question. Segovax replied hastily, patting her arm.

Abruptly she turned and walked away from the group, heading for an enormous blue-stone altar beneath the largest of the craggy pillars. She stood there, gazing upwards.

Ben Hur glanced at the warriors. Both men and women were subdued. Clearly they had heard the sad tidings as well. But none of them made any move to go and speak to the lonely princess.

'I have told her what happened.' Segovax informed Ben Hur. 'Her grief was beyond words. But I reminded her that she is now Queen. She has gone to the altar to pray for her mother's spirit and to ask for guidance.'

Segovax took Ben Hur by the arm. Tasgetius beckoned to the warriors, and the whole party withdrew to a respectful distance from Brigantia.

'Surely there is something we can do to comfort her,' Ben Hur said finally.

Tasgetius shook his head. 'It is best that we wait.'

'She must think,' Segovax explained. 'She has a great decision to make. My brother and I have advised her to flee north and seek refuge with the Caledonians. But she does not want to abandon the land of her ancestors. She is afraid the Iceni will no longer be a people. It is for her to decide. She is Queen.'

Time passed. At last Brigantia left the altar and started back to her people. Tasgetius and Segovax hurried forward to meet her.

An intense conversation began. Several times Brigantia pointed towards Ben Hur. One by one the other Iceni moved over to join the discussion, leaving Ben Hur alone. Soon a full-scale council was in progress, everyone speaking at once.

Then Brigantia uttered a sudden command and, with an imperious sweep of her hand, silenced the whole group. She began to speak, but two young men stepped closer to her, shouting loudly. Her face flushed with anger, she shouted back. In confusion the men retreated. Several of the older Iceni clearly found the situation amusing, and laughed at the younger men's discomfiture.

When the discussion ended, the uncles returned to Ben Hur, followed by Brigantia.

'She has made known her will,' Segovax announced. 'It remains for us to obey. We shall return to our tribal lands and start afresh. She wishes that you accompany us.'

Ben Hur shrugged. 'Very well.'

'It will be dangerous,' the old man warned. 'The Romans may still search for us and pursue their vengeance.'

'I will risk it.'

'There is more . . .' Segovax paused, then, pulling his eyebrow, he continued. 'Because she is the last of the royal family, Brigantia has decided that her first duty is to produce an heir. She wishes that you be the one to impregnate her.'

It took a moment for Ben Hur to absorb this.

'She insists it is fitting, for it is because of you that our royal house has not been destroyed,' the uncle explained. 'Furthermore she finds you agreeable. She hopes that you do not find her unattractive.'

Ben Hur glanced at Brigantia. She stood there regally, almost haughtily, but her eyes were unmistakably anxious.

Finally he smiled. 'No, I do not find her unattractive.'

CHAPTER TWENTY-ONE

Ben Hur moved restlessly. He hoped he had not wakened Brigantia, but she seemed fast asleep. A rasping snore came from the slumbering figure on the other side of him. He knew it was Segovax, for when Tasgetius slept he never made anything more than an odd, gulping sound. Ben Hur settled himself on the rushes, moving away from the elderly men, and sliding closer to Brigantia.

As he pulled the harsh blanket up over his chin, he detected the first rays of grey light filtering through a crack in the wattle wall of the Long House. The structure was new, and they had not yet had time to search out all the chinks and fill them. Brigantia had chosen this spot for the village because it was not far from the ancient Iceni capital. She had repeated to Ben Hur some of the legends about the place which her mother had told her as a small child.

He smiled at her dim shape by his side. She was already using many Latin words. Of course, he had picked up a great deal of her tongue as well, and they spoke to each other in an odd hybrid jargon culled from both languages.

Many aspects of life with the Iceni were not easy. He was having difficulty getting used to their customs. Brigantia was not yet his wife, for it was expected that an Iceni couple would live together for a season before marriage, to make sure they were congenial. Only then would the wedding ceremony be performed. There were times when Ben Hur felt as though he were on trial.

He had, of course, expected to enjoy sexual relations with his consort in bed, as Greeks, Romans and Jews did. But this was not to be. To the Iceni, bed and slumber were a communal activity to be shared by the whole family and guests as well. Ben Hur was grateful that Brigantia's family consisted only of Tasgetius and Segovax. Their body odours were not always pleasant and they were noisy sleepers, but this was infinitely preferable to sharing a bed with cousins, aunts, nephews and miscellaneous offspring, not to mention other close friends. Ben Hur knew of some beds in the village which contained at least a score of people.

As was the Iceni way, Ben Hur had intercourse with Brigantia in the daytime, seeking out trysting places in the forest. Inconveniences such as rain, frost or insects were to be ignored. Indeed, indifference to inclement weather was considered a measure of passion.

He sighed. In spite of these hardships, he found himself hoping that his time with her would not come to a sudden end.

'Why are you sighing?' came her low voice from the darkness.

'I did not know you were awake,' he whispered.

'How can I sleep with you flopping about like a fish?'

'It does not seem to disturb your uncles.'

'Nothing disturbs them. Now tell me why you were sighing.'

'A sad thought came to me. If I should be unable to give you an heir, I will have to go. Yet it will not be easy to leave you.'

She chuckled. 'You have grown attached to me . . .'

'In some ways,' Ben Hur admitted.

'If I chose another man to marry,' she stated, 'you would kill yourself!'

'You are a fool,' Ben Hur laughed. 'I am fond of you, but that is as far as it goes!'

'There will be no need to kill yourself,' she told him. 'You have given me an heir. I have known it for some time.'

For a moment, Ben Hur could find no words. Brigantia had an offhand way of delivering momentous information which never failed to take him by surprise.

'Why did you not tell me earlier?' he demanded.

'There is a problem. With whose Gods shall we raise the child? I wish to be fair.'

'Raise the child as you wish. I have no Gods.'

She gasped. 'No Gods! But . . . that cannot be!'

'I have found no God to whom I can give my complete allegiance.'

She sat up, staring at him. 'It is a terrible thing you have told me, Judah! No person should be without a God!'

'I had a God once.'

'What was he called?'

'Jesus Christ.'

'Jesus Christ was the God of your household?'

'No.'

Brigantia was clearly puzzled. 'No? Then how did you come to know him?'

'He appeared to us ... my friends ... my people, as another man.'

She snorted. 'All Gods – except the most feeble – can appear in human form!'

'You don't understand. This God was different from others. He wanted nothing from human beings, or so he claimed. No sacrifices or offerings – only that his followers should love each other and believe in him.'

'If he cared for his people so much, why did you turn away from him?'

'Because what he asked of men is more than they are willing to give.'

She gazed at Ben Hur for a moment longer, then she lay down again, drawing the prickly blanket over her body. For a time she was silent.

'The child must have a name,' she said suddenly.

'How can we name it until we know whether it is a boy or a girl?'

'We must think of a name for each. No infant should come into the world without a name.'

'What if you are bearing three – or four? It could happen.'

'You Roman-Judaean! I will think of the names! I should know better than to ask you for help.'

Suddenly Ben Hur was jolted as a body rolled into him. Tasgetius sat up, rubbing his eyes.

'Why are you lolling in bed so late?' he demanded. 'There is much to be done. There are provisions yet to bring in before the cold comes upon us.'

Tasgetius shook his brother. The other old man struggled to a sitting position, coughing, clearing his throat, and breaking wind loudly. The motion pulled the blanket from Ben Hur's body, and the sharp autumn air struck his limbs. Climbing out of the bed, he wrapped himself in his cloak, shivering.

He was getting accustomed to the morning ritual. All four of them hurried down the steps to answer the call of nature under convenient trees. When they had built the Long House, he had suggested to Brigantia that they place a Roman-style privy inside. But she had found the idea offensive.

When the Iceni re-entered the Long House, Ben Hur had to wait, as usual, while they cleaned their teeth with hazel shoots, then polished them with woollen cloths until they shone like ivory. Although Ben Hur would have no part of this bizarre habit, nothing would make the Iceni rush through it. The Britons were the only race Ben Hur had ever encountered who placed such importance on keeping the teeth in good condition. It was a strange preoccupation indeed.

Illogically, once this long and complex cleaning operation was finished, the three Iceni sat down for a sparse meal of hare cooked the night before, accompanied by thick milk. Ben Hur joined them for the food.

At last they descended the steps of the Long House to begin their tasks. Most of the Iceni were already in the forest, collecting wood for the winter. They were also foraging for acorns on which the tribe would have to subsist during the cold season, as their ancient ancestors had done. War had prevented Boudicca from gathering in the harvest.

For the last weeks they had been labouring to construct storage pits for these provisions, as well as new dwellings for the village.

Ben Hur paused to examine one of the cavernous holes they had dug the day before. Intended for the preservation of food, it was lined with hard clay to keep out the moisture and could be sealed on top. Nearby, ovens had been fashioned of the same clay. Here the meal made from the acorns would be dried before storage.

Just then a group of Iceni foragers emerged from the woods which extended halfway up the hillside. It was much too early in the day for them to be returning home, yet here they were, clutching tools and weapons, approaching at a run.

In a moment they had entered the citadel. Two youths spied Brigantia and sprinted towards her.

'Romans!' one of them gasped. 'They have just forded the river! They're coming this way! Hundreds of them!'

'I knew it was too good to last!' Tasgetius exclaimed. 'I warned you they would find us! We shall be butchered! At best, made slaves!'

Segovax regarded his niece reproachfully. 'You should have listened to us. We should have fled to the Caledonians and sought refuge with them!'

Brigantia shook her head. 'We did the right thing. It is what my mother would have done – stand where our ancestors stood.'

'If I remember rightly,' Segovax said sourly, 'you and your mother did not often agree. In those days you were more interested in Roman styles than our ancestral traditions.'

'That is true,' Brigantia admitted. 'But now I know that she was right.'

'She would not have insisted that we stay here to be taken away in chains and made slaves. No, never ... Now, if we had fled to the Caledonians –'

'This is foolishness!' Ben Hur interrupted. He had grown well enough acquainted with the Iceni to realize that they would argue all day about what might have been, regardless of any danger which happened to be descending on them at the moment. 'Are you forgetting? The Romans are only a few miles away! We must go into the forest. Separate into families. Hide. They will not find everyone. When the Romans have gone, the Iceni will return.'

'They will destroy this place,' Tasgetius protested. 'They will plunder all the provisions we have laboured so hard to gather.'

'Let them!' Brigantia cried. 'If we must start all over again – we will do so!' She took Ben Hur by the arm. 'Judah is right.'

Brigantia turned to the others who had clustered round, anxiously listening to the debate. 'Go! Gather your families. Your children! We will meet back here. Do not bring any belongings. We have no time.'

Hurriedly they began to move away. A few muttered as they went, throwing hostile looks at Ben Hur. He knew that many of them resented him, disliking the idea that a foreigner should have such weight in their affairs.

Ben Hur faced the young Queen. 'Brigantia,' he said gently, 'you must go without me.'

She stared at him, amazed. 'Without you? Why?'

'I will stay here and talk to the Romans. Perhaps I can persuade them that the Iceni are no longer a threat – that you wish only to live here in peace.'

'You are mad. They will kill you! You have committed a crime in the Roman army.'

'Suetonius spared me.'

'He will not do it a second time. Especially if you are coming to the Romans on behalf of their enemies.'

'There is no other way. You cannot keep hiding for ever. I do not want my child to come into such a life.'

'Then I will stay with you.'

'Now that is folly!' Ben Hur exclaimed vehemently. 'Suetonius has condemned every Iceni to death on sight!'

'If you remain here – so will I!'

Ben Hur appraised her stubborn face. He was reminded of her mother on horseback, sword in hand. He shrugged. 'Very well. I will go with you into the forest.'

He lay on his back, squinting to shut out the sunlight filtering through the trees, which displayed the last of their autumn finery. His eyes burned with weariness, but he could not sleep. How he envied the others. The whole group, Tasgetius, Segovax, half a dozen young people, were sprawled on the earth, sleeping soundly.

Though this hiding place was in deep forest, it was not far from the settlement, since Brigantia hoped to return quickly once the Romans had left. The Iceni had burned no fires and had subsisted on cold food. For the first night none of them had been able to sleep. Now another day had come, and exhaustion had caught up with everyone.

'Judah ...' Brigantia's eyes were open, but the lids were still heavy with weariness. 'Will the Romans find us?'

'They will certainly look. But even if they capture some, others will escape.'

There was a silence.

Then Brigantia spoke. 'Judah, I beg you ... pray to the God Jesus Christ to shield us from the Romans. I know you no longer follow him ... But our own Gods have turned against us ... The signs are clear.'

Ben Hur hesitated.

'Please, Judah ...'

Struggling to his knees, he took both her hands. Aware of her steady gaze, he uttered a prayer. 'Jesus Christ Almighty, in the name of your Heavenly Father, have mercy on the Icenian people.

Guard them from the vengeance of the Romans. Make the Iceni strong and give their Queen the wisdom to lead them ...'

He glanced at her solemn face. Suddenly he bent over and kissed her slightly parted lips.

'Rest, my little Queen,' he whispered. 'Sleep.'

The anxiety seemed to leave her face. Gradually her eyes closed, and soon she was breathing rhythmically.

For a long time he remained in the same position, holding her hands, not daring to move for fear of waking her.

He did not want to trust their fate to Gods. A God, after all, might just as easily ignore a man as help him. And if there was to be a conflict of divine powers, it would seem that the Roman Gods were stronger than any powers the Iceni could summon.

He must confront the Romans. Making a plea for the Iceni would be risky indeed, but he could see no other way. Another look round the little camp reassured him that the others were all still asleep. If he was to act now was the time ...

Yet he hesitated an instant, reluctant to leave this woman who was bearing his child. His thoughts flew back over his turbulent life. How distant that day seemed when he had buried Esther – when he had vowed in his grief that he would never take another wife. But the demands for procreation carried in Leah's sensuous vitality had challenged this vow. Yet the inexplicable twists of fate had taken him away from Leah too – and it was only here in the thick forests of this strange land that the opportunity had been granted him to refound the house of Hur. But now – would his legacy for the future be cut short, on the very threshold of fulfilment?

Grimly Ben Hur got to his feet. Summoning his reserves of strength, he glided silently into the trees.

He moved steadily at a slight trot, faster than a walk, but not quite a run. At all costs, he wanted to return to the settlement before the Romans left. Otherwise the whole futile process of flight, hiding, and rebuilding the settlement would be repeated the next time the Romans returned. And they would come back – they never gave up.

In spite of his weariness, the steady motion began to invigorate him. His eyes still ached from the strain of constant vigilance, but his head was rapidly clearing.

Before the sun was down, he reached the border of the woodland. In front of him rose the hill, crowned by its familiar fort. The ramparts were still standing, so there was hope that he was in time. Had the Romans already left, they would surely have demolished the defences.

He moved closer, keeping to the bushes. He detected the smoke of fires rising from the citadel, and the flash of sunlight on metal. Soon he could hear the sound of distant voices.

He would have to advance in the open. In his baggy British trousers laced up to the knees and his short leather jerkin, he knew he might easily be taken as an enemy. He took a deep breath. Stepping out of the shrubbery, raising his hands high to show that he bore no arms, he began to ascend the hill.

A soldier's helmeted head appeared over the palisade. A challenge rang out, echoing down the hillside. Ben Hur halted immediately.

'I am a Roman!' he shouted back. 'I come in peace! I want to see your commander!'

'Stand where you are!' the sentry replied.

The helmet disappeared from sight, and for an interval there was nothing but silence. Ben Hur was beyond the range of javelins or even arrows, but he prayed that they had no ballistae with them. He remembered a tale about a German warrior who had been nailed to a tree by a bolt from such a weapon shot from about a quarter of a mile away.

Finally both helmet and voice returned. 'Advance, but slowly!'

At every step Ben Hur's flesh crawled with anticipation of a hail of deadly missiles. Clothed as he was, he knew that his claim to be Roman might well be doubted. They could be encouraging him to come closer so that he would present a better target. There would certainly be many men behind that palisade who would have to be restrained from killing any Iceni on sight.

Finally he achieved the gate. It was open. Entering, Ben Hur paused. Lines of armoured Romans stationed behind the ramparts peered curiously at him.

In the clearing before the Long House, the lone figure of a Tribune stood waiting, feet apart slightly, hands on hips. He started towards Ben Hur. His limp was familiar.

'Paetus!' Ben Hur cried.

The two ran to each other, clasping hands warmly.

'Paetus, can it be you?' Ben Hur exclaimed. 'I thought you were dead!'

'Severus! You son of a goat! I thought the same about you. The story of your defying Suetonius has spread everywhere. You are the talk of Britain, by Jupiter! But no one expected you to survive the wilderness! And without arms!'

'It seems I was fated to live.'

Paetus gave him a knowing look. 'If I'm not mistaken, Fate had a little help! I'd be willing to wager every denarius I've hoarded these years – that barbarian female whose pretty neck you saved had something to do with it.'

'I won't deny it. But tell me about yourself, Paetus. I thought you must have been killed on the way to Postumus. Yet here you are – and a Tribune too!'

'Centurion was all I ever hoped for,' Paetus said wryly. 'When they told me I was a Tribune, I thought someone had made a mistake.' He took Ben Hur by the arm. 'There is no point in standing here in the sun. I have some fine Falernian inside.'

Paetus escorted him to the Long House, and they mounted the steps. Inside, Paetus crossed directly to the far corner and took up a skin of wine.

Ben Hur waited, now more hopeful for his mission. How curious, he thought, that his plea to spare the Iceni would be made in the very room where he had lived and slept with Brigantia.

Paetus returned with two goblets, one of which he thrust at Ben Hur. Taking the wine, Ben Hur raised the cup.

'I drink to your Lares. May there be no limit to your success!'

They drank.

'I'm glad you've advanced so high, Paetus, not only because I wish you well, but for selfish reasons.'

'Selfish reasons?'

'I need your help on behalf of the Iceni. It is unfair that the survivors are proscribed. They have suffered enough. They should –'

Ben Hur broke off, as Paetus began to laugh.

'I was not aware that I said anything amusing,' Ben Hur murmured.

'You did, Severus. Oh yes, you did indeed! But for a reason

beyond your knowing. It so happens your wish coincides with the will of our most Glorious and Radiant Emperor. In fact, I am here to grant a pardon to every surviving member of the Iceni tribe.'

Ben Hur gazed at him, surprised and pleased. 'How did Suetonius react to this?'

'Who knows ... Suetonius was relieved of his command. He's left Britain. You see, they sent out a Commission of Inquiry from Rome. One of Nero's freedmen was in charge of it. They decided that Suetonius' methods were too harsh. So they've replaced him with someone far more easy-going.'

'Who is he?'

'A man named Turpillianus. They say the Glorious and Radiant Nero grew tired of Turpillianus and welcomed the chance to kick him all the way to this cold island. Actually, he is not a bad old gentleman. But he drinks too much. To keep warm, he claims. He leaves all the work to me.'

'Then it is really *you* who governs the Province.'

Paetus shrugged. 'Behind the scenes, anyway ...'

'Britain is in good hands. I always knew you were a capable man, Paetus. No one could be more deserving of good fortune.'

Paetus put down his cup. 'No one could be *less* deserving,' he said quietly. 'It is those who are undeserving who get ahead in this world.'

'Surely you are too modest.'

Paetus regarded him soberly. 'Can I trust you, Severus?'

'I hope so.'

'I need to speak to someone,' he muttered. 'Severus – promise me that this will remain between the two of us only.'

'Of course.'

'You'll remember when Suetonius sent me for those reinforcements.'

Ben Hur nodded.

'I got through all right. But Postumus refused to obey. He was sure that Suetonius would be annihilated. My duty was clear – go back, report Postumus' disobedience, then die with my Legion. Instead I saved my neck. I stayed with Postumus.'

Pateus took a deep breath, then went on, spitting out the words as if ridding himself of a bad taste. 'The news came that Suetonius had won. Postumus, like a good Roman, killed himself to atone for his disgrace. Do you know what I did, Severus? I put the blame on *him*. I claimed he'd ordered me to stay. For my heroic efforts, I was made a Tribune.'

He fell silent, his face white and strained.

Ben Hur understood what a burden Paetus had been carrying. All his life Paetus had lived according to the harsh, demanding code of the Legions. He had worshipped the spirit of the Eagle and followed with complete faith wherever it led. Having violated the commandments of the Eagle, he had damned himself for ever.

'Is it true, Paetus,' Ben Hur asked finally, 'that you have been wounded eight times?'

'All in the front of my body,' he said with a rueful touch of pride.

'Men in the Legion told me you have been in every major battle in Britain since Caratacus was defeated.'

'It is true.'

'Then perhaps you have more than made up for turning your back once. Paetus, the Gods owe you one.'

Paetus shook his head. 'I have told myself the same thing ... It is no comfort ... I have made sacrifices, been to the augurs – but the omens are all bad. Perhaps I should follow Postumus' example ...'

Impulsively Ben Hur put an arm round his old comrade's shoulders. In a way he had travelled the same path as Paetus to disillusionment and loss of faith. Paul had once described faith as the substance of things hoped for – the evidence of things not seen. It was true. Brigantia had given Ben Hur new hope, and her love was evidence of things unseen. But could Paetus find the same sort of salvation?

'If I were you,' Ben Hur ventured finally, 'I would not follow Postumus' example.'

Paetus regarded him with tortured eyes. 'What other course is there for a Roman officer?'

'Better to cease being Roman than to cease living.' Ben Hur grinned. 'You can always follow *my* example – become an Iceni.'

Paetus began to laugh.

'Become a savage?' He looked at Ben Hur. 'Wearing rabbit skins like you?' He laughed again. 'I think I'd rather be dead!'

*

The common ground between the huts was jammed with Roman supply wagons, each filled with grain cultivated for the Roman army, but now diverted to the Iceni. Most of the drivers had left with their oxen, planning to return later when the wagons had been unloaded.

Thanks to the new Roman policy, generously administered by Paetus, the Iceni would not starve. If they could survive the winter, as all auguries signified they would, the tribe would be re-established.

Ben Hur descended the steps of the Long House, and moved towards Brigantia, who was supervising a group of young men and women energetically digging new storage pits. Others were constructing additional ovens for drying the sudden glut of grain. But abundance brought its own problems. Ben Hur hoped fervently that they could get the corn dried and packed securely in the pits before it began to spoil.

Passing the heavily built military wagons, he joined Brigantia. She gave him a warm look as he linked his arm in hers. Several of the Iceni workers nodded to him. Though they were not given to smiling, there was no longer any hostility in their eyes. He knew they held him responsible for their good fortune. At least they accepted him as their Queen's consort.

They had expressed this feeling in their own way. The old bard of the tribe had been killed in the great battle, but one of the young men was learning the art of minstrelsy. Already he had composed a ballad about 'Judah's' intervention with a Roman general to save Brigantia's life. It seemed the people would accept what was sung to the accompaniment of a harp more quickly than what was told them as precept by their elders.

Once again Ben Hur appraised the sacks of grain still packed in the wagons. He estimated the capacity of the clay ovens.

'You are a lucky woman to have a man like me,' he murmured to Brigantia.

She laughed. 'I have not married you yet.'

'You'll be in a hurry to do so when you hear what I have to say.'

'I am waiting. Speak.'

'We have been concerned that there will not be enough time to dry and store all this grain. Have you ever seen a Roman bath?'

'Yes. There were many in Londinium.'

'Do you know how they are heated?'

'No.'

'Come,' he said, guiding her towards one of the large clay ovens.

'Just outside the wall of a bath-house,' he explained, 'is a furnace which works in much the same way as this oven does. Where the furnace adjoins the building, there is an opening which allows the heat to flow under the floor of the bath-house.'

'The floor? The floor is raised?'

Ben Hur nodded. 'It is held up by many little stone pillars. The warmth flows in the space between these supports. The Romans call this heating system a hypocaust. Up against each one of our ovens we will build a house with a raised floor in the manner I have described. But our hypocausts will not be used for baths. We will fill the huts with grain. In this fashion, each oven can dry as much as twenty ovens did before.'

'Such thinking deserves a reward ...' She smiled meaningly.

Ben Hur grinned back. 'That is a most agreeable idea. I notice that your uncles have gone into the forest.'

'What does that have to do with it?

'The Long House is empty. The bed is empty.'

'You know our custom,' Brigantia admonished him. 'We cannot use the bed for a thing like that!'

'Today,' he announced, taking her firmly by the arm, 'I will introduce you to one of my customs ...'

Brigantia made no opposition as they mounted the steps. Ben Hur pulled the boarskin curtain aside, and they entered.

But both stopped short at the same instant. Standing by the bed was a black-robed, cowled figure.

'Dumnorix!' Brigantia exclaimed.

The Druid regarded them in baleful silence. Ben Hur could smell his fetid odour.

'What do you want?' Brigantia demanded.

The Druid appraised Ben Hur. 'So this is the Roman pig!'

'He is neither Roman nor a pig,' Brigantia replied with spirit.

'He is a foreigner. I heard that you had taken him as your consort, but I did not believe it. The blood of your ancestors runs thin! Does it not matter that your children will be debased seed?'

'What do you want?' Brigantia repeated.

'It is for your ears alone.'

'No,' she said firmly. 'You will say what you have to say to us both – or not at all!'

'Then listen well ... You are wallowing in the deceiving gifts of the Romans. I will accept that for the present – but only until your tribe grows strong again.'

'You have little say in what I will do! I am the Queen.'

For an instant their eyes held challengingly.

'Your mother made the mistake of opposing me,' the Druid warned. 'She came to a bad end ...'

'You have not said what you came to say,' Ben Hur interrupted harshly. 'Say it and leave us in peace!'

'I am not here to treat with you, Roman,' Dumnorix said contemptuously. He addressed Brigantia again. 'You must not ignore your ancient allegiance – the yearly tribute to the Druids. If you do not have gold – then pay us in grain.'

'We'll make the payment next year,' Ben Hur interjected. 'The Iceni must keep all their grain for the winter.'

'No!' Brigantia's voice was firm. 'Not next year! Not *ever*! I will no longer pay tribute to the Druids.'

Dumnorix spoke softly, but with great menace. 'Foolish woman! You will need the ancient Gods if your people are ever to rise again.'

Brigantia's eyes flashed. 'The ancient Gods abandoned us! Where were they when the Iceni wept and begged for life? Now I have a better God. He is called Christ. When the Iceni held out their hands to him, he came to help them. Yet he asks no tribute!'

Ben Hur stared at her in amazement. Brigantia had asked him once to pray to Christ on her behalf, but never had she given any indication that she had taken him as her personal God.

Dumnorix regarded Ben Hur balefully. 'This is your doing, Roman! You will be sorry ... The Iceni will be sorry ...' Abruptly, he strode from the Long House.

'We must be wary of him,' Brigantia said, a note of fear creeping into her voice. 'He is a powerful sorcerer. But I have made a decision, Judah. We will no longer go to the Stone Ring. From now on – Christ will be the God of the Iceni people!'

'Honour Christ if you wish,' Ben Hur said. 'But do not turn your back on your old Gods so hastily. They have been with your people for many generations.'

'Christ has proved his power,' Brigantia replied firmly. 'And my people shall do as I tell them.'

CHAPTER TWENTY-TWO

At least a score of the new circular huts with conical roofs had sprung up in the common ground of the citadel. Adjoining each one, below its floor level, was a large clay oven.

Surveying the smoking furnaces, Ben Hur savoured a moment of self-congratulation. The grain was drying swiftly. There was no longer any danger of its rotting.

He moved to another oven, where a young woman was piling wood into the flames. Tasgetius and Segovax were there also, eyeing the proceedings dubiously. Ben Hur grinned. Both of Brigantia's uncles were stroking their moustaches, which was a sign that they were in deep and mutual thought. In the past he had often wondered why they invariably shared each other's company and activities. Only recently had he discovered the reason. Many years ago, both had lost their wives within days of each other. Tasgetius' woman had died in childbirth. Segovax's wife had survived three births, but had fallen victim to a mysterious ailment. Shared grief had brought the brothers together in a comradeship which gradually became habitual.

Now Tasgetius noticed Ben Hur. He nudged his brother. There was a brief, whispered conference. Then, frowning, the ancients came over to him, continuing to stroke their moustaches.

'With these huts so close to the ovens – is there not a risk of fire?' Tasgetius murmured.

Ben Hur shrugged. 'That depends on the heat of the oven. That is why I am here – to make sure they are not overheated.'

Segovax scratched his head. 'An accident could happen.'

'Perhaps,' Ben Hur answered. 'But most of the grain has been dried and stored by now.'

Ben Hur knew that they were well aware of this. He also knew that they seldom came directly to a point. He waited for them to bring out their real concern.

'Actually,' Segovax began, 'there was another worry we were discussing ...'

Tasgetius nodded. 'The deep stones are not uncovered until you plough the field,' he said sagely.

'What is it now?' Ben Hur asked wearily.

Tasgetius cleared his throat. 'There is vexation ...'

'With the Druid,' said Segovax. 'He says that the old Gods are angry because Brigantia has put them aside and taken a new God. There will be retribution.'

'I see no sign of it yet,' Ben Hur observed. 'The Iceni are prospering.'

'Nevertheless,' Segovax insisted, 'the people are afraid the Druid will take vengeance on them because of Brigantia's sacrilege. Already some cattle have died.'

'The Druid directs his slanders at you most of all,' Tasgetius added. 'He says you persuaded her to espouse this blasphemy.'

'On the contrary,' Ben Hur replied, 'I have advised her against the religion. But she pays me no heed.'

'All this will lead to trouble,' Tasgetius warned.

Segovax nodded. 'It has already done so. Near Aquae Sulis there is a man who speaks of this same God Christ. His words have brought nothing but strife.'

Ben Hur was amazed. 'A Christian! In Britain!'

The brothers nodded again.

'Who is he?'

Tasgetius shrugged. 'Men call him the White Priest.'

Ben Hur recalled hearing Christ instruct his followers to make disciples of other nations. Was it happening? There was no denying that the message of Christ often had a compelling effect on people. Ben Hur himself had once been caught by it – and he had witnessed its impact on Brigantia. Now apparently there were others in this land who had also felt its touch ...

'Judah,' Tasgetius was saying, 'Fortune has smiled on the Iceni. After our terrible disaster, we are recovering at last – thanks in large part to you. And now you are the only one who can prevent us from falling into another disaster.'

Segovax added his entreaties. 'Persuade her to disavow this new God. If she will lead the tribe to the Stone Ring so that we may do homage to the Druids once more and perform the rites of winter – that will silence all criticism.'

Ben Hur did not immediately answer. He glanced at the ovens and their adjoining huts, the bald patches on the earth where the grain pits had been freshly covered. From the ashes of war, new life was springing up. If the rumblings of trouble over Brigantia's new religion should ever burst into flame, all this would be jeopardized, perhaps destroyed. Whereas a simple adherence to the ancient beliefs would surely lead the Iceni to unity and prosperity.

Finally he spoke. 'You are right ... I will ask her to return to the old Gods.'

'You must convince her,' Tasgetius insisted. 'She *must* lead us to the Stone Ring.'

Ben Hur nodded. Brigantia's uncles ducked their heads in gratitude and moved away.

Ben Hur gazed at the Long House. His task would not be easy. Brigantia had espoused her new faith with fervour and commitment. The day after she had announced allegiance to the new God, she had approached Ben Hur on the common ground.

'How do Christians marry?' Brigantia had asked with her customary directness.

'They have various ways. Sometimes it is arranged –'

'No! No! I mean – what is the *ceremony* of their marriage?'

'At first they followed the Judaeans, marrying in their temples called synagogues. But gradually the Christians came to realize that if a man and a woman wish to wed, all they need to do is take the vow – swear faithfulness to each other until death. That is enough in God's eyes. He is the only witness the Christians need.'

Brigantia had taken him by the arm, and they had left the settlement, making their way into the forest. Almost without thinking, their steps had guided them to the spot which was their usual trysting place.

'Say the words which will make us man and wife,' Brigantia had begged.

'God may not listen,' Ben Hur warned her. 'I am no longer a Christian.'

'You are a good man. He will listen.'

'Very well ...' Ben Hur had looked up at the canopy of green leaves above and for a moment believed her. 'In the name of Christ I take this woman to cherish and protect for all my days.'

Brigantia echoed him. 'In the name of Christ, I take this man as my husband for all my days ...'

Then they had embraced ...

Ben Hur took a deep breath. He could still feel the fervour of their lovemaking. Now he must persuade her to disavow the faith which had brought her such joy. Somehow he must make her realize that in doing so, she would not be rejecting the simple truth they had experienced that day in the forest glade.

Reaching the Long House, he slowly mounted the steps and entered. As usual, he paused, to accustom his eyes to the dimness within.

Then – with a choking cry, he lunged forward.

Just in front of the bed, Brigantia was sprawled on the floor in a pool of blood. She was still alive, but not for long. The glazed eyes and chalky pallor heralded approaching death. Her eyelids flickered slightly and her lips moved, but no voice came. He opened her gown. The hideous blue-red dagger wound was directly over her heart.

He cradled her limp form close to him. There was nowhere he could take her – nothing he could do.

'Brigantia ... Brigantia ...' he whispered. 'Who did this to you?'

The pale lips moved again. 'Dumnorix ...' she managed to whisper.

In despair he kissed her cold lips. It seemed to rekindle the last spark of life within her. Her eyelids fluttered once more, and the words came very faintly, as though from a voyager already far away. 'I will carry our child into the other world. One day you will join us there ... But you must go to the White Priest ... Serve Christ again ...'

'I will do it,' he whispered. 'I promise ...'

He could not accept this. It was not true! Surely he would awaken from this terrible nightmare to find Brigantia shaking him, with the morning sun behind her.

He could not weep. It was as if he had died with her. The only thing that lived within him was a merciless, vengeful demon. Only when it was exorcized could he try to keep his promise to Brigantia.

*

The great Stone Ring awaited its thralls, as it had for aeons. The sun was nearing the end of another day, and the misty winter air softened the outlines of the labyrinth, blurring its cabalistic design, understood only by Gods and a few select mortals.

Under a stone lintel, the Druid waited, his black cape melting into the shadows cast by the dying sun, making him almost invisible. It would be two days yet before the sun stood still in the heavens. Then the Druids from all over Britain would gather here, along with representatives from every tribe, to celebrate the winter solstice.

Dumnorix was early, waiting for another appointment. For days he had kept vigil here, living on acorns, dried meat and water. He knew that the Roman-Jew would come. And no doubt he would come early. The pig was searching for vengeance, and here, at the Stone Ring, during the winter solstice, was the only place he could be sure of finding it.

The Druid knew well that his foe was a formidable warrior, versed in every kind of weapon, immured to the death-games of the Roman arena. But Dumnorix had a potent ally – the power of the Necromancers.

There was a stirring in the bushes which grew at the edge of the forest about fifty paces away from the outer ring of the labyrinth. Dumnorix cocked his head, suddenly alert. He sniffed the breeze, and slowly his hands emerged from the folds of his cloak, clutching his dagger.

A fawn, still unsteady on its legs, emerged from the trees into the slanting rays of the golden sunset.

Dumnorix stood motionless. His throat began to quiver slightly. A soft sound came from his lips, a quiet, rhythmic bleat.

The fawn stiffened. As if drawn by an atavistic force, the little animal began to move towards the sound. When the humming grew louder, more demanding, the fawn advanced with light steps.

Still Dumnorix did not move. He waited until the creature was close. Then he pounced, seizing the startled animal round the neck, plunging his dagger straight into its heart. The fawn's death rattle was drowned in its own blood, and it pitched to the earth. Its legs thrashed for a moment, then it was still.

The Druid wasted no time. Picking up the creature's forelegs, he dragged the carcass to the inner ring. There, before a giant stone which pointed heavenwards like a huge finger, was the blue altar. Dumnorix pulled the dead creature over to it, and slashed the fawn's throat, allowing its blood to drain on the base.

Dumnorix lifted his blue face towards the sky. 'O Great Lugh of the Long Arm, accept my sacrifice! Set me aflame with your power. Make my voice and my legs and my arms lightning, so that I may blind and destroy my enemy!'

Reverently Dumnorix stooped, placing his lips against the animal's severed neck, drinking the warm, trickling blood.

Dumnorix stood up. Full of the God and exulting within, he returned to his vigil in the shadows.

Gulping the chilly air, Ben Hur toiled grimly towards the summit. The top of the hill was barely discernible through the gnarled trunks and bare branches. The ground was muddy and soft. Ben Hur slipped several times, but he hardly noticed.

The shadows of evening were rapidly darkening the sky, and sombre clouds heralded the approach of rain. He wanted to reach his goal before nightfall. Finding his way through the forest in the stormy blackness might prove difficult indeed.

Finally he reached the top. Peering through the web of denuded branches, he could see the valley below. There was the Stone Ring, symbol of the Druids – and death.

Without waiting longer, Ben Hur started down the slippery slope, picking his way through the trees.

Ever since Brigantia's murder, imprisoned in a morbid, tearless trance of grief, he had been moving like a sleepwalker. Immediately after the burial, he had gone to the Long House, collected a few of his belongings, only taking time for the careful choice of weapon. He had finally selected a long, pick-like dagger. The blade was made of the toughest iron known, and, if wielded properly, could be driven through any armour

The Iceni had watched his departure in silence. They knew where he was going; they were aware they would never see him again. But there had been nothing to say.

At last Ben Hur came to the base of the hill. He advanced slowly to the edge of the woods. There he paused. Before him lay the barbaric shrine.

If he were to come to grips with his enemy, surprise would be essential. He must explore the Stone Ring. He would learn its secrets and places of concealment. When the time came, he would be ready . . .

He glanced again at the sky. Dusk was falling rapidly. Leaving the cover of the trees, he trotted across the stretch of open ground towards the outermost circle of stone pillars.

Straining his eyes, Ben Hur surveyed the weird shapes outlined starkly against the purple twilight. Near the central circle was the huge finger of rock, standing like a crude, unfinished obelisk, marking the location of the altar – the holy of holies where all the Druids would congregate for their sacrifices.

Carefully Ben Hur moved forward, darting from stone to stone, utilizing all the concealment available. Since it was two days yet before the solstice, he doubted that anyone would be here. But he did not want to take unnecessary chances.

He arrived at the foot of the massive monolith. Circling its girth he came to the altar.

Suddenly he stopped. An inert form lay on the slaughter stone. Swiftly Ben Hur stepped to it and knelt beside it. It was a fawn, recently butchered, as the fresh blood attested.

His senses quivered. He rose, whirling, just as a shadow, like a huge bat, flew at him.

Ben Hur leaped to one side, but stumbled on a rock, falling flat. With the instinct of the arena, he rolled swiftly away, jumping to his feet, unsheathing his dagger, all in one motion. But when he spun to face his adversary, no one was there. The assailant had vanished. Ben Hur could hear his heart pounding as he glared at the silent stones.

A croaking laugh echoed through the misty air. Ben Hur had heard it before. Wrapping his cloak round his left forearm as an improvised shield, he advanced in the direction of the sound. But no one was there. It was only a pile of rock.

His heart raced even faster. He wondered if the misty twilight was playing tricks on him. Had the dark figure been an illusion?

A nerve on the base of his neck twitched. Obeying his old instinct for danger, he whirled. Dumnorix was there – aiming his dagger for a deadly thrust. Instantly Ben Hur raised his forearm, lurching away. The blow glanced off, slashing through the folds of the cape.

Now the enemies circled, facing each other, feinting with their blades. Dumnorix's features were indistinct in the evening light, but Ben Hur could smell his evil breath.

Hatred choked him. He wanted only to sink his dagger into his foe. It was all he could do to curb his urge to lunge forward rashly. But he held back. The slightest mistake – and the Druid would be gloating over another victim.

Slowly Dumnorix retreated, moving towards a strange cluster of stones, four or five slabs balanced together at odd angles. The Druid began to move faster, like a demoniac dancer. Ben Hur stepped up his pursuit. Dumnorix slipped behind the end pillar. Ben Hur followed, but stopped abruptly on the other side. Once again, the Druid had vanished.

Ben Hur circled the bizarre shapes, but there was no sign of Dumnorix. Was it the Sorcerer's black cloak which made him invisible, blending with the shadows? Or were the tales about his magic true? Ben Hur wished fervently for a magic of his own.

His fingers tightened on the hilt, as his eyes probed the darkness. Whatever power Dumnorix possessed, Ben Hur reminded himself, the Druid was still flesh and blood – as vulnerable to sharp iron as any other man.

The wild, croaking laugh rang out again. Ben Hur swung round. It had come from a solitary rock, not far away. There was something moving on top of the stone. He sprang towards it, but stopped abruptly. The phantom was merely a large black raven. With another croak, it flapped away.

Ben Hur spun, expecting Dumnorix to be behind him again, but there was nothing.

Then something moved near the monolith. The Druid's cloaked figure was approaching at a crouch, coiled to spring. Ben Hur advanced to meet him.

The adversaries were only feet from each other, each hesitating, seeking an opportunity to dart in and strike a fatal blow.

Ben Hur tried to see the sorcerer's eyes. In Ben Hur's youth, one of his tutors, an ancient and scarred Greek boxer, had taught him that the eyes would always reveal an opponent's next move. But the Druid had no eyes, not even a face, only a black shadow.

Dumnorix sprang, his blade swinging downwards in a silver arc. With a twist of his body, Ben Hur evaded the weapon.

Again they faced each other, each probing for an opening.

Suddenly a new sound intruded ... a soft scuffling ... the rattle of a dislodged stone ... It came from the monolith which loomed behind Dumnorix. The Druid's head flicked towards the noise. It was barely a movement, but it was enough. Ben Hur catapulted forward, seizing his enemy by the arm, driving his dagger into Dumnorix's neck. A gagging gasp from the Druid told Ben Hur he had struck the right spot. Ben Hur withdrew his blade, and the Druid pitched to the ground, twisting and writhing.

Ben Hur kicked the dagger from the Druid's hand, but it was unnecessary. Dumnorix had ceased his convulsions. He was dead.

Wonderingly Ben Hur's eyes searched for the cause of the sound which had distracted his enemy. There was nothing in sight. Cautiously he edged his way round the monolith until he reached the altar. There he stopped.

The forlorn silhouette of a doe stood over the body of its fawn, nuzzling it.

An immense weariness seized him. He wanted only to lie down and shut out the world with sleep. But he could not. He had another appointment to keep. And it would not wait.

For two sodden days and nights, he had slogged through the rain. His clothes were drenched, but he had long since ceased to care about the discomfort.

This morning, he had passed Aquae Sulis, being careful to give the town a wide berth. The place was becoming noted for its hot springs, often frequented by highly placed Romans and wealthier Britons. It was not hard to imagine that among these influential citizens there might be one from Rome who would recognize Quintus Arrius, a man wanted for plotting against the Emperor.

The sun was sinking towards the western horizon, bringing to a close yet another day. Ben Hur was nearing his destination. He had asked directions of a trader, and the man had described a hill exactly like the one Ben Hur was now approaching. Trees grew thickly up its slopes, but the top formed a curved green meadow, one side of which was terraced for cultivation.

Soon Ben Hur was rounding the base of the hill. Then, abruptly, he came upon the settlement. In a recently cleared section of land, marked here and there by tree stumps, about a dozen wattle huts were clustered, each with its own garden plot. A short walk took him to the dwellings.

Presently a woman emerged from a house, carrying a bucket. She set out towards the well, but at the sight of Ben Hur she stopped.

He moved closer to her. 'I am looking for the White Priest,' he said.

The woman gazed at him warily.

'Can you tell me where he is?' Ben Hur persisted.

Without answering, she fled back to the house and slammed the door behind her.

Almost immediately a short, leather-faced man of indeterminate age emerged from the house and approached Ben Hur truculently.

'What do you want?' he demanded.

'I am looking for the White Priest.'

'What do you want with him?'

'I will tell him when I see him.'

'Then tell me.'

Ben Hur frowned. 'You are the White Priest?'

'You may call me that.'

'You are the one who is teaching the faith of Christ?'

'Why should such teachings concern you?'

'I – I once knew something of these teachings. The time has come for me to learn more ...'

The other man studied Ben Hur, then finally nodded. 'Very well. I believe you. I will take you to the White Priest.'

'You led me to believe *you* were the White Priest.'

'I must be careful. There are many who would like to kill him. Are you armed?'

Ben Hur drew his dagger and offered it hilt-first. The other took it, and beckoned. 'Come.'

Leaving the settlement behind, they crossed some cleared ground, then reached the edge of the woods. Soon they were among the trees. A brief walk brought them to a wattle-and-daub structure half-hidden behind the foliage. An armed man, squatting by the door, rose at their approach. But at a gesture from Ben Hur's guide, he resumed his former posture.

'Wait here,' said Ben Hur's escort.

The guide stepped to the door, rapped softly, then entered. In a moment he returned. He nodded. 'The White Priest will see you.'

Ben Hur stooped and entered the hut, followed by the other man.

The shrine was small and homely, unfurnished but for an altar at the far end. The shutters of the two windows were closed, and the interior was dimly lit by a single taper.

A man stood waiting in the semi-dark. His hair and beard were white. Suddenly Ben Hur recognized him. It was none other than Joseph of Arimathea!

'Judah!' cried Joseph in disbelief. 'Judah!'

The two men embraced. 'I had given up hope of ever seeing you again!' Joseph exclaimed. 'Surely God must have guided your footsteps here!'

Ben Hur regarded his friend with wonder and affection. 'And you, Joseph! Here – in Britain! All the way from Judaea. It is hard to believe.'

'It is a strange story indeed,' Joseph agreed.

'Before you tell it – perhaps I should return this,' said a voice from behind Ben Hur.

He turned. The leather-faced guide who had brought him to the shrine was still there. But his expression was no longer hostile. He held out Ben Hur's dagger.

Ben Hur took it, murmuring his thanks. The other bowed and left the shrine.

Joseph grinned. 'You must not blame Julius if your reception was unfriendly. He was only protecting me.'

Ben Hur frowned. 'Then it is true what I have heard – the White Priest has enemies ...'

Joseph's face sobered. 'Indeed. Some officials of the Roman government have heard of my church. They do not like it. And among the Britons – the Druids have vowed to kill me.' He smiled at Ben Hur's expression. 'Don't look so dismayed! We are back together again. It's a marvel! We must celebrate.'

'You may not think it is such a joyous occasion when I tell you my story. I have nothing left. Faith was one of the first things I lost.'

'Then why are you looking for the White Priest?' Joseph wondered.

'Because I am trying to find a way back ...'

Joseph took Ben Hur by the arm and led him to the altar. There, gleaming in the light of the taper, was a solitary silver chalice.

'Judah,' Joseph announced reverently, 'this is the sacred relic round which I have built this temple.'

'Sacred? What sanctified it?'

'It is the Holy Grail. The cup from which Christ drank at the Last Supper. It is also the cup from which he gave the first sacrament. I have treasured it all these years. It was divinely ordained that I tell no one of its existence until it was placed in my temple.' A strange light came into Joseph's eyes. 'You see, Judah, I have always known that I must take the church to a far distant land. This cup must testify that he who built this church was witness to Christ's life and resurrection.'

Ben Hur gazed at the Grail. Its smooth surface was as enigmatic as Joseph's words. Was it true? Had Christ's face once actually been reflected in that polished silver?

He felt Joseph's reassuring hand on his shoulder.

'Stay here, Judah ... Work with me. When you help others, perhaps you will find your own answer.'

Ben Hur awoke. Quickly he threw off the blanket and rolled from his cushion of soft rushes. He blinked. He was alone in Joseph's thatched hut.

He rose and began to search for his tunic. He still felt sluggish from the large meal which Joseph had insisted on serving him. They had stayed up most of the night, recounting the adventures which each had experienced during their long separation. Ben Hur had been disturbed to hear of Joseph's estrangement from his daughter. It had been exceedingly difficult for Joseph to speak of it. Several times he had broken down and wept.

As difficult as Leah's life had apparently been, Ben Hur had a conviction that she would weather the storm. There was a stubborn determination in her character which would stand her in good stead. But Joseph was another matter entirely. He was old. He regarded himself a tragic failure as a father. He was convinced that his life was nearly over and that it was too late for him to heal the breach with Leah.

Ben Hur discovered his tunic in a corner just when Julius entered, bearing a bowl of steaming water and a towel. He placed it on the clay floor by the mat of rushes.

'A good day to you,' Julius said. 'I thought you might like a wash.'

'Indeed I would!' Ben Hur replied, eyeing the hot water eagerly. 'You are most thoughtful.'

Ben Hur stripped off his loincloth, picked up the towel, dipped it in the water, and began to scrub himself.

'Where is Joseph?' he asked.

'He is praying. But he will be here presently.'

Ben Hur felt a sudden concern. 'He is alone?'

Julius shook his head. 'Always one of us is with him.'

Using the dry end of the towel, Ben Hur removed the moisture from his body and began to dress. When he had finished, he turned to Julius curiously.

'You protect Joseph well. All of you in this village are Christians?'

Julius nodded.

'Then Joseph has made an auspicious start with his mission,' Ben Hur observed.

'We were Christians before Joseph came,' Julius replied. 'That is why he chose this spot for his church.'

Ben Hur was astonished. 'How did you become Christians?'

The other man smiled.

'All of us were soldiers – in the Second Augusta. Before the Legion was transferred to Britain, it was based in Syria. A cohort from our Legion was ordered to escort a Christian prisoner from Judaea to Rome for trial. He soon became our friend rather than our prisoner. On the voyage a great storm arose. For days we saw neither sun nor stars, and we despaired of our lives. But the prisoner prayed for us and we lived. Then he told us of Jesus. All of us on the ship vowed to follow his faith. None of us wanted to continue in military service, but we were bound by our oath. At last, here in Britain, we received our discharge.'

'This prisoner you spoke of – who was he?'

'A man called Paul.'

Ben Hur's heart leaped. 'Paul! Not Paul of Tarsus!'

Julius' features warmed immediately. 'The same! You knew him?'

Ben Hur nodded soberly. 'Paul was a good friend of mine. I only hope he is still alive.'

Julius picked up the towel. 'He will always live.'

Being careful not to spill the water, the ex-soldier moved delicately to the door and went out.

Thoughtfully Ben Hur slipped on his shoes. He felt the need to talk to Joseph.

Briskly he left the hut, crossing the clearing towards the woods. Once among the trees, he came quickly to the shrine. But there was no one standing watch outside.

With a slight sense of unease, Ben Hur pushed open the door. The place was empty.

He had not had the opportunity to examine the little temple. He studied it. It was unadorned, but sturdily built. A sweet fragrance permeated the sanctuary. But there was no incense burning, and Ben Hur could not find the source of the odour. The solitude, however, was soothing, and he did not want to leave.

His eyes moved to the altar, where the cup kept its vigil. An impulse drew him forward. He reached out and touched the Grail. It evoked memories of a world so long gone that it seemed another life. Momentous days of his youth in Judaea, with its tragedies and ecstasies, were real again. He picked up the chalice and held it in both hands. Warmth seemed to flow up his arms, giving him surprising strength. The Grail's silvery surface was like limpid water. Shimmering before him stretched a vast blue lake. Then he recognized it – the Sea of Galilee! He was in Capernaum again, and it was the carpenter's son who was approaching him, holding out his arms in greeting.

'Judah!' he exclaimed. 'It has been so long. What a joy it is to see you!'

He took Ben Hur by the arm, leading him to a well in the middle of the street. The stones surrounding it seemed to bake in the hot Judaean sun.

'You must be thirsty,' Jesus observed, as he began to draw the water.

Ben Hur nodded.

As the carpenter's son tugged on the rope, his warm, friendly eyes grew serious.

'Why have you forsaken me, Judah?' he asked softly.

'Then you know ...'

'If it is the truth, should I not know?'

'The faith I once had was too weak a weapon for this world.'

'Your way will be difficult, Judah, travelling unarmed in a hostile world.'

'I no longer have anything to fight for.'

In silence, Jesus pulled up the brimming bucket. He filled a cup and offered it to Ben Hur. Eagerly Ben Hur gulped the cool liquid.

'You have much to fight for,' said Jesus. 'Good can triumph over evil.'

'I wish I could believe that,' Ben Hur replied. 'I wish I had the strength I once had.'

'If you have faith, you will have the strength.'

'How can I have faith in something I do not know?'

'Think on one thing, Judah. You yourself have come close to death many times, yet you have continued to live. Did you ever wonder why? Do you see no purpose in this?'

Jesus turned away.

Ben Hur hesitated. He stood by the well for a moment, his mind seething with unspoken thoughts. Then he lunged after the departing figure.

'Wait!' he shouted.

He found himself in the midst of a crowd of people emerging from the marketplace. He recognized them. One was Nero, who paused thoughtfully, testing the point of a dagger on his finger. Agrippina was there too, watching her son with that odd little smile of hers. Peter emerged with one arm draped over Barnabas' shoulder, the other round Silas.

Ben Hur hurried over to Nero. 'You saw him! The one I told you about! The one who lived again!'

The Emperor did not seem to hear.

Frantically Ben Hur turned to the others. 'You saw him!' he cried.

But none of them paid any heed either. Ben Hur's desperation grew. He went from one to the other, shouting, pleading, but to no avail. Finally he wept, breaking down at last the wall of his grief . . .

The simple houses of Capernaum had vanished. He was back in the little temple, holding the Grail in his hands. His tears spent, he put the cup back on the altar and turned to go. Joseph was standing in the doorway. The patriarch's eyes were full of compassion and understanding.

'You have found your way . . .' Joseph murmured at last.

'Yes.'

'You no longer doubt.'

'The doubts will always be there, Joseph, but I must live with that.'

'And you are going back . . .'

'Yes.'

'Even if that means walking into the hands of your enemies?'

'I must, Joseph. *That* I do not doubt.'

The old man nodded. 'I understand . . .'

BOOK FOUR

ROME

CHAPTER TWENTY-THREE

Troubled, Peter strode past the bleak warehouses. His three companions were younger than he, but they had difficulty in keeping up with him.

Sextus pointed ahead, where masts of ships were visible over the roofs. 'Just over there ... that's where he is.'

'When I get angry, the worst part of me comes out,' Peter growled. 'I must remember to keep control of myself.'

'I would not blame you for losing your temper,' Sextus muttered. 'Antipater would drive Christ himself into a frenzy.'

They rounded a corner and paused. Dismayed, Sextus shook his head. 'It's too late. He's already started ...'

Down at the quay, a large grain ship was tied at its moorings. The vessel's hatches were open. Cargo was piled untended on the dock. The sailors and stevedores, who should have been at work, were clustered round a wagon, staring up at a man who stood on a seat. Dressed in a ragged cloak, he was a bizarre figure. Half his head was shaved, leaving a mop of hair on one side and a shining bald pate on the other.

'You are sailors!' he yelled. 'You come from all over the world! But I come from another world. I walked all the way! The forces of evil tried to stop me! I still have a Parthian arrowhead inside me – right here!' Dramatically Antipater opened his tunic, showing a scar on his hairy chest. 'But a greater force led me on!' he cried.

Peter and his companions moved down to the quay and stood indecisively on the fringe of the crowd.

'There is nothing we can do now,' murmured Sextus. 'It might be risky to stir up the dockers.'

In spite of his anger, Peter smiled. He was quite certain that if the dockers *were* stirred up, Sextus and Philip could more than hold their own. Apuleius, with the wispy beard and alley-cat swiftness, was not quite so formidable, but all three were obviously products of the Roman slums. Peter had never questioned them about their backgrounds. He knew all he needed to know – they were decent men with a zeal for the faith.

The rabble-rouser continued his harangue. 'I followed a star! It led me to the top of a mountain! There – I was blinded by a great light! I could not see, but I heard his voice. It was our Master! Amen! Amen!'

'Amen! Amen!' shouted four wolfish-looking men in the wagon behind Antipater. Their heads were half-shaved in the tonsure which was given to all criminals condemned to the mines – next to death, the most severe penalty prescribed by Roman law. Antipater, who claimed to have suffered this punishment, had told Peter that he had adopted the hairstyle to symbolize his 'revolution for Christ'.

'He's coming!' Antipater's fervour lifted his voice to a scream. 'He's coming!'

In exasperation, Peter looked away. He knew this part of Antipater's delivery by heart.

'Are you ready? Can you face him when he comes?' shrieked the evangelist. 'Can you look him in the eye and say you are without sin? For when he comes – he will cast down Caesar! He will sweep the Roman Empire from the face of the earth! *He* will be the new king! *He* will rule on earth!'

The words were too much for Peter. 'Antipater! Stop!' he bellowed.

The ragged missionary turned in surprise. 'Brother Peter!'

Peter elbowed his way to the wagon, followed by Sextus and Philip and Apuleius.

'Don't you "brother" me!' Peter snapped. 'Are you mad?'

With exaggerated astonishment, Antipater turned to his listeners. 'He calls me mad. Because I dare speak of the new king!'

'Quiet!' Peter hissed. 'You'll have the watch down on us with talk like that!'

'I am full of the spirit!' Antipater exclaimed righteously. 'Let me be!'

Peter yanked Antipater from the wagon.

'You witless Syrian! The place could be infested with informers! And you rave about casting down Caesar!'

There was an angry mutter among the onlookers. The sailors and dockers were moving forward threateningly.

'Who are you, you fat bully?' shouted one.

Others began yelling too. 'Let him be! Let him finish what he was saying.'

Immediately Peter thrust Antipater into the arms of Sextus and Philip, then clambered up on the wagon. Ignoring the baleful stares of Antipater's claque, he faced the dock workers.

'My friends,' he said disarmingly, 'I am Antipater's brother. I'm afraid he talks too much. His tongue gets him into trouble – that's how he got his hair cut.'

Only a few chuckled at Peter's little joke, but it was enough to break the tension. Encouraged, he went on.

'Antipater spoke of Christ's kingdom, but he does not understand what it means. It is a kingdom of the spirit and has nothing to do with Caesar's kingdom. As for Christ's promised return – we do not know when it will be. And it will happen in a way we cannot imagine. Go back to your work. Praise God. Rejoice in the thought that He loves you.'

The crowd began to break up, and Peter turned accusingly to Antipater's vulpine disciples.

'Why didn't you stop him?' he demanded.

'We do not accept your ministry,' one of them replied sullenly.

'We choose our own fruit in the garden of the Lord,' said another.

With a snort of disgust, Peter leaped from the cart, joining Sextus, Philip and Apuleius, who still clutched Antipater. The preacher's bloodshot eyes fixed on Peter defiantly.

'That mealy-mouthed talk of yours won't do any good,' Antipater taunted. 'Why do you think the church is in such a state? Because it is mealy-mouthed!'

'The church is in a bad state,' replied Peter, 'because of the drivel you and your friends spout on street corners.'

'Drivel? It is the truth!' Antipater drew a deep breath. The faraway look came into his eyes again. 'I was a slave in the mines of Elba! I know what the poor, desperate, starving suffering of this world want. They want sedition! They respect a man who dares to stand up and say treasonous things! They want hope – not empty promises. You tell them that Christ will come again? Excellent! But they want to know where! When? What will he bring them?'

'And I suppose you know where and when he will come?'

'Yes!' cried Antipater ecstatically. 'I walked all the way here! I followed a star! It led me to the top of a mountain! A bright light –'

'Enough!' Peter roared. 'You stink of cheap wine! Go and sleep it off!'

Antipater shook an admonishing finger at him. 'You tell me to go to sleep. I tell you to wake up! Stop and think. How many of our brothers follow you ... and how many of them follow me?'

Abruptly he twisted free from Sextus and Philip, giving them another scornful look. Then he strode off.

Sextus regarded Peter apologetically. 'I am sorry I had to interrupt your work for a thing like this.'

'You did right,' Peter assured him. 'I fear Antipater greatly. His boast was no idle one. He *does* attract more followers than we do. He is like the Circus. The shiftless folk love a show ... Of course they flock to him! But he is dangerous. He discredits us.'

'It's an unchristian thought,' Philip sighed, 'but I wish he were back in the mines of Elba.'

Perspiring furiously, Peter bent over the wheel pit, filing away at a rim. He had been so much away from the shop recently that he was falling behind on work.

Sometimes he wished that he were once again a simple fisherman on the Sea of Galilee. Several times he had considered abandoning this life and returning to Judaea. But his determination to do God's work here in Rome always made him put aside such thoughts. Perhaps the obstacles which continually seemed to stand in his way were a test of his faith.

A heavy footfall in the doorway interrupted his reverie. It was Varro, the rich tanner, who always stank of his trade. Varro did not look happy. With an impatient gesture he tossed the cartwheel he was carrying on to the floor.

'You call yourself a wheelwright!' Varro shouted. 'Take a look at this!'

Peter rose and examined the wheel.

'It looks all right to me.'

'All right!' Varro cried.

'What's wrong with it?'

'Look at the rim. It wiggles like a snake. I put it on my cart and it nearly overturned!'

Just then another customer entered the shop. He was a tall, bearded man. Peter gestured to a bench.

'I'll be with you in a moment ...'

The stranger sat down.

Peter turned back to the irate tanner. 'I am sorry, Varro. I see that something went wrong. Leave the wheel. I'll have it ready for you tomorrow.'

'I'll leave nothing. All I want is my money back.'

Embarrassed, Peter took Varro to one side.

'There is a problem ... I cannot return your money ...'

'Cannot!' Varro barked. 'I'll see that you do! I'll –'

'Please,' Peter interrupted. 'I had to spend the money the moment I laid hands on it. You see, I have a family to support.'

Angrily Varro snatched up his wheel. 'If you care that much about supporting your family, you'd do best to find yourself another trade!'

With that, the tanner was gone.

Peter regarded the waiting stranger sheepishly. 'You know how it is ... Sometimes customers don't appreciate good workmanship ...'

The other nodded and got to his feet.

'What can I do for you?' Peter asked.

'You might greet me ...'

Peter regarded him blankly. 'Good day to you, sir,' he murmured finally.

'Is that any sort of greeting for an old friend? You showed more warmth to those hyenas on the shores of Galilee!'

Peter stared at him incredulously. Then his face glowed with recognition. 'Judah!'

Letting out a shrill hyena cry, Peter seized Ben Hur in an enormous embrace, dancing round the shop, pulling Ben Hur with him. 'You're alive! You're alive! You're not dead!'

Urgulania appeared from the back. 'Peter! What is it? What's happened?'

Peter released Ben Hur and grabbed his wife, kissing her on both cheeks. He jabbed a thumb in Ben Hur's direction. 'Look who's back! It's Judah!'

She gazed at Ben Hur in wonder. 'It *is* Judah! God above ...'

Peter gave vent to another hyena-like whoop of joy.

Urgulania rounded on him. 'Shush! You'll wake the baby!' She dashed back into the room behind the shop.

Once again Peter hugged Ben Hur. 'I'm so glad to see you!' He held his old friend at arm's length, regarding him with deep affection. 'They couldn't kill you ... You're indestructible, by Yahweh! What a story you must have to tell! I'll wager it'll keep us awake for nights.'

'And what about you? Did I hear Urgulania right? You are a father?'

The joy left Peter's face. He avoided Ben Hur's eyes. 'In a manner of speaking ...'

Ben Hur frowned. 'Well, speak then! Is it a boy or a girl?'

'There was a boy. But he died. Shortly after he was born. Only for Urgulania – he still lives.' Peter took Ben Hur by the arm. 'Remember ... He has dark hair ... His name is Judah ... Come.' He escorted Ben Hur towards the inner door. 'She'll want you to see him.'

On the threshold Ben Hur paused. There was Urgulania standing near a cradle.

They went over to her. Ben Hur gazed into the crib. The wooden doll Peter had fashioned long ago lay there, neatly tucked in with a gay blanket.

'See ...' Peter murmured to his wife, 'there was nothing to worry about. I didn't wake him.'

'I must go and warm his supper,' Urgulania whispered. She slipped quietly out of the room.

Ben Hur gazed at Peter sombrely. 'I learned a lot about faith in Britain, but now I have learned even more.'

'So have I,' Peter replied quietly. 'It is good that you have rejoined us, Judah.'

'What has happened? The others? Where are they?'

The big man shook his head sadly. 'Barnabas died. It was a terrible shock! It seemed like nothing at first – a mere chill ...' He sighed. 'Silas and Phoebe went to Gaul to found a new church. And those who are with me in Rome – you will not know any of them, Judah.'

'Leah? Have you seen her?'

Peter hesitated. 'For a time I kept an eye on her. But I soon stopped. There was no need for concern. She has done very well for herself. At least in this world ...'

Leah surveyed her reflection in the mirror. She ignored her naked body, paying careful attention to her elaborate coiffure. Her hair was a crown of perfect little curls piled high on her head. It was certainly in style – exactly the way the Empress wore hers.

Now that Poppaea was Nero's wife, her rakish, seductive look was affected by everyone. Hair must be worn up, exposing plenty of neck, to be dramatically revealed when a lady removed her veil. For the Romans, unlike the Jews, considered the nape of a woman's neck the most attractive part of her body.

When Octavia had been Empress – before she had died so suddenly and mysteriously of an unidentified ailment – the chaste look had been popular, with a spray of ringlets demurely covering the provocative neck.

Teuta entered with the silk garments and placed them on the couch. The Illyrian woman appraised her mistress.

Teuta shook her head ruefully. 'Such beauty! You are truly blessed! I only hope the Gods never make you pay for it.'

Leah hurled a hairbrush at her, but Teuta dexterously ducked the missile.

'Go croak with the crows!' Leah cried. 'I never asked the Gods to make me beautiful. Why should I pay for it?'

Teuta did not answer. She held up a delicate silk stola. It was edged with purple and trimmed with pearls and rich gold braid round the neck opening.

'It is fit for Diana herself!' the Illyrian woman exclaimed. 'There will be no eyes for the Festival of Flowers – they will all be looking at you!'

Smugly Leah told herself that Teuta was right. She had ordered the gown weeks ago – just for this occasion. At last she was going to end her seclusion in this house.

Often she had wondered with exasperation why she had ever married Minucius. She might as well have stayed his mistress. He never introduced her to anyone, unless it was some misty-eyed philosopher who thought a woman was only something to bear a child or a cup of wine. Once he had brought home a famous rhetorician, who took Leah for a boy! It turned out the fellow had cataracts in both eyes. Well, this afternoon no one was going to take her for a boy!

She stroked the soft material of the stola. 'No one will notice me,' she said modestly. 'You forget – all the most beautiful women in Rome will be there. The *Empress* will be there.'

Teuta laughed coarsely. 'What a fraud you are! You know very well you outstrip all of them. And, if I'm not mistaken, you won't let your charms go unnoticed.'

'You're horrible! Why must you always think I have the worst motives?'

'Because I know you.'

'Be quiet and help me dress!'

Teuta picked up the inner tunic. It was made of transparent coan material – as delicate as any web a spider could spin. She helped Leah slide into the filmy garment, then fastened a light girdle round her small waist. Over this, Teuta slipped the stola, fastening a ribbon round its middle.

Leah sat on the couch, and Teuta slid delicate purple shoes on to her feet. These were trimmed with pearls as well. Then Leah rose, spinning a graceful pirouette before the Illyrian woman.

'You little demon!' Teuta exclaimed. 'You are really up to no good, aren't you?'

Leah grinned. 'I hear the voice of Jealousy . . .'

'You do indeed. *I* have to make do with the gardener, except on holidays, when everyone is drunk . . .'

Leah ceased her little ballet and once again studied her image in the mirror. On a sudden impulse, she jerked the pins out of her hair, allowing it to tumble over her shoulders.

Teuta gave a cry of anguish. 'What did you do that for? It took all morning to arrange it!'

'I have decided I do not like my hair up,' Leah declared. 'Now go and get my cloak!'

Teuta shrugged and sauntered out of the bedroom.

Idly Leah's eyes meandered along the painted spiral design which decorated the walls. It would be a mistake to look like Poppaea. Leah had a feeling she would create more of a stir if she adopted a different style. Now that she had cajoled Minucius into taking her to the Festival of Ceres, she was determined to make the most of it.

She moved back to the mirror for a final inspection, then turned as Teuta re-entered with the cloak.

'Where is my husband?'

'If he were my husband, I would certainly know,' Teuta said insolently.

'One day, Teuta,' said Leah, 'you will go too far.'

'One day, madam, so will you.'

Irritably, Leah went out. Why was it that whenever she sought her husband, he was never at hand? Yet when she wanted nothing to do with him, he was always fawning over her?

She had an idea where he might be. They never mentioned the Goddess these days, but Minucius still frequently went to the household shrine to read and seek quiet, or, as he put it, to contemplate the paradoxes of life.

He was there, poring over a scroll as usual. It was a moment before Minucius was aware of her presence.

'Leah!' he exclaimed. 'How gorgeous you look! Where are you going?'

Leah stamped her foot. 'The same place you are going! To the Festival of Ceres!'

'Oh ... I had forgotten.' He sighed. 'You do look lovely ...' Absent-mindedly, he glanced back at the scroll.

'Well?' asked Leah impatiently. 'Why do we wait?'

'Must we go?'

She caught her breath. 'Of course! We planned it.'

'Why don't we go to Capri instead?' he said suddenly. 'Just the two of us. We'd be alone there ...'

'We're always alone. We never see a soul. Are you ashamed of me?'

'Leah, please!'

'You may not have a taste for society, but I do. I don't want to read about life, I want to live it ... be in the centre of things.'

'That's the worst place to be.'

'Why?'

'Your Jewish forebears had a wise saying – "The fish stinks from the head." The court circle is a cynical little world where only flattery and self-advancement matter. Do not think those few hundred depraved people represent the real Rome! The true Rome lives among the traders, the craftsmen, the country gentry, in the smaller towns – people who pass their whole lives without ever setting foot in court. There you will still find the values which made Rome great.'

Leah tried to suppress her vexation. 'I am not interested in those good, honest citizens and their dull little lives. I want excitement.'

'What you want is dangerous. How do you think I have been able to preserve my family fortune intact? Or keep the comfortable, untroubled way of life you now enjoy? By keeping to myself! By arousing no one's interest or jealousy. So I resist all efforts to drag me to these social functions – in spite of the fact that my birth entitles me to attend.'

'Oh, Minucius! Please let's go! We won't speak to anyone. We'll just watch. We'll enjoy the good food and wine then return home.'

'You are very insistent.'

'Minucius! You promised!' She went up to him, placing her hands on his shoulders, regarding him pleadingly. 'Just this once ...' She kissed him.

'Is this so important to you?' he asked.

'Yes.'

'I do not understand.'

'It will be wonderful! There will be a ceremony at the Aventine Temple. Afterwards a parade through the city. And this evening – a reception at the palace.'

Minucius groaned. 'A reception at the palace! No! Not that!'

'All right,' Leah conceded hastily. 'We will not go to the reception. But we *must* see the ceremony, and the procession – please!'

He appraised her. 'Very well. But just the ceremony and the procession.'

'Then we must hurry.' She took him by the hand. 'It will be starting soon. Is the carriage ready?'

'Don't you want to say good-bye to the little fellow?'

Leah caught her breath. She had completely forgotten about Tarquin! 'Yes, of course. Let us find him.'

She followed her husband out into the hallway. How curious it was, she thought, that Minucius seemed to love the boy even more than she did. During the months she had carried the infant in her womb, she had worried constantly about the way Minucius might respond to the child – the offspring of another man. But she need not have feared. After the birth pains had subsided and Leah lay exhausted in bed, the midwife had cleansed the baby boy and laid it at Minucius' feet for the ceremonial acceptance. With no hesitation, he had picked him up and cradled him in his arms. On the ninth day, he had taken the baby to the Pontiffs, and given it the name Tarquinius Superbus Maximus Minucius. Leah could still remember Minucius' expression when he had placed round his adopted son's neck the sacred locket to ward off the Evil Eye. That moment was the only time Leah had ever come close to feeling genuine affection for Minucius.

He had been the best of fathers. Long before it was necessary, he employed a Greek tutor to give his son the proper intellectual environment.

Though she liked the child well enough, Leah did not share Minucius' passion for parenthood. Without her husband's knowing, she had been successfully employing the method Teuta had taught her for preventing pregnancy.

Now, passing through the gorgeous triclinium, they reached the entrance hall, and emerged through the front door into the bright sunlight.

Leah always loved the sight of the well-manicured lawn which stretched to the pine grove, concealing the house from the main road. It was somehow a symbol of comfort and security.

While Isidorus, the tutor, dozed on his stool, Tarquin was happily driving round in a miniature cart, pulled by a large grey mastiff.

The boy caught sight of his parents' approach. 'Watch me!' he shouted.

Flicking the cords which served as reins, he urged the panting dog to a trot, then whipped him into a run. Leah noticed that the tutor had awakened and risen to his feet, doing his best to appear alert.

'Stop that, Tarquin,' called Minucius, striding forward. 'Ares is a good dog. You want him to be your friend, don't you?'

'Yes.'

'You can see he is tired. Do not drive him so hard.'

Obediently Tarquin tugged on the reins, and the animal halted, tongue hanging out.

'Can I drive him slowly?' Tarquin asked.

'No. Give him a rest.'

Minucius stooped and unhitched the dog, patting its heaving sides.

Tarquin climbed from the cart. 'Then will you play ball with me?'

'All right. But only a few tosses – because your mother and I have to be going.'

'Here, sir,' called Isidorus briskly. The tutor picked up an inflated pigskin, and, with a great show of vigour, tossed it to Minucius, who lobbed it gently to the excited boy. Tarquin was only four years old, but Leah could already detect a marked resemblance to Paris – he moved with the same feline grace. Whatever happened, Leah prayed fervently, Tarquin must never grow up to be anything like his true father! Though Leah did not love Minucius, she would much prefer that the boy should mature to be like him.

A movement caught her eye. It was among the trees. On the far side of the lawn, partially hidden behind the trees, a man was standing. Unobtrusively Leah moved across the green to the spot where the tutor was sitting, hoping to get a better view.

The interloper was tall, bearded, and apparently interested in the activities on the grass. There was something familiar about him.

'Isidorus!'

The Greek stood up respectfully and came to her. 'Yes, illustrious lady.'

'That man . . . who is he?'

'What man?'

'Over there – in the trees.'

Blankly Isidorus peered, then shook his head. 'I see no man there.'

Leah's glance went sharply back to the pines. The intruder had vanished.

Suddenly she knew why the stranger had seemed familiar. It was Judah Ben Hur!

But even as the thought came to her, she dismissed it. The idea was preposterous! She was reliving the silly infatuations of an adolescent! If it were Judah, he would have come forward and made himself known. But Judah was long dead. There could be no other explanation for so many years of silence.

As Ben Hur crossed the Vicus of the Wheelwrights, he could see Peter in the open front of the shop, still working away on the unfinished rims.

The big man looked up, mopping the sweat off his brow, as Ben Hur approached.

'Well?' Peter demanded.

'I saw her – and her husband. It looks as though they have a son.'

'You didn't speak to her?'

'No. I must find a way to see her alone.'

'For God's sake, Judah. Your position is risky enough as it is!'

'I think I can trust her. I must try to reconcile her with her father. It is the greatest sorrow of Joseph's life that he has lost his daughter. Hearing from her once more might heal the wound in his soul.'

Peter sighed, picking up the rim, sighting along its surface. 'I think Urgulania has some food for us. Tell her I will be there as soon as I have finished this.'

Ben Hur nodded and left Peter to his toils.

The back room was empty. He sat down at the rough wooden table. The sight of Leah had been disturbing. He had forgotten how lovely she was. And now that she had reached the full bloom of womanhood, she was more enticing than ever.

Urgulania appeared, carrying a steaming pot. She hurried to the table, put it down, then extracted a ladle which was stuck in her girdle.

She smiled. 'Judah, I hope you are hungry.'

Ben Hur was not hungry. But he forced himself to nod. 'Indeed I am. And Peter will be here to join us shortly.'

Urgulania regarded Ben Hur with ill-concealed curiosity.

'Did you see her?'

'From a distance.'

Urgulania began filling wooden bowls with thick black soup. 'Poor Leah . . .' Urgulania placed a bowl in front of Ben Hur, handing him a large wooden spoon. 'Possessions were always important to her. When little Judah grows up, I hope he will always find joy in life – even if he has no possessions.'

Wiping her hands on her tunic, Urgulania moved over to the crib, peering into it. 'How your namesake sleeps: I hope he will be like you.'

Ben Hur got to his feet. 'I'll tell Peter his soup is getting cold.'

He hurried into the outer shop and wearily slumped on to a stool. He looked at his hands. They were shaking.

Peter glanced at him with an understanding smile. 'I know,' he murmured, 'but she loves the child very much ...'

The sound of running feet came to them. Three young men appeared at the front of the shop. Ben Hur recognized them as Sextus, and Apuleius, the newcomers Peter had introduced to him.

'What is it, Sextus?' asked Peter, putting aside the wheel.

'Antipater,' replied Sextus sourly. 'He asked us all to be here.' Sextus glanced back towards the street, where the sound of bells could be heard, accompanied by the chant of many voices.

Coming through the archway into the Vicus was a group of twenty or thirty barefoot men, clad in ragged tunics. Ben Hur noted that their heads were all half-shaven. They walked with an odd movement, shifting their weight from one foot to the other in a shuffling little dance, chanting the whole while. In their right hands they held little bronze bells which they jangled in time with their song. At the head of the procession was a man who looked much like the others. But he carried a larger bell, mounted on a staff, which he rang by striking the pole on the ground.

Ben Hur glanced at Peter. 'Is this the troublemaker?'

'I thought I was rid of him!' Peter groaned.

Antipater's motley band reached the open shop front, but they did not stop. Instead they made a ritualistic circle, then finally drew up near the doorway.

With no preamble, Antipater strode into the shop, pointing his staff at the wheelrim which Peter had been straightening.

'I see you still serve Mammon! You are a thrall in the marts of commerce.'

'I have to eat,' said Peter.

'I eat! The Lord feeds me! I beg for my bread. I walked all the way here! I followed a star! It led –'

He suddenly became aware of Ben Hur. 'There are strangers among us. I do not know you, brother. But like our Master – I welcome everyone into my arms.'

The evangelist embraced Ben Hur. 'I am Antipater, Herald of the Second Coming! Who are you?'

'I am called Judah.'

'Judah? Just Judah? Surely there is more to your name than that.'

'The rest of my name must remain secret.'

Antipaper nodded knowingly. 'You are a fugitive – I can smell them.'

'I did not say that.'

A gleam showed in Antipater's eyes. 'The condemned are thrice blessed in the eyes of the Lord! Christ himself was condemned. You are a kindred spirit, Judah! I was a slave in the mines of Elba!'

He spread open his tunic, pointing to the scar on his chest. 'See here – the marks of their chains!' He grinned. 'So because you are a fugitive, we welcome you as one of us, Judah. We will lead you to Christ!'

'That is hardly necessary,' Peter commented drily. 'Judah saw Christ and heard him speak.'

Antipater was taken aback, but only for an instant. He seized Ben Hur and kissed him on both cheeks. 'God has brought you to me! I know it! You will help me herald our Master's return!'

He swung round, addressing the group at large. 'Today we must strike a blow for Christ! The Emperor of Rome is celebrating the Festival of Ceres – that holiday of demons. We will assault that shrine of iniquity! We will smash the idols they worship. We will cast down the Emperor of Rome – for we are the agents of God! Amen!'

'Amen!' cried Antipater's entourage.

Peter's face was red with anger. 'You are a madman! If you attempt anything like that – you'll only end up with a rope round your neck, or nailed on a cross!'

'Yes!' Antipater shouted ecstatically. 'I welcome the cross! I welcome the death of a martyr! I want to die in no other way!'

Tactfully Ben Hur moved forward. 'Antipater ...'

'Yes, brother?'

'You say you are a Christian.'

'God is my witness – I am a Christian!'

'Then if you are – surely you care about the fate of the church . . .'

The Evangelist gazed incredulously at Ben Hur. 'You ask if *I* care about the fate of the church? *I*, Antipater? My brother – I want to see it envelop the earth, trailing clouds of nectar and ambrosia. I walked all the way here –'

'Heed me!' Ben Hur broke in sharply. 'An action like the one you are planning will only turn everyone in Rome against the Christians. It will harm the church beyond repair.'

A sadness seemed to come over Antipater. 'Your faith is weak. You hide it behind locked doors. That is the way Pharisees worship. The mission of all Christians is to go out and convert others. We must destroy false Gods and their shrines.'

'I forbid this!' Peter thundered.

'Who are you to forbid me?' Antipater demanded.

'I am head of the Roman church!'

'I do not recognize you as head of anything,' Antipater said haughtily. He faced Ben Hur. 'What about you, Judah no-name – will you come with me?'

'No.'

Antipater's eyes probed in turn Sextus, Philip and Apuleius. The young Romans shook their heads as well.

'I am sad for you,' Antipater said with contempt. Banging his bell-stick on the ground, he stalked out. He beckoned to his companions, and the whole procession shuffled away.

Bleakly, Philip watched them go. 'We must stop him . . .'

'How?' wondered Apuleius. 'There are more than a score of them.'

'We can go to the Temple of Ceres,' replied Philip. 'We can try to keep him away from the ritual.'

Ben Hur stared at him. 'Have you lost your head? He will only greet us as "brothers" and brand us as his followers. Nothing worse could happen to us.'

CHAPTER TWENTY-FOUR

Perched on the Aventine Hill, which rose to the south of the Circus Maximus, were the two small temples of Diana and Ceres. These brightly painted dwellings of Goddesses were almost submerged in a sea of tenement houses, with their shabby inhabitants congregated outside to watch their betters. Diana's shrine seemed neglected and almost forlorn, for there was no festival in honour of her today. The Temple of Ceres, however, was surrounded by the people of the court.

Minucius had found a place for Leah immediately before the steps, where she was actually rubbing elbows with some of the most powerful people in the Roman Empire. Here were senators, equestrians, magistrates and priests. Their women were dressed in surpassing finery, bedecked with garlands of flowers, filling the air with scent. Leah glanced down at her own modest bouquet. How like Minucius to give her only violets!

But a small thing like flowers did not matter now. She was trembling with excitement, for the Emperor himself had not long ago passed just in front of her – almost close enough to touch! She had never imagined him so young and so handsome. Accompanied by the Empress, his family, his household and an odd group of toga-clad equestrians, Nero had mounted the temple steps and was now inside performing the ceremony.

It was impossible to see what was going on inside, for a select detachment of the Praetorian Guard lined the top of the steps, blocking the view. The soldiers were a magnificent sight, dressed in their highly polished armour, wearing helmets topped by gay plumes. Dull by comparison were the brown uniforms of the city watch, who were busy holding back the curious multitude.

Leah could hardly wait for the grand procession to start. The Emperor and his entourage would be in the lead, surrounded, of course, by the Praetorians, followed by the senators, then the equestrians, among whom would be Minucius and Leah. And the whole gorgeous parade would be inundated by flowers thrown from the buildings lining the route.

'The worship of Ceres is very important to ensure the fertility of crops,' Minucius was saying. 'For, as I have told you, Ceres is the spirit of the grain. Ceres' worship came to Rome five hundred years ago, when there was a terrible famine –'

'Minucius!' Leah interrupted.

He glanced round in bewilderment. 'What?'

She pointed up the steps of the Temple. 'That officer, just to the right of the guards. The one wearing the breastplate and the purple plumes. Who is he?'

'Tigellinus – the new commander of the guard. He recently replaced Burrus.'

'He's very dashing.'

'They say he's well qualified for his post. He's utterly depraved. The story is – Nero was tired of Burrus' interference. Tigellinus obligingly had Burrus poisoned. Your dashing officer wanted to do away with Seneca too. But Nero wasn't quite ready for that – not yet anyway.'

'Is Seneca here today?'

'Not likely!' Minucius eyed her sadly. 'You are very fond of gossip. But you were not a bit interested in what I was telling you about the festival.'

'Of course I was!' Leah exclaimed hastily. 'It was fascinating! Please continue.'

Somewhat mollified, Minucius nodded. 'Well, to be brief, there was a terrible famine. The Augurs consulted the Sibylline Books – where they find most of their prophecies. They announced that a shrine must be built here on the Aventine for Ceres.' He pointed to the building. 'The Temple you see standing before you today was erected as a result of the decree. It is one of the most ancient temples in Rome. Ever since that day it was built five hundred years ago, it has been under the care of Aediles, the officials who are in charge of the city's grain supply. Another interesting –'

'Minucius!' Leah squealed, seizing his arm. 'Look!'

At a gesture from Tigellinus, the Praetorian Guard was opening its ranks, taking up positions on both sides of the steps. A moment later Nero himself appeared, his neck and hair festooned with garlands. A roar went up from the onlookers. With both arms uplifted, the Emperor acknowledged their adulation.

Now the Emperor's family and household appeared beside him. Lining up just behind Nero were the twenty equestrians whom Leah had noticed earlier.

Impatiently Nero gestured for silence. He waited until the cheers of the crowds subsided, then he spoke. 'My fellow Romans! I thank you for coming here today!'

The equestrian claque applauded energetically, and the crowd followed obediently with cheers. Once again the Emperor held up his hands for silence, and the tumult died away.

Nero continued. 'May all the Gods shower the Roman People –'

'Son of Satan!' screamed a voice.

There was a stunned silence. All heads turned in the direction of the cry. A bizarre-looking man with his head half-shaved, wearing a long, ragged cloak, pushed his way to the front of the crowd, near the outermost rank of nobles. He was followed by twenty or thirty others, who were similarly attired, jangling the little bells they were carrying.

'I am Antipater the Blessed!' cried the leader. 'The Herald of the Second Coming of Christ!'

Minucius glanced at Leah. 'This madman appears to be one of those Christians – the sect you said your father belonged to.'

Leah shuddered. 'Don't remind me! My father had some queer friends, but I've never seen this one before ...'

'You are worshipping false Gods! Demons who lead men to damnation!' Antipater cried, as he and his followers advanced towards the Temple. 'I am the messenger of God! And in his name I will destroy these false idols! Christ is coming! Prepare!'

'Prepare! Prepare!' chanted his acolytes.

Tigellinus bounded down the steps two at a time. 'Prefect of the Watch!' he shouted. 'Get them out of here!'

Before the city watch could deploy, Antipater and his men were rushing towards the Temple. Apprehensively the senators, equestrians and those surrounding the Emperor drew back, huddling in groups on either side of the steps. The Praetorian Guards descended, forming protective lines in front of them. Leah searched for the Emperor, but she could see no sign of him. Minucius took her by the arm, and pulled her right up behind the line of soldiers.

The watch, gripping their wicker shields and batons, dashed up the steps after Antipater and his men. In a moment they had overtaken the Christians, and were striking them with their cudgels. A few of Antipater's half-bald disciples managed to writhe away, and push over some of the statues on the portico. But these men too were overwhelmed. Antipater, knocked sprawling by one of the watchmen, seemed to lose his fervour. He rolled down the steps with the agility of an acrobat, then quickly wriggled away on all fours into the mob. Some of his fellow agitators were following their leader's example, breaking and running. Only a few were captured.

An animal roar burst from the rabble lining the road. A shower of stones and other objects began to rain down on the steps, forcing the watchmen to raise their shields for protection.

Leah had been told about the volatile nature of the Roman mob. Indeed she had experienced it herself at Paris' theatre. The street people were shiftless and idle, supported by the state on the grain dole, entertained almost daily in the arena or circus, and always ready to join a riot – no matter what its cause.

Now with ferocious curses and shouts of glee, the whole mass began to surge forward, engulfing the watch, who were pinioning their prisoners on the steps.

'Kill the Christians!' someone cried.

The shout was taken up by the rabble.

'Kill the Christians! Kill the Christians!' they chanted.

The few shaven-heads who had been arrested by the watch were protected by their captors, but the intensity of the violence was increasing. It seemed to Leah that its original object, the Christians, had been forgotten, and now the mob, worked up into an uncontrollable frenzy, was attacking the watch, or each other.

The Praetorian Guards tightened their ranks, linking their shields. But they made no move to join the mêlée.

'Why don't the soldiers help the watch?' Leah yelled at Minucius, her voice barely audible over the din.

'Because their job is to protect the Emperor and the Senate,' Minucius shouted back. He tugged her arm. 'This will get worse! We must find a way out.'

'Can we get to the carriage?' Leah asked.

'It's not far. I think I can reach it. But you stay here – as close to the soldiers as possible. I'll bring the carriage up behind the Temple.'

She started to argue, but Minucius, ignoring the danger, wormed away through the crowd. In a moment, he had disappeared.

Leah swung round, watching the brawling in front of the Temple. The wild confusion banished all sense of time. She could not stifle the apprehension she felt. She had a fear that Minucius might not return.

Then she forgot all about Minucius. For nearby, standing not ten feet away, was the Emperor himself!

He had come part-way down the Temple steps and was watching the rioting. He seemed to be enjoying it. His eyes were sparkling with excitement. Then he caught sight of Leah. A little smile began to twitch the corners of his mouth. Leah smiled back. Surely that story about poisoning which Minucius told her was not true! On a sudden impulse, she tossed Nero the bouquet she was still holding. Deftly he caught it, and, without taking his eyes from her, he raised it to his lips.

Tigellinus appeared beside him and began to speak urgently, but Nero waved him away. The Emperor took a step towards Leah, then paused abruptly. Minucius had returned. He put a protective arm round her.

'Hurry!' he urged. 'I have the carriage.'

Leah followed him glumly. Now she wished Minucius had taken longer. She threw a quick glance over her shoulder. Nero was still gazing after her.

The bushes of the imperial gardens were sculptured into an elaborate maze, and even Epaphroditus sometimes had difficulty finding his way. Nevertheless, he hurried forward with the confidence of long experience. There was a stone seat at the centre of the maze. No doubt the Emperor would be there.

The freedman paused at the sound of voices. They were very near, just over the hedge flanking the path. 'You are certain these Christians are subversives?' Nero was saying.

'There is no doubt about that,' a nasal voice replied. It was Tigellinus, whose insolent tone was so habitual it persisted even in conversation with the Emperor.

'You tortured them?' Nero wondered.

'There was no need. They were only too willing to talk.'

'Then how do you know they were not lying?'

'Because their words were too damning for anything but the truth. And they admitted their ties to Paul, the Christian agitator we're holding in prison. All of them say they owe allegiance to a King in Judaea, whom they claim to be a God. They predict he will overthrow you.'

Nero's laugh echoed from the palace walls. 'What fools they are!'

Epaphroditus had heard enough. He circled the final bend of the maze, and approached Nero and Tigellinus.

'It took you long enough!' Nero exclaimed, rising from the stone bench.

Epaphroditus nodded. 'But I have been successful.' He flashed his most winning smile. 'If you will permit me to say it – successful, as usual.'

'Who is she?' Nero demanded.

'Exalted Sir –' Tigellinus broke in.

'Be quiet!' Nero snapped.

The commander persisted. 'What do you want me to do about the Christians? Execute them?'

'Execute Paul. But let the others go.'

'Surely –'

'I said let them go! But watch them. See how many they are – who their friends are.'

The Emperor turned back to Epaphroditus. 'Now tell me . . . who is she?'

'The wife of Ostorius Minucius, a wealthy Equestrian.'

'Do I know him?'

'No, Exalted Sir. He does not go about much in society.'

Nero glanced back at Tigellinus. 'What about you? Do you know this Minucius?'

Tigellinus shook his head.

'Well, you should! His wife is the most unbearably gorgeous woman I have ever laid eyes on. By all the Gods – if I do not see her again – I will die!'

He turned back to Epaphroditus. 'There has been much gossip about me – so I shall have to approach this with care. Jupiter's eyeballs! Why do all beautiful women have husbands? Does hers have any friends whom I know?'

Epaphroditus chuckled. 'Indeed he does.'

The freedman savoured the moment. He was going to puncture Tigellinus' inflated confidence. Since Burrus had died – suddenly and mysteriously of an unidentified ailment – Tigellinus' rise in the Emperor's favour had been meteoric. But Epaphroditus despised this new favourite, with his barrack-room arrogance and contempt for others.

'Well?' Nero demanded impatiently. 'Tell me. Who?'

'Surely you have not forgotten Seneca?'

Epaphroditus did not look at Tigellinus, but he could sense the Prefect stiffening at the mere mention of his old enemy.

Nero frowned thoughtfully. 'Perhaps I was a little hasty in banning him from court.'

'No – you were right!' Tigellinus exclaimed. 'He was a friend of Burrus. He was plotting against you.'

Epaphroditus did not take his eyes from the Emperor. 'I beg to disagree with the Most Eminent Prefect. I never believed Seneca was guilty. Sometimes a man makes odd alliances because he cannot afford to make enemies. I happen to know Seneca still thinks highly of you, Exalted Sir.'

'Have Seneca brought here,' Nero decided. 'I will speak with him.'

'You must not!' cried Tigellinus.

Nero rounded on him furiously. 'Must not! Must not! You presume to tell me what to do?'

Epaphroditus placed a conciliatory hand on Nero's arm. 'I think we should hear Tigellinus out. If he has any objections to Seneca – let him tell us what they are.'

'Very well,' Nero replied impatiently. He glanced at Tigellinus. 'What do you have against Seneca?'

'It's no personal grudge,' the Prefect muttered defensively. 'But there are rumours ... suspicions. We are having him watched.'

Nero pondered this.

Epaphroditus relished playing the role of magnanimous arbitrator, since he knew what the Emperor's decision would be. Nero was avid to meet this new woman. His lusts seemed stronger than ever these days – especially since his relationship with Poppaea was deteriorating. Ever since she had lost Nero's first child at birth, the Emperor had grown more disgruntled with her.

The freedman had manoeuvred Tigellinus into an impossible position. For his own security, the Prefect would have to oppose the return of Seneca. And yet his opposition could only end in defeat.

Nero faced Tigellinus decisively. 'You have not given me one shred of actual evidence against Seneca. Until you do – I do not see why he should be ostracized further.' He gestured to Epaphroditus. 'Send for him.'

The freedman bowed. 'I have taken the liberty of doing so already.' Again he favoured the two men with his most winning smile. 'Seneca is waiting in the palace at this moment.'

'Splendid!' cried Nero. 'You are a gift of the Gods, Epaphroditus! You always seem to know my wishes – even before I have said a word.'

The freedman shrugged modestly. 'I try, Exalted Sir. I try.

'I'll be in the music room,' said Nero, plunging off into the maze.

Tigellinus spoke quietly. 'You dropping from a diseased donkey ...'

Epaphroditus mimed a shocked expression. 'Control yourself, Prefect!'

Tigellinus was trembling so violently that he had difficulty again finding his voice. 'Joining forces with Seneca, are you? Surely you know where he is going to end up? You'll end up there too. I promise you that.'

'Do not make promises you cannot keep. You think you enjoy the Emperor's confidence. Many have thought that – Agrippina, Otho, Young Arrius, Seneca, Burrus. What about those people, Tigellinus? Every one reached the highest pinnacle. Where are they now?

The Praetorian Prefect had no words.

'I am not threatening you,' Epaphroditus pointed out. 'I am merely telling you the facts of life. I will be useful as a friend, but fatal as an enemy.'

But even as he made the peace offering, Epaphroditus decided it was too late for Tigellinus. The Prefect had shown his true colours, and he would show them again. One could not wait for that.

The floor of the music room was a brilliant mosaic. Scores of dolphins swam in many coloured circles towards the centre where the Emperor lay on his back. The heavy iron plates balanced on his chest moved up and down rhythmically, as he sang the scale.

Seneca entered and paused near the door, his heavy-lidded eyes showing no signs of surprise.

Nero heaved the weight off his chest, placing it carefully on the floor, and sat up.

'Seneca!' he cried. 'My dear old tutor! Come in.'

Seneca bowed. 'Exalted Sir, how good of you to see me!'

'Exalted Sir? My name was always "Lucius" to you.'

Seneca bowed again. 'After such a long separation I was not sure if I could still claim that privilege of personal address. I have been trying to see you for quite some time – but it seems I no longer have access to the imperial ears.'

'It is nothing of the kind,' Nero protested. 'It is merely that I am busy. Affairs of state.'

'You may remember,' Seneca said drily, 'I was once the guiding spirit of affairs of state. In those days, you would never approach them without me. But the rumour is – I have fallen from favour.'

'Like most rumours, it is completely untrue. I shall always be in need of your wisdom and guidance.' Nero scrambled to his feet. 'You say you have been trying to see me. Nothing urgent, I hope?'

'Modestly urgent, perhaps. I have been wanting to make you a gift.'

'What sort of gift?'

'Everything I have. My estates, wealth, servants and slaves.' He smiled. 'Even the flamingoes at my Alban villa.'

'Astonishing! Why should you give these things to me?'

'I am getting old. I might die suddenly and mysteriously of an unidentified ailment – as Burrus did.'

Nero ignored the innuendo. 'You are in excellent health. You must not give away your property. What will you do to support yourself?'

'A man who intends to devote what remains of his life to Philosophy has few material needs. As Zeno says, "Follow nature and you will feel no need of craftsmen." It is we humans who have made everything difficult to come by – through our disdain for what is easy to come by.'

Nero sighed wearily. 'You are an avalanche of words. You haven't changed, have you?'

'Not in my loyalty to you. I beg you to accept my offering.'

The Emperor eyed him speculatively. 'I *would* accept it – in fact, I am a little short of cash – but unfortunately I cannot.'

Seneca's jowls quivered slightly. 'Indeed? When I was a trusted member of your council, there was never any provision against the Emperor receiving gifts. Or has the administration developed a conscience?'

Nero chuckled. 'Nothing of the kind. My freedmen are more unscrupulous about my finances than ever. And believe me – they would love to get their sticky fingers on that property of yours. But the trouble is – if I accepted your gift, no one would believe it was voluntary.'

'Very well,' Seneca agreed. 'It seems I am destined to pursue my studies in luxury, a handicap I will endeavour to overcome.'

The Emperor laughed and reclined on the floor again, placing the weight on his chest. He drew three breaths and sang a high quavering note, not breaking it until his face was purple from lack of air. He repeated the exercise once more, then put the weight back on the floor, and sat up.

'I have a new voice teacher. He claims that singing with a heavy weight on the chest is the best thing for the lungs. My voice is developing power it never had before.'

He got to his feet. 'You know a man named Minucius?'

'I do,' Seneca replied guardedly.

'You pick wealthy friends, don't you?'

'As Plautus says, "Where there are friends, there is wealth."'

Nero grinned. 'Minucius is wealthy indeed. His greatest treasure is his wife.'

'You say *I* have not changed. Perhaps so. But I see that *you* have not changed either.'

'When I cease to admire beautiful women,' Nero replied, 'I will cease to live.'

Seneca nodded knowingly. 'If one can judge from your past, you will have a long life. But why this particular female?'

'Have you ever seen her?'

Seneca nodded.

'Then you have seen Aphrodite herself.'

*

The seductive warmth caressed her skin. She lay sprawled by the pool, receiving the full force of the sun through the open roof. Her eyes were closed, but she could hear Teuta moving about the atrium, watering the plants which grew in boxes set up against the walls.

For the thousandth time Leah relived the incident in her mind. She savoured every detail of the encounter over and over again. The vivid memory filled her with sheer delight. She would never forget how he had caught the flowers, pressed them to his lips.

'What are you thinking about?' came Teuta's voice.

Leah opened her eyes to see the Illyrian woman standing over her.

'I wasn't thinking about anything,' Leah replied truculently. She closed her eyes, hoping the other woman would go away.

'Yes, you were,' Teuta insisted. 'You had that look about you.'

'What look?'

'That lascivious, lustful look!'

Leah's eyes flew open. 'You are a crude baggage!'

Teuta laughed. 'I can always tell when you are thinking about fornication.'

'You insolent bitch!' Leah cried. 'How could you know a thing like that?'

'Because your nipples stand up.'

Before Leah could reply, Minucius' slave boy hurried into the atrium. As usual, he ignored Leah's naked body.

'Eminent lady,' he announced, 'the master wishes to see you.'

'Tell him I am taking the sun!' Leah snapped. 'I will see him later.'

The boy regarded her dubiously. 'I beg your pardon, eminent lady, but he said it was very important. He is waiting now in the triclinium.'

Leah was startled. The triclinium! Minucius never went there.

'Very well,' she said. 'Tell him I will be there immediately.'

The boy bowed, and scurried out.

Leah slipped into the stola which Teuta held out for her, then padded barefoot into the dimness of the hallway.

The mosaics and paintings of the triclinium shimmered in the sunlight which poured through the windows. Minucius was reclining on a couch, waiting for her. Across the room, seated on a curule chair, was another man. With dismay, Leah recognized the guest as Seneca. Of all her husband's friends Leah found him the most pompous and boring.

'I greet you, Renowned Sir,' she said. 'Please excuse the way I am dressed, but I was taking the sun.'

Seneca's jowls quivered slightly. 'The sun's loss. My gain.'

Minucius indicated a couch. 'I sent for you because Seneca requested to speak with both of us together.'

Seneca nodded. 'That is correct. It concerns both the husband and the wife. The good husband and the good wife ought to be good friends. Is it not so?'

Minucius nodded.

'And you will agree that good friends ought to share in all things?'

'Quite,' murmured Minucius.

'Therefore the good husband and the good wife ought to share in all things,' Seneca concluded. 'And Plato sums it up the same way when he says that the female sex ought to partake equally in the work of the male sex. Zeno, however, was ambivalent on this point. He –'

Minucius cleared his throat discreetly. 'You said you had a matter of great importance to discuss with us ...'

The philosopher's expression did not change. He nodded. 'I had not forgotten. I was coming to that. I was merely creating the proper groundwork.' He paused. 'I have come to announce a great opportunity for you.'

Minucius gazed at him. 'Opportunity? What is it?'

'The Emperor requests the presence of you and your wife at a banquet this evening. An intimate affair – just the three of you.'

Leah felt a thrill. The Emperor's invitation could have only one meaning.

'But we do not even know the Emperor!' Minucius exclaimed.

'That is a condition His Exalted Majesty would like to rectify.'

'I still do not see why he should seek our company,' Minucius persisted.

Seneca got ponderously to his feet. He began to pace, staring downwards thoughtfully.

'A splendid floor you have here, Minucius,' he murmured. 'The man who created it must have been a real craftsman.' He sighed. 'But it is just as Zeno said – "No matter how deft a human artist, he cannot compare with the architect of the universe."' The bulky senator looked up. 'The Emperor knows you are talented, a man of ability, and that your wife is very beautiful. He does not want to see such assets go to waste.'

'Waste!' Minucius exclaimed. 'I think my wife and I lead very full lives. We are rearing our family. We have our interests.'

'He wishes that your talents be put to a more public use,' Seneca insisted. 'He is considering a high office for you, Minucius. Perhaps a governorship. It is possible that our legate in Cappadocia will be replaced.'

'This is all very flattering,' Minucius replied. 'But I am not a political person. Besides, Cappadocia is a long way off. I do not want to be so far from Rome.'

'It could be any post you wish. The Emperor needs good advisers. Think it over. You do not have to decide now. You do not even have to come to the palace tonight. Provided your wife does.'

Leah caught her breath, as Minucius' face went white. When he finally spoke, his voice came in a croaked whisper. 'I thought you were my friend. Get out of my house!'

Seneca did not move. 'My dear Minucius, I *am* your friend! I have spoken to you in such a shocking fashion because I know the way things are – and some things are inevitable.'

'This is *not* inevitable!' Minucius said savagely. 'You can tell the Emperor that!'

'I am only concerned with your profit,' Seneca protested.

Minucius thrust his face close to Seneca. 'You think I would profit by selling my wife? What a contemptible man I would be!'

Seneca laughed. 'Do not underestimate the value of being contemptible. As Zeno says, "To be held in contempt is the last refuge of a wise man."'

'The answer is no. My wife happens to mean something to me. You can also tell him that –'

'Minucius!' Leah said suddenly. 'Since I am the subject of this discussion, perhaps I should speak. You have no choice. You must bow to this – otherwise I shudder to think what will happen to you.'

A sudden change seemed to come over him. He shrugged, and smiled bitterly at Seneca.

'Perhaps I will follow my wife's prudent advice,' he murmured. 'It has been said, "We should assume that whatever happens was bound to happen, and refrain from railing at nature."'

'You have read my last essay!' Seneca exclaimed.

Minucius nodded with the same bitter smile.

'What a pity it is, Seneca, that you do not live as you write.'

Seneca spread his hands urbanely. 'It is impossible to live as one writes. Beside, as I have always said, a virtue is best appreciated from its exact opposite.' He turned to Leah and bowed. 'A carriage will be here for you at sunset.'

Seneca nodded to both of them, then strode out.

Leah could feel Minucius' eyes on her, but she could not look at him.

'Thank you,' he said in a low voice.

'There is nothing else to be done,' she muttered.

He did not answer. He stood, as if listening for something. Then the sound came – horses' hooves, moving rapidly away down the path outside the house.

Now he stepped swiftly to her side. 'I know why you did this – but you won't have to make such a sacrifice! The Tiber is a very short walk from here. A boat ... we can take one to Ostia. Several of my ships there will be leaving on the tide. We only need choose which one to board. Fetch Tarquin! We have little time.'

'It is impossible!'

'We can do it! We'll sail for Spain. There is strong sentiment there against the Emperor. Among the highest officials. Galba, Otho, others. All the soldiers in Spain are with them.'

Leah regarded him grimly. She had always known that the day would come when she would have to let Minucius know the truth. Now that the day had arrived, she was surprised to find that she did not want to hurt him.

'I will not go with you,' she said quietly.

His eyes were incredulous. 'Not go?'

'I have just accepted an invitation from the Emperor.'

'But surely – that was to protect me. You were forced.'

She shook her head. 'I *want* to go, Minucius.'

Unable to meet his stricken eyes, she turned and hurried from the room.

CHAPTER TWENTY-FIVE

At last she was ready. She had forced herself to take time over her dressing. Deliberately, she had chosen the same purple stola edged with pearls which she had worn to the Festival of Ceres.

She gave herself a final appraisal in the mirror, then adjusted her stola to expose more of her neck and breasts. On impulse, she pulled up the gown and massaged more of the fragrant nard into her thighs.

At last she started towards the door, but paused. Minucius might try to stop her. She could not bear the idea. If she did encounter him, she would rush out of the house and wait by the road for the carriage.

The door moved, but it was only Teuta bringing Leah's cloak.

'It is still too much to believe!' Teuta exclaimed. 'You and the Emperor! What a triumph!'

'Give me my cloak. There is no time to lose.'

'You must take time for one more thing.'

'What is that?'

The Illyrian woman held up a small vial. 'This potion – drink it. It will make you irresistible. Even eunuchs will hunger for you!'

Leah shook her head impatiently. 'I do not need that sort of help.'

'You are young and arrogant. We *all* need help – in one way or another. Now that you have won the Emperor's attention, you want to keep it, do you not?'

'Why shouldn't I keep it?'

Teuta laughed crudely. 'How little you know! He'll enjoy you for one night – and discard you.'

Leah was piqued. 'He chose *me*, out of all those women at the Festival! And he has gone to all this trouble – just to find me again. Is that the act of a man who seeks me for just one night?'

'For the Emperor, yes. It is common knowledge he will turn heaven and earth just to conquer a single beautiful woman. It pleases him to use his power to seduce women in ways no other man can. Once he has attained his object – the interest is gone.'

'All right,' Leah said. 'Give it to me.'

She grabbed the vial and swallowed its contents, grimacing at the bitter taste.

'Gods! What is in that brew?'

Teuta smiled archly. 'If I told you, it would not work.'

Leah grabbed her cloak and hurriedly pushed her way out of the room.

Minucius was not in the hall. Leah darted through the rooms of the house until she reached the front door.

Outside there was no sign of the imperial carriage, but Tarquin was sprawled on the grass, playing his flute under the watchful eye of his tutor, who squatted nearby, keeping time with a baton.

Neither had noticed her, and Leah was tempted to go on her way without calling attention to herself. But something prevented her. The sun was low, and the air was getting cool. The boy had been down with a sniffle recently.

She hurried over to them.

'Isidorus!' she called.

The tutor got to his feet. Tarquin also jumped up.

'Mother,' the boy cried, staring at her dress, 'are you going out?'

'Only for a little while.' She faced Isidorus. 'Take him inside. I don't want him in this damp air.'

Isidorus bowed. 'I beg your pardon, eminent lady. Tarquin was doing so well with the flute, I lost sight of the sun. I will take him in immediately.'

'Mother!' Tarquin burst out impatiently. 'Aren't you going to sit with me at supper?'

'I cannot –'

'But you will come in and kiss me good night?'

'Of course.' The lie came with difficulty and she avoided his eyes. 'But do not stay awake for me. I may be late.'

'But you will come. Even if I'm asleep.'

'I'll come.'

'Promise?'

'I promise.'

Only then did Tarquin allow the tutor to lead him inside.

As Leah watched them, she fancied she saw a movement at one of the shutters. Could it be Minucius?

There was a clatter of hooves. Leah turned. A carriage, pulled by two splendid white horses, appeared like magic through the pines.

It was dark when the carriage door was opened. She blinked in the light of torches.

A tall, impressive man of middle years, resplendent in a red cloak of Tyrian silk, assisted Leah to the ground. The most remarkable thing about him was his smile. It was warm, reassuring and made her feel instantly that this was a friend.

'My lovely lady,' he said. 'I extend you the quintessence of greetings. I am Epaphroditus, and I have come to conduct you personally to the Emperor.'

Leah was impressed. Epaphroditus was a name known to every household in Rome. He was Caesar's right-hand man, heading the complex web of the imperial household. Though a freed slave, he was more powerful than most senators. To be received by him personally was a signal honour. It was yet another proof the auspices were good.

Taking her by the hand, Epaphroditus led her up the imposing steps. They entered through tall doors. Once inside, Leah followed him down the torch-lit hall. Her eyes took in the magnificence of the paintings and statues which lined the way.

Soon they arrived at another pair of doors flanked by guards. At a gesture from the freedman, the sentries opened them. Epaphroditus conducted her into another room. It was large, with a high ceiling, and Leah guessed that it must be an audience chamber of some sort. But it was covered with bouquets of violets – columns, walls, ceiling, even the furniture.

And the Emperor himself wore a crown of violets. Clad in a purple tunic which matched the flowers, he was seated on a curule chair, next to a large table flanked by banqueting couches. He jumped up.

'At last you have come!' he exclaimed.

'I am overwhelmed to be in your Imperial Presence.'

'Epaphroditus,' said Nero. 'You have won my gratitude by bringing this delicious creature here – now win my undying affection by leaving us alone!'

The freedman bowed. 'Exalted Sir ... Faultless lady ...'

Epaphroditus backed from the room, smiling continuously, and bowing three or four times.

Nero led her to a table behind his chair. Its surface was of clear polished marble, and on it was placed a single gold bowl. The vessel contained a small and slightly wilted bouquet of violets.

Nero picked up the flowers reverently. 'You threw these to me at the Festival of Ceres. I will treasure them always.'

Leah was intoxicated, but she forced herself to choose her words with care. 'Exalted Sir. I can truly say that day was the most fortunate of my life. Being so close to your Exalted Person for the first time was an experience I shall never forget.'

'Let that memory be only the beginning of a host of joys!' Nero cried. He drew her to the dining couch. 'I am so delighted to see you again that I have forgotten my manners. Please ... make yourself comfortable.' With the poise of an accomplished host, Nero indicated a large bowl on the table. It was filled with snow.

'I had it rushed here from the peaks of the Apennines,' he told her. 'Of course, much of it melts on the way, but just enough survives.'

He filled two goblets with the snow, then poured wine over it. He handed one to her, then raised his own.

'If Helen's face launched a thousand ships, yours will conquer an empire. For the Emperor of Rome is already your prisoner!'

It was mid-day when the imperial carriage stopped in front of Minucius' house. A slave leaped down, opened the door, and Leah stepped out. She waited until the vehicle moved away.

Now she would have to face Minucius. She turned reluctantly towards the house.

Nothing had turned out the way she had expected. True, the night of lovemaking had seemed a triumph. The Emperor had been ecstatic over her charms. Yet when she woke this morning, she had been alone. She had seen no one until a servant had entered, announcing that a carriage was waiting to take her home. There had been a note of finality about it she did not like.

Perhaps the Emperor would summon her again. Perhaps not. She could not free herself of a nagging suspicion that she had been dismissed. Prudence suggested making her peace with Minucius, but that was probably no longer possible. Nevertheless, she was determined to try.

There was a peculiar stillness about the house. At this hour, the slave who trimmed the hedges was normally at work. And there were always voices – Teuta, the servants in the kitchen, or Tarquin making life miserable for his tutor. But now all was quiet.

Warily Leah entered the hall. She came to the triclinium and stopped in surprise.

There was Minucius, reclining on a couch, regarding her coolly. How unlike him to be lounging in this room! He made no move.

'You had a pleasant evening, I trust?' he said softly.

'I had to do it, Minucius ...' Leah began hesitantly.

'You wanted to. You made that clear enough.'

'I only told you I wanted to so that you would not try to stop me – and harm yourself in doing so.'

'How thoughtful,' Minucius murmured.

'Do not harden your heart against me now. Take me to Spain with you.'

He shook his head. 'It is too late. I have made other arrangements.'

'What arrangements?'

He did not answer.

She glanced round the room. 'It is like a tomb here. Where is everyone?'

'I sent them away to Seneca's house. Your little boy is there. I preferred to be alone while I was preparing my departure.'

'Departure?'

He did not answer. There was something about his twisted posture on the couch which did not look natural. And his face was excessively pale.

'Where are you going?' she wondered.

'A long way from here.'

With an effort, Minucius shifted his weight. Only then did Leah notice that his hands were resting in basins on either side of the couch. He lifted his arms. His veins were slashed, and blood flowed from his wrists. Then he let them collapse back into the bowls.

'No!' she cried.

She stepped forward in dismay. 'Minucius! Not this – not this! I'm not worth it!'

'No, you are not,' he murmured, 'but the thing is done.'

He paused, mustering his strength, then forced out the words. 'I have made a new will, leaving my possessions to the Emperor. Except for the sum I have given to Seneca in trust for the little boy when he grows up. And you, my lovely Aphrodite, will get nothing.'

The Flaminian Way seemed to be deserted. Ben Hur moved forward cautiously. Sometimes brigands or thieves violated the sanctity of tombs and used them for hiding places. He hoped this had not happened to the resting place of Arrius' wife, but he had to find out.

Reaching the marble structure, he mounted the three steps of the podium. Seizing the handles of the heavy doors, he twisted and pulled. They were stuck. He tugged, and only reluctantly did they grate open. The light flooded the little sanctuary.

He surveyed the bare chamber, with the marble sarcophagus in the middle of the floor. Once he was sure that the room was empty, he closed the double doors behind him, leaving them slightly ajar so that some light could enter.

Darting to the other side of the sarcophagus, he knelt, ran his hands along the flagstones, until he found the slight indentation. He pushed down hard, and the opposite edge of the slab lifted. He managed to get his fingers under it and slid the stone away. The tunnel below was a black hole. He crouched beside the aperture, peering down into the darkness. There was no sound or movement of any kind. Finally he took a deep breath, gripped the sides of the opening, and lowered himself into the passage. He edged forward, deliberately leaving the opening in the floor behind him uncovered, so that he might have some light to guide him on his return journey.

The air was stale. Creeping along at a half-crouch into the thick blackness was decidedly unpleasant. Some brigand's dagger might come slashing out of the gloom at any moment.

Ever since Antipater's reckless raid on the Festival of Ceres, Ben Hur had known they must sever all links with the extremists. So he confided to Peter the existence of the underground chamber. Peter had agreed that a secret sanctuary was necessary. But the first task was to determine whether it was still usable.

The air became less oppressive, and he knew he had reached the end of the tunnel and was now in the comparatively spacious chamber under Arrius' tomb.

He moved stealthily across the floor, relying on his sense of direction to take him to the other entrance. Soon his outstretched hands brushed the rough surface of the opposite wall. He found the lever and pulled. The stone moved. Ben Hur shifted it slightly, just enough to allow a ray of light into the chamber.

It was as he had always remembered it, an aisled hall cut off from the rest of the world – safe in the bosom of the earth. Thankfully it was empty. He moved along the walls, inspecting the room carefully. He could remember when there were altars in this miniature basilica, and burning incense, statues in each of the niches. Now, with all that gone, there would be space for at least twenty people. The niches could be used to store food and belongings. Rushes for mattresses, blankets could be placed in each bay along the aisles. The place was certainly usable and much less hazardous than the Vicus of the Wheelwrights.

He closed the trap leading to the tomb of Arrius above, then felt his way back along the passage.

In the tunnel he moved more rapidly than he had on entering, since he knew there were no lurking intruders. After an interval, he could see the dim light at the far end.

When he reached it, he hoisted himself into the tomb of Arrius' wife, then replaced the flagstone, concealing the existence of what was below.

Eager to get back to the city, he shut the doors of the tomb behind him, and started off at a brisk walk.

He had not gone far when something light brushed him in the face, then flickered to the ground. At first he thought it was a feather, but he stooped and examined it. It was a large piece of ash. More grey particles were floating in the air nearby. He looked up and caught his breath with horror. The whole sky to the north-west was black, rolling clouds of smoke stretching as far as the eye could see in either direction. Ahead the road rose over a slight incline. Ben Hur dashed forward, and soon he was on the higher ground.

There lay the city, sprawled over its seven hills. The black pall of smoke was darkening the sun. The city of Rome, as far as he could see, was in flames.

CHAPTER TWENTY-SIX

It was an appalling spectacle. Desperate crowds of refugees choked the Flaminian Way. Some were expressionless, numb with shock. Others were weeping. Women clutched bewildered children.

Grimly Ben Hur pushed his way among them. At first he had considered waiting in the fields outside Rome, on the assumption that Peter and the others would surely join the mass exodus. Then he had realized this might not happen. He and Peter had made arrangements to meet at the Vicus. In all probability Peter would still be there, waiting doggedly. Ben Hur must stick to his original plan – find his comrades and conduct them to their new dwelling. And, if he moved swiftly, he was confident he could still enter the city in safety. The area down by the Tiber, where the Vicus was located, was still untouched by the conflagration.

Crowds of refugees grew denser as Ben Hur drew abreast of the Field of Mars. On his left hand, flames and smoke were everywhere. On his right, the Pantheon and the Monuments of Agrippa were still intact.

The fire was blazing at its height in the vicinity of the Palatine, Caelian and Aventine Hills. The depression between the hills, where the Circus Maximus lay, was nothing but a vast blazing inferno. The sight filled him with mixed feelings. Much of his life as a charioteer, both triumphs and tragedies, had taken place in that great stadium. It seemed as if part of him was vanishing in those flames.

Deciding that it was too difficult to push through the throng, he hurried off across the Field of Mars. There were fugitives here as well, many just sitting hopelessly on the ground, watching their homes burning in the distance, but it was less crowded than the road.

He glanced back again. Clearly the fire was getting worse. It looked as though the whole city was doomed. There was a seven-thousand-man fire fighting force, established long ago by the Emperor Augustus. Yet Ben Hur had not seen one fireman. It was puzzling indeed.

Reaching the river, which was covered by a thick layer of floating ash, he quickened his pace. The Vicus was not far away now. After an interval of trotting along the bank, he left the Tiber. He made his way through the familiar twisting alleys until finally he was in the Vicus of the Wheelwrights. The flames, although clearly visible over the rooftops, were still some distance away. Despite this, frightened people were milling about in front of their shops, packing belongings, saddling animals, collecting their families. Ben Hur elbowed his way through the despairing residents. He found Urgulania waiting anxiously in the shop front.

At the sight of him, she ran forward. 'Judah! How awful this is! I am so worried –'

'Hurry!' Ben Hur cut in. 'The hiding place I mentioned to you – we can use it. Get Peter!'

'He's not here!'

Ben Hur was dismayed. 'Not here! But they –'

'Sextus came,' Urgulania interrupted, her eyes round with fear. 'I did not hear what he said – it upset Peter terribly. I have never seen him in such a rage! He told me to wait. He said he would be back.' She began to cry. 'Then the fire broke out ... He's been gone so long, Judah. I hope he is all right!'

'We cannot wait for him,' Ben Hur said urgently. 'We must leave *now*!'

She shook her head vehemently. 'I will not go without Peter!'

He seized her by the arm. 'Look! The fire is coming this way! It will soon be here!'

Urgulania pulled away from him, shaking her head.

Ben Hur thought quickly. 'What about your baby? Little Judah?'

The point struck home. She ran back into the shop, then reappeared, carrying the doll wrapped in a blanket.

Ben Hur, taking her by the arm, led her away. But she stopped abruptly, pointing across the street. 'Look!'

Four wine-soaked ruffians were looting one of the wheelwright shops.

'They will break into our place and steal everything!' Urgulania exclaimed.

'Let them,' Ben Hur replied. 'It will burn anyway.'

He propelled her towards the archway. The flames were approaching the Vicus from this direction, but it was worth the risk. Ben Hur was intent on reaching the Flaminian Way and escaping the city as soon as possible.

When they had left the Vicus behind, they hurried through the narrow alleys. The air was oppressively warm, and Ben Hur could smell the fire. Not very far to his right, the flames were now leap-frogging from building to building. The crash of falling timbers and the cries of people were clearly audible.

With a deafening roar, a tall tenement which abutted the road ahead erupted into tongues of heat.

Urgulania gasped, clutching her bundle tightly.

Ben Hur urged her towards the burning structure. 'Hurry! We must get past it!'

But before they could go any further, the spindly building across the narrow street seemed to swell, then burst into flames too.

They halted. Ben Hur glanced back. Flames blocked their retreat. The only escape was a narrow side-street which led towards the river. Pushing Urgulania ahead of him, he took this route. There was fire in front of them, but it was being contained. Here at last were some firefighters. Two of them were pumping water from a well on to a blackened, smouldering ruin. Right across the street, a tenement was still blazing fiercely. On the very top storey, fear-filled faces looked down on more firefighters, who approached at a run, pushing a hand cart. The instant the watchmen reached the tenement, they unloaded mattresses and cushions, and began to spread them on the ground.

They gestured to the people above. 'Jump! Jump!' they cried.

The terrified family continued to stare at the street, but they made no move. One of them, an older man, began to push the others. A woman with a child jumped as well. They landed hard.

Some were stunned and had to be helped to their feet. But most were able to walk away.

At last they were nearing the Flaminian Way. They passed more firefighters, who were beating the flames with soaked blankets.

Rumbles seemed to shake the road under Ben Hur's feet. A multi-storied dwelling buckled, collapsed in on itself, then spilled out on to the street, showering everything in the vicinity with a blizzard of hot cinders. Debris was flung everywhere, igniting two more buildings. A sheet of flame made the way ahead impassable.

Ben Hur fled to the right, with Urgulania following. He was lost, forced by the flames away from the route he knew, into an unfamiliar part of the city. All he could do was keep moving and stay as far away from the fire as possible.

They were now in a lane, where gangs of citizens and watchmen were feverishily demolishing wooden buildings before the searing heat could reach them. But then, with a noise like a thunderstorm, a hurricane of flames raced down the street. The firefighters fled as the district erupted into an inferno.

Desperately Ben Hur dashed down the only passageway free of the conflagration, pulling the woman after him. But he had only gone a few paces when he stopped short. The alley was blocked by a curtain of fire. They were trapped!

Wildly Ben Hur looked about. Nearby was a three-holed stone latrine.

'Give me that blanket!' he shouted at Urgulania.

'No!' she cried. 'It is protecting my baby.'

Impatiently he reached for it, but she drew away.

'Give it to me!' he roared.

He snatched it, but she clung to it. They struggled over the blanket, then, angrily, he jerked it away from her. The wooden doll was flung to the cobbles. Its head snapped off and rolled away.

'You have killed my child!' she screamed.

Ben Hur started for the latrine, but she flew at him, tearing and scratching.

'You killed my baby!' she shrieked hysterically. 'You killed him!'

He hurled her aside, but she came at him again. Ben Hur flung her away even harder and she stumbled into the gutter. Instantly he dashed to the latrine and stuffed the blanket down the centre hole. He prayed the water was still flowing – that the fire had not cut off the source of supply. He gasped with relief when he felt the moisture seeping round his fingers.

When the blanket was fully sodden, he pulled it out and turned back to Urgulania, who was still sprawled on the street sobbing.

Without preamble, he jerked her to her feet, draped the dripping blanket over their heads like a canopy. Pushing her ahead of him, he plunged into the flames which blocked the way. The air seared his throat and lungs. His legs were scorched. But suddenly they were through, staggering beyond the giant furnace.

He threw aside the smouldering blanket. Little flames had sprung to life on the folds of his cloak and on the hem of Urgulania's stola. With both hands he beat them out.

Now Ben Hur appraised their surroundings. Nearby was the Field of Mars. Safety was in sight, but he was almost too weary to feel relief. His glance went back to Urgulania.

She stood there, sobbing, apparently oblivious to everything.

'Urgulania ... listen to me,' he said gently.

She continued to weep, paying no attention.

He seized her, turning her forcibly to face him. He shook her.

'Urgulania! There was no child. The child died long ago. You must face that.'

She gazed at him blankly, her face still streaming tears. Then her head slumped forward. Her whole body swayed. Ben Hur had to support her to keep her from falling.

'You are right ...' she muttered finally. 'The little one is gone. He was with me such a short time.'

Desperately the sweating watchmen worked the pumps. The Decurions urged them on, shouting and cursing. Their faces and clothes were smeared with soot as they fought the losing battle against the flames.

More watchmen hurried up, pushing hand carts full of vinegar-soaked blankets.

At that moment, a chorus of shouts burst from the alley which led into the street. 'Idolators! Creatures of the devil!'

The workers paid no attention to the cries, but a motley band of men, their heads half-shaven, dashed from an alley into the street, brandishing cudgels and staves.

Mercilessly they attacked the watchmen, who ceased their fight with the flames and turned to protect themselves.

'Spawn of Satan!' Antipater yelled, lashing out right and left with his bell-staff. 'This is God's fire! Let it consume this city of sin!'

Abruptly Antipater turned away from the battle. He picked up flaming timbers, throwing them into one of the buildings the fire had not yet reached. He continued to fling his firebrands until flames began to lick out of the ground-floor windows.

He picked up another burning timber and started purposefully towards a shop, but paused. Hurrying towards him were four men – Peter, Sextus, Philip and Apuleius.

Peter's face was white with rage when he confronted Antipater.

'It is true then! Sextus told me – but I could not believe it! You *started this fire*!'

Antipater laughed. 'Yes! I started it – but I am only the hand of God!'

'Antipater!' Peter pleaded. 'Come to your senses! Call your friends away. Let the watch put out the fire.'

He advanced towards Antipater, but the evangelist retreated, holding Peter at bay with the flaming torch.

Leaving Peter to face Antipater, Sextus and his companions rushed to join the battle in the street, attempting to pull the shaven-headed men away from the firefighters.

'Do you realize what you have done?' Peter cried, his voice breaking with anguish. 'Thousands of people are being burned to death! A whole city is being destroyed!'

The wild-eyed man thrust the brand towards Peter's face, forcing him back.

'They killed Paul!' Antipater shrieked. 'Yesterday – they brought him from the dungeon and beheaded him!'

Peter was aghast. 'Paul ... he's dead?'

'Paul is in heaven!' Antipater shouted. 'But now the sons of Satan must join their master in the flames of hell!'

'It is your fault Paul died!' Peter burst out. 'You and your fanatics have turned the Romans against the Christians. But what you have done now is ten thousand times worse! You have *ruined* us! Everyone in the world will hate us!'

'No!' howled Antipater, thrusting the brand at Peter again. 'The end of the world is at hand! It is written that when the Lord comes again, the world will be consumed by fire! I am the instrument of God. I have prepared the way for the Second Coming!'

Peter's breathless comrades rejoined him. Apuleius had an ugly cut over his right eye. 'We cannot stop them,' he gasped. 'They are too many ...'

Antipater menaced all four men with his firebrand, but they ignored him.

'The city is doomed,' Sextus insisted. 'We'd better get out ourselves.'

Peter did not reply. He was gazing off at a massive line of arches, still visible through the flames, which reared their bulk over the Caelian Hill.

Sextus took him by the arm. 'Peter! Come!'

'Wait!' Peter breathed. 'There's still a hope. Nero's aqueduct. Look! We can dislodge one of those blocks on top of it – the water will come pouring down. It will flood the hill.'

'It is worth a try,' Philip agreed. 'I know that Marius' stables are nearby. He's got tools and crowbars. Let's get them!'

'It is God's fire! Let it burn!' Antipater yelled.

Again he waved his torch at them. With his free hand, Antipater stamped his bell-staff on the ground.

At the sound, his comrades broke off their battle with the watch. All came running to Antipater's aid.

'Hurry!' Peter hissed to his friends. 'The alley! Run!'

Sextus and the other two darted into the narrow passageway behind Peter just as Antipater's followers rushed up. Peter obstructed them, completely spanning the entrance with his outstretched arm.

'Stand aside!' bellowed Antipater.

Peter wrenched the torch from Antipater and threw it at him. Instantly the shaven-heads fell on Peter, bearing him to the ground by sheer weight of numbers.

Suddenly, out of the smoke, watchmen came charging up, attacking Antipater's men from behind. Surprise was on their side, and soon many of the shaven-heads were subdued. Others began to slink away.

'Come back!' Antipater screamed at them. 'You are forsaking the fight of the Lord!'

At that moment two watchmen seized him.

'Take your hands off me!' Antipater snarled.

Then came the call of a trumpet. Marching down the road was a company of Praetorian Guards, their armour gleaming even in the smoke-shrouded light.

'At last!' groaned one of the begrimed firefighters with relief. 'It took them long enough!'

The Praetorians clattered up, seizing Antipater and his men, beating those who continued to resist. Several guards took Peter, pinioning his arms, in spite of his protests. An officer strode up. It was Tigellinus himself. He was exhausted and furious. His grim eyes surveyed the prisoners, then came to rest on the firefighters.

'Which one of you is in charge here?' he demanded.

'I am,' one of the watchmen replied.

'You sent for the Guard?' Tigellinus persisted.

The man nodded.

'You were lucky that your messenger managed to reach us.' Tigellinus gestured at the half-shaven prisoners. 'I gather these are the arsonists.'

'Yes, Most Eminent Sir,' the watchman replied.

'I suppose I should offer my thanks,' said Tigellinus gruffly. 'We've been trying to get our hands on this gang of madmen all day.' He turned to one of his centurions. 'Give the watchmen ten sesterces each.'

While the soldier counted the money, Tigellinus strode up to Antipater, clutching him by his half-head of hair. Savagely he jerked it, then dealt Antipater two stunning blows across the face.

'You pig's offal! Who are you?' snarled Tigellinus.

'I am the hand of God!' Antipater gasped. 'I come in the name of Christ.'

'A Christian!' sneered one of the Praetorians.

Tigellinus did not seem to hear him. He was staring fixedly at Antipater's face, still gripping him by the hair. 'By Jupiter!' he exclaimed. 'I know this troublemaker! He's the same maniac who caused that riot at the Festival of Ceres!'

Roughly he shoved Antipater against the guards who held him, and turned, gesturing to the soldiers. 'Take them.'

'Wait!' cried Peter, struggling against the men who held him.
Tigellinus swung round again.

Peter faced the officer with dignity. 'You are making a mistake. I am not one of these men.'

'Then what were you doing here? Warming yourself by the fire?'

'I was helping the watchmen,' Peter insisted.

The Praetorian Commander glanced questioningly at the watchmen. They shook their heads.

'I didn't see him,' one of them muttered.

'I have told the truth,' Peter protested.

'With all this smoke,' interjected another watchman, 'we couldn't see much.'

A soldier laughed mockingly. 'Maybe they're all innocent!'

Tigellinus continued to examine Peter. 'Perhaps he is telling the truth ... His head is not shaved like the others.'

'That's right!' agreed Peter quickly. 'I am *not* one of them. On my honour, I am not!'

'Then you are not a Christian.'

Peter hesitated.

'Out with it! Answer me!' Tigellinus snapped. 'Do you deny that you are a follower of this Christ?'

Peter met the Prefect's gaze defiantly. 'No! Him I will not deny! Never again!'

Impatiently Tigellinus turned away. 'Take him away with the others.'

Bleakly Ben Hur surveyed the pile of charred timbers – all that remained of what had once been Barnabas' shop. He picked up a half-burned wheel, glanced at it, then tossed it aside. His gaze fell on something else. It was the scorched remains of the cradle.

The whole city was destroyed. How many lives had been lost? And Leah? What had happened to her and her husband and her child? Ben Hur resolved that as soon as he found Peter, he would pass by Minucius' house to see if all was well.

Impatiently he turned to Philip.

'When you came back to the street where you left Peter, surely some of the watch was still there?'

Philip shook his head. 'I saw no watchmen. No one. You understand, Judah – we were gone a very long time. We were searching for tools to use on that aqueduct, but we were unsuccessful.'

Ben Hur's lips tightened. 'I hope Antipater did not do Peter any harm.'

The young man squeezed Ben Hur's arm encouragingly. 'Take heart. The watch must have helped him. Believe me – Peter will be here. If not, the others will find him.'

'You have given me hope.'

'Peter would not want you to worry,' Philip asserted. 'He would say – the worst which can happen in this world is only momentary for a good man, insignificant in comparison with eternity.' He sighed. 'If only we all had Peter's faith!'

Ben Hur regarded Philip with interest. 'I have been observing you and your friends for some time. The church is indeed fortunate to have three young men like you. Tell me – what turned you to Christianity?'

Philip shrugged. 'I am a child of this city.' He smiled self-consciously. 'I have never known anything outside it. The Empire was just a word to me. It still is.

'My father was a blacksmith. We lived not far from this spot. When I grew up, I was apprenticed to him. My father and I were very close; I wanted nothing more than to follow in his footsteps.' Philip paused. 'When he became desperately ill, it was the end of the world for me. No doctor could help. I prayed to every God I knew. But my father grew worse.

'One afternoon, Barnabas the wheelwright, a customer of my father's, took me aside. He told me about Christ, who had suffered on this earth, but had showed men the way to the true God. I begged Barnabas to pray to Christ for my father. He said that he would, but he cautioned me first. My father would live, he told me, only if it were God's will. It might also be God's will that he pass from this world. But if that should happen, it would not mean that he was truly dead. A man's soul lives for ever.'

Philip shook his head ruefully. 'I did not understand, and I told Barnabas so. I did not care about my father's soul. All I wanted was for my father to live. Not in some other world – in *this* world!

'Barnabas just looked at me, then he promised he would pray.

That was the last I ever saw of him. A month later my father was dead, and so was Barnabas.

'There was no money ... nothing. I did not even have enough to eat. I'll admit it – I became a thief. I joined two other thieves.' He grinned. 'You know them as Sextus and Apuleius.'

Ben Hur laughed. 'Your companionship has persisted, I see, but I hope your habits have changed.'

'Thank God they have! But for a long time, we were thieves. We broke into houses, even temples, picked pockets. We didn't make a bad living. But one day I thought I had been caught when I ran foul of someone who recognized me. It was an old friend of my father's.

'It turned out, however, that he had been looking for me. Long ago my father had given him money when he had needed it. There was no expectation of repayment. Yet even though there was no necessity – even though my father was dead – this man insisted on paying me the debt.

'Suddenly I knew what Barnabas had meant. My father had been a good man, and his good had lived on after his death. If this was possible – was it not also possible that his soul still lived?

'It was that simple. I became a Christian, and so did my two comrades. We all went to Peter and offered our services. It was fortunate –'

He paused, staring off at something. Ben Hur looked in the same direction.

Sextus and Apuleius came hurrying through the stone arch, the only structure still standing in the Vicus.

'At last we've found you!' Sextus gasped. 'We must flee!'

'Why?' Ben Hur demanded.

'The Emperor has issued a public proclamation outlawing the Christians!' Apuleius exclaimed. 'The Praetorians have caught Antipater – all the others. Peter too.'

Ben Hur could hardly bring himself to ask the dreaded question. 'What have they done with him?'

'The worst,' muttered Sextus. 'He was condemned with the others. There was torture. Some may have talked. We may be implicated. One thing is certain – *all* Christians are blamed for the fire!'

Philip fought to control his emotion. 'We must find where they are keeping Peter. There may be some way we can help him.'

'It is too late,' Sextus insisted. 'He may already be dead. They have been putting them on crosses all morning.'

'Where?' Ben Hur demanded.

'The Field of Mars.'

Ben Hur started off, but Sextus and Apuleius seized him.

'Judah,' Sextus begged, 'we *must* leave the city! The watch is scouring the streets.'

'He's right,' Apuleius agreed. 'Do not walk into their hands.'

'You go!' Ben Hur said savagely. 'I am going to the Field of Mars.'

They released him and he strode away.

Ben Hur trudged along through the charred ruin of a once proud capital. Desolation and destruction were everywhere. Not a single standing building was in sight. The world was as black as the night of his soul.

At long last, the Field of Mars appeared. He stopped, his heart constricting. There silhouetted against the sky, which was still smeared with smoke, were at least thirty crosses. Ben Hur felt the presence of his companions and realized they had been following him. Indeed they were loyal. It was too late to send them back now.

With a great effort he forced himself to approach the terrible scene.

Half-shaven heads, hanging limply, were visible among the victims. Some of them were not yet dead; they moved weakly. A few feeble groans were audible. But the guards posted round the area paid no attention.

Coming to the nearest cross, Ben Hur stared up into the inanimate features. Then he moved on. The third cross bore the body of Antipater. The triumphant Herald of the Second Coming seemed pitifully insignificant in death.

Then – the dreaded sight. He did not have to go closer to know that it was Peter. But his mind was numb. His legs seemed to move of their own accord.

He stood under the cross, allowing the full torrent of his grief to pour from his soul.

'Peter ... Peter ...' he wept. 'Give me some of your faith!'

'There is no need,' whispered a tortured voice.

Ben Hur stared up in shock. It was Peter who had spoken. There was still a flicker of life in him!

'I have been waiting for you ...' came the faint words.

'God ...' prayed Ben Hur. 'End his pain!'

'The pain is ... only a doorway through which I will pass, to the garden beyond.'

'If only I had come sooner!'

'You came when you could ...' Peter faltered. Finally his bloodless lips moved again. 'My burden is less because you will carry on my work. Our master gave me the keys to the kingdom ... I pass them to you, Judah ...'

'I cannot fill your place, Peter. I am not the rock you are.'

'You do not know yourself, Judah. Since your return to Rome ... your faith and purpose have been stronger than ever. The holy spirit has entered you ...'

There was no more pain in Peter's drawn face – only peace.

CHAPTER TWENTY-SEVEN

The torches, set in their metal holders on the pillars, flickered fitfully in the close air of the underground basilica. Shadows danced across the faces of Sextus, Apuleius and Philip. Ben Hur handed each of them a small bag.

'Always have this barley with you when necessity calls you outside,' he said. 'If anyone should ever stop you, say your parents belonged to Arrius' household. You have come here to make offerings of barley at the tomb of Arrius' wife. I need not remind you,' he added warningly, 'to leave this place as seldom as possible.'

The young men placed the little bags in the pouches of their belts.

Sextus looked dejected. 'The pagans have won. If we must spend our lives in hiding, we cannot go out among others. Peter's church in Rome will die.'

'There is still much we can do,' Ben Hur replied. 'We have ink and papyrus. We can write. The spoken word vanishes into the air – but things written outlive a man.'

The three faces brightened considerably. Ben Hur realized that after the utter misery of the last four days, they were hungry for hope.

'I do not want to be the voice of gloom,' Sextus murmured, 'but a disturbing thought has occurred to me. I only have *three* sesterces.'

'You are rich by comparison with me,' Philip stated. 'I only have one.'

'I have no money at all,' said Apuleius.

All looked at Ben Hur.

'I'm afraid I am in the same situation. I lost my money-pouch in the fire.'

There was a bleak silence.

Finally Apuleius gave voice to the thought they were all sharing. 'Even our combined resources will not be enough to feed us for very long. A few days at the most.'

'There may be a solution,' Ben Hur mused quietly. 'Some years ago, before my exile, I hid away money in the villa.'

'But the villa is no longer closed up,' Apuleius warned. 'Someone is living there now. Peter told me.'

'Nevertheless I think it is worth the risk to retrieve the money.'

'How much is it?' Sextus wondered.

'A considerable amount. If it is still there.'

'What if it is not there?' Apuleius inquired caustically.

Ben Hur shrugged. 'We will think of something else.'

'And I will tell you what it is,' said Philip.

All turned to him hopefully. With a crafty little grin, Philip pointed to Sextus and Apuleius. 'We three will return to our old profession!'

Ben Hur was surprised. 'Stealing?'

'Helping the church,' Philip said. 'Apuleius was once the best pickpocket in Rome!'

'We cannot do that, Philip,' Sextus insisted. 'It is against the teachings of Christ.'

'He's right,' Apuleius agreed.

'It will be for a good cause,' Philip replied.

'The end never justifies the means,' Sextus stated firmly. 'Is that not true, Judah?'

Ben Hur frowned. 'That's a dilemma. Certainly stealing is a sin, but on the other hand Christ said we may be forgiven for our sins.'

Sextus gazed at him. 'Are you saying that stealing can sometimes be justified?'

'No, but if circumstances force us to steal, we are not necessarily damned. Provided, of course, we confess the crime to God, and pray for his forgiveness.'

'I think we will be doing a great deal of praying,' Sextus commented drily, 'unless you can find that money you spoke of.'

Thoughtfully Ben Hur moved a few steps to the sealed entrance of the crypt. The stone which covered it was not quite closed, leaving a tiny crack for observing the outside world. Ben Hur squinted through it.

'It is still day out there. I'd best wait for darkness.' He pointed to a pile of fresh rushes. 'In the meantime, let us spread these. The air is stale in here.'

All four picked up the sweet-smelling branches and began to strew them over the floor.

As Ben Hur worked, he counted the skins of water piled up against the right-hand wall. They would not need refilling for several days. He assessed the six metal pots set out on the floor near the entrance to the tunnel. It was not an ideal way to dispose of their natural wastes, but it was better than fouling the floor. The pots had to be carried carefully the entire length of the tunnel, then emptied outside, a task they shared in equal turns. It was not only unpleasant but risky as well.

Despite the hardships of their fugitive lives, Ben Hur had noticed an increased determination and will to survive among his comrades. After all, the element which had divided the church in Rome was now gone. In a certain sense the disaster of the fire had separated the wheat from the chaff.

But Peter's loss was a terrible blow. Ben Hur's thoughts went to Urgulania. She had received the shocking news with amazing calmness. She had merely insisted that Peter would still be with them. They must continue to carry out his work.

Ben Hur knew that Urgulania's stoic reaction reflected no lack of love for her dead husband. Perhaps the shock of facing the death of her child had made the second blow easier to bear.

He reminded himself to give the remaining bag of barley to Urgulania – after all, she was the one who left the crypt most frequently, having taken on the task of obtaining provisions for the others.

He looked round. She was nowhere in sight. He realized that he had not seen her for some time.

'Sextus!' he called. 'Where is Urgulania?'

The young man put down his bundle of rushes and turned.

'I don't know. Perhaps she went to get food.'

'No,' said Ben Hur. 'She did that yesterday. She would not have gone out again.'

He had warned Urgulania – as he had the others – about the dangers of leaving their hiding place more often than necessary. Another thought chilled him. Had the equanimity with which she had heard the news of Peter's death been deceptive? Suddenly he was afraid.

'I'd better find her,' he said.

He strode to the opening which led into the murky blackness of the tunnel, stooped and entered. For a time he made his way along. Then he perceived a light glimmering ahead. It was not light from the outside – it was the flickering glow cast by an oil lamp. Ben Hur quickened his pace.

With great relief he came upon Urgulania. She was on her knees, painting a picture on the rough stones of the wall. Intent on her task, she was unaware of Ben Hur when he reached her side.

'Urgulania,' he said softly.

Startled, she looked round, then got to her feet. She seemed almost embarrassed.

Ben Hur gazed at her handiwork. It was an awkward, childish, stick-like figure of a man clad in a golden tunic. With his staff, the figure was striking a rock from which poured a stream of water. And over the head of the figure the name 'Peter' was inscribed in crude letters.

Ben Hur indicated the painting. 'What have you done here?'

She pointed to the drawing. 'Moses brought a fountain of water in the desert by striking a rock. And Peter is the rock upon which Christ built his church. In the scriptures Moses was the shepherd of God's people in the desert. Peter was the shepherd of Christ's church here in Rome.'

Ben Hur stared at the picture again. It did not reproduce Peter's features at all. Yet there was something about it which captured his essence. Even if Urgulania had not written Peter's name in her clumsy letters, Ben Hur was certain that he could never have mistaken the identity of the man in the golden tunic.

'If this is to be our place,' she said, emotion creeping into her voice, 'I wanted to leave something – something to remind those who come after us of Peter.'

The night did not offer much cover, with the full moon pouring its silver light over the landscape.

Taking a deep breath, Ben Hur darted across the short stretch of grass until he reached the hedge growing right up against the wall of the villa. He crept along until he came to the bath-house. He breathed a silent prayer that the money would still be where he had hidden it under the floor. He glanced up at the small shuttered window. It was closed tight.

Drawing a small knife from his belt, he inserted it between the shutters, fishing for the wooden bolt on the other side. He found it and attempted to work it free. But nothing happened. It was wedged too tight. He moved the blade up and down in an effort to loosen it – but to no avail. Impatiently he pulled the handle of the knife sideways, trying to break the end of the latch. Suddenly it gave, the shutter banging open – but the blade of his knife had snapped.

The noise seemed preternaturally loud in the stillness of the night. He crouched there, motionless, hoping he had not awakened anyone. There was no further sound.

Finally he slid the shutter open the rest of the way, wormed through the opening and dropped inside. The room was hot and steam rose from the pool. Clearly it had been in recent use. Ben Hur made his way to the furnace doorway. Just short of it, he knelt and ran his hands along the floor.

At that moment the door on the other side of the room swung open. A bulky man stood there, framed by the moonlit columns of the portico outside.

Ben Hur leaped for the window, but the newcomer charged in and seized him by the legs. Ben Hur grabbed his assailant's arm, twisting it behind him, then flung the fellow into the pool. Once again he started for the window, but now four other men shoved their way in, attacking Ben Hur. He struggled, but was borne to the ground by sheer weight of numbers. He kicked and twisted madly, but his efforts ceased abruptly when the first man, who had climbed out of the pool, held a dagger to his throat.

Two of his captors hoisted him to his feet, while the man with the dagger continued to keep the point of his weapon in Ben Hur's face.

'Looking to steal something, are you?' he growled. He gestured to one of his fellows. 'Run and fetch the master.'

Ben Hur said nothing. These men appeared to be servants, and no doubt the owner would be some highly placed Roman. Ben Hur tried to think of a convincing explanation to account for his breaking into the villa, but none occurred to him.

At last the sound of footsteps was heard on the portico. The owner, wrapped in a long cloak, strode in, accompanied by the man who had summoned him, along with still more servants bearing lamps. With a shock, Ben Hur recognized him. It was Phaon! The old freedman was equally astounded.

'Young Arrius! By the sacred hearth of Vesta! I thought you were dead!'

'I have returned to life.'

'Thank the Gods for that!' He turned to the servants. 'Release him!' he ordered sharply.

Clearly bewildered, the servants obeyed.

'You've come back!' Phaon breathed with wonder.

'Perhaps my method of entrance was a little unorthodox,' said Ben Hur.

Phaon laughed, a little too heartily. The servants seemed more mystified than ever at Phaon's unexpected familiarity with an intruder.

'Come, young Arrius,' Phaon insisted, taking Ben Hur by the

arm, leading him out on to the portico. 'We have so much to tell each other.'

Outside, Phaon studied Ben Hur anxiously. 'You look tired. Would you like some food? ...'

Ben Hur shook his head. 'Not at present ...'

'You must have something. I insist.'

Before Ben Hur could refuse, Phaon darted back into the bathhouse. Ben Hur could see him through the door, as he addressed the servants in low tones. The words were inaudible, but Phaon's manner was clearly that of a master addressing his inferiors.

Returning to the villa, Ben Hur realized, had been a reckless mistake ...

An instant later, Phaon was back on the portico, linking his arm with Ben Hur's, escorting him to the tablinium door.

On the threshold, Ben Hur paused. 'And Electra? I hope she is well.'

'She hasn't changed a bit. She sleeps as soundly as ever. As you see – all this commotion hasn't disturbed her in the least.'

'Perhaps we should wake her and tell her I am here.'

Phaon shook his head. 'I'd rather not. She's very highly-strung ... She'd be hysterical if she saw you back from the grave in the middle of the night. But do come in and sit down. You must tell me what has happened to you.'

Ben Hur followed Phaon into the tablinium. As Phaon lit the oil lamp, Ben Hur surveyed the room. It was much the same as it had always been, but for the addition of an expensive set of new chairs.

'How extraordinary this is,' Ben Hur murmured. 'You may know, Phaon, when I left Rome, I was not in the highest favour with the authorities. I fully expected that all my property would have been confiscated.'

'It was,' said Phaon. 'For some time. Boarded up. Until Electra and I finally managed to get permission to move back.'

Something about Phaon's uneasy stance transported Ben Hur's mind back to that day, years before, when after an incriminating conversation with Agrippina he had come face to face with Phaon – Phaon who was supposedly at the market but instead was standing uneasily on the path, the same way he was standing in front of Ben Hur now.

'The authorities paid you well for your betrayal, didn't they?' Ben Hur murmured.

Phaon licked his lips.

'And Electra doesn't know,' Ben Hur persisted. 'That's why you didn't want to wake her, isn't it?'

Phaon shrugged weakly. 'She thinks you are dead ... That you willed me the property.'

There was a moment of silence. Ben Hur stared at Phaon. He had treated the freedman with kindness and consideration, and Phaon had certainly chosen a strange way to repay it.

'You hate me, don't you?' Phaon burst out. 'You despise me! I am worse than a worm under your foot!' His voice rose in intensity. 'But they didn't threaten you! They weren't going to cut *your* head off! Yes – I betrayed you! I was wrong, I know. A man should be courageous and defy such threats! But I am not like you! I am only a servant. I am not a brave man and I don't want to be!' Tears showed in his eyes. 'It doesn't mean I don't love you ... It's only that I – I cannot stand pain ...' He began to weep openly.

Ben Hur gazed at him wryly. 'Let's forget the past. At the moment I'm only concerned with the present. Forget that you have seen me tonight. As far as you know, I am still dead.'

Phaon's tears ceased. Again he could not meet Ben Hur's eyes. He shook his head. 'You ask the impossible.'

'Surely you cannot mean that! You would betray me again?'

The freedman stared at the floor. 'I have little choice. The servants have seen you. The word will get out that you were here ... If I protected you, I would suffer the very fate I have striven so hard to avoid.'

Ben Hur struggled to control his fury. There was no time for anger. Unless he could escape, this was the end. And a hideous end it would be. The Emperor, frustrated so long in his vengeance, would not be inclined to mercy.

'Phaon,' he said earnestly. 'Listen to me. There is no need for your fears. Your servants do not know me. You can tell them I am an old friend of yours.'

Phaon shook his head slowly.

'It is too late, young Arrius,' he whispered. 'I didn't send those servants for food . . . I sent them for the watch . . .'

Ben Hur did not wait for more. He lunged for the door and pulled it open.

But there, outlined starkly on the portico in the moonlight, were six armed men, their drawn swords glittering dangerously.

A vast congress of the homeless was encamped on the Field of Mars. Tents had been pitched. The air resounded with the cries of children and the grunting of livestock.

Her eyes smarting from the smoke of giant cooking fires, Leah elbowed her way towards the Pantheon and the Monuments of Agrippa. These buildings had been thrown open and were swarming with refugees from the burned-out city. Great awnings had been rigged up beside the Baths of Agrippa, sheltering unclaimed belongings. In front of the portico of the Pantheon, food was piled on long tables, and wagons filled with vegetables and fruit were waiting to be unloaded. Members of the city watch were doling out the provisions to long queues of people.

At last Leah caught sight of the imperial party circulating among the forlorn humanity on the grass. Praetorian Guards formed a protective ring round the glittering dignitaries of the court. The Emperor himself stood out among the rest, dressed in a golden cape and long Germanic pantaloons.

Leah paused, mustering her courage. She had to do something soon, before the property assessors came to take possession of her husband's estate. Right after Minucius' death she had gone to the palace to seek help from the Emperor, but she had been informed that the entire court was away at Antium. But now that Nero had returned, she was determined to try again.

She pushed her way through the crowd until she reached the Praetorians surrounding the court entourage. She tugged one of the soldiers by the leather bands which covered his sleeve.

'I must see the Emperor,' she said urgently. 'It is very important.'

The man shook her off, but she reached out and took his arm again.

'Please,' she begged. 'Let me through.'

'Go away!' snapped the Praetorian.

Leah stepped back, but she had no intention of leaving. Carefully she manoeuvred her way round the soldiers until she came nearer to the Emperor. Throngs of refugees were trying to get close to him, but the Praetorians were pushing them back. The imperial attention was directed towards a small boy who stood, crying mournfully, ignored by his family who squatted wretchedly nearby.

Nero strode over and knelt beside the boy. Immediately the family scrambled to their feet, ducking their heads respectfully at the imperial presence.

'Do not cry, little fellow,' said Nero. 'I know you have lost your home, but we must bear up under misfortune.'

'Pluto is gone!' the boy wailed. 'I have lost Pluto!'

The Emperor seemed puzzled. 'Pluto?'

One of the boy's kin took a timid step forward.

'Exalted Sir ...' he explained hesitantly. 'Pluto is a goose – it was my son's pet.'

'He shall have another one!' the Emperor declared. He turned back to the boy. 'Would you like a swan too?' Nero gestured to Epaphroditus, who hovered nearby. 'See to it.'

The child's tears vanished.

'Bless you, Caesar,' the father murmured.

Now the golden-cloaked Emperor faced the ragged multitude on the grass.

'My poor people!' he cried. 'When even a single Roman suffers, I suffer. You can imagine how I feel now. You are homeless. I am one of you. I too have lost my home. My palace has been burned to cinders!

'But we shall rebuild the city! It will be more magnificent than ever – a fitting capital of the world. No more rickety tenements! I'm putting a new code of fire regulations before the Senate. All buildings must have stone partitions. There must be firefighting equipment in every other house.

'In the meantime – until you find new places to live – all public buildings will be open to you. We will help you in every way possible.'

There were cheers. Nero waved benevolently to his audience as Epaphroditus passed him a bag. The Emperor delved into it and pulled out a fistful of coins, which he hurled to the people. Again and again he repeated the gesture, sending the desperate refugees scrambling for gold.

Finally he stopped, turning to confront his entourage. 'These people sitting out here in the open – surely there is some shelter for them?'

The Prefect of the City shook his head lugubriously. 'The tents are all full.'

'Then open the Temple of Saturn! House as many people in there as you can. Saturn won't mind.'

Doggedly Leah ventured forward again, but hesitated when she noticed a palace official tugging anxiously at the Emperor's cloak. Leah could hear his words.

'Exalted Sir, we're having trouble with the purveyors. The men from the Treasury haven't paid them for the food yet.'

'Jupiter's eyeballs!' Nero yelled. 'I'm drowning in incompetence!'

He strode off towards the massive columned front of the Pantheon. The gaping mob followed, with Leah tagging after them.

The purveyors at the long tables bowed when the Emperor came up. He hurled a handful of coins at them.

'Take your money!' Nero bellowed in a voice loud enough for the multitude of onlookers to hear. 'Just keep the food going out to the citizens! I want my good people fed! If you need any more funds, I'll pay you out of my own pocket!'

The Emperor moved over to a cart of vegetables not far from where Leah was standing and inspected the produce. Desperately she tried to get past the soldiers again. But a medallion-studded Centurion blocked her way, seizing her by the arms.

'You may be beautiful, honey-pot,' he growled. 'But you're no hungrier than the others. Now be off! If you want food, go to the end of the line.'

This time, however, the commotion had attracted Epaphroditus' attention. The freedman came over, then beamed with recognition. He bowed. 'Faultless lady! What a delight to see you!'

Amiably he turned to the soldier. 'Why were you troubling this lady, Centurion?'

Defensively the Centurion released her. 'She was trying to push her way through. I have orders to let no one approach the Emperor.'

Epaphroditus' smile broadened. 'Excellent! I like soldiers who obey orders. But in the case of this woman you may ignore your orders.' He patted the Centurion's arm. 'Nevertheless – keep up the good work.'

The freedman took Leah by both hands.

'What brings you to this scene of sadness, may I ask?'

'Please, Epaphroditus!' Leah said breathlessly. 'I must speak to the Emperor! I know how busy he is – but I will not take more than an instant of his time. I am in a desperate situation.'

For a moment Epaphroditus studied her thoughtfully as if considering the implications of her request.

'In that case,' he murmured finally, 'we'll do something about it.' His smile came back. 'Not because you are desperate, but because you are desperately lovely.'

He escorted her towards the imperial group by the vegetable cart. Nero snatched a large radish, sniffed it and bit into it. He scowled. 'This tastes like a piece of wet leather! I want only the freshest food for the people!'

'Exalted Sir,' the Prefect reminded him gently, 'we are bringing in everything we can get our hands on, and it is still not enough. We are in no position to be choosy.'

Epaphroditus stepped closer to the Emperor and whispered into his ear. Nero turned. He regarded Leah blankly for a moment, then his face brightened. 'The lady of the violets! How marvellous! Do you have some more violets for me?'

'I am afraid not.'

'Never mind that. It is enough just to lay eyes on you. I have missed you, by Jupiter!'

'I did not get that impression,' said Leah, unable to conceal the note of bitterness which crept into her voice.

'You refer to my absence the morning after our glorious evening together.' He sighed. 'You do not understand. Business took me off to Antium. Then this awful fire! My dear – I have not had a moment to breathe!' He snatched another radish from the cart and popped it into his mouth. 'One day I shall write an epic poem about it. But it is too close to me now – the pain is still too sharp.'

Abruptly he stopped chewing, regarding Leah penetratingly. 'Don't tell me you were burned out too! Are you homeless like the rest of us?'

'I am homeless, but not because of the fire.'

'Whatever happened?'

'My husband died.'

'In the fire?'

Her voice was harsh. 'He killed himself. It was the morning after I came back from being with you. He took vengeance by disinheriting me. I don't care about myself – but I have a little boy to support, and a faithful servant. I won't have any money to feed them.'

The Emperor seemed hurt. 'What a paradox life is! I acted only out of love, and tragedy has resulted!'

'You speak of love,' Leah blurted. 'You have shown no love for me.'

'How little you know me! But there are ways to rectify that.' He glanced round quickly. 'I think my business here is finished, in fact.' He turned to Epaphroditus. 'Call my carriage!' His questing eyes returned to Leah. 'Since we are both homeless, perhaps we can seek shelter together.'

Leah reclined lazily on the couch, watching Teuta sweep the mosaic floor of the triclinium. The Illyrian woman paused to open the shutters wider. Sunlight flooded the room with glittering splendour.

The dancing colours lifted Leah's spirits. Only now was she beginning to emerge from the depression caused by Minucius' death. But for some time she had been bound by a net of remorse and guilt, combined with a bitter resentment.

She had petitioned Nero for title to the property, but the Emperor had so far avoided committing himself, explaining that he was already under criticism for bestowing too many state possessions on his favourites. But at least the threat of eviction had been avoided.

'Teuta,' she called, 'what food have you prepared this afternoon?'

The servant woman shrugged. 'Enough ...'

'I did not ask that. I want to know what sort of food.'

'Peacock brains, flamingo tongues, lamprey milt. Of course, if he needs an aphrodisiac, we could serve him some pike livers.'

Leah stretched. '*That* he does not need.'

Teuta regarded Leah warmingly. 'It won't last, you know.'

'You are so negative!' Leah cried with exasperation. 'Do you never see anything hopeful? Must everything be a bad omen?'

'In this case the bad omen is obvious. You are just too blind to see it, silly girl that you are!'

'What are you talking about?'

'You are having your affair in the very house where you lived with your husband. That is not fitting. Minucius will come back. His ghost will find a way to ruin it for you. Not that I am opposed to the affair – on the contrary. But do your rutting where it will not anger the dead.'

'Stop your babbling!'

Teuta picked up the broom with another shrug. 'Never say I failed to warn you,' she muttered direly as she went out.

Leah sprawled in silence. But something made her flesh tingle. There was another presence in the room. Her eyes swept round, but nothing was visible. Yet she was certain that she was not alone. She could feel it.

Her glance fell on a blue silk hanging in one corner, which concealed some Samian pots. Leah could have sworn that it stirred slightly.

Abruptly she strode over and pulled it aside. There stood Tarquin.

The boy regarded her solemnly. 'My father *is* coming back ...'

'Why do you say that?'

'Teuta said so. I just heard her.'

'Pay no attention to Teuta. I have told you – he is dead. He will never come back. And I have told you before – he was *not* your father.'

'Who is my father? The man with the red hair who comes here?'

'No!' she replied sharply. 'The man with the red hair is the Emperor. And Emperors have to be very careful about who their children are. Never, never suggest that he is your father!'

'Who *is* my father?'

Leah did not answer immediately. She took him by the arm and led him over to the couch. She made him sit beside her, then clasped both of his hands in hers. Her son was one of the few beings in this world who had ever mattered to her. Even though her life was uncertain, the boy must not suffer.

'Tarquin,' she said, 'you did have a father once. But there is no point in my telling you about him, because I think it will be better if he is never a part of your life.'

'Will I ever have a father?'

'Perhaps.' Impulsively she hugged him. 'There is something much more important I must tell you now. You are nearly six years old. You are getting to be a big fellow, big enough to know what to do if anything should ever happen to me.'

'I will do whatever you tell me, mother.'

'Good. There is a man named Seneca . . . He is well-known. He is wealthy and important. Remember the name.'

'Seneca.'

'He is holding money for you. When you come of age – when you are fourteen years old and take the toga virilis, the money will be yours. Go to him then.'

At that moment Teuta entered excitedly. 'There is a chair here for you! The bearers say they've been sent by the imperial freedman.' Teuta shook her head. 'But I do not understand it – it is a *public* chair.'

'Did they say why I was to go with them?'

'No. They said nothing – except that you are to hurry.'

An inexplicable apprehension gripped Leah, but she fought to appear calm. 'Fetch my cloak.'

Obediently Teuta started for the door, but paused. 'What am I going to do with all the food?'

'Eat it yourself.'

With a snort, the Illyrian woman disappeared.

'Will you be gone long, mother?' Tarquin asked in a small voice.

She hugged him again. 'No, Tarquin. I'll be back soon.'

The bearers placed the chair on the ground in front of a rambling house on the far side of the Gardens of Maecenas.

Epaphroditus emerged from the gate in time to bow Leah out of the litter with his usual studied politeness.

'Faultless lady,' he said. 'I regret that I was not able to send a carriage for you, but we have still not replaced the conveyances we lost in the fire.'

'I am afraid I was delayed,' she said apologetically. 'When the message came, I was with my little son. I hope nothing is wrong.'

'Why should anything be wrong?'

'It is only that I expected the Emperor to come to my house as usual.'

'I am sure you have nothing to worry about. He awaits you impatiently.'

Epaphroditus paid the bearers, then, waving away the Praetorian Guards, conducted Leah through the gate into the vestibule.

Inside, they passed two liveried servants, then stopped short as Nero himself hurried up to meet them. He seized Leah in an extravagant embrace.

'How cruel are the beautiful!' he cried. 'How could you keep me waiting so long! But no matter – you will never do so again.'

Leah regarded him warily. 'Exalted Sir, I pray that I have not displeased you too much.'

'You have. You have tortured me! In fact, you do not deserve the wonderful gift I have waiting for you.'

'Gift?'

'Yes, greedy girl.' He snatched her arm. 'Come!'

She had to run to keep up with him, as he led her down a narrow corridor.

'I need no gifts,' she said tactfully. 'Only your esteem.'

'You have imprisoned that for ever,' he asserted, quickening his pace.

At last they reached a door. Nero hurled it open and beckoned for Leah to enter.

She found herself in a spacious chamber complete with couches, tables, braziers, and gay wall paintings. A large window flooded the place with light and fresh air.

He grinned at her. 'Not bad for temporary accommodation. Let me show you the other room.'

Nero slid aside a wooden partition and conducted Leah into a bedroom. It was simply furnished but pleasant.

'The sleeping couch is a little crude for my taste,' said Nero, 'but every scrap of furniture in the palace was burned in the fire.' He indicated another sliding door. 'On the other side of that is *my* bedroom.'

'And whose bed is this?' Leah asked, realizing already what the answer would be.

He regarded her mischievously. 'My little nosegay, you will occupy this bower. These are your apartments.'

Impulsively Leah seized him round the neck and kissed him.

He blushed with boyish pleasure and led her back into the other room. 'Naturally you can visit your son as often as you like. I hope you find this as comfortable as your husband's house.'

'I like it better – because you are here.'

'It will be more convenient – your staying here with me. As you know, business never leaves an Emperor alone. Travelling back and forth to that house of yours takes too much time.'

'I am sure we will be very happy,' Leah murmured, trying to keep excessive elation from her voice.

'You'll be even happier when the new palace is built,' Nero went on. 'I am going to call it the Golden House. It will bring the country into the city – the plans include parks, streams, even an artificial lake! In the very middle will be a statue of me – one hundred and twenty feet tall! My architects are men of rare genius – they saw what I wanted right away. They designed a circular triclinium which can actually revolve to face the sun throughout the day. And miles of porticoes meandering through the parklands – mineral baths, walls of brick-faced concrete. At last I can begin to live like a human being!'

He paused with a frown. 'That reminds me – I am due to meet the architects now. I have kept them waiting too long.'

He hurried to the door. 'I shall return shortly – on wings of love.'

Leah was left alone to contemplate the dazzling life which lay ahead. She began to inspect her new surroundings. She wondered what sort of accommodation the Empress had . . .

But she warned herself not to be too confident. The Emperor was notoriously promiscuous. Her fortunes could sink as rapidly as they had risen.

There was a soft rap on the door.

'Come in,' said Leah.

Epaphroditus entered, holding a bundle of papyri. He bowed. 'Faultless lady . . .' His eyes flickered round the room. 'Forgive the intrusion, but I was looking for the Emperor.'

'He went to consult with an architect, but he'll be back soon.'

The freedman held up his documents. 'These demand his immediate attention. If you don't mind, I'll leave them here.'

He stepped over and placed them on the table. Then he turned to her with his usual smile. 'I hope you find this accommodation satisfactory . . .'

'Very.'

'If there is any way I can be of service,' he went on, 'I shall be most gratified. Your slightest wish – you must tell me.'

'You are very kind, Epaphroditus. I appreciate that.'

'It is my deepest hope that your relationship with the Emperor will prosper. Actually that is why I convinced him that this apartment for you would be a convenient arrangement.'

'That was your idea?'

He nodded.

'Why should you be so concerned about me?'

'As I have said, I have great regard for you.'

Leah studied him. 'If there is ever any way I can repay your generosity, I wish you would let me know.'

For a particle of time his smile was gone, and she saw another being beneath the mask – stern and implacable as death.

'May I be open with you?' he asked.

'Openness is what I seek.'

'I need not point out that it would be foolish to betray my confidence.'

'I will not betray you.'

The radiant smile flooded back. 'You have heard of the estrangement between the Emperor and the Empress?'

'Yes.'

'Poppaea and I are not on the best of terms. I was not displeased when she and the Emperor quarrelled, but now she wishes a reconciliation. As long as you are here, there is little likelihood of her return.'

'I only hope my influence is as strong as you think.'

'With Nero one is never sure of anything,' he said candidly, 'but this much is certain. Of all the women he has known recently, none but you has aroused such an extravagant response.'

'That is very encouraging to hear.'

'It follows that what you say and do can be of great importance. Naturally I will continue to foster your cause – and, in return, I hope you will foster mine.'

'Gladly – but it surprises me that you, the Emperor's closest confidant, would need help from someone like me.'

'Being close to the Emperor has made me many enemies. Some of them I cannot strike at directly. You will have ways of reaching Nero which are denied to me.' He added with elaborate delicacy, 'In some positions, a woman can be more convincing than a man.'

Leah smiled. 'You can count on me.'

'Then let us consider our unholy alliance sealed,' he said, offering his hand.

She clasped it. He bowed as effusively as ever and left.

Leah sank on to a couch. For some time she pondered the strange conversation, but her thoughts were interrupted when Nero reappeared. His face was flushed and excited.

'I shall make both those architects equestrians!' he cried. 'You should see their plans for the reception room. It will have a sliding ceiling from which perfume and flowers will shower the guests.'

He took her passionately into his arms and kissed her neck. Gently she extricated herself, and indicated the documents on the table. 'The freedman told me to bring those to your attention ...'

Instantly his euphoria vanished. He moved over to the table and glared balefully at the pile. 'Jupiter's eyeballs! The life of an Emperor is a slavish existence! I do not belong to myself. I am at everyone's beck and call.'

'If the task displeases you,' Leah suggested, 'why not leave it until later?'

'Impossible. It could be important.' He shrugged and spoke with wry humour. 'The Roman mob could be causing disturbances again. Another one of my tax collectors may have been strangled – or stuffed down a well in some village. There may be trouble on the Danube frontier. Or perhaps someone wants to sell me some choice gladiators.'

He sat down, and took up the stylus with a sigh. 'I really should abdicate. I should go to Greece and become a poet and spend the rest of my life playing the lyre.'

'Would you take me with you?' she asked.

'I swear I'll never again go anywhere without you.'

'If only I could believe that!'

He winked. 'I'll convince you in just a moment – as soon as I finish with these beastly documents.'

He began to sift through the petitions, muttering or making humorous comments about each one. Some he signed and stamped with his seal ring. Others he placed aside.

There was something boyish and charming about him when he was in a good humour. The unruly copper-coloured hair, which was never quite neat, made him seem younger than he was. Leah knew that she could never learn to love him. Yet, at times like this, she found his company agreeable.

Just then he stiffened, staring at the document he was holding.

'No!' he gasped.

He glared at the papyrus in front of him, rubbing his forehead as if suffering from some terrible inner pressure.

'What is it?' Leah ventured timidly.

He did not answer.

'Tell me what is wrong,' she insisted.

'Death warrants!' he growled savagely. 'I hate them! I can never accustom myself to signing the cursed things! Sometimes I wish I had never learned to write!'

'Who is to die?'

'A man called Arrius.' Nero rose and began to pace grimly. 'His real name was Judah Ben Hur. He was condemned in absentia some years ago.'

For an instant Leah could not credit her ears. Judah Ben Hur alive? And was now to die? She clutched the table for support, astounded at the violence of her own emotions. But he was alive! That mysterious figure who had been lurking near Minucius' house – it *had* been Judah! The thoughts tumbled over each other in her confused mind. Why had he come back? Why now and not before? But if it was Judah, why had he not come forward and presented himself? And what circumstances had caused his condemnation?

She spoke in almost a normal voice. 'Why is he to be executed?'

The Emperor did not answer. He was so preoccupied with his own gloomy reflections that he had not noticed her agitation.

She repeated the question. 'Why has this man been condemned?'

She was astonished to see that there were tears in his eyes. She moved close to him and touched his arm.

'You are weeping ...'

He brushed her hand away and resumed his pacing. 'We were so close!' he blurted out. 'Arrius and I. We were the best of friends! I thought I had found the one man I could trust!'

Suddenly he spun round, his face contorted with rage. 'He *betrayed* me! He ought to die!'

Striding to the table, he took up the stylus again.

Leah came quickly to him and restrained his hand.

'Don't.'

He glared at her. 'Don't? Why do you say that?'

'Because you should not be hasty.'

'But he deserves to die!'

'I was not thinking of him. I was thinking of you.'

'Of me!' His scowl deepened.

Gently Leah stroked his head. 'I think you would *like* to spare him because he was once your friend.'

'This man conspired against me – to *murder* me! After I showered him with favours!'

'That is all the more reason to spare him,' Leah declared, her voice recovering some of its strength. 'It will show the greatness of your heart. You may not know it, but you are widely held to be the finest ruler Rome ever had. Your place in history is assured, not only as an Emperor, but as an artist too. Surely mercy – not vengeance – is worthy of such a man.'

He slumped into the chair.

Her hand moved down his neck, caressing it. Then she kissed his ear. 'Surely you have better things to think of than a man's death,' she whispered.

'I cannot put it out of my mind. After all those years ...'

He glared balefully at the document again.

Delicately Leah reached out and took the stylus from his fingers. 'I think I can put it out of your mind.'

He rose slowly, staring at her. 'You surprise me.'

'I do?'

'Yes. You have more than beauty. You have a certain untutored intelligence.' He grinned wryly. 'It seems I am destined to be ruled by women.'

CHAPTER TWENTY-EIGHT

Ben Hur did not know how many days had passed. There were no windows in the fetid little cell, only a barred aperture in the heavy wooden door, admitting a dim flicker from the oil lamps burning unceasingly in the corridor outside. It was perpetual night in this filthy damp prison.

It was the existence of a caged beast. The walls were damp. He was always cold, wrapping himself in his threadbare cloak to conserve any last vestige of warmth. At least a pot had been provided for his natural wastes, but it was rarely emptied, and it grew unbearably foul. Once they had changed the straw which covered the stone floor, but this had hardly affected the teeming population of insects and vermin. He had long since abandoned the futile attempt to keep them off his person. They crawled under his tunic, infested his hair, and their bites were a grim reminder that he was still alive.

Preternaturally, his ears had become attuned to the sounds in the corridor outside. Every time he heard footsteps he was certain that his executioners were coming at last. Yet he tried to sustain himself with the feeble hope that he was being kept alive for a purpose. It had been this hope which had brought him back to the perils of Rome. Surely this destiny had not yet been fulfilled! The Roman church had been virtually destroyed by Nero's purge, reduced to three pickpockets and a grief-stunned woman, scrounging like moles for their existence in a forgotten crypt. If they ever needed his inspiration and help, now was the time.

His belief in his mission was being put to the ultimate test. With every breath he drew, he was staring death in the face. But it was not this which terrified him. He had seen death's visage too often – it had almost become an old friend. What filled him with fear was the thought that his life had been an utter waste.

The lethal sound broke his reverie. It was the tramp of footsteps, echoing in the corridor outside. Somewhere a door grated open, then shut with a hollow boom. The steps came steadily closer. His heart beat with each footfall. He prayed they would go past his door. But they stopped outside. The jailer's face filled the opening.

'A visitor for you,' he grumbled.

Ben Hur rose and went to the door. A hooded figure was waiting in the hall outside. When the jailer disappeared, the visitor approached Ben Hur's cell. The hood was drawn back.

'Leah!' Ben Hur exclaimed.

For a moment, neither could speak.

'Can it be you?' Ben Hur wondered. 'How did you know I was here?'

'Never mind that now. Your life has been saved!'

He stared at her.

'It is true, Judah. You will be kept in prison, but not put to death. It is the Emperor's command.'

'How can you know this?'

'I am very close to the Emperor ...'

He studied her lovely face, framed by the iron bars. God only knew how Leah and Nero had met! But however it had happened, Nero would not be the one to pass up such a woman.

'You think me evil,' she said in a low voice.

'No,' he replied with feeling. 'You are the hand of God!'

She smiled cynically. 'I have risen in the world – but not that far yet.'

'Does Nero know you are here?'

'Of course not.'

'Then how did you get into prison?'

'Nero's freedman, Epaphroditus, arranged it. I have done him a service – we trust each other.' She glanced furtively up and down the corridor, then reached into her pouch and took out some gold coins, passing them to Ben Hur through the bars. 'Use these. They might buy you better treatment from the guards.'

He gazed at the money in his palm, then looked back at her, searching for some hint of what she had become. He felt a worldliness in her, a sophistication and weariness that came only after much living.

'I hardly know you any more,' he murmured.

'I have grown up. I have seen much. I have been through harsh times. I have reared a son. My husband died. Now I am sharing an emperor's bed. Yes, Judah, I have known these men, but I have loved only one.'

Ben Hur hesitated. 'I never thought I would see you again, Leah. Even so, I have only known one woman. But I loved her dearly.'

Anger darkened Leah's face for a moment.

'Who is she?' Leah demanded.

'It does not matter. She is dead.'

Leah's resentment seemed to vanish. 'Tell me one thing, Judah. I saw you watching my husband's house. If you felt nothing for me, why were you there?'

'I never said I felt nothing. Once I was planning a whole life with you.'

'Is that why you came? To abduct me?'

'No. I had no desire to intrude on your marriage. I wanted only to speak to you on behalf of your father.'

She stiffened. It was almost as if he had slapped her face.

'I didn't come here to discuss my father,' she said tightly.

'Why are you so bitter? He gave you everything.'

'Yes! And took it away from me! With no reason. Without telling me. He destroyed my life!'

'You do your father an injustice. You do not understand his devotion.'

'Eat your devotion for supper!' she blazed. 'I hope it sustains you here in this rotting cell!'

She turned and hurried away down the corridor.

'Leah!' he cried.

'I don't want to speak to you again!' she shouted back.

Leah banged on the door at the end of the corridor. The guard opened it and she went out.

He turned back into the darkness of his cell. In despair, he sank on to the pallet of straw which served as his bed. Leah had come back like a ghost of his past to bring him hope. But now he had angered her. He would never see her again.

'Judah!'

He looked up. She had not gone! Her face was there framed in the bars. Quickly he rose and crossed to the door.

'I am sorry!' she begged. 'Please forgive me!'

He reached through the bars to touch her shoulder comfortingly. She took his hand in both of hers and held it fiercely.

'It was the anger in me speaking ... I wanted you to say you loved me. I expect too much, perhaps ... But you don't know what you have meant to me, Judah ... ever since I was a child. You have always been my idol. I have measured every other man against my memory of you ... and they were all wanting. If only we had been married! My life would have been different.'

Ben Hur was silenced by the violence of her emotion, but, before he could answer, she kissed his hand and fled.

Long after she had departed, he stared out into the darkened passage.

Despite the afternoon heat, Leah kept the hood of her cloak up as she drew closer to the hovels clustered under the grim wall.

She paused a good distance from the postern, watching it carefully. Epaphroditus had warned her never to approach if anyone was in the vicinity. But now a female fruit seller was lingering by the gate, conversing with the guard. Leah fumed with impatience. Finally the woman pushed her barrow away. Only when the hawker had disappeared from sight round the corner did Leah start forward again.

As Leah neared the postern, however, the guard held up a hand.

'You'll have to wait today,' he grumbled. 'There's an execution ...'

Leah clenched her teeth. This had happened once before, and she had been forced to stand outside in the sun until the grim business had been completed. But any delay was better than running the risk of being seen by those in the courtyard.

Once again she waited in the heat. Finally there was a hollow knock from the inside of the gate. The guard unlocked it. There stood the familiar, dour figure of the jailer. He beckoned curtly, and Leah followed him along the path leading to the inner gate.

She was careful to keep her eyes away as they passed the dreaded steps from which the bodies of the condemned were thrown.

Only when they descended into the damp corridor of the prison itself did Leah breathe more easily. Nevertheless, she was worried.

Up until now she had been almost too lucky. Nero apparently accepted that she was spending her absences from the imperial residence with her child. And the Emperor had not been paying much attention to her anyway. It was not from lack of ardour, but from preoccupation with seemingly endless troubles – signs of revolt among the Roman armies in the provinces, the revelation of a dangerous conspiracy which involved half the Senate and a good number of Praetorians as well. But in spite of this, every time Leah came to the prison, the risk of some misadventure and discovery increased. Epaphroditus had warned her not to come too often, but it was impossible to stay away.

Paradoxically, in these fetid surroundings, Leah had felt happy for the first time in years. It was like a return to the far-off dreams of her youth. True, it was hard to see the once proud Prince of Hur reduced to the wretched existence of a prisoner. But it spite of everything he was still the same man who had commanded her adoration since childhood. Even now he was the legendary figure who could make all things happen. She could not believe that he would not somehow free himself from his predicament.

At last the jailer stopped at the door to the cells. He drew back the heavy wooden bolt, and Leah entered the musty passage.

She ran the last few steps. Immediately Ben Hur's haggard features appeared in the barred aperture. He squeezed his hand through the narrow space. Leah clasped it in both of hers and kissed it.

'Judah ... Judah ...'

'It has been an eternity since you were here!' he exclaimed with feeling.

'I will always come. Never doubt that. *Never!*'

'I believe it when I see you – when you touch me. But when you are gone, I am afraid ... something could happen. You might never return. Leah, your visits are everything to me.'

'For me it is the same. My life away from you is hateful. I live only to come here. I even think I love this cell.'

They regarded each other helplessly.

Finally he spoke. 'What is it like outside?'

'Just another day.'

'Is the sun shining?'

'Yes. It is shining ...'

'And your boy, is he well?'

She nodded.

'He still plays with his cart?'

Suddenly she pulled her hand away from his. 'Judah, I can't stand it!'

'What can we do?'

'Surely there must be something. You are an innocent man!'

'Who will believe that?'

'I'll face the Emperor myself! I'll tell him you have been wrongly condemned. I'll *make* him believe me!'

'Don't try, Leah,' he warned. 'You'll destroy yourself. You think *that* will help me?'

'You never had a chance to present your case. If I speak to him, he'll listen to me.'

'You don't know what kind of man he is.'

'I think I know better than anyone,' she replied heatedly. 'He's not what people say. I think he is capable of decency. I'll appeal to him.'

He stared at her. 'Then why haven't you suggested it before now?'

Leah did not answer.

'You know it won't work,' he insisted.

'I must try!'

She turned away and strode down the passage.

'Wait!' Ben Hur cried.

But she did not heed him. The door banged behind her with finality.

Nero stared at her coldly. 'Now I understand why you took the stylus out of my hand. It wasn't any concern for me. It was concern for Arrius.'

'Concern for both of you,' Leah replied. 'I have thought about him often. His life in that prison must be hideous.'

'Why did you conceal that you knew him?'

'I should have told you at the time,' Leah admitted. 'But I was afraid you'd misinterpret it ... as you are doing now.'

He rose slowly from the couch. 'Was Arrius a lover of yours?'

'No!' she exclaimed. 'He was a relation of my family. I was a child when I last saw him. I did not even know he was still alive.'

Nero seemed somewhat mollified. Then his eyes narrowed. 'You know all about the conspiracy – the reason why Arrius was condemned ... But how is that possible? I never told you. Indeed – the whole episode has been a well-kept secret ever since it happened.'

Leah felt a moment of confusion, but she recovered herself hastily. 'I only learned about it the other afternoon. I was playing with my boy when an old beggar came with a letter. It was from Judah. Apparently it was smuggled from prison. He swore he was innocent and begged me to plead with you.'

Nero gazed at her steadily. 'Odd – Arrius knowing of your friendship with me.'

'Lots of people know. There are all sorts of rumours. But I'll admit – I thought it was strange too.'

Abruptly his expression changed. He grinned. 'That's why I believe it. Because it is strange. Life is like that.'

Leah was amazed at his shift of mood. 'Oh, Lucius! You mean – you *will* help him?'

He regarded her mysteriously. 'I might. When I'm near a pretty woman, my reason becomes clouded.

Suddenly the door banged open, and Epaphroditus rushed in. It was the first time Leah had ever seen him agitated.

'Jupiter's eyeballs!' Nero yelled. 'How dare you barge in here without knocking! How –'

'It is an emergency!' Epaphroditus cut in. 'She won't listen to reason. She ...'

He trailed off helplessly as a lovely woman strode into the room. Leah had only seen her from a distance, but she had no trouble in recognizing her deadly enemy. Involuntarily, Leah bowed to the Empress.

Nero was not so respectful. 'You arrogant, presumptuous, conniving bitch! I did not send for you!'

Poppaea spoke grimly. 'I could not wait for your summons. My news is too wonderful for that.' She smiled maliciously at Leah. 'There is no need for introductions. I know who you are. And I know what I have to say will interest you as well.'

She faced Nero. 'I am pregnant again. You'll have an heir after all. Or have you reached the point where not even fatherhood pleases you?'

He surveyed her disparagingly. 'Whose bastard is it?'

'It is not a bastard. I have been two months without my cycle. Two months ago, we were together – or have you forgotten?'

'You always were a liar.' He stabbed Leah with a bitter glance. 'I am surrounded by liars!'

'It is your child,' Poppaea said flatly. 'You think I would be fool enough to have an affair?'

'Passions make people foolish.'

'You know your accusations are false,' she shouted. 'Your agents have been watching me night and day.'

Nero did not reply.

'They would have informed you of any indiscretions on my part.'

'Very well ... you've told me,' the Emperor said finally. 'I thank you for the good news – in spite of the rudeness of your entrance. The child will have every consideration. You can be certain of that! Now kindly remove yourself from my sight.'

Poppaea pointed at Leah. '*She* is the one who is going. *I* am staying.'

Nero slammed his fist on the table with exasperation. 'Vulcan's forge! Am I destined to be hag-ridden all my life?'

Poppaea laughed. 'Hag-ridden! You bring all the hags upon yourself. You are intent only on seduction. You don't care how many lives you ruin. And the people know it. Oh, I know ... they put on a big show of enthusiasm at the sight of you. But why are there stirrings in the provinces and conspiracies here? Because they hate you! They hate me!' She flicked her hand at Leah. 'They hate her too! The one they loved was Octavia – whom you murdered!'

The words stung Nero into an incoherent fury. His mouth worked convulsively. He lunged at Poppaea, seized her by the neck and shook her. Then he choked her until her eyes bulged.

Terrified, Leah watched Nero hurl Poppaea against the wall, and batter her furiously with his fists.

Instinctively Leah started to go to her rival's aid, but a hand caught her by the arm. She turned to find herself facing Epaphroditus. He shook his head and drew her away.

Now Poppaea slumped to the ground. Nero kicked her repeatedly. Suddenly she screamed in agony, clutching her belly. 'The child! The child!' she screamed.

Nero stopped, frozen with horror. Blood was staining Poppaea's stola. He looked round in panic. 'A doctor!' he gasped. 'Hurry!'

He swung round and grabbed Epaphroditus, roughly shoving him towards the door. 'Run! Get a doctor! Quick!'

Epaphroditus nodded and started away. At the door he paused and looked back, then finally went. Leah sensed that help would be a long time in coming.

Weeping now, Nero sank to his knees beside the stricken woman. 'Please! Don't let it happen! I'm sorry, Poppaea! I'm sorry! Oh, Jupiter – help me! Gods –'

Leah remembered the silk under-tunic lying on her sleeping couch. She dashed into the adjoining room, seized it, and returned, tearing the garment into strips. She knelt beside Poppaea, pulling up her garment, determined to stop the bleeding somehow.

A stinging blow caught Leah across the head. She tried to protect herself as he flailed at her. Scrambling to her feet, she retreated.

'You've done it!' he spat. 'You and your ambitions. I wish I'd never seen you!'

'Lucius! Stop!' Leah begged desperately, cowering to avoid the blows.

'You evil witch! It never would have happened but for you!'

Screaming incoherently, hysterical with grief and rage, he grabbed her by the hair and jerked her head back and forth. The room swam before Leah's eyes as he propelled her brutally towards the door.

He pulled it open, disclosing the anxious faces of servants, who had gathered outside. With a last, agonizing twist of her hair, he pushed her out of the room.

'Get her out of this house!' he yelled. 'I never want to see her again!'

The door banged shut.

Two of the servants took Leah's arms. She shrugged their hands away, and moved with dignity towards the main door. They kept pace with her. Hot with pain and indignation, she strode out, leaving the house without a backward glance.

Two days of anxiety, wondering what to do, concocting lame explanations to satisfy little Tarquin, sleepless nights – all had combined to wear Leah down. The first thing she had done was to visit the prison. As she had hoped, no word of her disfavour had yet reached the jailer, and she had seen Ben Hur once more. But the meeting was only an anguished farewell, for she knew she would be unable to return to him again. In spite of this he had tried to encourage her, assuring her he would gain release somehow; but his words had been hollow indeed.

The memory did not improve Leah's mood. The last thing she felt like doing was trudging along this road in the dusty heat. Nevertheless she had refused to yield to the temptation to hire a chair. She knew that she must conserve her precious remaining funds.

Finally Seneca's villa lay before her. Debilitated and dispirited as she was, Leah could not restrain a gasp of awe at its magnificence. Even the Emperor's residence could not match this splendour. Gilded Corinthian columns flashed everywhere in the sunlight. The entrance portico seemed to stretch endlessly before her, and at its far end was the stately house itself.

Leah passed a circular outbuilding, near which several horses were tethered, then advanced tentatively along the portico.

As she went, she became aware of the shouts of men at work. A group of slaves, watched by an overseer, carried furniture across the portico and down a short flight of steps to the lawn.

A large wagon was positioned in front of the portico. The slaves were loading it with chairs, tables and other furnishings. Nearby, watching the progress of the work, stood an equestrian wearing a toga with the distinctive narrow purple stripe. From time to time, he checked a scroll.

Leah left the portico and approached him. 'Where will I find Seneca?'

The man stared at her as though she had said something odd.

'Isn't this his house?' Leah demanded.

'It was.'

'Was?'

'I see you haven't heard,' the equestrian observed. 'This is the property of the state now.' He smiled, appraising Leah's figure. 'I am Manlius, assistant to the City Prefect. I am in charge of removing the effects here. Can I be of service?'

'Where is Seneca?'

Manlius wagged his head sadly. 'He's dead . . . A large conspiracy against the Emperor has been uncovered among the senators. Seneca was one of them.'

The equestrian noticed Leah's dismay. 'You seem very upset. Is there something I can do to help?'

'You can indeed,' said Leah. 'Seneca was given some money to hold in trust for my little son. How can I go about getting it?'

'I'm afraid that's impossible,' Manlius said. 'Any money the senator had is now the property of the Emperor. You'll have to petition him about it.'

Despair and weariness overwhelmed her.

Manlius patted her arm. 'Do not be distressed. Petitioning the Emperor is complicated, but in your case it might not be so difficult.' He winked. 'You have a pretty face. They say he has a weakness for lovely women.'

Leah turned away in disgust.

Just then a proud horseman rode up, his cloak of Tyrian purple flowing behind him. He reined in. It was Epaphroditus.

With relief, Leah ran towards him.

He dismounted and bowed with his usual extravagance as she came up. 'Faultless lady! How good to see you again, after all these melancholy events!'

'I have been to the residence a number of times to speak to you. But you've been unavailable.'

He looked surprised. 'I was never told that you had come!'

'I need your help, Epaphroditus.'

'Of course. I shall do anything within my power. But I am afraid we will have to discuss it later. I have important business with this estate.'

Epaphroditus started away. She seized his arm.

'It cannot wait,' she insisted. 'Please arrange for me to see the Emperor.'

'It might have been possible if Poppaea had not died.' He shook his head pityingly. 'What a sad accident – her falling like that. I'm afraid he's in mourning. He will see no one.'

'He'll see you!'

'Nevertheless, I would not attempt to go against his will. If I brought up your name, he might get even more upset.'

'But you are my friend. We agreed to help each other.'

'There is nothing I can do.'

'At least, speak to him for me,' she pleaded. 'Some of the money confiscated from Seneca belongs to me.'

'For me to be involved in any way with Seneca's affairs would be most impolite.'

'I suppose, then, our "unholy alliance" is no longer in effect?'

'Regrettably, events have made it obsolete, but you still have my highest regard.'

'I'm grateful for that,' Leah said bitterly.

CHAPTER TWENTY-NINE

The Prison Prefect noted that the Emperor's hair was redder than before. Had it been dyed to hide the premature grey? Nero also seemed heavier, as he waited uneasily in the middle of the grim chamber with the air of a man who did not want to soil his person by touching anything.

'Exalted Sir,' the Prefect said nervously. 'I was led to believe that you were still in Greece.'

'As you can see,' Nero snapped, 'I am not. Jupiter's eyeballs! It's taking them long enough.'

'I beg your pardon,' ventured the Prefect timidly. 'But the prisoner is on the lowest level. It will take some time . . .'

There was another uncomfortable pause. The Prefect's eyes flickered desperately round the cheerless barrack-room. It was almost as if he were seeking some means of escape.

'What condition is he in?' the Emperor wondered.

'I have no idea, Exalted Sir,' said the Prefect. 'I have not seen him.'

Nero scowled. 'You are sure he is alive?'

'So the guards tell me.'

There was a knock. Nero nodded to his Praetorian escort, who opened the door. The prisoner was pushed into the chamber.

Ben Hur had to cover his eyes against the light flooding in through the window. The brightness was sheer agony. At last the discomfort grew less acute. Cautiously he removed his hands from his face and half-opened his eyes, until he could make out the waiting figure of Nero.

Ben Hur was not surprised. He had known something unusual was afoot when they had dragged him from his cell, given him a rudimentary wash, cut off most of his beard, and dressed him in a clean tunic.

'Leave us!' the Emperor commanded.

The Prefect looked doubtful. 'Exalted Sir ... I feel unsure about leaving you alone with the prisoner.'

'Just do as I say.'

Bowing profoundly, the Prefect went out, followed by the Praetorians.

The Emperor waited until the door was closed. Then he approached Ben Hur. He circled him, inspecting him, but said nothing.

'Are you satisfied with what you see?' Ben Hur asked finally.

Nero stopped. His eyes became angry. 'You are fortunate to be alive!'

Ben Hur laughed. He was surprised at the sound. He had not laughed in a long time.

'I? Fortunate? You came here to tell me that?'

'No. I came to ask you a question.'

There was a silence. Ben Hur waited. Finally Nero spoke.

'Since the day I was born I have been surrounded by treachery. my mother ... my wives ... my friends. All the people I have favoured. Whatever I have granted them, they have used against me. They take, but they give nothing.'

He regarded Ben Hur balefully, his face sullen with rage. 'Now the whole world is turning against me! There is rebellion in Gaul. In Spain, Galba and Otho are massing more and more men. I know what they're up to. Everywhere I turn, it is the same story.'

He moved to the window and stared out.

'I wish I dared to abdicate!' he exclaimed fervently. He turned back to Ben Hur glumly. 'Poppaea died, you know ...'

The news took Ben Hur by surprise. 'I did *not* know. We are poorly informed here in prison.'

Nero did not seem to hear him. 'I still cannot get over it,' he murmured. 'I went to Greece, you know ...' He glanced at Ben Hur.

'No . . . I don't suppose you know that either. I went, thinking that if I took part in the great festivals, my pain would grow lighter. But it did no good. I could not forget that look on her face when . . .' He shook his head. 'I loved her . . . I really did. Of course, she didn't love me. She was out to get what she could, like all the others.'

There was another gloomy silence.

'You came to ask me a question,' Ben Hur reminded him.

Nero gazed at him. 'You were different. I always knew that You weren't trying to cultivate me for what you could gain, like the others. But even you were treacherous. Now – with everything collapsing about my ears – I suddenly need to know the answer. Why did you try to kill me?'

'I did not try to kill you.'

'That's what she said . . .'

'Leah?'

'Yes . . . I wanted to believe her at the time. But I did not.'

'Then why are you asking me?'

'Because I have to hear it from your lips, Arrius. Tell me the truth. Whatever it is – I promise you won't suffer.'

'I am not on trial. It is too late for that.'

'Arrius . . . I need a friend. Now, of all times, I need the truth!'

Ben Hur had no words. He did not feel capable of answering.

'There was another reason I came here,' Nero muttered. 'I am afraid, Arrius. I have a premonition that my days are numbered. I remembered something you said. About a man in Judaea who died, yet returned to life.'

Ben Hur nodded.

'Who was this man? I want to know more about him.'

'Have you heard of Christ?'

'Christ! Surely not the one the Christians follow!'

'The same.'

'But the Christians are criminals! They burnt the city! They commit every sort of abomination!'

'Those who do such things have usurped the name of Christians. Christ was a messenger of peace. He came to show men how to reach God.'

Nero studied him. 'Am I right in supposing that you are a Christian?'

'Yes, I am.'

'You dare to admit that? Even though the sect is proscribed?'

'I have little left to fear.'

'When you first told me about this Judaean of the miraculous life – were you a Christian then too?'

Ben Hur nodded. 'You wondered why I never sought personal gain from my friendship with you. I'll tell you – because Christ's teachings forbid self-seeking.'

'I think I am beginning to understand ...'

'There was another reason I wanted your friendship. I saw you as the hope of the world. I wanted to bring you to the faith. But even to approach such a task was beyond my power.'

The Emperor grew even more thoughtful. 'Perhaps I need a new God ... The old Gods seem to have deserted me.' With sudden decision, he faced Ben Hur. 'I want to hear more of this. I will sit at your feet, and you will instruct me. You are now pardoned. I will restore you to your estates. As for that pederast of an informer who once served you – I'll have him crucified.'

'No!'

Nero looked surprised.

'There is no need to take vengeance on Phaon on my account.'

'Very well. I will spare him. Now let us see the last of this foul place.' He moved towards the door.

'One moment ...' Ben Hur said.

The Emperor paused.

'Where is Leah?'

'I do not know. I have not seen her for a long time. Which is all for the best. She was gorgeous, but an evil witch.' He regarded Ben Hur penetratingly. 'She claimed she was a relative of yours. Is that so – or was it more than that?'

'Her family was close to mine.'

'She was ravishing, I'll say that,' Nero mused. 'There was no denying her anything.'

'You have no idea what became of her? Not even a clue?'

Nero shook his head. 'For all I know she may be dead. Probably is. Women that beautiful seldom live long.'

Ben Hur felt like a man visiting his own past. The atrium was the same as it had always been. Electra's toneless voice could be heard singing in the kitchen. As before, multicoloured fish cruised lazily in the familiar pool. Ben Hur noticed one with a distinctive black stripe, half hidden under a floating lily. It looked exactly like the one Seneca had remarked on years ago. If it *was* the same fish, its world had changed not at all. Yet how utterly different was the world outside that pool! But, in its own terms, each was equally real. There were so many different realities. Surely, behind these myriad diversities there must be an answer. A final truth. Somewhere.

His mind wandered to Leah. What had happened to her? The moment he had been released from prison he had searched for her, but with no success. She had vanished without trace. Had Nero been right? Perhaps she was no longer even alive.

A discreet footfall interrupted his thoughts. He turned. Phaon stood respectfully in the doorway.

'I beg your pardon, Eminent Sir, but your guests are waiting for you in the tablinium as you requested.'

'Thank you, Phaon.'

Ben Hur started for the door, and Phaon moved aside to let him pass.

'Eminent Sir ...' the freedman ventured.

Ben Hur paused.

Phaon spoke hesitantly. 'Once again I must express my undying gratitude for your kindness to me.'

'You have already done so quite enough, Phaon. Consider it forgotten.'

'I will never forget. I assure you of that.'

Ben Hur smiled and turned towards the portico.

'Another thing, sir ...'

'Yes?'

Phaon seemed more uneasy than ever. 'Do your guests know that I was an informer?'

'Yes. They are very close to me. I confide everything to them.'

The freedman nodded ruefully. 'I see the hostility in their eyes. *They* have not forgiven me.'

'I am sorry for that, Phaon. Perhaps you expect too much.'

Ben Hur left the atrium. He walked along the portico to the tablinium door.

Inside Sextus and Apuleius were waiting by the window. Philip sat in a chair, while Urgulania, never idle, busied herself scrubbing the soot from a wall stained by an oil lamp.

'You ought to be more pleasant to Phaon,' said Ben Hur curtly, as he closed the door. 'That goes for all of you.'

'I've said nothing to him,' Apuleius replied defensively. He glanced at his comrades. 'I think we've all been more than generous, considering.'

'He feels your dislike.'

Apuleius shook his head. 'You're too kind to him. I have learned that when a man betrays you once, he's liable to do it again.'

'Have we not made it our rule of life to forgive those who wrong us? Or am I mistaken?'

There was an awkward silence.

'Have you found any trace of Joseph's daughter?' Philip asked finally.

'None. But I intend to keep looking.'

'I have some friends who live near the old Vicus,' said Urgulania. 'Perhaps they would know something of Leah. I'll talk to them.'

'Please do. I would appreciate that.'

'I'll go now.'

She took up her cloth and walked out of the room.

'Joseph's daughter may have left the city,' Philip speculated. 'Many people are doing so. You have heard, I suppose, that Galba is marching on Rome with an army. He can only be aiming at supreme power.'

'I have heard talk about it,' Ben Hur admitted. 'But since Nero is finally showing us signs of favour, I'm hoping it is only a rumour.'

'Galba's army is no rumour,' said Philip. 'The city is full of the news.'

'Nero is not exactly helpless,' Sextus pointed out. 'He has Tigellinus and the Praetorians behind him. They'll defeat any army Galba can bring up.'

'Whatever hardships lie before us, we must endure them,' Ben Hur stated. 'The days ahead are crucial for us.'

'In what way, Judah?' wondered Apuleius.

'We have an opportunity which may not exist much longer. A number of those who followed Christ and heard his actual words are still alive. We must find them. We must have them put in writing the things they heard Christ say. These men are carrying with them a precious testament for the future. We must not let it die with them.'

'You yourself heard Christ,' Philip pointed out.

'But my knowledge of his words is as imperfect as my faith. I only saw him in the last days of his ministry. We must find men like Matthew, James, Thomas – as many of them as we can – who were with him from the very beginning.'

'We'll bring them here to Rome,' Philip agreed eagerly. 'They'll share their memories with us. We can hide their testaments in the crypt with the rest of our writings.'

There was a loud rapping on the door. 'Come in,' Ben Hur called.

Phaon stumbled into the room. He was very agitated.

'Eminent Sir, you must come quickly. The Emperor ... the Emperor ...'

'Here?' Ben Hur exclaimed.

'Hurry!' Phaon insisted. 'He's in the hall. He demands to see you – says it's very urgent!'

Ben Hur turned to the others. 'Wait.'

He followed Phaon. They crossed the portico, entered the atrium and came to the entrance hall.

There stood Nero and Epaphroditus.

The Emperor looked haggard. Both men were dressed in rough countrymen's cloaks with their hoods thrown back. At the sight of Ben Hur, Nero ran up to him and seized him by both arms.

'Arrius!' he gasped. 'Thank the Gods I've found you! If ever I needed a friend, it is now! Everything is lost! My enemies are hunting for me. As if I were an animal – not an Emperor.'

'Phaon!' Ben Hur ordered. 'Go out to the front and keep watch.'

Phaon obeyed instantly.

'I will stand guard behind the house,' Epaphroditus offered.

The Emperor patted the freedman's shoulder. 'I am unspeakably grateful for the loyalty you have shown.'

'Loyalty is my only choice,' Epaphroditus said. 'I have made too many enemies.' A ghost of his old smile flickered across his face. 'It is too late for me to change colours now.'

'Nevertheless,' Nero replied, 'the fact remains that you have stayed with me until the end.'

'It is not the end!' said Epaphroditus fervently. 'At least I pray that it is not!'

He hurried away.

Ben Hur took Nero by the arm.' 'Come ...'

Hurriedly he conducted the Emperor through the atrium and down the portico to the tablinium door. Opening it, he beckoned for Nero to enter.

The Emperor stopped short on the threshold, staring at the three men inside. Apuleius glanced dubiously at his friends, then bowed. The others did the same.

Nero regarded Ben Hur accusingly. 'You didn't tell me there were others here! Who are these men?'

Ben Hur pulled Nero into the room and closed the door. 'These are my comrades, Lucius. There is no time for hesitation. You must accept my word that they are trustworthy.'

Nero stared at Ben Hur's friends as if trying to fathom their feelings. Then he nodded. 'Very well. Nothing really matters anyway. I am destroyed, Arrius! I sent Tigellinus with the Praetorians to stop Galba. But he went over to the rebels – the pederast! I woke up in the first watch of the morning. It was the quiet which wakened me – you have no idea how quiet it was! I soon found out why. There was no one there. Even the servants had fled. Only Epaphroditus has stayed with me. Then I thought of you. I humbly beg you, Arrius, to shelter me here.'

A thought was taking shape in Ben Hur's mind. There *was* a place – the crypt. But that would mean sharing his secret with Nero. If they should succeed in saving the Emperor's life, would the knowledge of their sanctuary be safe with him?

Almost pleadingly, Nero touched his shoulder.

'Arrius! You are silent! Speak! Do something. You are my last hope!'

Ben Hur nodded. 'I have a place for you to hide.'

'Judah!' cried Sextus. 'No! Not that!'

'Enough, Sextus,' Ben Hur said firmly. 'I have already decided. We must help him.'

The others looked anxious, but they made no further protest. Ben Hur faced Nero.

'I have money. Hidden in this very house. It will be enough to sustain you when you escape from Italy. In the meantime, you will be safe here.'

Nero gripped Ben Hur by the arms. 'You are my true friend! If I can only get to Egypt, my position will be restored. I have always been popular there. I can get more money ... support ... raise an army!' He was suddenly euphoric. 'You won't regret this! I'll reward all of you! I'll make you consul, Arrius, then governor of Asia!'

Ben Hur shook his head. 'We need no rewards. It is sufficient for us to help people. It is the command of Christ.'

Abruptly Nero became solemn. 'I vow that if I live – if I triumph over my enemies – I will take your faith and your God as my own. By Jupiter, I will!'

The door opened, and Phaon hurried in, all formalities forgotten. 'Sir! There are soldiers on the road! I fear they are coming this way.'

Nero groaned with dismay. 'Pederasts! It didn't take them long! They'll torture me! They'll ...'

'Stay here!' Ben Hur ordered. 'I'll see what I can do.'

Without waiting for an answer, he rushed out after Phaon. They dashed through the house until they reached the front door. Cautiously Phaon opened it a crack, and Ben Hur peered out.

There were indeed soldiers on the Flaminian Way, and the leaders were already turning on to the path to Ben Hur's villa. Their elaborate, well-polished armour and expensive equipment proclaimed them as Praetorians. They were at least two centuries strong.

Ben Hur opened the door and strode boldly out on to the path. The Centurion in charge saw him coming and signalled his men to halt. The officer advanced to meet Ben Hur.

'What is your business here, Centurion?' Ben Hur demanded.

'Who are you?'

'Quintus Arrius. I own this house.'

'I have orders to search this property.'

'Whose orders?'

'The new Emperor. Galba.'

'Galba? Emperor?'

'The army has taken the oath of loyalty and the Praetorians also. Soon the Senate will proclaim him.'

'May I see your orders?'

'They are right here,' said the Centurion.

He tapped the polished ivory hilt of his sword and stepped forward. Ben Hur prudently allowed him to go by. He followed the Centurion up the path towards the villa. The heavy tread of hob-nailed feet and the clink of arms told him the soldiers were keeping pace close behind him.

Reaching the front door, the officer pushed it open unceremoniously. But he stopped short on the threshold and turned to his men.

'It appears someone has done our work for us,' he announced grimly.

Ben Hur elbowed past the Centurion. Nero lay sprawled on the floor of the hall, bleeding, a knife in his chest. Sextus, Philip and Apuleius were crouched beside him, while Phaon hovered fearfully in the background. Sextus rose, his face bleak.

'Judah ... we could do nothing. He rushed out after you. When he saw the soldiers, he stabbed himself. We had no time to stop him. We did not even know he was armed.'

The Centurion unsheathed his sword. 'Move aside. I have to finish him off.'

Ben Hur caught him by the shoulder. 'No!'

The officer wrenched away. 'I have my orders.'

'Surely you see he is dying. Let him die in peace!'

The man hesitated, lowering his weapon slightly.

Ben Hur regarded him with contempt. 'It is a small favour to grant the man who was your Emperor only yesterday.'

The Praetorian avoided his eyes, sheathing his blade. 'Very well. But you are under arrest for harbouring him.'

Ben Hur shrugged. 'Then I am your prisoner. But let me be alone with him now.'

The Centurion indicated his men. 'We'll be waiting. The house will be surrounded.'

He turned away and his men clattered after him.

Ben Hur knelt beside the dying Emperor.

Nero mustered a small caricature of a smile. 'What an artist the world is losing ...'

Ben Hur could find no words to answer him.

'This Christ ...' Nero whispered. 'The one who died and yet lived again. If only I could do that!'

'You can, Lucius. You must believe it. Embrace Christ and confess the evils of your life. Repent them. Death comes from evil. If we free ourselves from evil, we will live again, just as Christ did. You must ...' He groped for further words to comfort the dying man.

Nero's voice came with heart-rending weakness. 'I confess willingly ... I have been the worst of men. I repent that. I truly do ... If only he will forgive me ... my soul will be the most humble of souls.'

Ben Hur gestured to Sextus. 'Fetch me water! Quickly!'

The young men darted into the adjoining atrium. He picked up a pot used for watering plants, filled it from the pool, and hurried back to Ben Hur. Taking the vessel, Ben Hur dipped his fingers into it and sprinkled water on the dying man's forehead.

Nero's breath was increasingly laboured. His eyes flickered open again. 'What ... What ...' he murmured.

'I am baptizing you in Christ. Freed of your sins, you are the temple of God. The spirit of God dwells within you ...'

Even as he spoke, he realized that Nero had not heard the words.

CHAPTER THIRTY

The Forum was a sea of silent people watching the spectacle in their midst. Ben Hur surveyed their expressionless faces with loathing. He knew that they were waiting to see him condemned like the others who already had been led to their deaths this same morning.

His eyes shifted back to his judges, sitting behind a temporary wooden table set up in front of the Curia. Presiding was the new Emperor himself, who had insisted on this summary justice. Even now, while Galba sat here in his moment of triumph, purging the city of his enemies, Ben Hur had a premonition he would not last long. A fat, elderly man, he was busy stuffing little cakes into his mouth from a plate of delicacies. He had been devouring food during the whole of Ben Hur's statement to the court.

Now there was a long pause while Galba finished the last of his cakes, shaking his head dubiously. Finally he swallowed and fixed Ben Hur with his pale blue eyes.

'Your statement is utterly unconvincing,' he said flatly.

'It is the truth,' Ben Hur replied.

'Silence!' Galba snapped. 'The only part of your defence which can be substantiated is the fact that you were in prison. How you got there doesn't matter. It is the way you got out which is important to me. You were *let* out, by that incubus Nero ... that enemy of the Roman people, who usurped the title of Emperor. He restored you to your estates! And when my soldiers tracked him down, where did they find him? At *your* house!'

An ominous quiet shrouded the blood-hungry Forum. Ben Hur felt helpless. There was so much he had to leave unsaid for fear of incriminating the Christians. There was nothing for it but to remain silent and accept whatever fate was going to hand him.

Galba drew himself up and surveyed the assembly. 'Before I pass judgement, does anyone wish to speak?'

'I do.' A tall, handsome figure disengaged himself from Galba's entourage and stepped forward. It was Otho.

Ben Hur watched him with dismay. He had noticed Otho earlier, staring at him implacably during the proceedings. Whatever Otho might say would surely destroy any chance of clemency. If the court should hear now that Ben Hur refused to join a conspiracy against Nero, *that* would be the end.

Otho approached, took the oath before the Pontiff, then faced Galba.

'Exalted Emperor, my services to you and your cause should certainly be proof enough that my testimony is disinterested. I have shown –'

'All right! All right!' Galba interrupted testily. 'Get to your point!' He reached for another cake, but the plate was empty. With irritation, he pushed it away.

'Gladly,' said Otho. 'I have listened to Arrius' defence. Not a word of it is less than the truth.'

Ben Hur was amazed. Otho was speaking in his favour!

Otho continued. 'I was a close friend of Arrius when he was Nero's favourite. It is a fact that he became disenchanted with the Emperor. His disapproval of Nero was so strong and so open that he had to flee into exile.'

'The defendant has already made that claim,' Galba interrupted again. 'But there are no witnesses to back up his story.'

'I have a very reliable witness, who will substantiate that Arrius did indeed spend years in exile. And no one will question the qualifications of this witness – a man without whose help neither you nor I, Exalted Sir, would be standing here now.' Otho cleared his throat. 'I call Suetonius Paulinus, General of our Legions – who marched into this city at our side.'

A figure stepped forward from a nearby group of military officers. It was Suetonius indeed!

Ben Hur felt a twinge of apprehension. He had deliberately avoided mentioning his military service in Britain, fearing that it would only cast unfavourable light on his testimony. The ignoble ending of his army career would not endear him to Romans.

A deafening cheer burst from the crowd as the General made his way towards the Pontiff. Ben Hur was aware that Suetonius' legendary campaigns had virtually turned him into a folk hero. As he watched the veteran's approach, he realized that Suetonius must be even older than Galba, yet he hardly showed the years which had passed since Ben Hur had last seen him. If anything, he seemed leaner and tougher than ever.

Just before reaching the judges' table, Suetonius stopped and faced the massed audience, giving them the clenched fist salute of the Roman army. If the applause had been loud when the General appeared, this gesture raised it to such a thunderous pitch that the very temples surrounding them seemed to shake.

At long last the acclaim died down, and Suetonius went up to the tribunal. After the pontiff had administered the oath, Suetonius stared for a moment at Ben Hur, then turned to the court. The voice which commanded legions echoed through the Forum.

'This man called Arrius served under me in Britain. I knew him by another name which need not concern us here, except to say that he was using it because he was a fugitive from Nero. I promoted him to Tribune on the field of battle for bravery. And he was also brave enough to disobey my orders, for which I expelled him from the Legion. Only two things prevented me from inflicting the supreme penalty on him – the fact that he once saved my life, and the knowledge that he was an enemy of Nero. It was fortunate that I spared this man, for afterwards he killed one of Rome's deadliest enemies – Dumnorix, the Druid High Priest.'

The General's eyes went back to the prisoner. Ben Hur thought he detected a grudging glimmer of respect in the older man's glance.

An expectant hush fell over the Forum as the General rejoined his soldiers. Discreetly a servant approached, placing another platter of cakes on the table. Galba took one and crammed it into his mouth.

'Exalted Sir,' said Otho. 'I may point out that Arrius will be of great use to us. Not only is he the proprietor of the Arrius estate here, but he is also the heir of an ancient and noble house in Judaea.'

'You don't think I would allow such considerations to prejudice my opinion, do you?' Galba said sanctimoniously. 'I am only concerned with justice. That is why I have answered the call of duty and led this revolution against the forces of tyranny. And justice demands this man be acquitted of all charges. Next case!'

With relief Ben Hur turned, a free man again. Otho strode up and took him by the arm, leading him away from the tribunal.

'That was a near thing, Arrius,' he murmured. 'I am sorry you had to go through it.' He grinned. 'But at least it ended well ...'

'I am deeply grateful for your help,' Ben Hur replied. 'But I still find it hard to believe that you took such a risk on my behalf.'

'You might say I paid Agrippina's debt,' Otho murmured. 'You took a spear through your body defending her.'

'How could you possibly know about that? You were already in exile!'

'True. But Petronius wasn't. Later on Nero discovered his involvement. Poor Petronius was invited to commit suicide – it was an invitation he could not refuse. But before his end, he wrote me a long, long letter, describing everything that had happened.'

Ben Hur regarded Otho curiously. 'Why didn't you show this letter to Galba?'

'Because Galba is mentioned in it – most unfavourably. And I may have occasion to use the letter later. You see, we regard Galba as merely a temporary expedient. We had to accept him because he commands the Spanish Legions. However, Galba has pledged to designate me as his heir. Once I've assumed the purple –' he nudged Ben Hur – 'I'll be able to use some loyal friends. Or perhaps even before my elevation.'

'Judah!' called a familiar voice.

Ben Hur's eyes swept the onlookers until he spotted Apuleius and Sextus, along with Philip and Urgulania. They had worked their way to the edge of the crowd, where the line of soldiers prevented them from going any further.

Otho grasped his hand. 'Visit me whenever you can, Arrius.'

Ben Hur nodded, then walked over to his comrades. Emotionally they embraced him.

Urgulania bestowed a moist kiss on his cheek. 'God bless you, Judah!' she cried.

Philip glanced darkly at the tribunal. 'Thank God it is over ... And thank God you have powerful friends, Judah.'

'Powerful they are,' said Ben Hur in a low voice. 'But if they were to know my true allegiance, I wonder if they would still be my friends. I assure you – I never mean to put the issue to the test. We do not dare to trust any of them.'

He started off, but Urgulania laid a hand on his arm. 'Judah ... I found Leah.'

Momentarily Ben Hur was unable to speak. He was unprepared for the almost violent surge of gratitude which went through him.

'Found her! Where?'

'Wait!' Urgulania warned. 'She is not in happy circumstances. The servant woman who had looked after her child caught fever and died. Leah entrusted the little boy to me.'

'Where is she?'

'She does not want to see you, Judah. She begs you to forget her and think only of the boy.'

Astonished, Ben Hur stared at her. 'I – I find this hard to believe. Did she give you a reason?'

Urgulania avoided his eyes. 'She said only that the past cannot be relived.'

'Where is she?' he repeated.

'She made me give my word I would not tell you.'

'But you must,' he insisted.

'Would it be right for me to break my word?'

Ben Hur sighed with exasperation. 'You think it is right for the child to grow up apart from his mother – knowing she sent him away?'

Urgulania said nothing, but the stubborn set of her face suggested that she was not about to yield.

'Urgulania,' he pleaded, 'there are times in this life when it is necessary to choose between two evils. It is the duty of a Christian to choose the lesser.'

'In this case,' Urgulania stated, 'the lesser evil is to respect her wishes.'

Ben Hur scrutinized her. 'What are you hiding? What has happened to her?'

Urgulania remained stubbornly silent.

Phaon and Electra waited in front of the villa. Tarquin, a thin child of seven or eight, stood between them. He was smartly attired in a fresh boy's toga. Ben Hur wondered where they had procured the garment at such short notice.

He was glad they had prepared the boy to be presented to him. It would be an excuse to get away from Urgulania. Even though he had ceased questioning her about Leah, Urgulania had remained sullen for the entire journey homeward, and he was heartily sick of her company.

'There is no need for me to inquire the outcome!' Phaon exclaimed, hurrying forward, followed by Electra. 'I see you here alive and well standing before me! Thank the Gods!'

'The Lares of your household have protected you!' Electra cried.

Ben Hur smiled. Phaon and Electra had not yet learned about the God of the Christians, but he had no doubt they would find a place for Christ among the many other deities they worshipped.

Everyone's spirits were high, and for the first time Ben Hur's companions seemed friendly to Phaon. As they related how the trial had gone and expressed over and over again their joy at Ben Hur's deliverance, the boy stood by quietly, watching the others with his large, serious eyes.

Ben Hur went over to him, kneeling beside him. 'You must be Tarquin ...'

'Yes, Eminent Sir,' he replied solemnly.

'I am Judah Ben Hur.'

'My mother says I am to obey you in all things.'

Ben Hur smiled. Tarquin had a poise and maturity which were surprising in one so young.

'Phaon,' Ben Hur called. 'Have you shown Tarquin his new home?'

The freedman shook his head. 'There was no time, Tarquin has spent the morning eating and sleeping.'

Ben Hur turned back to the child. 'And have you eaten enough?'

'Yes, Eminent Sir.'

'Would you like me to show you the villa?'

'If it is your wish.'

Ben Hur beckoned for Tarquin to follow, and they entered the house. They passed through the hall, atrium, portico and the inner garden. The whole time Tarquin remained reserved and silent, only speaking in reply to a direct question. Ben Hur sensed that Tarquin was on guard, still uneasy in his new surroundings. The lad had the hollow-eyed look of privation, but obviously someone had taught him manners. Perhaps this was a vestige of the time when Leah's husband was alive and Tarquin had been given the benefit of a tutor's guidance.

'Would you like to see where I sleep?' Ben Hur asked.

Ben Hur entered the room, and Tarquin followed, looking round politely. Then he caught sight of the charioteer's helmet and harness, which still hung on the wall. His face lit up, and he turned to Ben Hur eagerly.

'My mother said you raced in the Circus Maximus!' he blurted out. 'Did you wear these?'

'Indeed I did.'

'I had a chariot once,' Tarquin confided. 'Well, actually it was a cart. My father had a big dog named Ares, and Ares used to pull me round the lawn as quick as boiled asparagus!'

'Would you like to drive a real chariot?'

'A real chariot!' Tarquin gasped. 'When?'

'I have several chariots in the stables. You look old enough to drive the light one. I'll tell you what – it is yours.'

Tarquin was speechless, but his eyes made clear he had found a new deity. Ben Hur took him by the arm. They left the bedroom, walked down the portico, and entered the bath-house.

Freed of all inhibitions now, Tarquin marvelled at the round pool. 'What a monstrous bath! It looks like a lake. We had a bath in my father's house – but nothing like this.'

'Would you like to go in?' Ben Hur inquired.

Tarquin needed no second invitation. In an instant, his clothes were off, and he dived into the pool, swimming like an eel.

He surfaced, spouting water. 'Once I caught a fish with my bare hands!'

'A remarkable feat! Where did this take place?'

'In the river where I lived with my mother.' He dived under again.

Ben Hur stared thoughtfully at the shape swimming under the surface. Clearly more information was there for the asking. Ben Hur was not above obtaining it. Removing his tunic, he lowered himself into the pool. In a moment, Tarquin had surfaced and was floating nearby.

'Do I assume that you lived in a boat with your mother?' Ben Hur inquired casually.

'Half a boat. On the mud flats. It was upside down, and it had a hole in the bottom. We used one of my mother's old tunics to cover it up, so the rain would not get in.'

'Where is this boat?'

Tarquin was suddenly suspicious. His old reserve was back. 'My mother said I was not to tell you ...'

'Then, of course, you must not,' Ben Hur assured him hastily. 'Come. We'll dry ourselves and look at that chariot.'

Tarquin nodded eagerly and vaulted out of the pool. The boy was at ease again.

The river was low. Wide expanses of mud steamed in the late afternoon sun. Ben Hur picked his way along, avoiding the tide-pools. The stench of rotting vegetation filled the thick, clammy air.

The familiar arches of the Milvian Bridge spanned the river not far ahead. A number of boats were drawn up on the mud beside it. If the one he sought was not among them, he would have to cross the bridge and continue his search on the opposite bank.

Cautiously he advanced until he reached the beached vessels. They all seemed well equipped and capable of use, filled with the fish traps which the boat people were always setting up in the river, an endless source of complaint to the navigators.

Then he saw it. Right by the stone bridge itself was a derelict remnant of a barge. Turned over, its hull served as a roof. The open end, where the hull had been broken off, was propped up by two stakes. Under the rotting timbers was the figure of a woman, indistinct in the deepening dusk, crouched over a small fire.

Ben Hur approached quietly, but froze as her head turned in his direction. Immediately she leaped up, disappearing under the shelter of the boat.

He lurched forward into a run.

Reaching the upturned hull, he stooped and peered in, trying to adjust his eyes to the stale gloom. He could make out the crouched figure of the woman in the shadows at the far end.

'Leah?' he called tentatively.

There was no answer.

'Leah ... I know it is you ...'

'Please! Go away!' came her voice.

'I must speak to you.'

'No. I beg you! Leave me!'

Ben Hur was bewildered. 'You came to me in that prison ... You were a blessing from heaven. You gave me hope for life. And now you want me to go away, without telling me why?'

The shadowy figure moved and came towards him. She stepped out from under the rotten hulk and faced him defiantly in the light.

He gasped. What had been the face of a goddess was terribly disfigured. Her finely chiselled nose had been cruelly broken. A livid scar covered one cheek.

'Now will you go?' she demanded.

'Who has done this to you?' Ben Hur breathed.

'Does it matter?'

'Yes, it matters.'

He reached out to touch her, but she drew away.

'Then I'll tell you,' she said savagely. 'There is a house of pleasure run by a woman named Calpurnia. When I had no more money, I went there. I did whatever any man wanted – until one day a noble gentleman did this to me.'

She thrust her face close to him, the words spilling out of her. 'He beat me up and poured scalding oil from a lamp on me! I am on the streets now, but I make a living.'

She pointed to her face bitterly. 'Yes, Judah, there are still men who do not mind this!'

'You think that makes any difference to me?'

'I don't want your pity!'

'It's not pity. I want you ...'

Tears showed in her eyes, but she spoke harshly.

'I dreamed of being married to you. You were a king to me. And I knew I was beautiful enough to be your queen. Now that can never be. I'm hideous! Something you'd want to hide from people!'

She tried to turn away, but he held her fast.

'Leah,' he cried, 'you still think of beauty as if it were a gown of many colours to be displayed to the world. That's only beauty on the outside.'

Leah was silent.

'Believe me,' he insisted. 'You were a slave to that beauty. It had to be fed all the time. It was a cruel master. I was afraid it would destroy you. It would have been a barrier between us. One man's love would never have been enough for you. But now there is no barrier. We'll be happy, you and I ...'

She burst into sobs. He drew her closer.

For a long time he held her, looking out over the mudflats. The sun had vanished and with it the distinction between the water and the land. Nothing had boundaries or limits.

Suddenly Leah spoke. 'In the prison, you wanted to tell me about my father. I wouldn't listen to you ... Now I would like to listen. I only wish there was some way I could let him know ... I realize now how much he loved me.'

In the distance a small figure was approaching. It was Tarquin, running, nimbly avoiding tidepools. Behind him hurried Sextus, Philip, Apuleius and Urgulania.

The boy came up breathlessly. His solemn eyes surveyed Ben Hur and his mother. Then he grinned knowingly. 'I guessed you'd be here.'

The others clustered round excitedly.

'We had to find you, Judah ...' Philip gasped.

'Momentous news!' cried Sextus. 'Listen!' He pointed towards the city.

Ben Hur heard it – a sound like distant thunder. It was the muffled roar of a vast multitude.

'Galba is dead!' Sextus announced.

'Dead!' Ben Hur exclaimed. 'How?'

'A revolt! Otho is Emperor! Otho! The Senate has proclaimed him! He's your *friend*, Judah! Our day has come!'

'No,' Ben Hur said quietly.

Their exuberance turned to dismay.

'Once we reveal ourselves, there is no turning back,' Ben Hur stated. 'We will be prey to all those who fear and hate what we are. I know Otho well, but he's not the man for our purpose. He's not evil – but he's an opportunist.'

'Then we must continue hiding ... running ... pretending to be what we are not ...' Apuleius muttered glumly.

'There is no other way,' Ben Hur replied. 'We must wait until the right man is in power. One day it will happen – a Christian will rule Rome. But now we must dedicate ourselves to building a secret society – a society which cares for its members and keeps them close to God while they live on this earth. It will be a state within a state – stronger than even the Roman Empire, because it will be cemented by the bond of faith.'

He gazed at each of them.

'Its roots are here in Rome,' Ben Hur declared. 'Its branches shall extend throughout the world. And the fruit of this tree will nourish the humble and meek, wherever they are ...'

Their faces told him they had found comfort in his words. He hoped one day he might find the same comfort. But he knew it would not happen. The doubt was still there. It always would be. It would only end with death.

MORE ABOUT PENGUINS AND PELICANS